PROLOGUE

ILIOS MANOS looked out across the land that had belonged to his family for almost five centuries.

It was here on this rocky promontory, stretching out into the Aegean Sea in the north east of Greece, that Alexandros Manos had built for himself a copy of one of Palladio's most famous creations. Villa Emo.

Manos family folklore said that Alexandros Manos, a wealthy Greek merchant with his own fleet trading between Constantinople and Venice, had done business with the Emo family, and had been seized with envy for the new Emo mansion. He had secretly copied Palladio's drawings for the villa, taking them home to Greece with him, where he had had his own villa built, naming it Villa Manos and declaring that both it and the land on which it stood were a sacred trust, to be passed down from generation to generation, and must be owned by no man who was not of his blood.

It was here that Alexandros Manos had created what was in effect a personal fiefdom—a small kingdom of which he was absolute ruler.

Ilios knew that this promontory of land, surrounded on three sides by the Aegean Sea and with the mountains of northern Greece at its back, had meant everything to his grandfather, and Ilios's own father had given his life to keep it—just as his grandfather had forfeited his wealth to protect it. To protect *it*. But he hadn't protected the sons he had fathered, sacrificing them in order to keep his covenant with both the past and the future.

Ilios had learned a lot from his grandfather. He had learned that when you carried the hereditary responsibility of being descended from Alexandros Manos you had a duty to look beyond your own emotions—even to deny them if you had to—in order to ensure that the sacred living torch that was their family duty to the villa was passed on. The hand that carried that torch might be mortal, but the torch itself was for ever. Ilios had grown up listening to his grandfather's stories of what it meant to carry the blood of Alexandros Manos in your veins, and what it meant to be prepared to sacrifice anything and anyone to ensure that torch was passed on safely.

His was the duty to carry it now. And his too was the duty to do what his grandfather had not been able to do—and that was to restore their family's fortunes and its greatness.

As a boy, when Ilios had promised his grandfather that he would find a way to restore that greatness, his cousin Tino had laughed at him. Tino had laughed again when Ilios had told him that the only way he would pay off Tino's debts was if Tino sold him his half-share of their grandfather's estate to him.

Ilios looked at the building in front of him, the handsome face imprinted with the human history of so many generations of powerful self-willed men. It was set as though carved in marble by the same hands that had sculpted images of the Greek heroes of mythology. The golden eyes were a legacy of the wife Alexandros had brought back with him from northern lands, and they were fixed unwaveringly on the horizon.

Tino wasn't laughing any more. But he would be plotting to get his revenge, just as he had since their childhood. Tino had always wanted what little his cousin had, and would not take this humiliation lightly. As far as Tino was concerned, being born the son of a younger son was to labour under a disadvantage—something he blamed Ilios for.

Ilios knew the reputation he had amongst other men for striking a hard deal, and driving a hard bargain, for demanding the impossible from those who worked for him in order to create the impossible for those who paid him to do exactly that.

There was no black magic, no dark art, as some seemed to suppose in the means by which he had made his fortune in the construction business—other than that of determination and hard work, of endurance and driving himself to succeed. The graft that Ilios employed was not oiled by back-handers or grubby deals done in shadowed rooms, but by sheer hard work. By knowing his business inside out and from the bottom up—because that was where he himself had started. Even now, no commission that bore the name of Manos Construction did so until he had examined and passed every smallest detail. The pride and the sense of honour he took from his work, which he had inherited from his grandfather, saw to that.

Ilios knew that the journey he had made from the poverty of his childhood to the wealth that was now his filled other men with resentment and envy. It was said that no man could rise from penury to the wealth that Ilios possessed—counted in billions, not mere millions—by honest means alone, and he knew that few men envied him more, or would take more pleasure in his downfall, than his own cousin.

The rising sun struck across his profile, momentarily bathing it in bright gold reminiscent of the mask of the most famous of all of Greek Macedonians—Alexander the Great. He had been born in this part of Greece, and according to family lore had walked this very peninsula with his own forebears.

Several yards away from him one of his foremen waited, like the drivers of the heavy construction equipment behind him.

'What do you want me to do?' he asked.

Ilios gave the building in front of him a grim look.

'Destroy it. Pull it down and level the site.'

The foreman looked shocked.

'But your cousin—?'

'My cousin has no say in what happens here. Raze it to the ground.'

The foreman gave the signal to the drivers, and as the jaws of the heavy machinery bit into the building, reaching out to the morning sun, Ilios turned on his heel and walked away.

CHAPTER ONE

'So, what are you going to do, then?' Charley asked anxiously.

Lizzie looked at her younger sisters, the familiar need to protect them, no matter what the cost to herself, stiffening her resolve.

'There is only one thing I can do,' she answered. 'I shall have to go.'

'What? Fly out to Thessalonica?'

'It's the only way.'

'But we haven't got any money.'

That was Ruby, the baby of the family at twenty-two, sitting at the kitchen table while her five-year-old twin sons, who had been allowed a rare extra half an hour of television, sat uncharacteristically quietly in the other room, so that the sisters could discuss the problems threatening them.

No, they hadn't got any money—and that was her fault, Lizzie acknowledged guiltily.

Six years earlier, when their parents had died together, drowned by a freak wave whilst they were on holiday, Lizzie had promised herself that she would do everything she could to keep the family together. She had left university, and had been working for a prestigious London-based interior design partnership, in pursuit of her dream of getting a job as a set designer. Charley had just started university, and Ruby had been waiting to sit her GCSE exams.

Theirs had been a close and loving family, and the shock of losing their parents had been overwhelming—especially for Ruby, who, in her despair, had sought the love and reassurance she so desperately needed in the arms of the man who had abandoned her and left her pregnant with the adored twin boys.

There had been other shocks for them to face, though. Their handsome, wonderful father and their pretty, loving mother, who had created for them the almost fairytale world of happiness in which the family had lived, had done just that—lived in a fairytale which had little or no foundation in reality.

The beautiful Georgian rectory in the small Cheshire village in which they had grown up had been heavily mortgaged, their parents had not had any life insurance, and they had had large debts. In the end there had been no alternative but for their lovely family home to be sold, so those debts could be paid off.

With the property market booming, and her need to do everything she could to support and protect her sisters, Lizzie had used her small savings to set up in business on her own in an up-and-coming area south of Manchester—Charley would be able to continue with her studies at Manchester University, Ruby could have a fresh start, and she could establish a business which would support them all.

At first things had gone well. Lizzie had won contracts to model the interiors of several new building developments, and from that had come commissions from homebuyers to design the interiors of the properties they had bought. Off the back of that success Lizzie had taken the opportunity to buy a much larger house from one of the developers for whom she'd worked—with, of course, a much larger mortgage. It had seem to make sense at the time—after all, with the twins and the three of them they'd definitely needed the space, just as they had needed a large four-wheel drive vehicle. She used it to visit the sites on which she worked, and Ruby used it to take the boys to school. In addition to that her clients, a small local firm, had been pressuring her to buy, so that they could wind up the development and move on to a new site.

But then had come the credit crunch, and overnight almost everything had changed. The bottom had dropped out of the property market, meaning that they were unable to trade down and reduce the mortgage because of the value of the house had decreased so much, and with that of course Lizzie's commissions had dried up. The money she had been putting away in a special savings account had not increased anything like as much as she had expected, and financially things had suddenly become very dark indeed.

Right now Charley was still working as a project manager for a local firm, and Ruby had said that she would get a job. But neither Lizzie nor Charley wanted her to do that. They both wanted the twins to have a mother at home, just as they themselves had had. And, as Lizzie had said six months ago, when they'd first started to feel the effects of the credit crunch, she would get a job working for someone else, and she still had money owing to her from various clients. They would manage.

But it turned out she had been overly optimistic. She hadn't been able to get a job, because what industry there was in the area geared towards personal spending was shedding workers, and with the cost of basics going up they were now struggling to manage. They were only just about keeping their heads above water. Many of her clients had cancelled their contracts, and some of them still owed her large sums of money she suspected she would never receive.

In fact things were so dire that Lizzie had already made a private decision to go to the local supermarket and see if she could get work there. But then the letter had arrived, and now they—or rather *she* was in an even more desperate situation.

Two of her more recent clients, for whom she had done a good deal of work, had further commissioned her to do the interior design for a small block of apartments they had bought in northern Greece. On a beautiful promontory, the apartments were to have been the first stage in a luxurious and exclusive holiday development which, when finished, would include villas, three five-star hotels, a marina, restaurants and everything that went with it.

The client had given her carte blanche to furnish them in an 'upmarket Notting Hill style'.

Notting Hill might be a long way from their corner of industrialised Manchester, on the Cheshire border, but Lizzie had known exactly what her clients had meant: white walls, swish bathrooms and kitchens, shiny marble floors, glass furniture, exotic plants and flowers, squishy sofas…

Lizzie had flown out to see the apartments with her clients, a middle-aged couple whom she had never really been able to take to. She had been disappointed by the architectural design of the apartments. She had been expecting something creative and innovative that still fitted perfectly into the timeless landscape, but what she had seen had been jarringly out of place. A six-storey-high rectangular box of so-called 'duplex apartments', reached by a narrow track that forked into two, with one branch sealed off by bales of dangerous-looking barbed wire. Hardly the luxury holiday homes location she had been expecting.

But when she had voiced her doubts to her clients, suggesting that the apartments might be difficult to sell, they had assured her that she was worrying unnecessarily.

'Look, the fact is that we bargained the builder down to such a good price that we couldn't lose out even if we let the whole lot out for a tenner a week,' Basil Rainhill had joked cheerfully. At least Lizzie had assumed it as a joke. It was hard to tell with Basil at times.

He came from money, as his wife was fond of telling her. 'Born with a silver spoon in his mouth, and of course Basil has such an eye for a good investment. It's a gift, you know. It runs in his family.'

Only now the gift had run out. And just before the Rainhills themselves had done the same thing disappearing, leaving a mountain of debt behind them, Basil Rainhill had told Lizzie that, since he couldn't now afford to pay her bill, he was instead making over to her a twenty per cent interest in the Greek apartment block.

Lizzie would much rather have had the money she was owed, but her solicitor had advised her to accept, and so she had become a partner in the ownership of the apartments along with the Rainhills and Tino Manos, the Greek who owned the land.

Design-wise, she had done her best with the limited possibilities presented by the apartment block, sticking to her rule of sourcing furnishings as close to where she was working as possible, and she had been pleased with the final result. She'd even been cautiously keeping her fingers crossed that, though she suspected they wouldn't sell, when the whole complex was finished she might look forward to the apartments being let to holidaymakers and bringing her in some much-needed income.

But now she had received this worrying, threatening letter, from a man she had never heard of before, insisting that she fly out to Thessalonica to meet him. It stated that there were 'certain legal and financial matters with regard to your partnership with Basil Rainhill and my cousin Tino Manos which need to be resolved in person', and included the frighteningly ominous words, 'Failure to respond to this letter will result in an instruction to my solicitors to deal with matters on my behalf'. The letter had been signed *Ilios Manos*.

His summons couldn't have come at worse time, but the whole tone of Ilios Manos's letter was too threatening for Lizzie to feel she could refuse to obey it. As apprehensive and unwilling to meet him as she was, the needs of her family must come first. She had a responsibility to them, a duty of love from which she would never abdicate, no matter what the cost to herself. She had sworn that— promised it on the day of her parents' funeral.

'If this Greek wants to see you that badly he might at least have offered to pay your airfare,' Ruby grumbled.

Lizzie felt so guilty.

'It's all my own fault. I should have realised that the property market was over-inflated, and creating a bubble that would burst.'

'Lizzie, you mustn't blame yourself.' Charley tried to comfort her. 'And as for realising what was happening— how could you when governments didn't even know?'

Lizzie forced a small smile.

'Surely if you tell the bank why you need to go to Greece they'll give you a loan?' Ruby suggested hopefully.

Charley shook her head. 'The banks aren't giving any businesses loans at the moment. Not even successful ones.'

Lizzie bit her lip. Charley wasn't reproaching her for the failure of her business, she knew, but she still felt terrible. Her sisters relied on her. She was the eldest, the sensible one, the one the other two looked to. She prided herself on being able to take care of them—but it was a false pride, built on unstable foundations, as so much else in this current terrible financial climate.

'So what is poor Lizzie going to do? She's got this Greek threatening to take things further if she doesn't go and see him, but how can she if we haven't got any money?' Ruby asked their middle sister.

'We have,' Lizzie suddenly remembered, with grateful relief. 'We've got my bucket money, and I can stay in one of the apartments.'

Lizzie's 'bucket money' was the spare small change she had always put in the decorative tin bucket in her office, in the days when she had possessed 'spare' change.

Two minutes later they were all looking at the small tin bucket, which was now on the kitchen table.

'Do you think there'll be enough?' Ruby asked dubiously

There was only one way to find out.

'Eighty-nine pounds,' Lizzie announced half an hour later, when the change had been counted.

'Eighty-nine pounds and four pence,' Charley corrected her.

'Will it be enough?' Ruby asked.

'I shall make it enough,' Lizzie told them determinedly. It would certainly buy an off-season low-cost airline ticket, and she still had the keys for the apartments—apartments in which she held a twenty per cent interest. She was surely perfectly entitled to stay in one whilst she tried to sort out the mess the Rainhills had left behind.

How the mighty were fallen—or rather the not so mighty in her case, Lizzie reflected tiredly. All she had wanted to do was provide for her sisters and her nephews, to protect them and keep them safe financially, so that never ever again would they have to endure the truly awful spectre of repossession and destitution which had faced them after their parents' death.

CHAPTER TWO

No! It was impossible, surely! The apartment block *couldn't* simply have disappeared.

But it had.

Lizzie blinked and looked again, desperately hoping she was seeing things—or rather not seeing them—but it was no use. It still wasn't there.

The apartment block had gone.

Where she had expected to see the familiar rectangular building there was only roughly flattened earth, scarred by the tracks of heavy building plant.

It had been a long and uncomfortable ride, in a taxi driven at full pelt by a Greek driver who'd seemed bent on proving his machismo behind the wheel, after an equally lacking in comfort flight on the low-cost airline.

They had finally turned off the main highway to travel along the dusty, narrow and rutted unfinished road that ran down to the tip of the peninsula and the apartments. Whilst the taxi had bounded and rocked from side to side, Lizzie had braced herself against the uncomfortable movement, noticing as they passed it that where the road forked, and where last year there had been rolls of spiked barbed wire blocking the entrance to it, there were now imposing-looking padlocked wrought-iron gates.

The taxi driver had dropped her off when the ruts in the road had become so bad that he had refused to go any further. She had insisted on him giving her a price before they had left the airport, knowing how little money she had to spare, and before she handed it over to him she took from him a card with a telephone number on it, so that she could call for a taxi to take her into the city to meet Ilios Manos after she had settled herself into an apartment and made contact with him.

Lizzie stared at the scarred ground where the apartment block should have been, and then lifted her head, turning to look out over the headland, where the rough sparse grass met the still winter-grey of the Aegean. The brisk wind blowing in from the sea tasted of salt—or was the salt from her own wretched tears of shock and disbelief?

What on earth was going on? Basil had boasted to her that twenty per cent entitled her to two apartments, each worth two hundred thousand euros. Lizzie would have put the value closer to one hundred thousand, but it still meant that whatever value they'd potentially held had vanished—along with the building. It was money she simply could not afford to lose.

What on earth was she going to do? She had just under fifty euros in her purse, nowhere to stay, no immediate means of transport to take her back to the city, no apartments—nothing. Except, of course, for the threat implied in the letter she had received. She still had that to deal with—and the man who had made that threat.

To say that Ilios Manos was not in a good mood was to put it mildly, and, like Zeus, king of the gods himself, Ilios could make the atmosphere around him rumble with the threat of dire consequences to come when his anger was aroused. As it was now.

The present cause of his anger was his cousin Tino. Thwarted in his attempt to get money out of Ilios via his illegal use of their grandfather's land, he had now turned his attention to threatening to challenge Ilios's right of inheritance. He was claiming that it was implicit in the tone of their grandfather's will that Ilios should be married, since the estate must be passed down through the family, male to male. Of course Ilios knew this—just as he knew that ultimately he must provide an heir.

Ilios had been tempted to dismiss Tino's threat, but to his fury his lawyers had warned him that it might be better to avoid a potentially long drawn-out and costly legal battle and simply give Tino the money he wanted.

Give in to Tino's blackmail? *Never.* Ilios's mouth hardened with bitterness and pride.

Inside his head he could hear his lawyer's voice, saying apologetically, 'Well, in that case, then maybe you should think about finding yourself a wife.'

'Why, when Tino doesn't have anything resembling a proper case?' Ilios had demanded savagely.

'Because your cousin has nothing to lose and you have a very great deal. Your time and your money could end up being tied up for years in a complex legal battle.'

A battle which once engaged upon he would not be able to withdraw from unless and until he had won, Ilios acknowledged.

His lawyer had suggested he take some time to review the matter, perhaps hoping Ilios knew that he would give in and give Tino the one million euros he wanted—a small enough sum of money to a man who was, after all, a billionaire. But that wasn't the point. The point was that Tino thought that he could get the better of him by simply putting his hand out for money he hadn't earned. There was no way that Ilios was going to allow that.

He had been attempting to vent some of the fury he was feeling by felling branches from an old and diseased olive tree when he had seen a taxi come down the road to the headland, stopping to let its passenger get out before turning round and going back the way it had come.

Now, still wearing the old hard hat bearing the Manos Construction logo he had put on for protection, his arms bare in a white tee shirt, his jeans tucked into work boots, he walked out from the tree line and watched as Lizzie looked out to sea, his arms folded across his chest.

Lizzie turned back towards the flattened ground where the apartments had been, shock holding her immobile as she saw the man standing on it, watching her.

'You're trespassing. This is private land.'

He spoke English! But the words he had spoken were hostile and angry, challenging Lizzie to insist with equal hostility, 'Private land which in part belongs to me.'

It wasn't strictly true, of course, but as a partner in the apartment block she must surely own a percentage of the land on which it had been built? Lizzie didn't know the finer points of Greek property law, but there was something about the attitude toward her of the man confronting her and challenging her that made her feel she had to assert herself and her rights. However, it was plain that she had done the wrong thing. The man unfolded his arms, revealing the outline of a hard-muscled torso beneath the dirt-smeared tee shirt tucked into low-slung jeans that rode his hips, and strode towards her.

'Manos land can never belong to anyone other than a Manos.'

He was savagely angry. The hardness of the gaze from golden eagle eyes fringed with thick dark lashes speared her like a piece of helpless prey.

Lizzie stepped back from him in panic, and lost her footing as she stumbled on a rough tussock of grass.

As she started to fall the man reached for her, hard fingers biting into her jacket-clad arms as she was hauled upright and kept there by his hold on her. The golden gaze raked her with a predatory male boldness that infuriated her. He was looking at her as though…as though he was indeed a mythical Greek god, with the right and the power to take and use vulnerable female mortal flesh for his own pleasure as and when he wished. Sex with a man like this would be dangerous for the woman who was drawn to risk herself in his hostile embrace. Would he take without giving, or would he subjugate a woman foolish enough to think she could make him want her by overpowering her with his sensuality and leaving her a prisoner to it whilst he remained unmoved? That mouth, with its full bottom lip, suggested that he possessed a cruel sensuality that matched his manner towards her.

Lizzie shivered, shocked by the inappropriateness and the unfamiliar sensuality of her own thoughts. She tried to concentrate on something practical.

Somehow as he'd moved he'd also found time to push back the protective hard hat he was wearing, so that now she could see the thick darkness of his hair. She was five foot six. He was much taller—well over six foot—and of course far more powerful that her. Lizzie could see that the effort of holding her had hardly raised the biceps in his powerful arms, but that didn't stop her from trying break free of him.

He stopped her with contemptuous ease, pulling her closer to him. He smelled of earth, and hard work, and of being a man. From somewhere deep down, in the place where she kept her most special memories, she had a sudden mental image of being held in her father's arms in the garden at her parents' lovely house in Cheshire, laughing in delight as she looked down from that height to where her mother was kneeling beside her two younger sisters. Those had been such wonderful years—years when she had felt safe and secure and loved.

But this man was not her father. With this man there would be no safety, no security, and certainly no love.

Love? She was so close to the dirt-streaked tee shirt that she could see the dark shadow of his body hair through it. She could almost feel the force of his hostility towards her. And she felt equally hostile to him. That was why her heart was banging into her chest wall and why her senses were recoiling from the intense awareness of him that his proximity was forcing on her.

What kind of awareness? Awareness of him as a man? Awareness of his maleness? Awareness of his sexuality? Awareness that within her something long denied, something starved of the right to express itself, was pushing against the barriers she had erected against it. Because of this man?

No, of course not. That was impossible. Her heart was thudding even more frantically, pumping adrenalin-fuelled denial through her veins. Why was she reacting to him like this? She had no interest in his sexuality. She *must not* have any interest in his sexuality. She must not want to stay here in his arms.

The panic caused by her own feelings had Lizzie demanding fiercely, 'Let go of me.'

Ilios wasn't used to women demanding to be set free when he was holding them—quite the opposite. Normally women—especially women like he knew this one to be: selfish, shallow, self-seeking women who cared nothing for others—were all too keen to inveigle themselves into situations of intimacy with him. Which was, of course, why he felt so reluctant to release her.

When she pulled back against him the movement of her body released the scent she was wearing, delicate and light. Deep down inside him something visceral and unfamiliar jerked into hot molten life. Desire? For a woman like this? Impossible. He released her abruptly, stepping back from her.

'Who are you?' Lizzie asked unsteadily, struggling for balance both physically and emotionally.

'Ilios Manos,' Ilios told her curtly.

This man was Ilios Manos? The man who had sent her that letter? Lizzie's heart thumped into her ribs, its sledge-hammer blow fired by shock.

'Ilios Manos, the owner of this land on which you have no right to be, Miss Wareham,' Ilios told her grimly.

'How do you know who I am?' The question had been spoken before Lizzie could stop herself.

'Your name is on your suitcase strap,' Ilios pointed out curtly, gesturing towards the brightly coloured strap wrapped around the handle of the small trolley case she had abandoned in the shock of discovering that the apartment block had gone.

'What's happened to the apartments?'

'I gave orders for them to be knocked down.'

'What? Why? You had no right.' Her shocked disbelief deepened her anger, and also in some illogical way her awareness of him—as though she had developed some unwanted new sense designed exclusively to register everything about him and make her intensely receptive to that information. From the way the narrowing of his eyes fanned out fine lines around his eyes to the shape of his mouth as he spoke and her extreme awareness of the powerful maleness of his body.

'I had every right. They were on my land. Illegally on my land.'

Lizzie struggled to clamp down on her awareness of him.

'The land belongs to my partner, Tino Manos, not you.'

'My cousin has ceded his right to the land to me.'

'But you can't just knock down a block of apartments like that. Apart from anything else, two of them belonged to me.'

'Yes,' he agreed, 'they did.'

There was something about the way he was looking at her that made Lizzie feel extremely uneasy—as though she had unwittingly stepped into some kind of trap.

'Tell me, Miss Wareham, what kind of greed makes a person ignore the normal rules of law to grab at something even when they know it must be fraudulent?' His voice was deeply cynical, his whole manner towards her menacing and iced with bitter contempt.

'I...I don't know what you're talking about.' Lizzie protested truthfully.

'Of course you do. You were in partnership with my cousin. You have said so yourself. You must have known about the building regulations that were broken, about the suppliers and workmen left unpaid in order to build the apartments at a minimum cost to your partnership, and for the maximum ultimate profit.'

'No, I didn't,' Lizzie insisted. But she could see that he didn't believe her.

'Have you any idea of the damage your greed has caused? The hardship it has inflicted on those you cheated?

Or do you simply not care? Well, I intend to make sure that you *do* care, Miss Wareham. I will make sure that you pay back everything you owe.'

Ilios was angrier than he could ever remember being. His cousin had systematically tried to cheat him and manipulate him at every turn, and now Tino was even daring to challenge his legitimacy to what was rightfully his. Ilios could feel his fury boiling up inside him. His cousin might not be here to pay for what he had done, but his partner in crime, this Englishwoman who actually dared to lie to him, *was* here, and she would bear the brunt of his fury and his retribution, Ilios decided savagely.

'Everything I owe?' Lizzie objected, her heart sinking. 'What do you mean? I don't owe anybody anything.'

Her determination to continue lying to him hardened Ilios's resolve to inflict retribution on her. She was everything he most disliked and despised in her sex. Dishonest, and attempting to cloak her dishonesty with an air of pseudo-innocence that manifested itself in the way she was dressed—simply, in jeans worn with a tee shirt and a plain jacket—and in her face with its admittedly beautiful bone structure, free of make-up.

Just as that damn elusive scent she was wearing had made him want to draw her closer, to pursue it and capture it, so the pink lipstick that deliberately drew his attention to the fullness of her mouth made him want to capture her lips to see if they were as soft as they looked. Where another less skilled woman might have tried to use artifice to mask her deceit, Elizabeth Wareham used art—the art of appearing modest, honest, vulnerable. Well, it wouldn't work on him. Anyone who did business with his cousin had to be as dishonest and scheming as manipulative as Tino was himself. Like attracted like, after all. She could try using her sexuality to disarm him as much as she liked. He wasn't going to be taken in.

When Ilios Manos didn't respond, Lizzie stiffened her spine and her resolve and repeated, as firmly as she could, 'I don't owe anyone in Greece any money, and I don't understand why you think I do.'

'I don't *think* you do, Miss Wareham. I know you do—because the person you owe money to is me.'

Lizzie gulped in air and tried not to panic. 'But that's not possible.'

Ilios was in no mood to let her continue lying to him. 'You owe me money, Miss Wareham, because of your involvement with the apartments built by my cousin on my land. Plus there is also the matter of the outstanding payments for goods and services provided by local suppliers to you.'

'That isn't my fault. The Rainhills were supposed to pay them,' Lizzie defended herself.

'The contract supplied to me by my cousin states unequivocally that *you* are to pay them.'

'No—that can't be possible,' Lizzie repeated

'I assure you that it is.'

'I have my copy of the contract here with me, and it states quite plainly that the owners of the apartments are to pay the suppliers direct,' Lizzie insisted.

'Contracts can be altered.'

'And in this case they obviously have been—but not by me.' Lizzie's face was burning with disbelief and despair

'And you can prove this?' Ilios Manos was demanding, the expression on his face making it plain that he did not believe her.

'I have a contract that states that my *clients* are responsible for paying the suppliers.'

'That is not what I asked you. The contract I have states unequivocally that *you* are responsible for paying them. And then there is the not so small matter of your share of the cost of taking down the apartments and returning the land to its original state.'

'Taking down the apartments?' Lizzie echoed. 'But that was nothing to do with me. You were the one who ordered their destruction—you told me that yourself...'

Lizzie badly wanted to sit down. She was tired and shocked and frightened, but she knew she couldn't show those weaknesses in front of this stone-faced man who looked like a Greek god but spoke to her as cruelly as Hades himself, intent on her destruction. She was sure he would never show any sign of human weaknesses himself, or make any allowances for those who possessed them. But there was nowhere to sit, nowhere to hide, to escape from the man now watching her with such determined intention on breaking her on the wheel of his anger.

'I had no choice. Even if I had wanted to keep them it would have been impossible, given their lack of sound construction. The truth is that they were a death trap. A death trap on *my* land, masquerading as a building constructed by *my* company.'

As he spoke Ilios remembered how he had felt on learning how his cousin had tried to use the good name of the business Ilios had built up quite literally with his own bare hands for his nefarious purposes, and his anger intensified.

His company. Lizzie automatically looked at his hard hat and its logo. She remembered Basil Rainhill smirking when he'd told her that Manos construction was 'fronting' the building of the apartments, and that they had a first-class reputation. Then she had assumed his smirk was because of the good deal he has boasted about to her, but now…

'I don't know anything about how the apartments were built. In fact, I don't understand what this is about. I was contracted to design the interiors of the apartments, that's all.'

'Oh, come, Miss Wareham—do you really expect me to believe that when I have a contract that stages unequivocally that payment for your work was to be a twenty per cent interest in the apartment block?'

'That was only because the Rainhills couldn't pay me. They offered me that in lieu of my fee.'

'I am not remotely interested in how you came by your share in the illegal construction my cousin built on my land, only that you pay your share of the cost of making good the damage as well as what you owe your suppliers.'

'You're making this up,' Lizzie protested.

'*You* are daring to call *me* a liar?' Ilios grabbed hold of her, gripping her arms as he had done before. How had she dared to accuse him of lying? His desire to punish her, to force her to take back her accusation, to kiss her until the only sound to come from her lips was a soft moan of surrender, pounded through him, crashing through the barriers of civilized behaviour and forcing him to fight for his self-control.

She had said the wrong thing, Lizzie knew. Ilios Manos was not the man to accuse of lying. His pride lay across his features like a brand, informing every expression that crossed his face—and, Lizzie suspected, every thought that entered his head.

He was still holding her, and his touch burned her flesh like a small electrical shock. Her chest lifted with her protesting intake of air. Immediately his gaze dropped to her body with predatory swiftness—as though somehow he knew that when he had touched her, her flesh had responded to his touch in a way that had flung her headlong into a place she didn't know, brought her face to face with a Lizzie she didn't know. Her heart was thumping jerkily, her senses intensely aware of him, and her gaze was drawn to him as though he was a magnet, clinging to his torso, his throat, his mouth.

She swung dizzily and helplessly between disbelief and a craving to move closer to him. Beneath her clothes her breasts swelled and ached, in response to a mastery she was powerless to resist. How could this be happening to her? How could her body be reacting to Ilios Manos as though…as though it *wanted* him? It must be some weird form of shock, Lizzie decided shakily as he released her, almost thrusting her away from him.

'I'm not calling you a liar,' Lizzie denied, feeling obliged to backtrack, if only to remind herself of the reality of her situation. 'I'm just saying that I think you've got some of your facts wrong. And besides—why aren't you demanding recompense from your cousin, instead of threatening and bullying me?' she demanded, quickly going on the attack.

Attack was, after all, the best form of defence, so they said, and she certainly needed to defend herself against what she had felt when he had held her. How could that have happened? She simply wasn't like that. She couldn't be. She had her family to think of. Being sexually aroused by a man she had only just met, a man who despised and disliked her, just wasn't the kind of thing she had ever imagined being. Not ever, and certainly not now.

Determinedly she martialled her scattered thoughts and pointed out, 'After all, I only owned twenty per cent of the apartment block. Your cousin, from what the Rainhills told me, owned the land, most of the apartments and was responsible for the building work. I never even met him, never mind discussed his business plan with him. I was given the apartments and made a partner in lieu of payment for the work I'd done. That's all.'

Ilios knew that that was true, but right now it didn't suit his mood to allow her any escape route—especially now that his cousin had increased his fury by continuing to plot against him. Ilios wanted repayment, he wanted retribution, he wanted vengeance—and he would have them. Ilios hated cheats, and he hated even more being forced to let them get away with cheating.

'My cousin has no assets and is heavily in debt. The Rainhills, as I am sure you have discovered yourself, have disappeared. And, whilst you might only own twenty per cent of the apartment block's value, the partnership agreement you signed contains what is called a joint and several guarantee—which means that each partner is both jointly and severally liable for the debts of the whole partnership. That means that I can claim from you recompense for the entire amount owing.'

'No, that can't be true,' Lizzie protested, horrified.

Ilios looked at her. There was real panic in her voice now. He could see that she was trembling.

An act, he told himself grimly. That was all it was. Just an act.

'I assure you that it is,' he told her, ignoring her obvious distress.

'But I can't possibly find that kind of money.' She couldn't find *any* kind of money.

'No? Well, I have to tell you that I intend to be fully recompensed—not just for the money I am owed, but also for the potential damage that could have been done to my business. A business for which I have worked far harder than someone like you, who lives off the naïveté of others, can ever imagine. You own your own business?'

'Yes,' Lizzie acknowledged. 'But it is almost bankrupt.'

Why had she told him that when she hadn't even told her sisters just how bad things were? That every spare penny she had had been placed into their shared joint account to ensure that the mortgage was paid, the household bills met, and food put on the table at home.

She looked really distraught now, Ilios could see, but he refused to feel any sympathy. Showing sympathy was a sign of weakness, and Ilios never allowed himself to be weak.

'You have a property? A home, I assume?' he pressed

'Yes, but it is mortgaged, and anyway I share it with my sisters, one of whom has two small children and is dependent on me.'

Lizzie didn't know why she was admitting all of this to him, other than because she was in such a state of shock and panic. She wasn't going to let herself think about the last few months of long nights, when she had lain awake worrying about how she would manage to protect her family and continue to provide for them financially. They knew that things were bad, she hadn't been able to hide that from them, but they did not know yet just how bad.

'Your sister does not have a husband to support her and her children? You do not have parents?'

'The answer to both those questions is no. Not that it is any of your business, or relevant to our discussion. There is no way I can find the money to repay you. The only thing I own that is my own is my body…'

'And you wish to offer *that* to me in payment?'

Lizzie was horrified.

'No! Never!'

Her immediate recoil, coupled with her vehemence, inflamed Ilios even further. Was she daring to suggest that she was too good for him? Morally superior to him? Well, he would soon make her change her tune, Ilios promised himself savagely.

'You deny it now, but the offer was implicit in your declaration that your body is the only thing you have.'

He was determined to humiliate her. Lizzie could see that. Because he had somehow sensed her sexual reaction to him?

'No. That is, yes—but I didn't mean it the way you are trying to suggest. I only meant that I do not own anything via which I could raise the money to pay you.'

'Except your body.'

'I didn't mean it like that,' Lizzie repeated, mortified. 'I just meant that…' She lifted her hand to her head, which was now pounding with a mixture of anxiety and despair. 'I can't pay you.'

Ilios had had enough. His temper was at breaking point. He would have what he was owed—one way or another.

'Very well, then,' he began, causing Lizzie to go weak with relief at the thought that he was finally going to accept that there was no point in him continuing to press her for money.

'If your body is all you have with which to repay me, then that is what I will have to take—because I promise you this: I *will* have repayment.'

CHAPTER THREE

LIZZIE's head jerked back on the slender stem of her neck as she looked up at Ilios in shocked disbelief.

'You—you can't mean that!' she protested. But even as she protested, something fierce and elemental was flaring up inside her—a desire, an excitement, a wild surge of female longing that shook her body with its force and shamed her pride with what it said about her. She couldn't want him—and most especially she could not want him under circumstances that should have been making her recoil with revulsion.

'I do mean it,' Ilios assured her.

'I can't believe that anyone could be so…cruel and inhuman, so lacking in compassion or understanding.'

The sudden explosion of sound from Lizzie's mobile phone, announcing the arrival of a text message, momentarily distracted them both.

Watching the way Lizzie reached frantically for her mobile to read it, Ilios gave her a look of cold contempt.

'You are obviously eager to read your lover's message, but—'

'It's from my sisters,' Lizzie interrupted him abstractedly, without lifting her gaze from the small screen. 'Wanting to know if everything is all right.'

'And you, of course, are going to reply and tell them all about the my so called cruelty and inhumanity.'

'No,' Lizzie told him. 'If I did they'd worry about me, and that's the last thing I want. I'm the eldest. It's my job to look after them and protect them. Not the other way around.'

Ilios digested her response in silence. An eldest sister determined to protect her younger siblings wasn't the way he wanted to think about this woman.

'The light's fading,' he told her, gesturing towards the horizon where the winter sun, half obscured by clouds, was starting to dip below the horizon. 'Soon it will be dark. I have to return to Thessaloniki. We can continue our discussion there.'

Over her dead body, Lizzie thought rebelliously, suddenly seeing an opportunity to put some much needed distance between them. She hated the thought of running away instead of staying to fight and prove her innocence, but with a man like this one, hell-bent on extracting payment from her—in kind if he could not have cash—the normal rules of engagement didn't seem the best course of action.

'Very well,' she agreed, reaching for her mobile again.

'What are you doing?' Ilios demanded.

'Telephoning for a taxi,' Lizzie answered.

Ilios shook his head. 'There's no point. You won't get one to come all the way out here—and anyway it isn't necessary. You can travel back with me.'

'No! I mean, no, thank you. I prefer to make my own arrangements,' Lizzie insisted, whilst her heartbeat raced in panicky dread in case he guessed that the reason she was so reluctant to travel with him was not that she was afraid of the intimacy between them it would entail, but that she was afraid a part of her might actually welcome that intimacy.

'You can drop the prim stance,' Ilios told her. 'I can assure you that I have no intention of using my car as a makeshift brothel—and besides, the amount you owe me would require far more in repayment than a single fumble in the back of a car.'

As he finished speaking Ilios reached for Lizzie's trolley case, his swift possession of it leaving her with no option other than to nod her head in unwilling acceptance of his offer.

'This way,' Ilios commanded.

He had walked over the headland from Villa Manos, and it would be easier to walk back there rather than him leaving Lizzie here whilst he went for the car. And besides, he didn't trust her not to try to cheat him a second time by attempting to leave without paying her debt.

The path was narrow and single track, climbing over the headland, and Ilios was making it plain that he expected her to go first, Lizzie could see. In normal circumstances she would have enjoyed such a walk, in the crisp early evening air, and even as it was when she reached the top of the incline she couldn't help being tempted to take a few steps off the path towards the edge of the headland, drawn there by the magnificence of the scenery.

Ilios watched as the wind buffeted Lizzie, whipping her hair into a tangled blonde skein, and then he realised what she was doing.

Lizzie had only gone a few feet when she heard Ilios commanding, from behind her, 'Don't move. Stay where you are.'

It was too much to be denied such a small pleasure on top of everything else, so Lizzie ignored him, determined to defy him and have her moment of small rebellion and triumph even though she had been forced to give in to him on the bigger issues.

When Lizzie ignored him and continued to head for the edge of the promontory, Ilios let go of her case and raced after her.

Too late, Lizzie learned the reason for Ilios's command. The ground was shifting beneath her feet, moving. The edge of the headland was falling away—and she was going to fall with it. She *was* falling, in fact—but not, Lizzie recognised with relief, into the sea with the rock and earth. Instead she fell onto hard, firm ground, clear of the headland, wrapped in Ilios Manos's arms as he grabbed her in a flying tackle, dragging her backwards with a speed and force that sent them both falling to the ground. He had saved her life.

'Are you crazy? What the hell were you trying to do?'

'Not throw myself off the cliff, if that's what you thought,' Lizzie answered. 'Apart from anything else, I haven't got any life insurance. So there wouldn't be any point in trying to kill myself.'

'So you weren't planning some dramatic gesture, claiming you'd rather have death before dishonour?' he taunted her. 'That's just as well, because you'd have been wasting your time since you have already dishonoured yourself with your debt to me.'

'I wasn't trying to do anything other than look at the view.' Lizzie defended herself. 'I didn't know it was dangerous. There aren't any warning signs.'

'There don't need to be any. It's private property, exclusively mine, for my own use and pleasure.'

Lizzie was still in his arms, with the weight of his body pinning her to the ground. She should try to move, she knew, but those words he had used—*private property...exclusively mine...for my own use and pleasure*—had set off a trail of lateral thinking inside her head. Applied to herself, in the context of his insistence on her repayment of the debt she owed him, they were now conjuring up the kind of sensual scenarios that turned her body weak with a reckless longing and filled her with excitement and apprehension.

She wasn't used to feeling like this about any man. She didn't *want* to feel this way about any man—especially not Ilios Manos, who would, she felt sure, take her desire for him and use it against her to punish her. Wanting a man she barely knew wasn't something she had ever imagined would happen to her—her whole way of life, her entire way of thinking, was diametrically opposed to such a possibility. Not for her own protection, but for the protection of her family. To have such feelings now alarmed and terrified her. Lizzie desperately wanted to ignore what she felt, to deny it completely if she could. But it wouldn't let her. It was too strong for her, too determined to make its need felt.

Her heart was thudding under his hand, Ilios recognized, like the beat of the wings of a trapped bird, frantic for its freedom. But, like this land and everything on it, she was his by rights so ancient they were imprinted on every cell of his body. She was his. He was still holding on to her, and against the palm of his hand he could feel the soft, warm swell of her breast, more rounded and fuller than her slenderness had suggested.

Automatically, of its own accord, as though divorced from his thoughts and answerable only to its own need, his palm curved closer to her flesh, the pad of his thumb-tip moving experimentally over a nipple soft at first, but rising immediately to his touch. He cupped her breast fully, stroking her nipple, and his other hand tightened its hold to draw her closer. His body moved so that he could thrust one thigh between the jean-clad flesh of hers.

The world—her world, the world she had thought she knew—had gone crazy, Lizzie acknowledged. The heat burning through her body was surely global warming gone into overdrive. Her breasts—both of them, not just the one he was caressing—were aching to be enjoyed, whilst the knowing male thigh thrusting between her own made her want to lean against it, move against it, open herself to it and to all the delicious sensual possibilities its presence signposted.

This man was…

This man was her enemy!

What was he doing? Ilios had never had any taste for casual, meaningless sex, and yet here he was touching this woman who was lying beneath him as though he was starved for the sensation of her female flesh beneath his hands—as though the desire he could feel pounding through him was so strong, so all-important and demanding, so beyond his own control, that he had no choice other than to submit to it.

As Lizzie pushed him away Ilios released her, infuriated both with himself for his unacceptable and inexplicable need and with her for being the cause of it.

'You had no right to do that,' Lizzie told him fiercely, desperately anxious to establish that *she* was not the one who had started what had happened.

'That wasn't what your body was saying.'

Of course he was bound to have known what she was feeling, a man like him, with that aura he had of sexual power and knowledge. Lizzie's face burned hot with self-conscious awareness of how he had made her feel. She wasn't going to allow him to get the better of her, though. She couldn't afford to.

'You can think what you like,' she told him defensively. 'But I know the truth.'

Of course she did. And the truth was...

She didn't want to think about what the truth was, or what it had felt like to be held in his arms, to be touched by him, to have her senses set alight and her defences laying down their arms in willing surrender. She didn't want to think of anything other than putting as much distance as she could between herself and Ilios Manos as fast as she could.

CHAPTER FOUR

'WHERE are we going?' Lizzie asked uncertainly, once she was back on her feet and Ilios was a safe distance away from her.

'Not to some secluded grotto so I can imprison you like some Greek nymph awaiting the gods' pleasure, where you will be obliged to answer to my every sensual need, if that is what you are imagining. We are merely returning to Villa Manos, which is where I left my car.'

'Villa Manos? That is where you live?' Lizzie queried—after all, it was far safer talking about a villa than it was thinking about the dangerous effect his previous comments had been having on her.

'No. I have an apartment in Thessaloniki, at the top of the Manos Construction office block. The villa is very old, and the building has fallen into disrepair. It was Tino's hope that he could insist that it be bulldozed, because it might present a danger to the holidaymakers visiting the complex he planned to build here—but then I am sure that you already know all about that, since you are partners.'

They had almost reached the top of the incline now, and even though she was slightly out of breath Lizzie turned to face him, her normally calm grey eyes sparkling quicksilver-bright with temper as she objected. 'I have already told you. I have never even met your cousin, never mind been the recipient of his confidences with regard to his business plans.'

'Business plans which included manipulating me into selling him my half of our grandfather's land once he had forced me to remove our ancestral home from it.'

Ilios had started to climb the last few feet of the path, so Lizzie did the same, coming to an abrupt halt as she saw what lay below them, bathed in the last dying rays of the day's light.

At the far end of a long straight drive, lined with tall Cyprus trees and surrounded by Italianate gardens, slightly elevated from the surrounding terrain, set like a pearl against the dark green of the Cyprus and the blue of the Aegean Sea beyond it, perfectly framed by its surroundings was—

'Villa Emo,' Lizzie announced breathlessly in a slightly dazed voice as she stared at the building. She turned to Ilios to say in disbelief, 'It looks exactly like Villa Emo—the house Palladio designed for the Emo family outside Venice.'

To either side of the main house long, low, arcaded wings—which on the original Villa Emo had been farm buildings—extended in perfect symmetry, capped at both ends with classically styled dovecotes, whilst the main building itself was a perfect copy of the Italian original.

'It's so beautiful,' Lizzie whispered, awestruck by the wonderful symmetry of the building and wondering how on earth Palladio's beautiful villa for the Emo family had somehow transported itself here, to this remote Greek Macedonian promontory.

'A deadly beauty, some might say, since it was someone

else's desire to possess it conflicting with my grandfather's determination to keep it that cost my father and Tino's father their lives.' His voice was openly harsh with bitterness.

Without waiting to see if Lizzie was following him he started off down the steep path towards the house. Automatically Lizzie followed him, unable to stop herself from asking, once she had caught up with him, 'What happened—to your father?' She had lost her own parents, after all, and she knew the dreadful pain of that kind of loss.

'What happened?' Ilios stopped so abruptly that Lizzie almost cannoned into him, only stopping herself from doing so by placing her hand on his forearm to steady herself. She snatched it back again for her own safety and peace of mind as she felt the now familiar surge of sensual longing that physical contact with him brought her. How was it possible for this one man to do what no other man had ever done, without actually doing anything to arouse the desire she felt for him? Lizzie didn't know, and she didn't really want to know either. She simply wanted it not to happen.

Ilios was speaking again, and she forced herself to concentrate on what he was saying and not what she was feeling.

'The ruling Junta at the time believed that since my grandfather would not agree to sell the villa to one of their number he should be forced to make a choice between the villa and the lives of his sons. They misjudged my grandfather, I'm afraid. He chose the villa.'

'Over his own flesh and blood?' Lizzie couldn't conceal her horrified disbelief. 'How could he do something like that?'

They had reached the gardens now, and were taking a path that skirted past them, but instead of being disappointed at not being able to see them in more detail Lizzie was too appalled by what Ilios was telling her to think about them.

'He had no other choice,' Ilios told her as they emerged from the shadow of a tree-lined walkway into the gravelled courtyard where he had left his car.

'So what happened—to…to your father?' Lizzie had to ask the question.

'He was shot. They both were. But not at the same time. Tino's father, the younger of the two, was set free initially. It seemed he had convinced the Junta that if they set him free he would persuade his father to change his mind. When he couldn't, the only difference it made to their ultimate fate was that my father was blindfolded and shot by the firing squad he was facing whilst my uncle was shot in the back trying to escape them.'

Lizzie couldn't stop herself from shuddering.

'How awful—your poor mother.'

'I doubt she cared very much one way or the other. She and my father had only been married a matter of months—a dynastic marriage of sorts—and by the time she had given birth to me the Junta had been overthrown.'

Lizzie was appalled.

'So you never knew your father?'

'No.'

'And your mother?'

'She remarried—a cousin with whom she was already in love. I was handed over to my grandfather.'

'She gave you away?'

The pity that had been growing inside her with every terse answer Ilios had given her had grown into an aching ball of shocked compassion. She and her sisters had known such love from their parents, had had such happy childhoods, and Lizzie couldn't help but feel the contrast between her own childhood and the one Ilios must have had.

'As she saw it she had done her duty in marrying my father and producing a son, and so she deserved to follow her own heart, which did not lie with me.'

'Where is she now? Do you see her?'

'She and her second husband were killed in a freak storm when they were out sailing.'

Lizzie could understand why a person would want to keep such a beautiful home in the family—but surely not at the price of one's own children? How could a man have sacrificed his own sons the way Ilios's grandfather had?

'Villa Manos isn't just an inheritance, it is a sacred trust,' Ilios told her coldly, obviously guessing what she was thinking. 'It was said by our ancestor when he had it built that as long as it remained in the hands of the Manos family our family would survive and thrive, but that if it should be lost to the family our line would shrivel and turn to dust. It is the responsibility of the Manos who holds the key to Villa Manos to ensure that there is someone for him to pass it on to. Since he is the elder or the two of us my cousin grew up believing—as I did myself—that our grandfather would pass on the key to him.'

'So why didn't he?' Lizzie couldn't resist asking.

'I went out into the world and made something of myself, whilst Tino preferred to live off what little our grandfather still had. In the end our grandfather decided that our history and out future would be safer in my hands. The land he divided between us, but the house he left to me.'

It was a tale of true Greek tragedy in many ways, Lizzie

reflected as Ilios headed for an expensive-looking car, which Lizzie could now see was a Bentley. He unlocked the passenger door and then opened it for her.

She had no option other than to go with him. Lizzie knew that, but she still hesitated.

In the end it was her compassion for the child he must once have been as much as her awareness of his power over her that had her sliding into the richly luxurious leather seat. Ilios stowed her trolley case in the boot before getting into the driver's seat and starting the car.

What a terrible, tainted inheritance he had received, Lizzie thought sadly as they bumped down the rutted lane.

The March day had darkened into early evening by the time they reached the main road that would take them back to Thessalonica. It had been a long day for Lizzie, who had been up at five in the morning to catch her flight, and the anxiety she had endured added to her tiredness now. Combined with the comforting hum of the expensive car, they had her drifting off to sleep and then waking herself up again as she fought the longing to close her eyes. She might feel appalled by the story he had told her, and filled with compassion for the lonely child he must have been, but that did not mean she felt comfortable about falling asleep in his presence. Far from it. There was something too intimate, too vulnerable about sleeping in his wakeful presence to allow her to do that.

And yet inevitably in the end she was unable to prevent her eyes from closing and her head dropping against the leather headrest, with her face turned towards the man who now had command of her life.

Ilios studied her. The bone structure beneath the pale skin was elegantly formed, her beauty quietly classical and enduring. Her loyalty to her family matched one of the most important tenets of traditional Greek society. She was, he recognised as he looked at her, the kind of woman a man would marry rather than simply want to bed for momentary sexual satisfaction.

Ilios exhaled on the sudden realisation of where his own thought processes were taking him.

The car hit a pothole in the road, waking Lizzie up.

What had she told herself about not betraying any more vulnerability than she had to? she cautioned herself as she sat up, and then frowned as she glanced at her watch and realised what time it was.

'Please excuse me, but I must send a text,' she told Ilios, reaching for her phone.

'To your lover?' Ilios challenged her.

'No! I don't have a lover!' Lizzie denied immediately.

The dark eyebrows rose. 'Such a vehement, almost shocked denial—and yet surely it is perfectly natural that a woman of your age should have a man in her life and her bed. You are what? Twenty-four? Twenty-five? After all, you can hardly still be a virgin.'

'Of course not. And I'm twenty-seven,' Lizzie told him.

Of course not. But her last sexual relationship—her only sexual relationship, in fact—had been when she had been at university. And it had existed more because it was the done thing than because she and the boy in question had envisaged spending the rest of their lives together. Things had been different then. She had been young, and life had been fun. Fun had died out of her life with the loss of her parents.

'And I wasn't shocked. It's simply that I have more important things to think about than men.'

'Such as?'

'My family—my sisters and my nephews. It is actually the boys I need to text. I promised them I would because I won't be there to read their bedtime story—it would have been my turn tonight.' Emotion choked Lizzie's voice. 'My family are far more important to me than any man ever could be. I have to put them first. They depend on me, and I can't let them down. They matter far more to me than some…some fleeting sexual pleasure.'

Automatically Ilios wanted to reject, to push away and in fact deny his awareness of the emotion in Lizzie's voice when she spoke of her family. There was no place for that kind of sentiment in his present life or in his plans for his future life. Nor would there ever be.

'If your only experience of sexual pleasure has been fleeting then it is hardly surprising it doesn't bother you to give it up,' he told Lizzie coolly instead. 'A good lover makes it his business to make his partner's pleasure as enduring as she wishes it to be.'

'That's easy to say,' Lizzie responded, desperate to try to hold her own and appear as nonchalant as Ilios himself. The reality was that his casual observation was having an intense and unwanted effect on her. It was making her ask questions of herself that she knew she could not answer. Questions such as what would it be like to be Ilios Manos's lover?

'And I assure you easy to do, when one knows how,' Ilios came back slipping the comment up under Lizzie's guard and drawing a soft gasp of choked reaction from her.

Of course Ilios Manos would be an experienced lover. Of course he would know exactly how to please his partner—even if that partner was an untutored as she was herself.

She was floundering now, going down under the flood

of awareness surging through her, a flood of dangerous sensations, longings, and—heavens, yes—images as well, of two sensually entwined naked bodies, one belonging to her and the other to Ilios. Stop it, Lizzie warned herself, beginning to panic. She could not afford this kind of self-indulgence. It was far too dangerous.

Determinedly Lizzie concentrated on texting the twins, adding a few words for her sister, telling her that she was still involved in discussions about the letter and would be in touch again as soon as she had something concrete to report to them.

'I take it that your sisters are aware of the purpose of your journey to Greece?' Ilios asked Lizzie.

'Yes,' she agreed. 'They saw your letter.' The thought of how her sisters would feel if they knew what Ilios had said to her—what he had demanded of her—brought a lump to Lizzie's throat. They would be dreadfully shocked—and worried too, for their own security.

That thought had her turning impetuously towards Ilios to beg him emotionally, 'Surely we can come to some kind of sensible arrangement that would enable me to repay you?'

'What do you mean by "sensible"?' Ilios asked.

Lizzie shook her head. 'Perhaps I could work for you as an interior designer?'

'The constructions in which I am involved are very large-scale commercial projects—schools, offices, corporate buildings, that kind of thing. However…' Ilios paused, turning to give her an assessing look in the shadowy darkness of his car. 'There is an alternative means by which you could clear the debt between us.'

Lizzie moistened her suddenly dry lips with the tip of

her tongue, before asking in a voice that was slightly hoarse with tension, 'And that is?'

The Bentley picked up speed as Ilios overtook the car in front of them. The delay in answering her ratcheted up Lizzie's tension.

It seemed an aeon before he turned towards her, his profile outlined by the moonlight beaming into the car. It was an undeniably handsome and very sensually male profile, Lizzie admitted, but there was a harshness in the downward turn of his mouth, that made her shiver inwardly. She wasn't sure which she feared the most: the effect of his harshness on her too easily bruised emotions, or the effect of his sensuality on her equally easily aroused senses.

'Marriage,' Ilios told her.

CHAPTER FIVE

'MARRIAGE?' Lizzie repeated unsteadily, feeling that she must somehow have misunderstood him.

'According to my solicitors I am in need of a wife,' Ilios informed her curtly. 'And since you claim you cannot repay me in cash, and since I have no appetite for the kind of woman who so easily shares her body with any man who has had the price to pay for it, I have decided that this is best way for me to recoup what I have lost and take payment from you.'

Lizzie felt as though glue had been poured into her brain, locking it together and jamming her ability to think.

The only words she could summon were the words, *Ilios Manos*, *marriage*, and *danger*—all written large in bright red ink.

'No,' she told Ilios shakily, before she could do the utterly reckless, dangerous and unthinkable and say yes. Whatever the reason Ilios might want her as a wife, it was absolutely not because he wanted *her*, and she had better hang on to that fact, Lizzie told herself, not start spinning crazily foolish fantasies and daydreams about Mr Right, Cinderella and happy ever after, filled with nights of sensual delight and days of blissful joy.

A categorical no was not the answer Ilios wanted, and nor was it the answer he had expected. He knew of a dozen women at least who would have been delirious with joy at the thought of becoming his wife, quite apart from the fact that Lizzie Wareham was in no position to dare to refuse him anything. She was certainly not going to be allowed to do so. Didn't she realise the position she was in? A position in which he held all the aces and she held none. If not, then perhaps it was time he made that position completely clear to her.

'No?' he challenged her coldly. 'So it is just as I thought. All that you have said to me about your desire to protect your sisters—your family—is nothing more than lies and total fiction.' He paused. A man of action and powerful determination, Ilios did not waste time analysing his decisions once he had made them, or asking himself what might have motivated them—even when they involved the kind of turnaround that had taken place inside his head since that very morning. He had decided Lizzie would be his wife.

He also hated not winning; once he had decided upon a course of action he stuck to it, no matter what obstacles lay in his way. Obstacles could be crushed and then removed. It was simply a matter of finding the right method to do so, with speed and efficiency, and Ilios thought he knew exactly the right method to shift the obstacle to his plans that was Lizzie's 'no'.

'I was about to say—before you were so quick to refuse me—that I am also prepared to pay you a bonus of one hundred thousand pounds, on the understanding that for your part you conduct yourself in public at all times during our enforced relationship as you would were that relationship real. In other words I expect you, in your role as my fiancée and then my wife, to behave.'

A bonus? What he meant was a *bribe*, Lizzie acknowledged, feeling sickened as much by her awareness of how little she could now afford to refuse as by her personal feelings swirling through her at the thought of being married to him.

'To behave as though I'm in love with you?' Lizzie supplied lightly, determined not to let him see how humiliated she felt. The thought of having to act as though she loved him filled her with an immediate and self-defensive need to refuse.

It was bad enough that he was humiliating her by offering her money, without her own painful awareness of her fear that the physical longing he aroused in her so easily might overwhelm her.

A truly brave person did not turn and flee from their own fear and danger, Lizzie reminded herself. A truly brave person stood their ground and fought to overcome it, to make themselves even stronger. And besides, how could she turn down the money he was prepared to offer her when she knew what it would mean at home. It would clear the mortgage, for one thing, and leave nearly ten thousand pounds' much needed 'rainy day money'.

It meant that she would be quite literally selling herself to him—a man she already knew affected her as no man ever had. But she had to accept his offer for the sake of her family. How could she live with herself if she didn't, knowing the huge difference it would make to their lives?

'To behave as though our relationship is genuine and desired by both of us,' Ilios told her. 'Very, well, then.' he continued, when Lizzie remained silent. 'If you prefer to have your family stripped of the roof over their heads—'

What kind of fool was she to dare to try and refuse him? What was she expecting? That he would turn into some kind of white knight in shining armour? Some kind of saviour who would generously let her off any kind of payment? It was time she grew up and learned as he had had to learn that saviours didn't exist. The only way to escape from the burdens life presented you with was to dig your own way out from under them—with your bare hands, if necessary, as he had. No doubt she expected him to feel sorry for her, with her tale of how her family had suffered and how she believed it was her duty to protect them. Why should he? Who had ever protected *him* when he had needed protection? No one. Hardship made a person stronger, unless they were so weak in the first place that they went to the wall. She must know that herself, since she had strength.

Ilios frowned. When and how had he decided, without knowing more about her, that Lizzie Wareham had strength? Strength was something he admired and respected, after all. Especially when that strength was hard-won.

'No, of course I don't,' Lizzie told Ilios fiercely, immediately tormented by the horrific images his callous words had conjured up. 'I just don't understand why you should want to marry me.'

It was the wrong thing to have said.

'I don't,' Ilios assured her, and the look he gave her sliced her pride to the bone. 'It is my lawyers who believe that the best way for me to protect what is rightfully mine from my cousin's greedy machinations is for me to marry. Tino needs money. He thinks he can blackmail me into giving him that money by threatening to challenge my right of inheritance under our grandfather's will. He knows that I will never give up what is in effect a sacred charge on me, a duty to both the history of our name and its future, so he thinks I will give in to him. But I shall not. He claims that the fact that I am known to have sworn never to marry and do not have a wife means I have broken an unwritten article of faith—namely that Villa Manos must be passed down through the male line of our family. Villa Manos and its lands are a sacred trust. They have been in our family for over five hundred years. They are the essence of what we are. Manos blood, my father's blood, was sacrificed for them. There is nothing I will not do to hold my duty and to meet it. *Nothing!*'

His fury, and the pride that went with it, filled the air around her so that she could almost feel and taste them, Lizzie recognized.

'Tino believes that he has backed me into a corner,' he continued angrily. 'That I will be prepared to buy him off in order to keep Villa Manos. My solicitors advise me that the best and only guaranteed way to block Tino's plans is for me to marry. After all, with blackmail one payment is never the end, it is merely the beginning. If I were to give in to him now—which I have no intention of doing—Tino would think that he has me in his power.'

Privately Lizzie found it impossible to imagine that anyone, male or female, would be foolish enough to think they could control a man like Ilios Manos.

'Why don't you simply find someone you genuinely want to marry?' she suggested. 'After all, a man with your—'

'With my what?' Ilios stopped her. 'With my wealth? That is exactly why I am not married and why I never intend to marry. Only a fool voluntarily puts himself in a position where a woman can enjoy a rich man's money both in marriage and then out of it, after they both discover that they no longer want one another. The curse of wealth is that it has the same attraction for sharks as fresh blood. My marriage to you will be different. You will already have been paid to wear my name and my ring. My cousin does not have the temperament for a long fight. Once he sees that I am married he will lose interest and the marriage can be annulled.'

Lizzie shivered as she heard the implacable merciless coldness in Ilios's voice. It reminded her all too well of what the reality of her situation was.

Once, before their parents' death, she might have been an impulsive eager young woman who believed that one day the sensuality of her nature would find joyous fulfilment with a man who was her soul mate. But that had been a long time ago. Since then she had believed that sensuality and its satisfaction were things she had put to one side without regret. Now, though—albeit against her will—she suspected that Ilios Manos had reignited her female desire. That made her vulnerable to him in a way that could not be countenanced.

For her own sake she should protect herself by returning to England and never thinking about him or seeing him again. For her own sake. But what about her family? For them, for their sake to protect them, she needed to stay here and accept the terms that Ilios was forcing on her. How could she possibly put herself first?

As though he had access to her private thoughts, Ilios told her unkindly, 'You have two choices. Either you agree to marry me, and in doing so give your sisters the financial protection you claim is all-important to you, or you refuse and face the consequences. Because I will pursue you for repayment of your debt to me, with all the power at my command. And I warn you—do not make the mistake of thinking I do not mean what I say or that I will not carry out my retribution.'

Two choices? He was wrong about that, Lizzie admitted bleakly to herself. She had no choice at all.

Even so, she managed to keep her head held high as she told him, 'Very well, then. I shall marry you—although there seems to be something you have overlooked in your calculations,' she couldn't resist adding.

'Which is?' he demanded.

'You said that Villa Manos and its lands must be passed from father to son,' Lizzie pointed out to him.

'And so it shall be,' Ilios agreed. 'We are living in the twenty-first century now,' he told her matter-of-factly. 'A child can be created without its parents having to meet, never mind get married.'

'But what about love?' Lizzie couldn't stop herself from asking. 'You may fall in love, and then—'

'That will never happen. I don't believe in what you call "love", and I don't want to. I would never trust any woman to have my children and not at some stage use them as pawns for her own benefit.'

The harshness in his voice warned Lizzie that this was a dangerous subject, one which raised strong emotions in him, even though she suspected that Ilios himself would refuse to accept that. But not to believe in love—of any kind... Lizzie shivered at the thought of such a cold and barren existence. Love could hurt the human heart—badly—but surely it was also woven into the weft and warp of human life in a way that made it as essential as air and water.

'When the time comes,' Ilios continued, 'I shall ensure that I become the father of one or possibly two sons. They will carry my DNA along with that of a woman who will provide the eggs before being carried by a surrogate. Neither women will know who I am, because it will not be any of their business. My sons will grow up with me, knowing that I am their father.'

'But they will never know their mother.' Lizzie's shock couldn't be hidden. 'Aren't you concerned about how that might affect them?'

'No. Because they will grow up knowing that they were planned and wanted—by me—and why. They will know too that I have protected them from exploitation by any woman using them for her own financial advantage. They will be far too busy learning what it means to be a Manos to worry about the absence from their lives of a woman they can call "Mother". Unlike many other children they will never be in the position of believing that their mother loves them above all else only to find that she does not…'

Was this the reason he refused to believe in love?

'Is that what happened to you?' she asked softly, driven again to feel pity for the child he must have been, despite the way he had behaved towards her. The words were spoken before she could check them.

The softness of Lizzie's voice touched a previously un-recognised area of raw pain within him that immediately had Ilios fighting to deny its existence—furious with himself for having such a vulnerability, and even more furious with Lizzie for so accurately finding it.

'Don't waste your time or your pity trying to psycho-analyse me. All I want from you is payment of your debt to me. Nothing less and nothing more,' he told her coldly.

It was all too much for her to take in, Lizzie admitted numbly. Physical and emotional exhaustion claimed her as the miles flew by, and her eyes ached to be closed just as her mind ached for the panacea of sleep, so that it could escape for a little while from the daunting prospect ahead of her. If it was cowardly to allow herself to find that escape in sleep, then she would just have to be a coward, Lizzie told herself, and she allowed her eyes to close.

He had got what he wanted, so why wasn't he feeling a greater sense of triumph? Ilios wondered. Why wasn't he filled with a sense of righteous satisfaction in having forced Lizzie to make reparation? He had the right and the justification for feeling both of those things, after all.

Some sense he hadn't known he possessed alerted him to the fact that Lizzie had fallen asleep again. He glanced at her. At least she would make a convincing wife—which, of course, was exactly why he had hit on this method of making her pay what she owed him. It was a perfectly logical and sensible decision for him to have made, and one which would leave him with the balance sheet of his pride healthily in credit. That was why he had been able to offer her the additional inducement of a cash payment. There *was* no other reason. No question of him actually having felt some sort of ridiculous compassion for the plight of her family. He simply wasn't that kind of man and never would be. If Lizzie Wareham *was* the victim of circumstance rather than her own greed, as she insisted to him she was, then what was that to him? Nothing.

He had no duty to take the woes of others onto his own shoulders. His duty was solely to himself alone. Because there was only himself. Alone. That was what he was—alone. And that was the way he preferred it, and it always would be.

Ilios put his foot down on the accelerator. His need to focus on the increased speed with which he was driving might be giving him an excuse not to focus on the woman sleeping at his side, but it was not an excuse he needed, he assured himself. Nor was it anything to do with *him* if the angle at which she was sleeping was likely to give her a stiff neck. But his foot was covering the brake in the minute gap between him recognising her discomfort and refuting his need to become involved in it.

Some instinct told Lizzie that something had changed and that she needed to wake up. A scent—alien and pulse-quickening, and yet also familiar and desired—caught at her senses, like the warmth of the heat from another body close to her own, the touch of a hand on her skin. Slowly Lizzie opened her eyes, her heart banging into her chest wall as she realised that she was practically lying flat in the front seat of the Bentley, with Ilios leaning over her. The soft light illuminated the interior of the car, and with it the carved perfection of his features.

Inside her head a tape played, trapping her when she was too vulnerable to stop it, tormenting her with images of herself reaching up to touch his face with her fingertips, exploring its chiselled features. Surely it should be impossible for a real live man to have such classically perfect male features?

She wanted to touch him, to run her fingertips over his face as though he were indeed a marvellous sculpture, created by hands so skilled that one could not help but yearn to touch the masterpiece they had created.

She could almost feel the hard-cut shape of his mouth— the lower lip full and sensual, the groove from the centre of his top lip to his nose clearly marked. A sign of great sensuality, so she had once read. His skin would feel warm and dry, and as she explored the pattern of his lips he would reach out and take hold of her wrist, kissing her fingers.

Frantically Lizzie struggled to sit upright, panicked by Ilios's proximity and the unwanted images inside her head to which it was giving rise.

His sharp, 'Be still', was harshly commanding, his eyes a deep dark gold in the soft light of the interior of the car. Hadn't it been the Greek King Midas whose touch had turned everything before him to gold, thus depriving him of life-giving water and food? Even his son had been turned into a golden statue by his touch, leaving him unable to return his love. Was that what had happened to Ilios? Had the circumstances of his birth and the burden of his inheritance deprived him of the ability to feel love? What if it had? Why should that matter to her?

'There is no cause for you to act like a nervous virgin. I was simply adjusting your seat so that you could sleep in it safety.'

Lizzie's 'Thank you', was self-conscious and stilted.

As he moved back from her to his own seat Ilios told her in a clipped, rejecting voice, 'There's no need to thank me. After all, had you fallen across me my safety would have been compromised as much as yours.'

Lizzie could have kicked herself. Of course he hadn't been thinking about her personal safety. Why should he?

Ilios had noticed her recoil from him—obviously instinctive and unplanned. But he was certainly not affected by it. Far from it. The last thing he wanted was a sexual relationship between them to add complications to the situation. Ilios looked out into the darkness beyond the car. He should perhaps make that clear to her. Not because of his own pride, of course. No. It was simply the sensible thing to do.

Restarting the car, he informed Lizzie dispassionately, 'I should have made it clear earlier that our marriage will merely be a business arrangement. If you were thinking of adding to your bonus payment by offering a sexual inducement, then let me warn you not to do so.'

As Lizzie exhaled in angry humiliation, Ilios continued bluntly, 'I do not want either your body or your desire. Should you be tempted to offer me either one of them, or both, then you must resist that temptation.'

There—that should have made the position clear to her, Ilios decided. It would certainly remove any future risk of his body reacting to her unwanted proximity.

He had obviously realised the effect he was having on her, Lizzie thought miserably.

Annoyingly, now that her seat was reclined and she could have slept comfortably, she felt too self-conscious to do so. So she found the buttons Ilios had used and brought her seat upright again, informing him in as businesslike a voice as she could, 'My sisters will be expecting to hear from me. I think it will be best if I simply tell them I shall be working for you as an interior designer, rather than trying to explain about our...the marriage.'

'I agree. However, where *my* friends and acquaintances are concerned the marriage will obviously become a public reality, and for that reason I think we should agree a suitable history of our relationship. I suggest we say simply that we met when I was on business in England and that our relationship has progressed from there. I kept it and you under wraps, so to speak, until I decided that I wanted to marry you.'

'Until we decided that we wanted to marry one another,' Lizzie corrected him firmly, refusing to give way and break eye contact with him when he flashed her a look of arrogant disbelief that said quite plainly that in his book *he* made the decisions.

'We shall soon be back in the city,' he continued, breaking the challenging silence. 'Which hotel are you in?'

'I had intended to stay in one of the apartments,' Lizzie was forced to admit.

'You mean you haven't booked anywhere?' His tone was critical and irritated, making Lizzie feel foolish and unprofessional. She had so much else on her mind to worry about that she'd completely overlooked the fact that she now didn't have anywhere to stay.

'Like I said, I was expecting to stay in one of the apartments,' she defended herself, telling him, 'Just drop me off somewhere central and I'll find somewhere.'

The last thing she wanted was for him to take her to some five-star hotel she couldn't afford.

Ilios fought back his irritation whilst mentally calculating the risk of how likely it was that someone he knew would see Lizzie and remember her later if he booked her into a hotel. He decided the odds were too high for him to take. It wasn't that he particularly cared about the fact that his wife-to-be wasn't wearing designer clothes, full make-up and expensive jewellery, but local society liked to gossip, and he didn't want anyone asking awkward questions.

They were travelling down a wide thoroughfare, passing a spectacularly well-designed tall glass and marble building, but before she could comment on it Ilios had turned into a side street and driven down a dark ramp, activating a door in the black marble of a side wall that opened to allow him to drive inside.

'Where are we?' Lizzie asked uncertainly.

'The Manos Construction building,' Manos told her. Under the circumstances I think it will be best if you stay in my apartment. There are certain formalities that will need to be dealt with—and quickly, if my cousin's suspicions are not to be alerted. Since you don't already have a hotel booking, it makes sense for you to stay with me.'

Stay with him? Lizzie's mouth had gone dry with tension and anxiety.

'Nothing to say?'

'What am I supposed to say? Thank you?' Lizzie's voice was filled with despair, and her emotions overwhelmed her as she demanded, 'Have you any idea what it's like to be in my position? Not to know whether or not you can pay your bills, or even where your next meal is going to come from? Not having anyone to turn to who can help?'

'Yes. I have known all those things and more—far more than you can ever imagine.'

His answer silenced Lizzie in mid-sentence, leaving her with her mouth half open.

Ilios hadn't intended to allow himself to speak about his most deeply buried memories, but now that he had begun to do so he discovered that it was impossible for him to stop. Emotions—anger, bitterness, resentment—fought with one another to tell their story, bursting from their imprisonment in a torrent of furiously savage words.

'World War Two and everything that followed it destroyed our family fortunes. What it didn't take the Junta did. I left home when I was sixteen, intent on making my fortune as I had promised my grandfather I would. Instead I ended up in Athens, begging from rich tourists. That was how I learned to speak English. From there I got work on construction sites, building hotels. That was how I learned to make money.'

'And you worked your way up until you owned your own business?'

'In a manner of speaking. Only the way I worked myself up was via a spell in prison and a few good hands of cards. I was falsely accused of stealing materials from a site on which I was working. In prison I found that I could make money playing cards. I saved that money, and then I went back to the construction trade and started to put to use what I'd learned.'

He would make a very bad enemy, Lizzie decided, shivering a little as she heard in his voice the implacability that had made him what he was.

What was happening to him? Ilios wondered. Why was he suddenly talking about things he had vowed never to discuss with anyone? It must be because he wanted to ensure that Lizzie Wareham didn't get away with thinking that she was the only one to have had hardship in her life. Satisfied with his answer, Ilios got out of the car and went round to the passenger door to open it for Lizzie.

He looked immaculate, Lizzie noticed, whilst she felt sure that she must look travel-creased and grubby. Whilst she smoothed her jeans, and then tried to do the same to her hair, Ilios went to the boot of the car and removed her case from it. Hastily Lizzie went to take it from him, but he shook his head, carrying it as easily as though it was a sheaf of papers. She had no need to wonder where his muscles came from. All that work on building sites, no doubt.

'The lift's this way,' he told her, directing her towards a marble and glass area several yards away. He activated it with a code he punched into the lock, standing back to allow her to go into the lift first.

If he hadn't told her himself about his childhood she would never have guessed, Lizzie acknowledged. He had the polished manners and self-assurance she associated with someone born into comfortable circumstances, not someone who had come up the hard way. But then his background was obviously moneyed, in the sense that his family had possessed it at one time. Had that made things harder for him? Set him apart from those he'd worked with? Had he ever felt alienated and alone?

Lizzie tried to imagine how she would feel if she didn't have her sisters, and then warned herself that sympathy was the last thing Ilios Manos wanted. He was a man who stood alone because he wanted to stand alone. He had as good as told her that himself.

The lift soared upwards at speed, flattening her stomach to her spine. She'd never really liked lifts, and this one was all glass, on the inside of the cathedral-like space of the building. Even though it was now in darkness, it made her feel distinctly nervous.

The lift stopped swiftly and silently, its doors opening onto an impressive rectangular hallway. The walls and floors were covered in limestone, and concealed lighting illuminated the space, highlighting the pair of matching limestone tables either side of a pair of double doors, cleverly looking almost as though they had been carved out of the wall instead of standing next to it. Two marble busts—one on either table—were also illuminated by concealed lighting.

When he saw her looking at them, Ilios told her, 'They are supposed to have been brought back from Italy by Alexandros Manos at the same time as he returned with copies of Palladio's plans for the villa. If you know Villa Emo and anything of its history then you will know that the Emo family were said to be of Greek descent—hence the classical Greek appearance of the villa.'

'As a trading port, Venice was something of a melting pot for various nations back then,' Lizzie agreed.

Ilios nodded his head, then opened the doors and waited for her to precede him.

A corridor lined with black marble on one side and mirrors on the other, to expand the space, opened out into a large living area with floor-to-ceiling glass walls virtually all along its length. Through them Lizzie could see the night sky, studded with stars.

White sofas stood on a black-tiled floor, focussed on a modern fireplace in the centre of the room. Picking up a remote control, Ilios pressed a button and a wall of the black glass rectangular chimney surrounding the fire slid back, to reveal a large television screen.

Everything in the room was state of the art and a future collector's piece, Lizzie recognised. She could immediately put a name to the prestigious interior design partnership that was responsible for the interior, and even to the designer within that concern who had headed up the team.

'Walt Eickehoven.' Without thinking, she said his name out loud.

Ilios swung round. 'You know him?'

'No, but I know his style,' Lizzie answered. 'Those sofas and that unit are unmistakably his. I've heard that he's got a queuing list of clients that goes into months, if not years.'

Ilios shrugged. 'Queues can be jumped. I'll show you the guest suite, and then you'll need something to eat. I'll order something in—do you like moussaka? If so, we can eat in half an hour.'

Lizzie nodded her head. She was hungry, but she was also tired.

'This way,' Ilios instructed her.

'This way' led down another windowless corridor of marble and mirrors, this one with inset niches, each one containing a carefully lit piece of stone artwork.

The apartment was a work of art in itself, Lizzie recognized, but her heart ached over a private question. How would the two motherless sons Ilios Manos intended to bring up fit into such an environment? She didn't think she would actually want to live in such a polished and sterile atmosphere herself, even though as a designer she could appreciate its stunning design.

Ilios had stopped outside a door in the corridor and was indicating to her. 'I think you will find everything you need inside.'

Nodding again, Lizzie opened the door. By the time she had closed it she knew that Ilios had gone—not because she had seen him go, but because somehow she had sensed it. The air around her and her own body's reaction told her that he was no longer there. She frowned. Finding Ilios Manos sexually attractive was understandable, and she tried to tell herself to quell her growing panic about how she was going to cope living so closely with him. Obviously such a stupendously male man was bound to have that effect on most women. But she was not most women, and she was desperately afraid of her vulnerability. Discovering that he had made such an impact on her senses that even her skin could register his presence or the lack of it was frighteningly dangerous territory—dangerous and not to be risked territory, in fact.

Instead of thinking about the effect Ilios had on her, Lizzie told herself to try and focus instead on her surroundings. As a designer she could possibly learn something that she could take with her into her life, when her present enforced ordeal was finally over.

The guest suite, for instance, was exactly that—a luxurious, streamlined boutique-hotel-style open space, with a sleeping area at one end that contained a bed, and a living space at the other furnished with sofas, tables and a desk.

Like the living room, the guest suite also had a glass wall that ran its full length, but this one looked inward onto what she imagined must be an enclosed garden, since it was virtually on the roof of the building. Carefully placed soft lighting revealed a perspective view of the ruins of a small elevated Greek temple, which looked down into the garden with steps leading from it into a swimming pool. Along the far length of the pool ran a colonnade, planted with vines, which led to a grotto of the sort favoured by designers of the Italian Renaissance opposite the temple. Parterred greenery in intricate formal patterns separated the pool area from the space outside the glass wall, so that that space formed an almost private outdoor sitting area, with double doors from the living space opening out onto it.

Lizzie didn't like to think of the millions just the apartment and its garden must have cost. Professionally, she was in awe. This kind of commission was so far outside her level of operation that the only time she would normally get to view one would be in the pages of a magazine. But, as a woman who shared her own living space with two sisters and twin five-year-old boys, she was almost repelled by the cool, sleek hauteur of living space. It made her feel that as a human being her presence within it spoiled its sterile perfection.

Ilios had handed her trolley case before leaving her, and of course it looked ludicrously out of place.

Half an hour, he'd said. That meant she had the choice of showering and tidying herself up, or texting her sisters.

That choice was no choice, really. Lizzie smiled ruefully to herself as she headed for the double doors to one side of the enormous low-level bed, dressed in immaculate grey and white linen to tone with the slate-grey tiled floor.

Beyond the double doors was a dressing room-cum-wardrobe space—enough space to house the entire wardrobes of her whole family with room to spare—and beyond that, through another set of doors, was the bathroom, containing both a shower and a bath, and a separate lavatory. For the first time since she had entered the apartment Lizzie realised she was in a room that combined both modern artistic design and sybaritic sensuality. For a start, the glass wall continued the full length of the bathroom, making it possible to stand in the wetroom-style shower or lie in the huge stone bath and look out into the garden. Limestone tiles covered floor and walls; thick fluffy grey, white and beige towels were stacked on the inbuilt limestone shelving unit next to the double basins.

After a regretful look at the shower, Lizzie washed her hands and face and then returned to the bedroom, sinking into the white sofa as she quickly texted her family to tell them the good news about her new commission from the owner of Manos Construction.

That done, she only just had enough time to comb her hair and renew her lipstick before a quick glance at her watch told her that her time was up.

When she had made her way back to the living area, she suspected, from the quick frowning glance that Ilios gave her, that he had expected her to have changed clothes. No doubt he was used to women making an all-out effort to impress him, but even if she'd had time to change, Lizzie acknowledged, since all she had to change into was a different top she was hardly likely to have impressed him.

While he might not exhibit the tendencies one somehow expected to see in a man who had 'come from nothing'—for instance, whilst she had no doubt that both his clothes and the watch he was wearing were expensive, they were the opposite of ostentatious—she suspected that designer-clad females were his normal choice of arm candy. Which was perhaps why he considered her sex to be so rapacious.

Their food, delivered whilst she had been in the guest suite, was a simple moussaka-type dish. It was, Lizzie admitted as they sat opposite one another at the polished black glass table, absolutely delicious—as was the wine Ilios had poured to go with it.

It was merely necessity that had prompted him to decide that Lizzie could pay off her debt to him by becoming his wife. He had no personal interest in her whatsoever, Ilios reminded himself as he watched her enjoying her food, plainly not in the least bit concerned about the fact that she was still dressed in workmanlike clothes that did nothing to accentuate her figure and were obviously neither designed nor worn with the idea of arousing male desire. So why did it irk him so irrationally to recognise that she had not made the slightest attempt to attract his attention? Was he really such a stereotypical male? Or was it because, despite the fact that she was not making any attempt to attract him, *he* was very much aware of *her*?

If he was, then it was probably due to the fact that it was some time since he had shared his bed with a woman. He had ended his last relationship after his lover had started trying to pressure him into marriage—over a year ago now, in fact.

If Lizzie's manner irked him then it was surely because, even though his current contact with the female sex was via a variety of social and business-related events, and not on any personal level, he took it for granted that the women he met would be well groomed, dressed in such a way that pleasing the male of the species would be their clear intention.

Ilios looked at her and frowned.

'You will need a new wardrobe before you can appear in public as either my fiancée or my wife,' he informed Lizzie.

'I have plenty of clothes at home. I can ask my sisters to send me some.'

'No.'

'Why not?'

'Why not? Right now you are dressed as though you were a suburban matron whose sole concern is looking after her family. Jeans and a blazer, loafers… A woman who does not seek to attract the attention of a man, and who perhaps would even prefer to repel male attention.' He made a dismissive gesture which stung Lizzie's female pride.

'Not all women are so insecure that they want to advertise their sensuality to the world at large. Some of us prefer to keep that aspect of ourselves private. In fact we take a pride in it,' she told him fiercely.

'Meaning what, exactly?' Ilios demanded. 'Wearing dull clothes and so-called sexy underwear beneath them?'

Lizzie could feel her colour rising and bent her head over her wine glass, hoping that the soft fall of her hair would cloak her blush, as she absentmindedly ran her fingertip round the edge of the glass. The fact was that as her sisters often teased her because she was a silk, satin and lace undies fan, the more feminine the better.

Ilios observed her behaviour, knowing immediately the cause of her flushed face and her reluctance to meet his gaze. What was a matter of far more concern and disbelief to him was the effect knowing that beneath her sensible clothes Lizzie Wareham deliberately chose to wear sensual underwear was having on him physically. It might be over a year since he had last had a lover, but that was no excuse for the images that were filling his mind now, and the reaction they were causing within his own body.

Ilios couldn't remember previously being so glad that he was seated at a table, and was thus able to conceal from a woman's view his body's reaction to her. To have such a painfully hard erection was territory that belonged to young men not yet able to fully master their sexuality—not men in their mid-thirties, and certainly not him. The mind could play tricks on a person, he reminded himself, and his reaction was probably not to Lizzie Wareham but to images he himself had created. He did not desire her. He was, to put it bluntly, simply aroused. He could have put any attractive female body into those images and felt the same effect. Desiring Lizzie Wareham was not part of his plan, and therefore must not be allowed to happen.

'I have work to do, so I suggest that you take the opportunity to go to bed have an early night,' he informed Lizzie.

He didn't want her out of the way because her presence was disturbing him on an intensely personal and sensual level that he didn't like. Not for one minute.

Lizzie's head lifted, her face burning even more hotly as her body immediately responded to the word *bed*—and not in a way that had anything to do with going to sleep. Somehow her senses refused to accept that anything as mundane as sleeping could take place in a bed that was in any way connected to Ilios Manos. Which was, of course, totally ridiculous. She was reacting like some hormone-flooded pubescent teenager, quivering with embarrassingly super-strength lust.

'Yes, I am tired,' she managed to respond. She was doing the mental equivalent of running past something dangerous without risking looking at it, determinedly avoiding re-using the word 'bed', Lizzie derided herself. But what else could she do, with her body signalling with increasing intensity the excited pleasure with which it viewed the prospect of going to bed with Ilios Manos? Not that *that* was going to happen. He had told her so already. Theirs was purely a business arrangement, that was all, and that was the way it was going to stay. Somehow she would find the strength to make sure that it did.

CHAPTER SIX

'I HAVE a meeting in half an hour.' Ilios stood up to finish the cup of coffee he was drinking whilst Lizzie remained seated, seeing him glance at his watch before continuing.

'I've ordered suitable clothes for you via an online concierge service. They should arrive within the hour. Have a look through them. If there's anything that doesn't fit, let me know. There's no need to thank me.'

'I wasn't going to,' Lizzie assured him grimly.

Ignoring her comment, Ilios continued, 'We shall be attending a gallery opening this evening, so you'll need to wear an engagement ring. I'm having a selection couriered over to my office. Maria should arrive at some stage to do the cleaning.' He reached into the inside pocket of his suit jacket and removed his wallet, opening it and removing what looked to Lizzie like an obscene amount of one-hundred-euro notes.

'You'll need this, I dare say. And I've put my mobile number into your mobile's address book. I should have thought that in view of the fact that you're an interior designer you would have had a more stylish one. Appearances count, after all.'

'I agree, but paying for luxury gizmos costs money,'

Lizzie defended, Her out-of-fashion mobile was nonetheless perfectly effective.

Five minutes later, left to her own devices in a space in which the smell of rich coffee and maleness lingered dangerously to torment her senses, Lizzie decided to explore her new surroundings—starting with the garden.

She could see now in daylight that the living space did not overlook the city, as she had expected, but instead had views towards the mountains.

The intercom buzzing had her heading for the entrance of the apartment, mindful of what Ilios had told her. When she opened the door there was no sign of a delivery person, but there were several large boxes stacked next to the door.

Nearly two hours later, standing in the guest bedroom surrounded by the clothes she had unpacked, Lizzie wished more than anything else that her sisters were here with her, to stare in awe at the beautiful garments now covering the bed.

The clothes *were* beautiful, and in exactly the kind of style she had always secretly coveted.

Out of the corner of her eye Lizzie caught sight of the deliciously pretty and feminine underwear she had hastily pushed out of sight under some of the day clothes, her face warming. Obviously he had noticed her reaction to his observation the night before. Stunningly sensual undies in soft cream silk and satin, trimmed with lace—or rather laces, she amended ruefully, remembering the boned corset that laced up at the back which had been in one of the boxes. That was something that would quite definitely be going back! After all, she had no one to fasten her into it, even if she had wanted to wear something so constricting. Neither was she entirely sure about the French knickers that were little more than a satin gusset-cum-G-string attached to fluted sheer lace panels. On the other hand the pure silk-satin low-rise boxer shorts and matching bras were so delicious they had made her mouth water.

And as for everything else—how was she supposed to resist the allure of silk cashmere cut into the most flattering skirt and trousers she had ever seen, in her favourite shade of warm beige? The trench coat, in a sort of off-white—not grey, and not beige either—carrying a very famous label, was the exactly the kind of coat she had secretly lusted after ever since she had realised what good clothes were, and it fitted her perfectly.

There were sweaters and shirts, tops, beach clothes, evening clothes, new jeans by an über-fashionable designer, and shoes so plain and yet so beautiful that Lizzie had simply wanted to hug them tightly to her. These were clothes that spoke an international language—and that language was the language of discreet style and elegance and an awful lot of money.

Lizzie stroked the silk tweed of a three-quarter-length Chanel coat in black and white, with the trademark Chanel camelia attached to an equally trademark Chanel chain fastening. How could she accept all of this? She couldn't. It was too much. She needed clothes, yes—but far less than this.

With a small sigh she began to repack what she thought were the more expensive items, retaining only what she felt she would genuinely need. Packing away the silk cashmere skirt and trousers and the Chanel coat and skirt and blouse wasn't easy, but it had to be done, Lizzie told herself firmly.

She had just finished, and was about to carry the boxes to the front door, when she heard a firm knock on the bedroom door.

Maria, the cleaner, must have arrived, Lizzie guessed—but when she went to open the door it was Ilios, who was standing in the corridor, looking impatient.

'I'm sending these back,' Lizzie told him, indicating the boxes she had just packed.

Ilios surveyed them, noting that there were far more by the door than there were on the floor beside the bed.

'They didn't fit? You didn't like the style?' His voice sharpened slightly. He still didn't know why he had changed his mind at the last minute and told the concierge service to select clothes for a woman who preferred discreet stylishness to clothes that were sexy.

This wasn't the kind of man who liked being proved wrong—about anything, Lizzie acknowledged, even when it was the dress size of a woman he had only just met. Because he felt that he was being judged and found wanting? Because it was important to him to prove himself as a success in every aspect of his life? Because inside there was still a part of him that had grown up knowing that his father had been sacrificed for a building, with all the fear for his own safety and security that must have caused? Stop feeling sympathetic towards him, she warned herself. It will only make things worse.

'No, they were perfect—both in fit and style,' she assured him.

'So why are you sending them back?'

'I don't need them, and… Well, they were far too expensive. The kind of clothes I could never afford. I would have preferred it if the clothes had been less expensive.'

It took Ilios several seconds to adjust his own thinking and judgement to her words. A woman who genuinely did not want a man to spend money on her? Who did she think she was kidding? Ilios didn't believe that such a woman existed.

'You will not be living the kind of life you normally live. As my fiancée and then my wife I expect you to dress and behave as the kind of woman those who know me would expect me to marry. You must think of yourself as an actress and these clothes as your props. You will not feel confident amongst my friends if you are not dressed appropriately.'

'Clothes are only window dressing. True confidence comes from a person's belief in themselves as someone of value,' Lizzie felt bound to point out gently.

'I agree,' Ilios told her unexpectedly. 'But we live in a society in which we are judged by those who do not know us on our outward appearance. For my wife to be seen in chainstore clothes could cause the kind of gossip that might well ultimately lead to speculation in the press that Manos Cosntruction is in financial difficulty. It isn't just my own wealth that depends on the continued success of my business. It is the jobs of all those who work for me. In business, a good reputation can be ninety per cent of one's success—lose that and you stand to lose everything. You must know that.'

There was enough truth in what he was saying for Lizzie to nod her head.

'I have brought a selection of rings in different styles and sizes for you to look at. Whichever one you choose can be sized properly for you.'

Recognising that Ilios was waiting for her to precede him out of the room, Lizzie edged her way past the end of the bed, so desperate to avoid accidentally coming into physical contact with him that she bumped into the bed itself and half stumbled, provoking exactly what she had feared. Ilios reached out to steady her, his hand resting firmly against her waist. His attention, though, was focussed on the floor. Following his gaze, Lizzie's heart sank. There, lying on the floor at his feet, was the corset she had been looking at earlier, which she must have dislodged as she stumbled. Still holding her waist, Ilios bent down and picked it up. He looked at it.

'It's going back,' Lizzie told him immediately. 'I couldn't possibly wear it.'

Ilios looked at her. 'Why not?'

'Well, for one thing it's not the type of thing I would wear, and for another I'd need someone to fasten it for me—it laces up at the back,' she explained. 'And that means that I'd need…'

'A man?' Ilios supplied for her.

'Another pair of hands,' Lizzie corrected him. The warmth of his hand on her waist was causing havoc inside her body. An entire quiverful of tiny, fiery darts of sensual pleasure seemed to have been discharged into her body, unleashing a thousand pinpoints of sensory reaction—rivulets of female need that were speedily flowing into one another to form a dangerously fast-flowing flood of physical desire.

Inside her head that desire was painting dangerous images. As though by magic what she was wearing had been removed and she was reclothed in the satin underwear she had been admiring before Ilios had arrived. At the same time, equally magically, Ilios's hand was stroking from her hip up to her breast, whilst his lips caressed the equally eager curve where her shoulder met her neck and his free hand slid into the silk-satin to cup the rounded flesh of her bottom.

Frantically Lizzie wrenched her attention away from what was going on inside her head. Ilios was a very attractive man, and it had been a very long time since she had…

Well, it had been a very long time. But that did not give her imagination carte blanche to indulge itself with those kind of totally impossible scenarios—especially in view of what he had said to her about what he did and didn't want from their relationship.

Lizzie pulled herself free of Ilios's hold and headed for the door, leaving Ilios to look thoughtfully at the corset and then at her disappearing back view, before dropping the corset onto the bed and turning to follow her.

'These are the rings. I asked the jeweller to send a variety for you to choose from.'

Lizzie's eyes widened as she looked down at the rings in the large leather case that Ilios had opened.

There were solitaires in a variety of shapes and cuts, coloured diamonds surrounded by diamonds, diamonds surrounded by diamonds—so much, in fact, that the light reflected from the rings almost dazzled her.

'They're all beautiful,' she told Ilios. 'But they're so…so eye-catching and big. Couldn't I have something smaller?'

'How much smaller?' Ilios asked dryly.

Lizzie pointed to one of the rings and told him, 'About a quarter of the size of that one. And plain. Just a solitaire.'

'Something more like this, do you mean?' he asked, reaching into his pocket and removing a small box which he opened to reveal a plain, perfectly plain solitaire set in what Lizzie assumed must be platinum, on a narrow platinum band.

Ilios didn't really know why he had noticed the ring, nor what it was about it that had made him think of Lizzie, never mind why he had asked for it to be boxed separately, but he could see from Lizzie's expression how she felt about it.

The ring was so simple and so perfect that Lizzie fell in love with it immediately.

'Exactly like that,' she told him.

Ilios removed the ring from the box and held it out to her, and for some reason—automatically, really, without thinking about what she was doing—rather than take it from him Lizzie extended her finger towards him instead.

Ilios looked at her, and she looked back at him, and a quiver of something age-old and beyond logic shot through her. Neither of them spoke. Instead Ilios curled his fingers round her wrist and then slowly slid the ring onto her wedding ring finger.

It fitted her perfectly. It looked and felt as though it had been made for her—as though it had been meant for her.

'It's perfect.'

Emotion choked her voice and stung her eyes. The ring was an age-old symbol of human love and commitment, given to bind a couple together, and suddenly it seemed to possess a significance that touched her far more deeply than she had expected.

'I wasn't expecting you back until later. You said you had a lunch engagement.' How strained and vulnerable she sounded—like someone desperately trying to make polite conversation as a means of covering up the huge, yawning dangerous pit that had suddenly opened up in front of them.

'The lunch was cancelled.' He was not going to tell her that he was the one who had done the cancelling.

'This gallery-opening you said we'd be attending this evening, will it—?' Lizzie began

'It will be a high-profile media event—lots of society

faces and photographers,' Ilios interrupted. 'Lots of gossip and champagne—you know the kind of thing. I have to go. I've got a site meeting in half an hour.'

Lizzie just nodded her head.

CHAPTER SEVEN

SHE wasn't doing this for Ilios, she was doing it for herself—to prove to herself that she had the strength to deal with this latest obstacle in her life the same way in which she had dealt with all the others: that was with courage and fortitude and a determination that those who needed her and depended on her would not find her wanting, Lizzie told herself firmly as she studied her reflection in the guest suite's dressing room mirror.

Matt black jersey draped her body from her throat to her knees, the dress's long sleeves ending on her wrists. A discreet sparkle of tiny jet beads in the shape of a flower just below her left shoulder was the dress's only ornamentation, but the way the fluid Armani dress moved when she moved really said everything about it that needed to be said, Lizzie knew.

Having had the whole afternoon in which to get ready, and having slipped out to buy a selection of glossy fashion magazines so that she could study the social pages, Lizzie could now understand why Ilios had deemed it necessary to replace her existing clothes. Greek women she could see did not believe in cutting corners or making economies about when it came to making a style statement. Designer labels, expensive jewellery, impeccable make-up and enviably glossy hair were, it seemed, *de rigueur*, and it was something she had decided she could not match without professional help.

As a result, and with Ilios's warning very much to the forefront of her mind, she had gone back out in search of a hairdresser. Now, thanks to Ilios's euros and the welcome skill of a Greek hairdresser, her hair was framing her face in a soft 'up do' that managed to be both elegant and yet at the same time look softly feminine, with delicate loose tendrils of hair drifting round her temples and down onto her neck, and her nails were immaculately manicured. Lizzie had refused the dark red polish the manicurist had offered— somehow it hadn't seemed appropriate for a newly engaged woman: far too aggressive and challenging. However, conceding that anyone genuinely newly engaged to Ilios would want the world to know about it by showing off her ring, she had agreed to a muted pink polish, because it matched her favourite lipstick shade.

She looked at her watch. It was not the pretty Cartier her parents had given her when she had obtained her degree—she had passed that on to Ruby when the twins had been born—but a plain, serviceable chainstore watch. Half past six. Ilios should be back soon, and she didn't want him to have to come knocking on the bedroom door a second time to find her.

Picking up the black clutch bag that went with her high-heeled suede shoes, and the pure white cashmere coat that was surely the most impractical garment even created, Lizzie opened the door and stepped out into the corridor, giving Ilios, who was standing at the other end of it on his way to his own room, the perfect opportunity to study and assess her appearance.

'Well?' she challenged him. 'Do I look suitably high-maintenance and worthy of being your fiancée?'

To say that he was lost for words would be an exaggeration, Ilios decided, but to admit in the privacy of his own thoughts that the Lizzie standing at the other end of the corridor waiting for his response was a woman whose discreetly sensual elegant took his breath away would not.

When Lizzie saw Ilios frown her heart sank, even whilst her pride stiffened. If she wasn't good enough for him, then too bad. After all, *she* wasn't the one who had insisted upon their fake relationship.

'You'll need these,' Ilios announced harshly, holding out to her several boxes without answering her question, and then walking away from her in the direction of the master bedroom.

Unwillingly, Lizzie took the boxes from him. Don't you dare cry, she warned herself as she went into the living area. She didn't dare, with the amount of mascara she had on.

Would it really have been so difficult for him to tell her that she looked good, even if he didn't really think so? He must know how anxious she was feeling. How much she needed the confidence his support would have given her.

Dropping her coat onto one of the sofas, Lizzie opened the first of the boxes, her eyes widening in disbelief as she looked at the contents. The necklace sparkling on the velvet couldn't possibly be real, could it? All those diamonds—and a matching bangle. She closed the box quickly. Her dress might look vaguely *Breakfast at Tiffany's*, but she certainly wasn't going to risk wearing something that might be worth a king's ransom just to re-inforce that image.

She was about to open the other boxes when Ilios returned.

He'd obviously showered, because his hair was still damp—and not just on his head. Lizzie had to fight to drag her gaze away from the damp, dark silky body hair she could just see as he finished fastening his shirt. His unexpected request for help as he opened his palm to reveal a pair of cufflinks startled her as she refocussed her gaze. Her mouth instantly went dry as a slow ache uncurled inside her body—like woodsmoke, and just as dangerously pervasive.

Somehow she managed to scramble to her feet and go to him, taking the links from him. Rose-gold and plain, they felt soft and warm in her palm. The initials on them were slightly faded, although she could still make out the interlaced A and M. Almost absently she rubbed her fingertip over them.

'They were my father's.' She heard Ilios's voice somewhere above her head. 'The design is Venetian. It is a tradition in our family that when a boy reaches the age of maturity he is given a pair of such cufflinks by his father—a sign of his manhood. Since my father was not able to do that for me, I wear his instead.'

For the second time in less than half an hour Lizzie had to remind herself of the damage tears would do to her eye make-up.

Watching Lizzie's head, bent towards his wrist, the nape of her neck exposed to his gaze, Ilios had to resist the temptation to reach out and curl one of the small escaping fronds of hair round his finger. He could quite easily have fastened the cufflinks himself—far more easily than Lizzie, in fact—but for some reason he had decided to ask her to do it for him. As a test of her suitability to be his wife? he taunted himself. Or as a test to himself, to prove he was not as susceptible to her as his body insisted on repeatedly telling him he was?

She really wished she wasn't having to do this, Lizzie admitted. Her fingers were stiff with nervousness and yet at the same time they were trembling. She could smell the scent of Ilios's freshly showered body, mixed with some kind of discreet male cologne, and whilst she wouldn't have said that the effect it was having on her senses was making her want to rip open his shirt and bury her face against his torso, it wasn't far short of that.

It was a relief to finally complete her task and be able to step from him, draw in a gulp of hopefully steadying and non-Ilios-smelling air.

'You aren't wearing your jewellery.'

'I…I thought it might be a bit too much.'

The dark eyebrows rose. 'I disagree. You should wear it.'

Because if she didn't she'd look out of place. That was the unspoken message he was giving her, Lizzie recognised as she picked up the two smaller boxes and opened them. She had to blink at the magnificence of the diamond earstuds in front of her. They had to be at least a carat each, and so brilliant they dazzled her.

Quickly Lizzie slipped them into her ears. With her hair up she did need something, she acknowledged. But merely 'something'—not these dazzling and no doubt very expensive earrings.

'What's wrong?' Ilios demanded.

'I was just thinking how many families the price of these would feed. It seems wrong to wear something like this when so many people are going through such a hard time. It makes me feel uncomfortable.'

'So if I were to offer them as a gift you would rather I gave their value in money to a charity? Is that what you're saying?' Ilios taunted her.

'Yes,' Lizzie responded—truthfully and without hesitation.

'Put on the watch, and then we had better leave,' was all Ilios said in response.

She was lying, of course; she had to be. He wasn't deceived or taken in by her, nor would he ever be—by her or by any other woman.

The watch was discreetly expensive: a plain black leather band and a white-gold face was studded with small diamonds.

Since Ilios was already shrugging on his suit jacket, Lizzie fastened the watch quickly and went to pick up her coat—just as Ilios too was reaching for it. Their fingertips met and touched, his over her own, warm and strong, filling Lizzie with a need to simply curl her fingers into his in a silent plea for acceptance and comfort.

Frantically she pulled back, grabbing hold of her coat with her other hand and telling Ilios quickly, 'It's all right. I don't need to put it on. I'll just carry it until we get out of the car.'

She really didn't think she was up to any more physical contact right now, with a man whose mere presence seemed to have the ability to send her body's awareness of him to stratospheric levels.

The gallery, when they reached it, was ablaze with lights, and with the shine reflected from the stunning amount of diamond jewellery being worn. Ilios's hand was on Lizzie's arm as he guided her through the mass of paparazzi, waiting to snap photographs of the rich and famous as they made their way from the kerb to the door.

'I can see now why you aren't keen on my outfit. Obviously to be considered anything like worthy of you I'd have to have dressed very differently,' Lizzie was forced to admit reluctantly once they had stepped inside. She had seen how many of the other women were wearing tiny little dresses, bandaged—or so it seemed—to their equally tiny bodies. The dresses revealed lengths of lean bronzed leg and the swell of quite often implausibly taut and rounded breasts.

No wonder he had derided her choice of clothes if this was what he considered normal clothing for the female body.

'The women you are looking at are high-price tarts up for sale—on the hunt for the richest husband they can snare,' Ilios told Lizzie grimly. 'The clothes they are wearing denote their profession, as does their desire to be photographed. It's their version of newspaper advertising. Come with me.'

As though by magic the mass of bronzed flesh parted to let them through—although not without some very predatory and inviting looks being thrown in Ilios's direction, Lizzie noticed.

Beyond the call girls and the men hanging round them, in the interior of the gallery were several groups of people: men in business suits, and elegant, confident-looking women in beautiful designer clothes.

One of the men came forward, extending his hand.

'Ilios, my friend. It is good to see you.'

'You only say that, Stefanos, because you hope to persuade me to buy something,' Ilios responded, turning to Lizzie to say easily, '*Agapi mou*, allow me to introduce Stefanos to you. I should warn you, though, that he will insist on presenting us with some hideous piece of supposed art as a wedding gift.'

Agapi mou—didn't that mean *my love*? But of course she wasn't, Lizzie reminded herself, as she admired the clever way in which Ilios had announced both their relationship and their impending marriage.

Within seconds people were crowding round them, smiling and exclaiming, and Lizzie had no need to fake the sudden shyness that had her moving instinctively closer to Ilios, so that he took hold of her hand and tucked it though his arm.

'Ilios, how can this be? You have always sworn never to get married.'

The speaker was a woman of around Ilios's own age; she was smiling, but there was a certain hard edge to her voice that warned Lizzie she was someone who might have a shared history with Ilios. She might not entirely welcome the news of his supposed intended marriage, even though she was wearing a wedding ring and was accompanied by a solid, square-faced man who appeared to be her husband.

'Lizzie changed my mind, Eleni,' Ilios answered her, and the smile he gave Lizzie as he turned to look down at her made her suspect that if he had gifted her with that kind of smile and meant it she'd have been transfixed to the spot with delight.

'Well, you cannot cling together all evening like a pair of turtledoves.' Eleni replied. 'I want you to convince Michael that he should build me a new villa on the island— and you, of course, must construct it. There is no other builder to whom we would entrust such a commission. I have it in mind to copy your own Villa Manos for us, since you insist on refusing to let us buy the original from you.'

Immediately Lizzie felt Ilios stiffen, his arm rigid against hers.

So, if they had once been lovers the parting had not been an amicable one, Lizzie guessed. Because there was plainly ill feeling between them now. Eleni must surely know that Ilios would never sell his family home.

'Has Ilios shown you Villa Manos yet, Lizzie? Told you that he will expect you to make your home there once you are married? Personally, I could never live anywhere so remote. Certainly not all year round. And then, of course, one must wonder what one's husband is getting up to whilst he is here in Thessaloniki and you are stuck on a peninsula in the middle of nowhere.'

'I would never marry a man I couldn't trust implicitly,' Lizzie responded calmly, and with quiet dignity.

'My dear, how very brave of you.' Eleni was positively purring. 'I hate to tell you this, but whilst a man will promise anything whilst he is in the first throes of…love, marriage often brings about a sea change. When a woman is occupied with her home and her children her husband can start to look elsewhere for entertainment. Especially a Greek man. After all, they have the example of our Greek gods before them. Zeus himself could not be faithful to his wife. He had many adventures outside their marriage, if mythology is to be believed.'

'A man who is truly happy in his marriage does not seek satisfaction outside it, Eleni, and I know that with Lizzie I shall find all the happiness I need.' Ilios defended their relationship, turning to her to lift her hand to his lips and tenderly kiss her fingers whilst gazing into her eyes.

Ilios really should have been an actor, Lizzie decided, struggling against the tide of longing surging through her. She had to be strong, she reminded herself. She had to fight the effect he had on her. She had to prove to herself that she could endure and overcome the effect his closeness had on her.

'An ex, I take it?' she couldn't resist murmuring to Ilios once they had escaped.

'Of a sort,' he agreed, a little to her surprise. 'Although the prey she was hunting was my cousin, not me. When she discovered that he wasn't going to inherit Villa Manos she dropped him.'

'And turned her attentions to you?'

'She tried,' Ilios agreed. 'But without success. You handled Eleni extremely well,' he said, then paused. Unable to stop himself, he told her brusquely, 'You play your part well. I suspect that every man here is envying me.'

What on earth had made him say that, even if it was true? Why should he care if other men wanted her? The admiration he could see in their eyes was a benefit to him, because it meant that she was being accepted and accept-able as his wife-to-be.

Lizzie couldn't help smiling at him. There was a soft, warm feeling inside her body—a sweet, tender unfolding of something, happiness, that lifted her. Just because Ilios had—what?—complimented her? She must not feel like that. She must not.

What he had said to her was the truth, Ilios knew. But more than that she had a warmth that drew people to her. He had seen it in the eyes of his friends and in their manner towards her. Could he have been unfair to her, wrong about her and the way he had initially judged her? What if he had? He didn't owe her anything, after all. She was the one who was indebted to him, not the other way around.

Lizzie wasn't sorry when it was time to leave the restau-rant where they had had dinner with Ilios's friends, next door to the gallery. Whilst the other people she had met had more than made up for Eleni's bitchiness with their warmth and readiness to befriend her, and the food at the smart restaurant had been delicious, she had felt on edge—knowing that she was only playing a part, afraid of making a slip that would reveal the truth, and at the same time uncomfortable with the deceit she was having to practise.

A valet brought the car round, and within minutes of leaving, or so it seemed, they were back in the apartment.

'I've set everything in motion for our wedding,' Ilios told her. 'It will be a civil ceremony, conducted at the town hall. Normally couples having civil ceremonies go on to celebrate more traditionally with a family party, but in our case that won't be necessary. I have let it be known that it is because I am so impatient to make you my wife that we are dispensing with a more lavish affair.'

Lizzie nodded her head, relieved that she had her back to him and he wouldn't see the effect his words were having on her. Tonight, posing as his wife, sometimes almost forgetting that she was simply playing a part, she had felt filled with happiness and…

And what?

And nothing, Lizzie assured herself hastily as she removed the watch and then took out the diamond earrings. Her hands were trembling slightly as she remembered how she had felt tonight, standing at Ilios's side, wanting him, wishing that he would turn to her and look at her with that same longing and need she felt for him.

What she felt for him was quite simply lust. Very shocking, of course, but even so far safer than becoming emotionally drawn to a man who didn't want her.

One of the diamond earrings slipped from her fingers. Just in time Ilios put his palm beneath her own and caught it. Caught it, as somehow he had caught her in the net. If he knew he would throw her to one side, like a fisherman throwing back an unwanted catch. Lizzie looked up at him—and then wished she had not.

Not trusting herself to take the earring from him—because that meant touching him—Lizzie held out the jewellery box to him instead.

Exactly what point was she trying to make by refusing to take the earring from him? Ilios questioned as he dropped it into the box. That she was sexually indifferent to him? If so, why should it make him want to take hold of her and kiss her until her mouth softened beneath his and she was pleading with him for more than mere kisses?

Silently Lizzie collected the scattered jewellery boxes and offered them to Ilios.

'Keep them yourself. You will need to wear them again,' he told her curtly.

Lizzie shook her head. 'I'd rather not. As I said before, they are far too valuable, and they should be in a safe.'

It was gone midnight. There was no reason for her to remain here in the living room with him—not when being with him was so very dangerous for her, she reminded herself sternly, just in case she was tempted to linger. Her will-power seemed to have become far too fragile. She had spent the evening pretending that they were intimately close, as lovers, aided in doing so by the two and a half glasses of champagne she had drunk at the gallery. All those bubbles were bound to have an effect on anyone's system, never mind someone who was quickly discovering how vulnerable she was to the man in front of her.

Her brief, 'I'll say goodnight', merely elicited a brief nod of his head from Ilios. His back was already turned towards her as she opened the door into the corridor.

Maria had obviously been in, Lizzie noted, because the bed was made up immaculately, as though for a new guest.

She went into the dressing room and opened one of the wardrobe doors, intending to undress and hang up her clothes, only the wardrobe was empty. Quickly Lizzie checked the others, and then the drawers. They were empty too. And her case had gone. Along with her toiletries and her toothbrush.

She began to panic. What was going on? She'd have to tell Ilios.

She found him in the living room, standing in front of the glass wall in his suit trousers and his shirt, a glass of wine in his hand. When he turned round as she approached him the shirt pulled across the muscles in his back, causing an aching sensation to slide through her lower body.

'I can't find any of my things,' she told him helplessly. 'They've all disappeared—everything, including my case and even my toothbrush. The maid's been in, because the bed is made up.'

'I know.'

'You know?' Lizzie looked at him uncertainly. What was going on? Had he decided he didn't like her new clothes after all and sent them back?

'They're in my room.'

'What?'

Ilios shrugged irritably. It had been as much of an unwanted discovery for him to find Lizzie's things in the master bedroom as it had obviously been for her to discover that they were missing from the guest room. The main source of Ilios's irritation, though, was his own slip-up in not realising that this might happen.

'Maria obviously took it upon herself to move them. She'll have heard that we are to marry, and it seems she has decided that since we are probably already sharing a bed, she might as well make life easier for herself by moving our things into my room.'

'But we aren't. I mean we can't.' Lizzie was aghast. 'Everything will have to be moved back. I'll do it myself— tomorrow—when you aren't here—but you'll have to tell her.'

'I don't think that would be a good idea.'

'Why not?'

'Because the last thing we want is for her to start gossiping that we're sleeping in separate beds.'

'But you said our marriage would be…that it wouldn't be…that we wouldn't be sharing a bed.'

'I hadn't thought things through properly then,' Ilios was forced to admit.

He was actually admitting that he had got something wrong? Lizzie could scarcely believe it.

'If you're concerned about what Maria might say, then why don't you tell her not to come? I can do her work whilst I'm here,' she suggested helpfully.

Ilios was already shaking his head.

'And deprive Maria of her the money she earns? No. Maria's family are dependent on her wages, and Maria enjoys a certain status in her community because she works for me. It wouldn't be right or fair to deprive her of those things.'

Lizzie had to gulp back the chagrin she felt at being reproved by Ilios for her lack of awareness of the needs of others—chagrin that was all the more intense because previously *she* had seen the one to point out that lack of awareness to him.

'But I don't want to share a…a bed,' she protested. How ridiculous that she had to struggle to force herself to say the word *bed*. She, an interior designer, who in the course of her work was perfectly familiar with those three small letters. Familiar with the letters, but not familiar at all with the way the word *bed* made her feel when she was in the presence of Ilios Manos.

'Do you think I do?' Ilios challenged her, immediately making her feel humiliated. 'We don't have any choice. Fortunately it is a very large bed,' he told her grimly.

She should, of course, be delighted and relieved that her presence in his bed was so unwelcome, Lizzie told herself. She wanted and needed him not to want her—if only to protect her from her own feelings after all. But instead she was filled with an explosive mix of emotions and sensations—heady excitement, tingling suspense, an irrational and rebellious aching longing that defied all her attempts to subdue it, and that was only the start of it. She could have written a list a metre long of all the effects Ilios was having on her as a woman.

She wasn't immature or unread; she knew that it was perfectly possible for a human being to experience sexual desire without necessarily being in love with the person they desired. However, she had never somehow expected to be one of those human beings who *did* feel like that. She had assumed that only those women with a high sex drive were likely to have their hormones drooling with longing for a man to whom they had no intention of becoming emotionally attached. But now, of course, she knew better. Much, much better. And what she knew told her very definitely that she could not risk sharing a bed with Ilios. Not under any circumstances. Of course she could and would attempt to control her feelings, but what if she failed? What if she was tempted to—? But, no—she must not, under any circumstances, allow those tormenting images she had viewed before to slip into her head.

It was a large bed, Ilios had said. But far from tamping down the fire running riot inside her, his words had only fed it. A large bed meant more space in which to enjoy the sensuality of all the delights the human body could provide.

Lizzie could feel the prickle of the nervous sweat breaking out on her skin. This couldn't go on. If it did she might well end up doing something she would not only regret but which would cause her humiliation and shame. She felt sick with anxiety. She could not share a bed with him. She simply didn't trust herself to be able to do so without giving in to temptation. Even if by some miracle she could control herself whilst she was awake, who knew what might happen whilst she was asleep? It was horribly easy for her to imagine herself moving closer to him, seeking his body in her sleep, wanting him, and then waking to find herself touching him.

She drew in a shuddering breath of despair. 'I really don't think that we should share a bed,' she told Ilios carefully.

She could see immediately that he didn't like what she was saying.

'Why not?' Ilios demanded. Had she somehow guessed that she aroused him, despite his determination not to admit that even to himself? Did she think that she was so desirable, so irresistible, and he so weak that he wouldn't be able to stop himself from turning that arousal into something more intimate?

'I just don't think that it would be a good idea,' Lizzie responded, wishing desperately that he would stop pressing her.

'Because you dare to imagine that I might desire you?' Ilios accused her. 'Despite what I have already said about there being no intimacy between us?'

'No,' Lizzie denied immediately. 'It isn't that.'

'Then what is it?'

'I'm afraid I can't say.'

'And I am afraid that you are going to have to—or take the consequences,' Ilios warned her quietly.

Lizzie exhaled very slowly. What he meant was that she was going to have to share his bed unless she came up with a cast-iron reason why she should not do. Her reason might be solid, but her courage certainly wasn't. Of all the unwanted situations she could have had to face, this had to be the worst of them. She was now in a position where she had to defend herself from her own desire for a man who didn't want her by revealing that desire to him. It was her only means of protecting herself from it.

She had never felt more vulnerable or self-conscious, but the truth was that she needed Ilios's help to stop her from making her situation even worse. Once he was aware how she felt, she knew he would take all the steps necessary to ensure temptation was removed out of her way. Desperate situations called for desperate measures, and there was surely no more desperate measure than the one she was going to have to take now. Rather like firefighters tackling a fire that threatened to destroy everything in its path, she was going to have to create a fire-break by deliberately destroying part of her own defences in the hope that doing so would ultimately protect her from herself.

'It isn't *your* desire that worries me,' she told him truthfully, deliberately emphasising the word 'your'.

CHAPTER EIGHT

LIZZIE'S admission was so unexpected, so breathtakingly straightforward and honest, that it took several seconds for Ilios to accept exactly what she had said.

He looked at her, watching the way the colour came and went in her face, seeing the bruised look of misery that shadowed her eyes, and something came to life inside him that he didn't recognise.

Why didn't he say something—anything? Lizzie thought anxiously, even if it was just to reject her.

However, when he did speak it was slowly, spacing out the words.

'Are you trying to tell me that you don't want to share my bed because *you* want *me*?' he asked in disbelief.

Lizzie's throat had gone so tight that it ached with her tension.

'Yes. That is, I think I do. I'm not used to feeling…that is to wanting… I've never actually lusted after anyone before,' she admitted, red-faced.

'"Lusted after"?'

Now Lizzie could see that she had shocked him.

'I'm sorry!' she apologised. 'I didn't want it to happen, but now you can see, can't you, how difficult it would be?

I've really tried not to…to think about it, but sometimes it just sort of overwhelms me. I'm afraid that if we were to share a bed, then… Well, what I mean is I know that you don't want anything to happen between us. I didn't want to have to say anything.'

She gave a small twisted smile, whilst Ilios listened to her with a growing sense of incredulity and disbelief.

'What woman would?' Lizzie continued self-deprecatingly. 'But at least now that you do know, I can rely on you to…to help me…to ensure that—well, that nothing happens.'

Ilios could hardly believe his own ears. Was she really standing there and telling him that she wouldn't share his bed because she was afraid that the sexual temptation of his proximity would be too much for her self-control? Did she really think that he was the kind of man who would allow a *woman* to play the role of hunter in the chase between the sexes? Immediately Ilios wished he had not used such a metaphor, because it had somehow or other caused some very sensual images indeed to break loose inside his imagination—images that were having exactly the opposite effect on him he assumed Lizzie had expected her admission to have.

Her head bowed, Lizzie admitted, 'I know you must be shocked. I was shocked too. That was part of the reason why I didn't want to agree to marry you.'

'You knew then?' Ilios challenged her.

Lizzie swallowed against the painful lump of anguish lodged in her throat. *I knew the minute I saw you,* she could have said. But of course she mustn't.

'I knew that there was something…' she told him carefully. 'But I thought it would go away.'

'And it didn't?'

She shook her head. 'I thought that I could fight against it, that it would be like fighting the hurdles I had to overcome when our parents died, and I will, only at the moment, after tonight and the champagne, I just don't think…'

'So it's only tonight that you don't want to spend in my bed?'

'No, it's not just tonight.'

'So it isn't just the champagne either?'

Lizzie couldn't speak. She couldn't look at him, and she couldn't run from him either. All she could do was simply shake her head.

'I'd be lying if I said that I'd never been propositioned by a woman before, and I'd be lying even more if I said that I'd either welcomed or enjoyed the experience,' Ilios told her abruptly. 'As far as I'm concerned, I'm a man who does his own hunting, who selects the woman he wants and pursues her—not the other way around.'

Lizzie's head came up. 'I wasn't propositioning you,' she denied fiercely. 'I was just trying to explain—to warn you.' When he made no response she continued determinedly, 'I could sleep in the guest room, and then in the morning…'

Ilios was shaking his head.

'No. Now that I am aware of the situation you may rest assured that you can safely leave it to me to take the right steps to deal with it. That was what you wanted, after all, wasn't it? For me to take responsibility for the situation?'

'Yes,' Lizzie was forced to agree.

'Right. I have some work to do—costings to check—and some e-mails to send. So why don't you make yourself at home in what will now be *our* bedroom and stop worrying? It is a husband's duty to protect his wife, is it not?' Ilios's whole manner was dismissive, and indicated that he no longer felt the issue worthy of discussion.

'I'm not your wife—and anyway, a lot of women would take exception to the idea that they might need to be protected,' Lizzie felt bound to point out.

'This is Greece,' Ilios told her firmly. 'And you are both worrying needlessly and imagining problems where none need exist.'

If she did go to bed now, with any luck she would be asleep before Ilios came to join her. In all probability that was why he was staying up to do some work, Lizzie reflected, as she picked up her coat and nodded in acknowledgement of what he had said.

Ilios's bedroom was twice the size of the guest suite, with both a bathroom and a wetroom attached to it. Not that Lizzie allowed herself to spend any more time than was absolutely necessary in the modern bathroom, with its limestone floor and walls, and its huge bowl-shaped bath.

The bed, as Ilios had told her, was very big—wide enough, surely, for two parents and at least four children; plenty wide enough for two adults to sleep in totally separate. Even so, Lizzie looked at the large sofa on the other side of the bedroom and then, still wrapped in her towel, went over to it. One by one she carried the cushions from it over to the bed, where she laid them meticulously down the middle of the immaculate pale grey silk and cotton cover.

There! That should stop her, should she attempt to do anything silly in her sleep.

Now all she had to do was find the cotton pyjamas she had brought with her from home.

Ten minutes later, wearing the tee shirt top and cut-off trousers, Lizzie pulled back the bedclothes and got into 'her' half of the bed.

* * *

Ilios rubbed his hands over his face to ease the tiredness from it and then looked at his watch. Almost two a.m. Lizzie should be asleep by now. Had he really needed to do this? an inner voice scoffed at him. After all, he was perfectly capable of ensuring that nothing happened that he did not want to happen. Wasn't he? Or maybe, given the lengths he was going to to avoid joining her, he wasn't as sure as he'd like to be.

He looked at the sofa. If that was how he felt, then he had better not take any risks, hadn't he? Picking up the cashmere throw that was draped just so over one of the sofas, Ilios lay down with the throw over himself, flicking the remote to switch off the lights.

This was certainly not something he had envisaged when he'd decided that Lizzie would make him a perfect pretend wife, Ilios thought grimly. Sleeping on the sofa whilst she occupied his bed, in order to protect her from herself…

CHAPTER NINE

'COFFEE.'

It was a statement, not a question, and the familiar darkly smoky male voice in which it was delivered brought Lizzie abruptly out of her sleep.

Ilios, dressed in a white towelling bathrobe and smelling discreetly of clean, warm male flesh, was standing beside the bed—her side of the bed—holding out to her a stylish white china mug, obviously wanting her to take it from him. Obediently Lizzie struggled out of her warm cocoon of bedclothes to sit up, reaching for the mug with one hand whilst keeping the bedclothes pressed to her with the other.

'I'm still not safe, then?' Ilios drawled, a gleam of something approaching amusement in the golden eagle eyes that held Lizzie spellbound.

He was actually smiling! Delight flooded through her, causing her to smile back at him before she could stop herself as she took the mug he was holding out to her. Until recollection of their conversation of the night before made Lizzie groan inwardly, and curse whatever had been responsible for her reckless folly.

Unable to come up with a suitably crushing and mature

response, she looked away from him, almost sloshing coffee onto the bedding when she saw that the sofa cushions she had carefully put in place last night had gone.

Her eyes wide with disbelief and censure, she accused Ilios, 'You took the cushions away.'

'I had no other choice. I'm Greek! I have to think what it would do to my reputation as a man if Maria arrived and found that you had barricaded yourself on one side of the bed in isolation.'

'You could have told her that we'd had a quarrel.'

'I could have,' Ilios agreed. 'But there is a saying that you should never sleep with your anger or without your wife. Maria is of the old school, and she would believe that the more intense the quarrel, the more passionate the making up. In Maria's eyes a quarrel between man and wife can result in only one thing—the arrival of a new baby nine months later.'

Lizzie shuddered inwardly and trembled outwardly. Why had he said that? He must know the effect it was likely to have on her after what she had told him. If this was his way of ensuring that she didn't give way to her desire for him, then Lizzie didn't think it was going to work very well.

'There must be something you can say to Maria that would make her accept that we should sleep in separate rooms—after all, we aren't even married yet.'

'No, there is nothing,' Ilios told her. 'You must know that in Greece, especially this part of Greece, a man's maleness is something he must prove to all those who know him in order to win and maintain their respect. That means being the master of his own house. No Greek male would ever publicly admit that his wife's sexual advances were unwelcome.'

'I wasn't suggesting that you that you told her that,' Lizzie informed him indignantly.

Ilios looked down at the bed. Make-up free, with her hair down round her shoulders and the part of her body that wasn't swathed in bedcovers shrouded by what looked like an oversized tee shirt, Lizzie looked nothing like a temptress of any kind. So why was his body telling him in no uncertain terms that she was, and that it was very tempted by her?

Absently glancing around the room, Lizzie noticed something she had not taken in before—the bedding on other side of the bed was pristinely neat. Untouched, in fact.

She turned accusingly to Ilios. 'You didn't sleep with me, did you?'

When his eyebrows rose she corrected herself hastily.

'I mean you didn't sleep in this bed last night.'

'No. I didn't.'

'So where did you sleep, then?'

'On the sofa. It was late when I finished working, and I didn't want to disturb you. You see, you were sleeping on my side of the bed. I could have moved you in your sleep—without waking you, of course—but, given what you had told me, I didn't think it wise to run the risk of you waking up in my arms and thinking…'

'That I'd reached for you in my sleep?' Lizzie guessed.

'Something like that,' Ilios agreed tersely. What he had been going to say was that he hadn't wanted her waking up and thinking that he returned her desire and wanted her. Nor was he going to admit that the thought of holding her in his arms had tormented his body with such a savagely fierce sexual ache for her through the long, slow hours of the night that he hadn't been able to sleep.

'I've been thinking that perhaps we should just be engaged. Not actually get married. And then—well, you could tell Maria that I'm not the kind of woman who shares a bed with her husband before he is her husband,' Lizzie told Ilios.

'I need a wife, not a fiancée. You know that. And besides, it's too late.'

'Too late?' Lizzie's heart had started to thump uncomfortably heavily. 'What do you mean?'

'We've got an appointment at eleven-thirty this morning with the notary who has arranged all the paperwork for our wedding. He will accompany us to the town hall, so that the formalities can be finalized, and then we can be married.'

'Today? So soon? But surely that isn't possible? I mean, doesn't it take longer than that to arrange things?'

'Normally speaking, yes, but when I explained to my friends at the town hall how impatient I am to make you my wife, they very kindly speeded things up for us. Manos Construction is currently contracted to do some refurbishment work on certain parts of the city, and the local government is keen to get that work finished ahead of schedule.'

'You mean you bribed them into making it possible for us to get married so quickly?' Lizzie accused him.

'No, I did not "bribe" them, as you put it.' Anger flashed in Ilios's eyes. 'I do not conduct my business by way of bribes—I thought I had already made that clear to you. All I did was agree to do what I could to ensure the contract is finished ahead of time and to the highest standard. Something I always insist on. We are subject to earthquakes here. It is always important that this is taken into account on construction projects, although some less than scrupulous contractors do try to cut corners. Now, I shall get dressed whilst you finish your coffee, and then leave you in peace to get dressed yourself.'

* * *

Peace? How was it possible for her to have anything remotely approaching peace now that she had met Ilios? Lizzie asked herself grimly just over an hour later, when she stood in the dressing room she was now sharing with her soon-to-be husband, studying her own reflection.

She was wearing an off-white wool dress with a bubble skirt and a neat boxy matching jacket—the nearest thing she had been able to find amongst her new clothes that looked anything like 'bridal'. Not that this was a proper wedding, or she a proper bride, of course. She must remember that. She was hardly likely to forget it, was she? It had been a shock to learn that they were getting married so quickly, but she suspected that she should have guessed Ilios wouldn't want to waste any time putting his plans into practice.

She walked towards the door. It was a strange feeling to know that the next time she looked at her reflection in this mirror she would not be Lizzie Wareham any more. She would be Mrs Ilios Manos.

CHAPTER TEN

'REMEMBER that you agreed to this,' Ilios warned Lizzie as they stood together on the steps leading of the town hall.

Ilios's notary, who had been with them the whole time whilst the simple ceremony making them man and wife had been taking place, stood back discreetly as Ilios took her arm.

Not trusting herself to speak, Lizzie nodded her head and forced a brief tight smile. It was all very well telling herself that it wasn't a real marriage, nor a proper wedding, nor Ilios her real husband—there had still been that dreadful moment when they had stood together before the official marrying them and inside her head she had seen the small church in the village where she had grown up, and herself dressed in white, with her father standing proudly at her side, her mother fussing over her dress and her sisters laughing, Ilios watching them smiling, and she had felt a tearing, aching sense of loss strike her right to her heart.

'Come,' Ilios urged her.

The sun was shining, drying pavements still wet from the rain that had fallen whilst they were inside the building, and the breeze was cool. Summer, with its heat, was still many weeks away, and for the first time since she had agreed to marry Ilios Lizzie longed desperately for those weeks to fly past, so that she would be free to go home to her family. It had felt so wrong, so lonely getting married without them—even if it was a pretend marriage—and she ached with nostalgia for her childhood and homesickness for her sisters and the twins.

The sunlight shone brightly on the newness of her wedding ring. She must stop feeling sorry for herself and remember why she had agreed to marry Ilios, she told herself—why she had *had* to marry him. He was still cupping her elbow, very much the attentive bridegroom—no doubt for the benefit of the notary to whom he was now speaking in Greek. Both of them were looking at her, their conversation excluding her, reminding her that she was an outsider in a foreign land and very much alone.

The pressure of Ilios's hold on her arm urged her closer to him, as though…as though he had somehow sensed what she was feeling and wanted to reassure her—just as a real husband would have done. That, of course, was ridiculous. Even if he *had* guessed how she was feeling he was hardly likely to care, was he? She could feel his thumb lightly rubbing her skin through her jacket. He was probably so used to caressing his lovers that he didn't even realise what he was doing, Lizzie thought waspishly, as she tried to ignore the effect his absent-minded caress was having on her body. He was turning towards her, smiling warmly at her—a false smile, for his audience, of course.

'Forgive us for speaking in Greek, *agapi mou*,' he told her. 'We were just discussing some business. But now, Nikos, I am impatient to take my beautiful wife for a celebratory lunch.'

The notary had soon gone, and Ilios was handing her back into his car.

Lizzie had assumed that Ilios would take her straight back to the apartment, and leave her to go on to his office, but instead he parked the car in a convenient space outside an elegant-looking restaurant.

'I didn't think you were serious about us celebrating,' Lizzie told him.

'I wasn't—but we do have to eat,' he pointed out dismissively, before getting out of the car and coming round to her door to open it for her.

They might not be publicly celebrating their marriage, but the keen-eyed restaurant owner who had greeted Ilios so warmly on their arrival must have noticed something— her new wedding ring, perhaps? Lizzie acknowledged. Her heart sank as he approached their table now, with a beaming smile and champagne. Of course she couldn't possibly offend him by refusing to accept his kindness, but even so she couldn't help glancing at Ilios as their glasses were filled with the sparkling liquid.

She wished that she hadn't when he lifted his glass towards her own and said softly, and very meaningfully, 'To us.'

'To us,' Lizzie echoed weakly, quickly sipping her own drink to disguise the fact that her hand was trembling. She mustn't blame herself too much for her reaction, Lizzie tried to comfort herself. After all a marriage, even a pretend marriage, was bound to have some effect on a person's emotions—just as a man like Ilios was bound to have an effect on a woman's awareness of her own sexuality.

The toast didn't have to be taken as a toast to them as a couple, and she was sure the deliberate emphasis Ilios had put on it was a private reminder to her that he was toasting them as separate individuals rather than a couple in their newly official union.

She found that even though she had been hungry her emotions were now too stirred up for her to have much appetite for the delicious food. Desperate for something to distract her from her unwanted and growing awareness that, no matter how illogical it might be, the fact that she and Ilios were married had produced within her an unexpected feeling of commitment to him—a sort of protective, deeply female need to reach out to him and heal the damage that had been done to his emotions and his life—Lizzie glanced round the restaurant.

Her attention focussed on a family group at another table. The parents, a pretty dark-haired young mother and a smiling paternalistic-looking father, were accompanied by three children: a little boy who looked slightly older than the twins, a girl who Lizzie guessed must be about four, and what was obviously a fairly new baby in a car seat buggy combo drawn up to the table. Although the children were not all the same sex, the relationship between them reminded her of her own childhood. The little boy, serious-looking and obviously proud of his seniority, was keeping an older-brotherly eye on the little girl and the baby, whilst the little girl was leaning over the buggy, cooing at the baby. Over their heads the parents exchanged amused and tender smiles.

Hastily Lizzie reached for her champagne, to try and swallow back the huge lump of aching emotion forming in her throat. Not for herself—she and her sisters had experienced the kind of love she could see emanating from this family. No, her sadness and pain was for those other children—Ilios's sons.

Before she could change her mind she asked Ilios, 'Are

you sure there isn't some way that you and your cousin could mend the broken fences between you and get your relationship on a happier footing?'

'If that's a roundabout way of trying to tell me that you're anxious to bring our marriage to an end as soon as possible, then—'

'No, it isn't that.' Lizzie stopped him. 'It's the children—*your* children,' she emphasized, when she saw Ilios look frowningly towards the table she had been studying.

Leaning across the table, she asked him quietly, 'Have you thought about what might happen to them if anything were to happen to you? They'd have no one—no father, no mother, obviously, no family Ilios. No one in their lives to give them a sense of continuity and security and…and… They would have no one to tell them their history, no one to tell them about you. I know that financially they would be protected, but that isn't enough. They'd be dreadfully alone.'

Ilios was looking down at his plate. She had infuriated him, Lizzie expected, and no doubt he was going to tell her that the future of his sons was none of her business.

When he did lift his head and look at her Lizzie found it impossible to gauge what he was thinking from his grim expression.

'So you think that I should—what was the phrase you used?—"mend fences" with my cousin so that in the eventuality of my unexpected demise he will open his arms and his heart to my sons and become a second father to them?'

Put like that, what she had said did sound rather like something out of a sentimental film, Lizzie admitted.

'Family is important.' She insisted.

'What if I were to do as you suggest and my sons ended

up being humiliated and tormented by my cousin, just as I was myself? What if he abused the trust I placed in him for his own financial benefit?'

'That's what I meant about wondering if it was possible for you to mend fences with him,' Lizzie defended herself. 'Now, before it's too late.'

'I see. I become reconciled with my cousin, and you get a quick escape from a commitment and an agreement you're obviously already wanting to renege on?'

'No! I am prepared to stay married to you for as long as it takes.'

Ilios arched one eyebrow in a silent but unmistakably mocking query, and then asked her softly, 'As long as what takes?'

Lizzie felt like stamping her foot. Ignoring her own feeling of self-consciousness, she told him fiercely, 'You know perfectly well what I was trying to say. I am not attempting to renege on our agreement. If I did that you'd be within your moral rights to demand repayment of the money you gave me—money I need to ensure my family's financial security. I know you've said that you don't believe in love, but to deny your own sons the emotional protection they will need...' She hesitated, and then decided to ignore her anxiety about angering him. If she was to be his children's champion then she must do so without considering her own position. 'Surely you can't want them to suffer in their childhood as you did?'

Ilios looked at her in silence, whilst she held her breath—waiting for his response.

When it came, it was both unexpected and underhanded.

'Obviously it isn't only sexual lust for my body that champagne arouses in you, but a lust for plain speaking.'

'What I said doesn't have anything to do with me drinking champagne,' she said vehemently.

'No? Don't the words *in vino veritas* mean anything to you?'

In wine there is truth. But it wasn't the champagne that had loosened her inhibitions. It was seeing that small happy family. Only somehow Lizzie didn't think that Ilios would believe her—no matter how much she tried to correct his interpretation of the situation.

Mend fences with his cousin? Ilios thought grimly of the way Tino had deliberately tormented him as a child—the way he had taunted him by pointing out that he had a mother, aunts and uncles and cousins, whilst Ilios's own mother had hated him so much she had abandoned him. Of course Tino had had his own cross to bear. Their grandfather had never let him forget that his father had died a coward.

To their grandfather male descendants had simply been there to fulfil and continue the Manos destiny: to own Villa Manos, the land on which it stood, and continue their once proud history. Nothing and no one else mattered.

But Lizzie had had a point. No man was immortal, and if he *should* die before his sons were old enough to manage their own affairs there would be plenty of vultures waiting to pick at the vulnerable flesh of their inheritance.

He and Lizzie looked at life and humankind from opposite viewpoints. She believed passionately in the power of love, in parenthood and families. He did not. When called upon to do so she had put her siblings first, and every word she spoke about them showed that she would do anything and everything she could to safeguard and protect them. Just as she would her children, should she become a mother? Ilios frowned. That did not accord with his own beliefs about her sex. He could concede that Lizzie might be that one rare exception. But so what?

The trouble was there were beginning to be far too

many *so whats* in his reactions to Lizzie Wareham, Ilios acknowledged, remembering that he had asked himself the same question when he had been forced to admit that he was sexually aware of her—sexually aware of her and aroused by her presence. He had no rational explanation for the way she made him think and feel, and trying to find one only served to increase his awareness of the effect she was having on him and his desire to crush it.

And yet, as much as he wanted to impose his will on his awareness of her, his body refused to accept it. Quite the opposite in fact. The ache that had been tormenting him flared from a dull presence to a sharp, predatory male clamour. Totally against what he had believed he knew about himself, her admission of desire for him had increased his own desire for her rather than destroy it. Increased it, enhanced it, and made him want her with a suddenly very driven intensity that he had never experienced before.

Ilios looked at Lizzie's half-empty glass of champagne, and then at the bottle still in the ice bucket. Picking it up, he told her, 'You'd better finish this, otherwise we'll offend Spiros—and I don't want to end up never being able to get a table here again.'

Lizzie shook her head.

'I've already had one full glass,' she reminded him.

'And two might turn your thoughts to your uncontrollable lust for my body and a whole catalogue of things you'd like to do to it?' he taunted her.

Before Lizzie could formulate a suitable crushing response he continued easily, as he filled her glass, 'It seems to me that the best way to quench your sexual curiosity would be to satisfy it.'

What the hell had made him say that? Ilios challenged

himself grimly. But of course he already knew the answer. Lizzie wasn't the only one battling against a desire she didn't want. Maybe what he'd suggested was the best way for them both to rid themselves of a need that neither of them wished to have.

What was happening? Was she hallucinating or was Ilios actually suggesting…? No, she must be imagining it.

'Is…is that an offer?' she managed to ask Ilios, in what she hoped was a voice that suggested she knew it wasn't.

Only she was left thoroughly bemused at his response.

'If you want it to be.'

Did she? What was happening here? Was Ilios really implying that he wanted her? Physically? Sexually? In bed?

Lizzie refused to answer him. She simply didn't dare.

She didn't like the way Ilios was looking at her. And she certainly didn't like the way that look was making tiny rivulets of giddy excitement and longing rush through her body, like teenage fans rushing towards an idol, oblivious to reality or danger. Neither did she like the way she suddenly and overpoweringly wanted to look at Ilios's mouth and imagine… She could hardly breathe, barely think—at least not of anything that didn't involve her getting up close and personal with Ilios and discovering if that full bottom lip did mean what it was supposed to mean. What would happen were she to touch it with her fingertips, taste it with her tongue, explore it and…?

In desperation Lizzie took what she hoped would be a cooling gulp of her champagne. She certainly needed something to dampen down the sensual heat that had taken hold of her. Ilios was still looking at her—looking at her as though he knew every word she was thinking and every thing she was feeling. No, she did not like that look and all it suggested at all. Lizzie drew in a shaky breath of air as her conscience prodded her. Well, all right, she did like it—but she didn't like the fact that she liked it.

The truth was, Lizzie realised ten minutes later, as Ilios held opened the car door for her, that much as she ached for the experience of having sex with Ilios, and eager as she was to explore and appreciate every bit of him, she was still female enough to want *him* to make the first move and show her that he wanted her as much as if not more than she wanted him. She needed to know his desire for her. She needed to feel that he wanted her so much that he could not deny that wanting. Only then would she truly be able to indulge her own desire for him. And of course that was not going to happen—was it?

But what if it did? Ilios could be right, and the best way for her to get over the longing that was tormenting her *was* for her to go to bed with him. Hot excitement kicked through her body. She was a woman, she reminded herself—she was twenty-seven years old, after all—not a teenager. She knew perfectly well what the situation was and she couldn't claim any different. Did she really want to go back home without experiencing what Ilios offered her just because she had panicked and wanted to be wooed? Wouldn't she, years from now, look back in regret, or even worse in yearning, for what she had not had? It was perfectly safe, after all, and so was she. It wasn't as though she was in love with Ilios and thought that somehow having sex with him—making love with him—was going to change him and cause him to fall head over heels in love with her.

No, this was purely about sexual desire. It was about answering, exploring, satisfying the need that had been aching, growing inside her from their first meeting. No one but the two of them need ever know that she had briefly stepped out of the role she had cast for herself after the death of her parents—a role that meant that she must always be the responsible eldest sister, monitoring her own behaviour in order that she could set their family standards and guide her younger siblings. Here, with Ilios, it was safe for her to experience being what in her real life she could never be—sensually eager, responsive to her own desires and those of her partner, without having to think about anything or anyone else.

What possible harm could there be in it? If it happened it would be a one-off, that was all—an exciting, tantalising sensual adventure. If Ilios should repeat his offer, was she going to be brave enough to do what she knew she wanted to do? Or was she going to be a coward who would spend the rest of her life regretting her hesitation?

CHAPTER ELEVEN

THEY'D travelled back to the Manos Corporation building in silence, and in that same silence they had got out of the car and travelled in the lift to where they were now—outside the door to the apartment, with Ilios unlocking it.

'What's this?' Lizzie asked curiously, almost forgetting the reason for her earlier inability to speak as she bent down to pick up the small blue bead lying on the floor just inside the door.

'Maria's obviously been in, and equally obviously she must know the wedding was today,' Ilios answered, taking the bead from her and putting it back down on the floor. 'It's meant to ward off the evil eye—a Greek tradition that involves those who have something to protect doing so by means of the gift of one of these. Maria obviously approves of our marriage, and by leaving this is protecting it and us from bad luck.'

Lizzie nodded her head. She'd have liked to have changed out of her white wool dress and coat into something less high-maintenance, but she was concerned that any move towards the bedroom on her part might be wrongly interpreted by Ilios.

'Who designed the garden?' she asked him instead. 'I haven't been out in it yet, but—'

'I designed it. Or at least I copied certain elements of the gardens at Villa Manos and adapted them for here.'

Whilst they were talking they'd walked into the living room.

'Will I be safe if I offer you a walk round the garden?' Ilios asked.

Did he really think she would pounce on him? Was he expecting her to make all the running? She couldn't, Lizzie knew. Not without knowing that he wanted her too.

Lizzie wondered what he was really thinking—and feeling. Had he meant what he'd said in the restaurant, or had he simply been amusing himself at her expense? Even worse, had he actually been thinking about taking her to bed and then decided upon reflection not to bother? Maybe she had misunderstood what he'd said, or taken it too seriously, and now he was stepping back from that conversation because he hadn't meant it. Lizzie's face burned at the thought.

'If you don't mind my saying so, if you would like to see the garden you may want to think about getting changed first, into something less...'

The sound of Ilios's voice focussed her attention on what he was saying, and valiantly Lizzie tried to put her mixed-up feelings to one side and focus instead of reality.

'Something less white?' she offered brightly. She refused to use the word *bridal*, with all that it implied.

Ilios nodded his head.

'Look, I've got a couple of e-mails I need to send, so why don't you go and get changed? Take as long as you wish. There's no rush.'

* * *

If Ilios had actually known how uncomfortable she'd been feeling, both in her outfit and about saying she wanted to change out of it, and had wanted to put her at her ease, he couldn't have done so more effectively, Lizzie acknowledged several minutes later, as she stood beneath the shower in the bathroom off the master bedroom. Not that she imagined he *could* have known how she was feeling. In fact he had probably simply wanted her out of the way. The more she thought about it, the more she thought she had been a complete fool for thinking he had been suggesting that he wanted her.

She showered quickly, using her own favourite shower gel from Jo Malone, and noting as she did so that the container was almost empty. Jo Malone treats were something she wasn't going to be able to indulge in any more. No doubt the whole family would end up using something safe and suitable for the twins. Smiling to herself, Lizzie stepped out of the shower, drying herself speedily and then wrapping a towel sarong-wise round her body. Removing the cap she had put on her head to keep her hair dry, she opened the door to the dressing room and came to an abrupt halt almost in mid-step, her eyes widening as she saw Ilios opening his wardrobe. Like her, he had quite obviously taken a shower—only his towel sat low on his hips and finished midway down his thigh.

Her 'Oh!' was a soft, half-choked sound as betraying as the manner in which she clutched her towel protectively to her body. 'I thought you said you were going to be busy sending e-mails,' was all she could think of to say.

'I changed my mind and decided to have a shower instead.' He wasn't going to tell her that the ache she had induced within his body had made it impossible for him to do anything other than give in to the need to take a cold shower.

He must have used the guest room—which, of course, was why he was here right now, looking for his clothes.

'I'll…I'll wait in the bathroom until…until you've finished.'

Was that squeaky, nervous voice really her own?

'So that you aren't overwhelmed by your desire for me?'

Why had she ever said that to him about being concerned that she might be the one overcome with lust? Both the joke and her sense of humour were becoming stretched to breaking point.

'I'll tell you what…' Ilios's voice was muffled by the wardrobe door that he had opened between them, and Lizzie had to strain to hear what he was saying. Automatically she took a couple of steps towards him, so that she could hear properly.

What would he tell her?

'Instead of talking about your desire for me, why don't you come here and show me?'

The door swung closed. Ilios was standing far too close to her—or rather she was standing far too close to him. But even as she decided to step back his right hand curled into her towel and tugged—firmly.

What was she going to do? If she stayed where she was she would be in danger of losing her towel, and if she moved it would have to be forward, towards him, and that would mean…

'Nothing to say?'

She was up close against him, and his hand wasn't gripping her towel. Instead it was smoothing its way up her bare arm and over her shoulder, stroking her neck, cupping her face. One hand, and then both.

'Very well, then, why don't I do this instead?'

He finished his sentence in a whisper, practically forming the words against her lips with his lips—lips that were smooth and warm and expertly knowing as they moved slowly over hers, pausing, lifting to allow her to gasp in a shaken breath. His fingers smoothed the skin of her face, and then he was kissing her again, slowly and lingeringly, each second of his touch its own intimate world of pleasure, given and then removed. A tantalising, tormenting unbelievably erotic pleasure, nothing more than light skimming kisses but at the same time so deeply sensual that they transported her to a whole new world.

Each time he kissed her and then withdrew Lizzie moved closer, hungering for more. Her own hand lifted to his face.

'I've wanted to do this from the first moment I saw you,' she admitted breathlessly, touching his skin with her fingertips, absorbing its texture, learning the shape of the muscles that lay beneath the warm flesh, her eyes dark and hot with what she was feeling.

'Only this? Nothing more?'

Ilios's voice was as soft and warm, as erotic to her senses as the dark cross of fine silky hair that painted his body. His words, with their tempting invitation, made her tremble beneath the intensity of her own desire.

'Not this, perhaps?' he suggested, sliding his hand round the curve of her throat and kissing her bare shoulder, each movement of his lips setting off a firestorm of quivering delight.

'Or this?' His tongue stroked the sensitive flesh just behind her earlobe, making her shudder visibly and cling to him as though her flesh was so boneless and pliable that she could melt into him. She wanted him so much—which made it all the harder to bear when he stopped kissing her and released her.

That was it? He was going to leave her like this? Aching so badly for him that—

'Come on,' he told her. 'I'll show you the garden.'

The garden? Now? She didn't want the garden. She wanted him. But Ilios was reaching for her hand and drawing her with him as he headed for the door.

They had been late coming back from lunch, and now it was almost dark. Cleverly placed lights illuminated the garden, transforming it into a space filled with magical images. The ruined temple was highlighted against the evening sky, the colonnade woven with a net of tiny starry lights.

'It looks very pretty,' Lizzie admitted absently, still dazed by his kisses, and still wearing nothing more than the towel wrapped around her. It was true about the garden, but they were now in a bedroom that possessed a very large bed, and right now all she wanted was to be lying on that bed with Ilios, with nothing to come between them, or to come between her and her increasingly urgent need to explore every bit of him.

Ilios obviously didn't feel the same way, because he was leading her down a smooth path, the tiles cool beneath her bare feet. The raised walls protecting the garden made it pleasantly warm, and above them the evening sky was studded with stars like diamonds in velvet, their gleam reflected in the swimming pool.

It would have been on nights such as these that the gods came down from Olympus to mingle with mortal men— and women, Lizzie thought, remembering how some of the Greek myths involved human women being impregnated by handsome gods. She paused to touch the leaves of a small olive tree set into a tub.

'Olives and vines. Food and drink,' Ilios murmured.

'Ambrosia and nectar,' Lizzie whispered back.

They had reached the side of the swimming pool, and as she looked back at the ruin Ilios spoke teasingly.

'I think we can dispense with these, don't you?'

Lizzie sucked in her breath as he plucked away her towel, but the self-consciousness she had expected to feel was banished—melting away, she suspected, in the heat that filled her as his gaze stroked over every bit of her, just as though he was actually caressing her.

What was happening to her? She was with a man who made her feel as no man had ever made her feel before, and it was the most extraordinary, the most deliciously sensual and exciting feeling she had ever had. Her awareness of her own nakedness actually gave her an additional frisson of pleasure, made her want to stretch erotically beneath the warmth of Ilios's gaze. She watched as he removed his own towel, her heart thudding into a climax of fierce female anticipation as she waited for him to take her in his arms.

Instead he dived into the water, slicing it cleanly and surfacing a few feet out into the pool before turning to hold out his arms to her.

'Jump in. The water's warm.'

They were going for a *swim*?

Lizzie took a deep breath and jumped.

Ilios's arms closed round her. They were standing body to body, the water just covering her breasts. It lapped against them, a warm touch against her sensitised nipples and between her legs, as sensual as a lover's touch gently caressing her. Ilios's hands stroked over her skin, his movements vibrating in the water so that it felt as though he and the water were one. He had complete mastery over her desire, arousing it, compelling it, filling her with pleasure and then drawing it from her. Her body was a willing vessel, to be filled with the pleasure he was giving her. The sensation of his breath against her skin made her cry out softly, arching her throat to its touch just as she was arching her body to his possession. She was his to do with as he pleased—to give her all the sensual delight he was giving her.

Lizzie closed her eyes beneath the onslaught of the sweet agony of growing need, opening them quickly when Ilios moved to float onto his back, taking her with him so that she was lying on top of him, supported by him, her body pressing into his, every inch of her skin aware of every inch of his, where they touched and where they didn't.

He kicked out strongly through the water, his hands sliding down her back and then up again slowly, stroking her skin with his fingertips, moving lower with each caress.

Lizzie held her breath against the fever of her own longing. Only when he finally stroked past her hips to cup her buttocks was she able to exhale in shaky relief. Now, at last, against her own sex she could feel his, solid with muscle and arousal, pressing up against her as Ilios pressed her down against himself.

Within her the heat of her own desire seemed to be melting her flesh, so that it softened and expanded. Her body moved under his hands and their grip on her tightened. It couldn't be happening like this, without any need for anything other than the satisfaction of the compulsive drive that was now pounding through her, but it was. All she could think of—all she wanted—was the satisfaction of having the full deep thrust of him within her.

Ilios was like a mythical god, Lizzie thought dizzily. His

touch made reality and reason disappear and replaced them with the most ancient and relentless of human drives. The need he aroused in her possessed her and drove her, so that all she wanted was to wrap herself around him.

They had reached the far end of the pool, where water fell from the top of a cliff past the opening to a grotto with soft lighting that turned the water a rich blue-green.

When Ilios eased her away from his body and stood up Lizzie could see that the water here was shallower. Water from the pool ran down his body, and Lizzie's gaze followed each drop hungrily.

'What?' Ilios asked watching her gaze with his own. 'What is it you want to do? This?'

He leaned forward and held her waist, kissing his way down past her collarbone and between her breasts—light, lingering kisses accompanied by the curling movement of his tongue against her damp flesh, making her burn with longing to do the same to him. His hand dropped to her thighs. Lizzie gave a small moan that became a gasp of tortured pleasure when Ilios started to kiss the slope of her breast, and then to circle the tight ache of her nipple with his tongue-tip.

The heavy pulse of the ache low down in her body picked up tempo. She leaned into Ilios's hold, her thighs parting. In response he tongued her nipple, and then drew it between his lips. Wanting more, Lizzie pushed towards him, welcoming the heat of his hand between her legs, whimpering with pleasure when his fingers found her wetness, her body clamouring for urgent and immediate release.

But instead Ilios lifted her out of the water and put her down at the side of the pool, then getting out himself to join her. Lizzie's heart was thudding. Her body was aching with frustration at the interruption and the removal of his pleasure-giving touch.

She reached for him, wanting to show him how she felt, cupping his face as he had cupped her own earlier, and then kissing him fiercely and eagerly, arching her body into his. His arms tightened round her and he kissed her back.

'We need to go back inside,' he told her. His voice was thick with the desire she shared as he urged her towards the bedroom.

'I know,' she whispered back. 'But I don't want to let you go. I want you so much.' She kissed him again, her hands on his body, her own body on fire with all that she was feeling.

Somehow, between increasingly passionate kisses, they managed to make it to the bedroom, where Lizzie wrapped her arms tightly around Ilios and kissed him, tasting his mouth with her own. She smoothed her hands over his shoulders and his back, stoking the heat of her own arousal with every caress as her senses greedily absorbed the pleasure of their intimacy. Every bit of him was hers to explore and enjoy, and her fingertips memorised the smooth flesh at the back of his neck, the thick strength of his dark hair, the shape of his ears, whilst her senses recorded his response to her touch: the way he arched his head back into her hold, the small thick sound of pleasure he made when she caressed the tender flesh behind his ear, the accelerated sound of his breathing when she had kissed his skin. Small milestones on the longer journey they were sharing, each one faithfully monitored and logged within her heart.

Her *heart*? But that would mean... From the shocked thud of her heartbeat its reverberations spread out through her, carrying to every part of her body and mind a warning—a message of anxiety and apprehension laced with disbelief. Surely there was only one reason why her heart might want to log every second of her intimacy with Ilios? If her heart was involved, then so were her emotions. Emotions and Ilios did not and could not mix. They were incompatible. Just as she and Ilios were incompatible.

Lizzie turned to him, but before she could even think of what she might reasonably say to bring an end to something she knew now would put her in emotional danger, Ilios was scooping her up, carrying her over to the bed, and kissing her with such shocking sensuality as he placed her on it that he immediately awakened her previous urgent desire.

In its fierce clamour it was impossible for her to hear any other voice—impossible for her to think of anything other than the growing sensual tension possessing her body.

Leaning over her, Ilios caressed her body, lingering over each touch with a focussed intensity that was all by itself unbearably erotic, driving her to reach for him. His lips brushed hers; his hand brushed her sex. His tongue-tip parted her lips whilst his hand parted her thighs.

Lizzie could feel her heart hammering into her ribs. Supporting himself with his other hand on the bed, Ilios watched her face as he touched her slowly and intimately, until she was opening helplessly to him, arching up to him for more.

'I want you. I want you, Ilios. Now—please.'

Lizzie's words, gasped in eager longing, pierced Ilios's hot desire, chiming a warning within himself that automatically set off his own protective defences. He had no means of ensuring that their intimacy would be safe. From what Lizzie had told him he doubted that she used any form of contraception as an automatic course. The thought of the health of either of them being affected by them having sex was one he dismissed immediately. He had never taken any risks with his sexual health, and he doubted that Lizzie had had enough previous sexual experience to have risked her own. But they were not protected against unwanted pregnancy, and that meant that he should stop—right now. After all, he had his future planned—and the children that would be a part of it. His children—his sons—protected from the pain he had known as a child, protected from any mother who might reject them or subject him to her avaricious financial demands.

His children who, according to Lizzie, having been conceived in the sterile atmosphere of a laboratory and carried by a woman they would never know, would be deprived of love.

'Ilios?'

Lizzie reached up and touched his face, not understanding why he wasn't responding to her, stroking her fingertips along the length of his sweat-dampened torso, trailing the narrow line of dark hair across his flat belly.

The look of hungry and absorbed need the moonlight revealed in her expression re-ignited the desire Ilios had been trying to suppress. Like flames devouring dry timber it raced through him, overpowering everything that tried to stand in its way, including his own inner warning voice. His body moved of its own accord, his mind powerless to control its need. And Lizzie reached for him, drawing him down towards her, her lips parting in the same longing he could feel in the way she moved to welcome him between her thighs.

The first hot, slick, sweet taste of her sex against his own brought down what was left of his self-control as effectively as a tidal wave smashing down a sandcastle on the beach.

He was within her, taking her, giving to her as they began the swift surging climb towards immortality. On the journey there were brief seconds of time when the pleasure was so intense, like stars within reach on a journey to the moon, that Lizzie was almost distracted enough to want to reach out to them—but then the drive of Ilios's body within her own reminded her of the greater purpose, their ultimate shared destination.

It came for her with convulsive tightening of her body that quickened into her orgasm, just as she felt Ilios's surrender to its fierce embrace spilling hotly into her.

Into her? Like an annoying fly, intruding on the wonderful peace of a lazy summer afternoon, the two words buzzed agitatedly inside her head, ignoring Lizzie's attempts to brush them away so that she could enjoy the pure heaven of lying fulfilled and sweetly aching in the aftermath of orgasm in Ilios's arms.

They hadn't used any contraception. It might not be true that having sex standing up prevented pregnancy, but perhaps if she got up instead of lying there... She was a responsible adult, after all, and there was no place in her life for an unplanned pregnancy.

So why, instead of doing something, or even saying something, was she instead luxuriating in lying close to Ilios, her hand on his chest, registering the beat of his heart gradually returning to normal? Her fingers played with the soft damp hair on his chest, and she enjoyed the male possessiveness of the leg he had thrown across her own, as though wanting to keep her as close to him as she wanted him to be close to her.

Ilios was leaning over her, his hand on her neck, his fingers stroking her skin.

'Good?' he asked.

'Heaven,' Lizzie responded truthfully. 'Absolutely heaven.'

Ilios gathered her close, ignoring the inner voice that was warning him he had just done something that broke all his rules, and something he was going to regret.

CHAPTER TWELVE

'I've got to go out to the villa today, to meet with one of the contractors, and I wondered if you'd like to come with me?'

The sudden frown that followed Ilios's invitation made Lizzie wonder if he had spoken without thinking and was now regretting having done so. But, faced with the prospect of another day on her own, sightseeing in the city, when she could instead see the house that had such a fascinating history, she was not going to ask Ilios if he would like to withdraw his invitation.

'I'd love to,' she told him truthfully. After all, it wasn't just Villa Manos she would get to see properly. She would also be with Ilios. Her heart leapt even as her thoughts filled her with guilt.

It had been disquieting to wake in Ilios's arms in the early hours of the morning after they had made love— several days ago now. She'd known that she had crossed a barrier she had never intended to cross. Lying with her head on Ilios's chest, listening to the sound of his breathing, Lizzie had been forced to admit to herself what she had recognised earlier in the evening. Somehow emotion had become entangled in what she had truthfully believed to be merely physical desire. And that emotion was love. An emotion Ilios had already told her he did not want in his life.

But that was all right, she assured herself determinedly now. After all, she was not going to tell him about her love for him. She wasn't going to offer it to him. She wasn't going to do anything different because of it. When the time came she would still pack up her belongings, fold her love in tissue paper in her memory, and take it with her. It was hers, and if she wished to cherish it and protect it, and every now and again remove it from the place where she had hidden it to relive those memories she had made, then that was her business—wasn't it? She was mature enough not to allow it to intrude into what was in reality a business relationship, a business commitment. Ilios had paid her—not to sleep with him of course, but to marry him. In doing so she was providing him a means of outmanoeuvring his cousin, and preventing him from causing him difficulties and delays with regard to their grandfather's will.

What on earth had made him ask Lizzie for her company? Ilios didn't know—or rather he was determined not to know, because of what knowing the answer to his own question might mean.

The night he had taken her to bed had changed everything between them. And it had also changed him. Ilios knew that there were those who came into contact with him who considered him hard and demanding, but the demands he made on others, the expectations he had of them, were nothing compared with those he made on and had for himself.

In taking Lizzie to bed in the first place he had broken his own rules, and that was bad enough. However, even though he had known they were not using contraception he had still gone ahead—and it was that fact that most challenged his perceptions of himself. He could have stopped. His mind had given him a warning that had in turn given him the opportunity to stop. But he had ignored that warning. Why? Because at that point he had been too aroused to want to stop? He was thirty-six years old, dammit, not a teenager and he knew it. Now it was that knowledge that was rubbing a raw place inside his head. Like grit in a shoe, demanding attention, a question that wanted an answer.

Why, when he had been aware of what he was doing and the risk he was taking, and when he had had the opportunity to stop, had he not done so? Why had he, in fact, deliberately continued? Knowing what might result? His life was planned out—his way ahead clear. Impregnating Lizzie with his child was not part of that plan, and neither that child nor Lizzie herself had any place in his future.

And now, when surely he ought to be distancing himself from Lizzie, he had actually invited her to spend the day with him.

It would be both heaven and hell to spend the day with Ilios, Lizzie knew. What had happened to her determination to fight what was happening to her? She would recover it, she assured herself. But just for today she was going to allow herself to bask inwardly in the happiness she felt and the delight of being with him. Inwardly. Outwardly, of course, she must treat the day and Ilios himself in exactly the same way she would have done an appointment with any client she might be accompanying, to view a property they wanted her to restyle for them. All right, so Ilios wasn't going to be asking her to restyle Villa Manos, and for her own sake she must remember why he had married her. As soon as Ilios deemed that their marriage had served its purpose she would be on her way home, and their marriage would be brought to an end.

With that in mind, when she joined him in the living room half an hour after they had finished breakfast, she was wearing her 'professional uniform' of jeans and a white tee shirt—although the new jeans were part of her Mrs Manos wardrobe and were designer. They fitted her perfectly, just like the tee shirt. She carried a jacket over her arm.

Like her, Ilios was also casually dressed in jeans. When he turned his back on her to place his coffee mug in the dishwasher Lizzie had an excellent view of the way in which the denim fitted the muscular firmness of his buttocks, and shamefully she could feel her heartbeat increasing as her gaze lingered on him longer than it should have done. Her? Ogling a man's body? Since when? But Ilios was no ordinary man, was he? He was the man she loved. And the temptation to go up to him and lean against him, hoping that he would turn round and take her in his arms, was almost overwhelming.

It didn't help that Ilios was now coming to bed after she had fallen asleep and getting up in the morning before she was awake, making it very plain that he did not want a repetition of the intimacy they had shared. Although the one good thing about her discovering that she loved him was that she did not now need to fear being overcome by her lust—knowing that she loved him had changed everything. It meant that she would not and could not risk Ilios recognising how she felt.

Pinning a bright, businesslike smile to her face, she asked Ilios conversationally, 'Is the interior of Villa Manos modelled on Villa Emo as well as the exterior?'

This was another unfamiliar issue he was having to deal with, Ilios acknowledged. The fact that not once since he had taken her to bed had Lizzie made any reference to what had happened. Not so much as by a look, never mind a word. Because she regretted what had happened? Because her sexual desire for him, once satisfied, had vanished? Either of those alternatives should have been welcomed by him, and yet here he was feeling they were unsatisfactory—that the situation between them was unsatisfactory. It left him feeling that there was unfinished business between them, that he wanted...

He wanted what? To take her back to bed and repeat his reckless behaviour? Double the chances of her becoming pregnant? Was that really what he wanted? The ferocity with which his heart slammed into his ribs caught him off guard. It was the realisation of what could happen that had caused that surge of emotion inside him, that was all. Nothing else. The last thing he wanted was for Lizzie to be carrying his child.

Ilios forced himself to focus on Lizzie's question.

'Yes and no,' he answered. 'It is both similar and different—you will have to judge for yourself. However, what I can tell you is that structurally my ancestor followed Palladio's measurement ratio for the interior, just as he did for the exterior, so the villa follows Palladio's beliefs in the importance of architectural harmony. Internally, the living space forms a classical central square core, within which are six rooms that sizewise form repetitions of one of Palladio's standard modules. For instance, either side of the entrance hall are two rooms which are sixteen Trevisan feet in width by twenty-seven Trevisan feet in length.' He paused, in case what he was saying was going over Lizzie's head, but he could see from her expression that she was following what he was saying perfectly.

'To create a ratio of six to ten,' she agreed. 'The perfect numbers in Renaissance architecture. I've read references to Palladio's buildings being like frozen music, because he adopted the proportions that Pythagoras said produced combinations of notes that fall harmoniously on the human ear.'

Ilios gave an approving nod of his head. 'That Greek connection had great appeal for my ancestor, according to our family lore. As far as Villa Manos goes, in between the smaller rooms—the two I've already mentioned—facing east and the west of the villa, are four more rooms which together have the same Palladio measurements. The central grand salon comprises two of those modules side by side, and the floor plan of the piano nobile is repeated in a second piano nobile over it, with mezzanine rooms in between.'

'Like Villa Cornaro?'

'You're obviously a Palladio fan.'

'It's impossible not to be if you love classical architecture.' Lizzie smiled. 'I was half toying with the idea of training as an architect when my parents died. It hadn't been my first choice of career, but working as an interior designer showed me how important structure is. From there… What is it?' she asked, when she saw how his own expression had changed and hardened.

Reluctantly he told her, 'My father was an architect, and as a boy it was my ambition to follow in his footsteps in that regard—to build modern structures in celebration of Palladio's own style, based on his principles. Of course there wasn't the money, although as a boy I didn't realise that. The Junta imposed such heavy taxes and fines on those who antagonised them, as my grandfather did, that they beggared him. He was left with nothing, and he had to watch Villa Manos falling into disrepair, unable to do anything to halt that process. Keeping it in defiance of the Junta was something of a pyrrhic victory for him. By the time the Junta was deposed there was nothing left for him to sell or mortgage, and certainly no money to educate me to the standard necessary for me to train as an architect. He loved the villa more than he loved any living person.'

Abruptly Ilios stopped speaking, wondering why he had allowed himself to reveal so much about his childhood and his family, telling Lizzie things he have never disclosed before to anyone, much less a woman who had shared his bed.

What was it about her that caused him to react in the way he did? As though she was different—and special? He must not exaggerate the situation, or his own reactions to it, Ilios cautioned himself. It was the fact that Lizzie was knowledgeable about Palladio and his work that had led to him confiding in her the way he had, nothing more.

Lizzie fought back the emotional tears stinging the backs of her eyes as Ilios finished speaking.

'But he must have loved you as well. After all, he left you the villa,' she told him impulsively, wanting instinctively to ease what she knew must be his hurt. Who would *not* be hurt in such circumstances?

'No, my value to him lay in my genes, that is all,' was Ilios's harsh response.

Lizzie ached with sadness for him. Was his own childhood the cause of Ilios's determination not to marry and not to allow any woman to knowingly have his children? Had having to be so self-reliant, unable to trust the one adult he should have been able to turn to, left him so badly scarred that he was unable to trust other human beings himself? It would have taken great emotional strength and endurance and great maturity to have survived the childhood Ilios had had and emerge unscathed from it, far more than any young child could have been expected to have.

Lizzie felt desperately sorry for the little boy Ilios must have been—so sorry, in fact, that she wanted to gather that child up in her arms and hold him safe, give him the same loving childhood she herself had known. But of course that child no longer existed, and the man he had become would scorn her emotions as mere sentiment, she suspected.

'The past is over. Looking back toward it serves no purpose,' Ilios told her curtly. 'We live in the present, after all.'

'That's true, but sometimes we need to look back to what we were to understand what we are now.'

'That is self-indulgence and it also serves no purpose,' Ilios insisted grimly, looking at his watch and adding, 'If you are ready to leave…?'

Lizzie nodded her head. The subject of his childhood and the effect it must have had on him was obviously closed, and she suspected it would remain that way.

It would soon be spring, and the temperature was beginning to rise a little. Wild flowers bloomed by the roadside, the way they had their faces turned up to the sun making Lizzie smile as Ilios drove them towards the east and the peninsula where Villas Manos stood.

Since Ilios was a good driver there was no logical reason for her to feel on edge. No logical reason, perhaps, but since when have the emotions of a woman in love been logical? Lizzie asked herself wryly.

They passed the turn-off for Halkidiki and the famous

Mount Athos peninsula, with its monasteries and its rule that no female was allowed to set foot there, including female animals, and then had stopped briefly at a small tavern for a simple lunch of Greek salad and fruit. It was eaten mainly in the same silence which had pervaded since they had set out.

If Ilios was regretting inviting her to join him, then she was certainly regretting accepting his invitation. She felt rejected and unwanted, deliberately distanced from Ilios by his silence—a silence that her own pride would not allow her to break.

Ilios drove straight to the villa on the western side of the promontory, ignoring the fork in the road to the east where the apartment block had been.

It seemed a lifetime since she had first met Ilios there. Then she had been a single woman, her only concern for her financial situation and the future of her family. Her own emotions as a woman simply had not come into the equation. Now she was married and a wife—at least in the eyes of the world. Her family were financially secure, and her anxiety was all for her own emotions.

Ruby had sent her a photograph of the twins via her mobile, so that Lizzie could see the new school uniforms she had bought for them at Lizzie's insistence that she must do so and that they could afford it. A tender, amused smile curled Lizzie's mouth. The two five-year-olds had looked so proud in their grey flannel trousers and maroon blazers, their dark hair cut short and brushed neatly.

Lizzie loved her nephews. She had been present at their birth, anxious for her young sister, and grieving for the fact that Ruby was having to go through her pain without their parents and without the man who had fathered her children. But when the twins had been born and she had

held them all the sad aspects of their birth had been forgotten in the rush of love and joy she had felt.

They had reached the villa now, and even though she
had seen it before, and knew what to expect, Lizzie was
still filled with admiration and awe as she gazed at its
perfect proportions, outlined against the bright blue sky.

The warm cream colour of the villa toned perfectly
with the aged darker colour of the marble columns supporting the front portico and with the soft grey-white of the
shutters at the windows. The gravel on which the car was
resting exactly matched the colour of the marble columns,
and the green of the lawns highlighted the darker green of
the Cyprus trees lining the straight driveway. The whole
scene in front of them was one of visual harmony.

There was no other car parked outside—which Lizzie
presumed meant that the man Ilios had come here to see
had not as yet arrived.

'We're earlier than I expected, so I'll show you the
inside before Andreas arrives,' Ilios announced as he
opened the car door for Lizzie and waited for her to get
out.

They walked to the entrance side by side. Side by side
but feet apart, Lizzie thought sadly as she waited for Ilios
to unlock the magnificent double doors.

Above them, where in Italy there would have been the
family arms and motto, was an image of a small sailing
ship.

'Alexandros Manos earned his fortune as a maritime
trader,' Ilios informed her, following her gaze. 'It was his
fleet that paid for this land and for the villa.'

Ilios had opened the door, and was stepping back so that
Lizzie could precede him inside the villa.

The first thing she noticed was the smell of fresh paint,

unmistakable and instantly recognizable. Her educated nose told her that the smell came from a traditional lime-based paint rather than a modern one.

With the shutters closed the interior was in darkness—until Ilios switched on the lights, causing Lizzie to gasp in astonished delight as she spun round, studying the frescoes that ran the whole way round the double-height central room.

She had seen frescoes before, of course, many of them. But none quite like these.

'Are they scenes from the *Odyssey*?' she asked Ilios uncertainly after she had studied them.

'Yes,' Ilios confirmed. 'Only Odysseus bears a striking resemblance to Alexandros Manos. To have oneself depicted as the hero of the *Odyssey* was, of course, a conceit not uncommon at the time. I've had the frescoes repainted because of the damage they've suffered over the centuries. Luckily we had some sketches of the original scenes to work with. The work still isn't finished yet,' Ilios added, indicating the final panel of the fresco, where a woman was bending over a loom, unpicking a thread, with the outline of a large dog at her feet.

The fresco was badly damaged, with paint peeling from it and marks across it that looked as though someone had scored the panel angrily with something sharp. Even so it was still possible to see what the panel was meant to represent.

'Penelope? The faithful wife?' Lizzie guessed, remembering the legend of how Odysseus's wife Penelope had held off the suitors who wanted to marry her and take possession of Odysseus's kingdom by saying she would only accept one of them when she had finished her tapestry, and then unpicking it every night in secret so that it would never be finished, so sure had she been that her husband would eventually return.

Ilios's terse, 'Yes', told Lizzie that he didn't want to discuss the subject of the panel, so she turned instead to follow him into one of the smaller rooms.

Here scaffolding showed where craftsmen were obviously working to repair the ornate plasterwork ceiling, which Lizzie could see held a central fresco of a family group.

'I had to go to Florence to find the craftspeople to do this work,' Ilios told Lizzie.

'It's a highly skilled job,' Lizzie agreed.

Two hours later Ilios had given her a full tour of the house. The man he was supposed to be meeting had telephoned to say that he would have to cancel and make another appointment. He was unavoidably delayed because his wife had gone into premature labour.

'I hope she and the baby will be all right,' had been Lizzie's immediate and instinctive comment as they'd walked down the return staircase.

The villa would be stunningly beautiful when the restoration work had been completed—a true work of art, in fact. But Lizzie simply could not visualise it as a home.

'It won't be easy, bringing up your sons here,' she felt bound to say.

'I don't plan to live here,' Ilios told her.

Lizzie looked uncertainly at him. 'But I thought—that is, you said that the house had to stay within the family.'

'It does, and it will. But not as a family home. I've got other plans for it. There's a shortage of opportunities for young apprentices to learn the skills that go into maintaining a house like this. I found that out for myself. So I've decided that Villa Manos will become a place where those who want to master those skills can come to learn them. Instead of turning the villa into a dead museum, I plan to turn it into a living workshop—where courses are run for master craftsmen, taught by those who have already mastered those trades themselves.'

'What a wonderful idea.' Lizzie didn't make any attempt to conceal her approval.

'I shall build a house for myself on the other side of the promontory.'

'Where the apartments were?'

'Yes. There will also be an accommodation block, and schoolrooms and proper workshops for the students. They will be situated in the wooded area between the villa and the other side of the promontory—' He broke off as Lizzie's mobile suddenly started to bleep.

'I'm sorry,' she apologised, scrambling in her bag for it so that she could silence it. Her face suddenly broke into a smile as she looked at the image which had flashed up on her screen.

'It's the twins—my nephews,' she told Ilios. 'My sister sent me a photograph of them earlier, in their new school uniforms, and now she's sent me another picture of them.' Lizzie held up the phone so that he could see.

Ilios glanced dismissively at the screen, and then found that he couldn't look away. The young woman in the photograph, kneeling down and clasping a uniform-clad boy in each arm, had that same look of love and happiness on her face as Lizzie herself wore when she was talking about her family. There was no doubting the closeness her family shared, and no doubting Lizzie's love for her sisters and these two small dark-haired boys. Fatherless they might be, but they were laughing into the camera, confident in the love that surrounded them. Neither was there any doubt about Lizzie's determination to protect her family and provide for them. If Lizzie herself were to have a child then she would love it with the same absolute loyalty and devotion he could see on her face now. A child…his child… Absorbed in the enormity of what he was thinking, Ilios didn't notice Lizzie move towards him until he felt her hand on his arm as she told him, 'It's thanks to you that they were able to have those uniforms.'

Thanks to him? Ilios tensed against what was happening to him—against the savage dagger-thrusts of pain that tore into him with Lizzie's words. Because they reminded him of the truth. The only reason she was here with him was because he had blackmailed her into marrying him.

He shrugged off Lizzie's hand on his arm, stepping back from her as he told her, 'There are some interesting features in the garden. I'll show you.'

Feeling rebuffed, Lizzie switched off her mobile and returned it to her handbag. Ilios obviously wanted to make it plain that their relationship was strictly business. He didn't want to be forced to look at photographs of her family.

'How long do you think it will be before your cousin accepts that he doesn't have any grounds to try and overset your grandfather's will?' she asked Ilios as they headed for the garden at the rear of the villa.

Here, beyond a wide flagged terrace, steps led down to what must once have been intricately formal beds of clipped box, surrounding a pool with a fountain. But Lizzie wasn't really concentrating on her surroundings. Instead she was hoping desperately for a miracle—for that miracle to be Ilios telling her that he had changed his mind about ending their marriage because he wanted them to be together for ever.

He shrugged dismissively. 'You are, of course, impatient to return to your family?'

'I do miss them,' Lizzie agreed, her heart sinking. That wasn't the response she had hoped for at all. It was true that she did miss her family, but she was also finding it increasingly difficult to behave as though nothing had happened between her and Ilios. Take now, for instance. When they had come out of the house she had almost put her arm through Ilios's, just as if they were actually a genuine couple. Of course it was because she craved the intimacy of physical closeness with him, just as any woman in love would.

'Regrettably, my lawyers feel that we should remain married for the time being, as a divorce so soon after our wedding would look suspicious. However, you can rest assured that I am every bit as eager to bring our marriage to an end as you,' Ilios announced coldly, his response driven by pride and the need to defend himself from the alien emotions that were threatening him.

The cold words struck into her heart like ice picks. But it was her own fault if she had been hurt, Lizzie told herself resolutely.

'This is what I wanted to show you,' Ilios told her nearly half an hour later, when they had walked through the extensive gardens to the villa and emerged at the side of a pretty man-made lake. He gestured towards a grotto dotted with statuary and ornamented with a small fresh water spring.

'What is it?' Lizzie asked him.

'It's a nymphaeum,' Ilios explained. 'An artificially created grotto for which the statuary has been specifically designed. Villa Barbaro has one—some of its statuary executed by Marcantonio Barbaro, supposedly. It's a conceit, really. A way for the villa-owner to show off either his own talent as a sculptor or that of an artist to whom he was a patron. The lake here needs dredging, and the small temple on the island renovating.'

'The whole place is stunning,' Lizzie told him truthfully. 'I can understand why your ancestor wanted it kept in the family. I do think, though, that your plan to turn it into a living workshop is a wonderful idea—and so very generous. A wonderful gift to future generations, enabling such special skills to be carried on.'

'I'm not motivated by generosity. I've been held up on too many contracts by the lack of skilled artisans—that's why I'm doing it.' Ilios's voice was clipped, as though her praise had annoyed him.

Because he didn't want it? Just as he didn't want her? She mustn't dwell on what she could not have, but instead hold in her heart what they had briefly shared, Lizzie told herself. She mustn't let that joy be overshadowed or diminished.

Nor must she allow the fact that Ilios did not return her feelings to prevent her from behaving as she would have done had she not loved him.

'I've really enjoyed today. Thank you for bringing me and showing me the villa,' she told him, with that in mind, as they headed back to the car for the return journey to Thessaloniki.

He had enjoyed it too, Ilios acknowledged. When he had not been battling with the emotions his conflicting feelings towards her aroused.

On the way back to Thessaloniki they stopped at the same tavern where they had had lunch. The small village overlooked the sea, and the front of the tavern was protected enough from the breeze for it to be warm enough to sit outside.

They'd eaten plump juicy black olives and delicious grilled kebabs, and were just finishing their coffee when it happened. A dull noise like thunder, and the movement of the ground beneath their feet.

The trestle table shifted, spilling Lizzie's coffee, and then Ilios got up, coming towards her and taking hold of her, pushing her down to the ground, covering her with his own body as he warned her, 'It's an earthquake.'

'An earthquake?' she echoed.

'This area's notorious for them. It will be all right—just keep still.'

She had no other option other than to keep still with Ilios's body a protective weight over hers, pinning her to the ground. His hand was cupping the back of her head protectively, pushing her face into his shoulder, allowing her to breathe in the now familiar scent of him. Lizzie just hoped he would assume that the heavy sledgehammer thuds of her heartbeat were caused by her shock and fear of the earthquake rather than by the proximity of their bodies. How fate must be enjoying its joke at her expense, knowing that when she had longed to be held in Ilios's arms these were not the circumstances in which she had envisaged it happening. To be held by him in an embrace outwardly that of the most intimate and tender of lovers which in reality was nothing more than a means of safety felt painfully ironic, even if his prompt actions were for her own benefit.

'What's that?' she asked anxiously above the growing noise she could hear.

'Just a few stones and boulders dislodged by the quake rolling down the hillside.'

Lizzie gasped as the earth moved again, in a shudder she could feel right through her body, causing Ilios to tighten his hold on her. Had he loved her, this moment would have been filled with the most intense emotion—and surely would ultimately have resulted in them celebrating their survival and their love for one another in the most intimate way possible once they had had the privacy to do so. Sex was, after all, the only human activity that combined life, birth and even a small taste of death in that moment when it felt as though one flew free into infinity.

Ilios. Why had she had to fall in love with him? Why couldn't she have simply wanted him on a physical level and nothing more? Because she was a woman, and the female sex, no matter how much it might wish for things to be different, was genetically geared to making an emotional commitment?

The earth had steadied, and so had her heartbeat, slowing to match the sturdy tempo of Ilios's. In a situation that would normally have filled her with fear for her own safety she had felt completely secure, protected—safe because of him. But here in Ilios's arms there was no emotional safety for her, only emotional danger, Lizzie reminded herself.

Against her ear Ilios spoke again. 'That should be it now, but we'd better stay where we are for a few more minutes.'

The warmth of his breath sent small shudders of sensual delight rippling over her nerve-endings, and the knowledge that his lips were so close to her flesh made her want to compel them even closer. Memories of how it had felt to have him caressing her skin with the stroke of his tongue-tip broke through the embargo she had placed on them.

'Will it affect the villa?' Lizzie asked, genuinely concerned about the villa but equally intent on distracting herself from thinking so intimately about Ilios and how much she loved him.

'No. The promontory isn't affected by the fault line.'

Lizzie could hear voices as people called out to one another. Ilios lifted his body from hers. She badly wanted to beg him not to do so—and not because of the earthquake. He stood up, and then reached down to help her to her feet.

'You've got dust on your face.'

Before she could stop him he leaned towards her, brushing her cheek with his hand.

She wanted to stay like this for ever, Lizzie thought achingly. With Ilios's hand on her skin, his gaze on hers, his arm supporting her—just as though she genuinely did matter to him, just as though he cared about her and wanted to protect her because he loved her. She moved towards him yearningly, only to have him move back.

What was happening to him? Ilios asked himself grimly. Increasingly his own behaviour was so alien to what he knew of himself that witnessing it was like confronting a stranger wearing his skin. A stranger who was challenging him for full possession of himself? A stranger who owed his existence to the arrival of Lizzie Wareham in his life? A stranger whose first thought was to protect Lizzie? Why?

Because it was in his own interests to protect her. He had a vested interest in her safety after all.

No one in the village seemed particularly disturbed by the tremor. Everyone was going about their normal business, and men were working to clear the debris from the hillside from the road as Lizzie got to her feet.

'Are you okay?' Ilios asked her.

'Yes, thanks to you.'

Oh, yes, he was definitely withdrawing from her—rejecting her gratitude, rejecting anything remotely emotional between them, and of course rejecting her physically.

Ilios stepped back from her physically as well as emotionally with a brisk nod of his head. 'In ancient times they used to believe that it was the gods' anger that was responsible for these tremors,' he commented a few minutes later as he opened the car door for Lizzie. 'Now we construct buildings especially designed to cope with the movement caused by them.'

CHAPTER THIRTEEN

RIDICULOUSLY, since she had done next to nothing all day other than sightsee and enjoy the rooftop garden of Ilios's apartment, Lizzie felt incredibly tired. She tried to stifle a yawn and look instead as though she was enjoying the reception she and Ilios were attending as part of an incentive by the Greek government to attract new business to the area. Naturally Ilios, as head of a locally based business which was successful internationally, was in great demand, and he had apologised for having to desert her to talk business with someone who had asked to be introduced to him.

She wasn't the only wife left to stand alone nursing a drink, Lizzie recognised as she glanced round the elegant hotel ballroom where the reception was being held. But her glass merely contained water. Champagne was something she was determined to avoid for as long as she was married to Ilios.

A smile of recognition from one of the women she had met at the gallery opening had her heading towards her in relief. Now that she was a little wiser about Thessaloniki society she dressed accordingly—overdressed, in fact, by her normal standards. Tonight, in addition to her designer dress in yellow silk, she was also wearing the jewellery. Ilios had a position to maintain, after all, and not just for the sake of his own personal status. The employees of Manos Construction depended on him, and on the success of the business. An immaculately coiffed and groomed wife said that a man had both good taste and money—reassuring values where other businessmen were concerned, no matter how much Lizzie might wish for a simpler and more straightforward way of doing business.

Engrossed in her own thoughts as she wove her way through the crowded room, she didn't see Ilios's cousin—to whom she had been introduced by Ilios earlier—making a beeline for her, until he was standing in front of her blocking her way.

Lizzie's heart sank.

When Ilios had warned her that his cousin was likely to be present she had been curious to meet him. Her private view was that Ilios, for perfectly good reasons rooted in their shared childhood, had turned him into a more unpleasant figure than he actually was.

It had taken less than a minute in Tino Manos's company for her to recognise that she had been wrong. If anything, Ilios's cousin was even more unpleasant than Ilios had said.

'So,' he announced now, with an unpleasant leer, 'an opportunity to talk to the new bride, my cousin-in-law, without Ilios standing over us.'

As he spoke Tino's gaze was fixed on her breasts, discreetly covered by the high neckline of the silk dress which wasn't in the least bit provocative. Nevertheless, the way Ilios's cousin was looking at her made Lizzie feel like crossing her arms over her chest, to protect her body from his unwanted visual inspection.

It was strange how you could sometimes know the

minute you met a person whether or not you were going to like them, Lizzie reflected, and tried not to show how desperately she wanted to escape.

Short and thickset, with overly familiar sharp dark eyes, Tino Manos was the kind of man Lizzie knew she would have disliked no matter who he was related to. She could understand now all too easily why Ilios had spoken as he had when she had suggested that for the sake of his sons he should try to 'mend fences' with his cousin. No sane parent would ever want to entrust his vulnerable children's emotional wellbeing and future to a man like this.

'You are to be congratulated on having caught Ilios. You must have something very special indeed to have persuaded him to give up his freedom having always sworn that he would never marry.'

Lizzie fought hard not to show how offensive she found his unsubtle hints as to why Ilios might have married her and to remain detached. The way Tino was looking at her and the tone of his voice repelled her physically and emotionally, and it was with great relief that she heard Ilios answering his cousin in an even tone.

'Yes, she does, Tino—and that something is my love.'

There was no need for Lizzie to act as she turned to her husband and gave him a speaking look of gratitude for his intervention.

'Love? I thought that was something you'd foresworn.'

Tino was like a dog with its teeth into something it wasn't going to release, Lizzie recognized.

'So did I,' Ilios agreed. 'Until I met Lizzie.'

As he spoke he turned towards her, smiling tenderly down into her eyes, reaching out to take hold of her hand, rubbing his thumb gently over her skin in a gesture that both caressed and reassured.

'And married her with such speed that you didn't even have time to invite anyone to the wedding.'

Tino was suspicious, Lizzie felt sure. Her hand trembled against Ilios's, and the look she gave him mirrored what she was feeling.

'I didn't want to risk losing her,' Ilios responded, still smiling down at her. 'I never want to lose her.'

As he spoke he bent his head and kissed her, his actions taking Lizzie by surprise. She knew that Ilios was putting on an act for his cousin, but still she had not expected this. Beneath his, her own lips softened and clung. Without intending to do so she placed her hand on his arm and moved closer to him, her whole body succumbing to her love for him, yearning toward him. Beneath the silk of her dress she could feel her nipples firming and aching, desire stirring and then quickening in the pit of her stomach. Unable to stop herself, she lifted her hand from his arm to his face, tracing the line of his jaw with achingly longing fingertips.

Ilios lifted his mouth from hers, causing Lizzie to open her eyes and look up at him. Her hand trembled against his skin, betraying her emotions, and her chest lifted with the demand from her lungs for extra oxygen. The words *I want you so much* and *Let's go home* formed inside her head, but had to be denied speech.

'So, how did the two of you meet?'

Tino's voice was an unwanted intrusion, reminding Lizzie of her real role, as a paid-for pretend wife. She compared all the pain that that brought her with the impossible fantasy she longed for. A fantasy in which Ilios really did love, really had meant what he had just said, really had meant the way he had just kissed her…

'Fate brought us together, Tino,' Ilios answered his cousin, continuing, 'Now, if you'll excuse us…?'

Ilios was drawing her away, his hand resting against the hollow of her back as he guided her towards Ariadne Constantin—the woman who had smiled at her earlier.

CHAPTER FOURTEEN

LIZZIE had to wait until she and Ilios were in the car and on their way home, having arranged to have dinner with the Constantins later in the week, to tell him, 'You were right about your cousin. It would be impossible to entrust the future of your sons to him. Do you think he believed what you said about us?'

'I certainly hope so,' Ilios answered.

Because he wanted to get rid of her, of course.

Ilios was annoyed with himself. Lizzie's admission that she had been wrong about his cousin had reminded him of her earlier warnings about the vulnerability of his children should anything happen to him. Why should he be concerned about what she thought? Why should the dangerous thought that Lizzie would be a good mother find its way into his head? He knew he had made the right decision with regard to his own life, and Lizzie could have as many children as she wanted just so long as they weren't his.

'I'll say goodnight,' Lizzie told him at the apartment, as she went to put away her coat. 'After all, I'm sure you have work you want to do.'

Why had she said that? Ilios wasn't stupid—just the opposite, in fact. He was very perceptive, and he was bound to hear the acid note in her voice and guess that she was deliberately needling him. She held her breath, waiting for him to challenge her, but instead he turned away from her, leaving her feeling relieved that her reckless behaviour hadn't provoked any comeback.

In the dressing room of the master bedroom she hung up her coat and warned herself that if he *had* demanded an explanation of her comment, he might easily have worked out that it had been provoked by her longing for him to take her to bed again, for his love.

It was all because of that kiss he had given her earlier in the evening—the way it had made her ache with the pain of her unrequited love for him.

In the living room Ilios opened his laptop. Lizzie was right, he did have work to do—and, as he had discovered many years ago, for him work wasn't just the panacea that stopped all his pain, it was also his most constant and trusted companion, his closest ally in the fight to remain independent of all human emotional demands. It sustained and supported him, and he knew that within seconds of studying the screen in front of him all thoughts of Lizzie Wareham and the unwanted emotions she aroused within him would disappear.

Only they didn't. No matter how hard he focussed on the screen, all he could see was Lizzie's image inside his head.

What was going on? Whatever it was, he didn't want it, Ilios thought savagely. There was no place in his life for it—or for her. But the harder he clung to that thought, to his denial of what he really wanted, the more his body ached for Lizzie. His body. That was all. That was all it was—a physical desire conjured up out of a lack of regular sex and the fact that he was sharing his living space with a woman. Any woman would have had the same effect on him. Any woman? Then why was it *her* image he could see inside his head, *her* body he ached to hold, *her* love for which he now hungered?

No. He categorically refused to accept the thought that had somehow slipped into his head. If he wanted anything from her then it was merely sex. Nothing more.

Prove it, an inner voice challenged him. Go to her now and take her in your arms, hold her and caress her and prove that when you do those things all you feel is a clinical sexual response, without anything emotional to pollute its physical purity.

Ilios looked towards the door. This was ridiculous. He didn't have anything to prove to anyone—least of all himself. But somehow he was on his feet and heading towards the master bedroom.

Lizzie was just getting into bed when the door opened and Ilios strode into the room.

'I thought that tonight I'd have an early night myself,' he told her, before disappearing into the dressing room.

Lying beneath the bedclothes, her stomach quivering with a mixture of uncertainty and excitement, Lizzie tried to breathe normally and relax, warning herself that Ilios probably hadn't meant anything other than exactly what he had said.

There was no need for him to do this, Ilios assured himself, as he stood under the jets of the shower.

Was he afraid that he couldn't prove what he had claimed? that inner voice goaded him.

No! Ilios denied. He stepped out of the shower and reached for a towel. If she hadn't touched his face and looked at him the way she had earlier on this evening, when he'd been forced to put on that display of newly married bliss for Tino, then this wouldn't be happening. He wouldn't be aching the way he was for her now. No? If that was all that had made him ache for her, then what was his excuse for the fact that he had ached for her in the same way every night since that first time?

It was sex—that was all. Sex.

He flung down the towel. There was still time to stop this, still time to walk away and to use his will-power to silence the voice inside him.

There might still be time, but where was the desire? That, Ilios acknowledged as he opened the bedroom door, was all for Lizzie.

She was lying on Ilios's side of the bed. How could she have forgotten?

'I'm on your side of the bed,' she told him as he came towards her. 'I'll move over.'

'Why?' Ilios asked her softly. 'When we're going to be sharing the same space?'

Lizzie felt her heart give a gigantic thump, and then her body filled with an anticipatory pleasure that poured through her like melted honey.

That was nothing compared with what she felt when Ilios got into the bed and drew her close to him. Like her, he was naked, and the feel of his skin against hers was a sensual caress almost beyond bearing.

This shouldn't be happening. Not now, when she knew that she loved him. It had been different before, but now... Now she was deceiving him, taking from him something he would not want to give her. Ilios was touching her, stroking his fingertips down the sensitive flesh of her inner arm and making her shudder openly in responsive plea-sure. Lizzie lifted her own hand to his shoulder, intending to tell him they must stop, but somehow the sensation of the warm, firm ball of male sinew and muscle beneath her touch overwhelmed her good intentions, seducing away her will-power to do anything other than give in to her own need.

Closing her eyes, Lizzie shaped the muscles of his back, her own nerve-endings recording the pleasure of each touch. Was male flesh really different from female flesh— thicker, sleeker, more warm, sensual satin than soft silk, somehow intrinsically male in its construction? Or was it merely her own response to knowing that the flesh she was touching belonged to Ilios that made her feel that?

As he kissed her and held her Ilios's desire for her ran like ribbons of fire, until it filled his heart and his veins, spilling out into his touch so that it patterned his feelings for her on her flesh.

Cupped within his hand, the soft weight of her breast fitted as perfectly as though it had been created for his hold alone, and the erotic sensitivity of her nipple as it re- sponded to his caress was responsive in that way only to his touch. The arch of her body inviting the possession of his was aroused only by and for him, as though they had been made for one another and only one another.

How could such a delicate touch have the power to drain from him the resistance of a lifetime? How could it seem to offer sanctuary and comfort? How could it possibly have the power to transform him from a man to whom emotions were the enemy to a man who craved…? A man who craved what?

Ilios moved restlessly against his own thoughts, against his own weakness in allowing himself this unfamiliar need to give the essence of himself into the safekeeping of another. He cupped Lizzie's face so that he could kiss her. Kissing her and feeling her response to him re-established his role as the one in charge of what was happening. And his was the responsibility for them both, Ilios warned himself—a responsibility he had already neglected once.

Beneath Ilios's kiss Lizzie breathed a sigh of delight. It was impossible not to let her hand follow its own inclinations and drift down the lean length of his body, past the flat male curve of his hip, and then come to rest at the base of his spine. The pressure of Ilios's mouth on her own increased, his arms tightening around her as he half rolled her beneath him. Eagerly Lizzie parted her lips, her tongue caressing his, her fingertips stroking the shallow hollow where his spine ended.

Was it her love for Ilios that made the intimacy they were now sharing so heart-achingly intense? Lizzie wondered emotionally. It must be; there could be no other explanation, surely, for the sense of deep intimacy and connection she felt towards him.

She moaned softly with delight as Ilios moved over her, answering the pressure of her growing need. The pleasure from his hands spreading her thighs and his lips tasting her sex took from her both the ability and the will to do anything other than give herself over to him as he moved up her body, his flesh gleaming in the moonlight, erect and taut. Lizzie reached out towards it, encircling the swollen head of his sex, engrossed in the sensation of possessing him.

What had been pleasure had now become a fierce beating urgency—a primeval drive strong enough to crush all obstacles in its way.

How could the pleasure of another's touch be so intense that it invaded every part of him, making his nerve-endings cry out within him under its onslaught? He wanted Lizzie to go on caressing him as she was for ever. He wanted her to stroke and know every bit of him. He wanted— As if a sheer drop had appeared out of nowhere in a misty landscape Ilios's thoughts skidded to a halt as he recognised the danger he was facing. He could not, *would* not allow himself to feel like this. It went against everything he had worked for and planned for. It must not happen. It had to be destroyed.

Abruptly Ilios forced himself to release Lizzie, pulling back from her, leaving her without a backward look or a word of explanation.

Ilios had gone. She was alone in the bed that had so recently been such a wonderful place of intimacy and shared desire but which was now a place of harsh reality and emptiness.

Curled up against her pain, Lizzie tensed her jaw against the agonised cry of despair burning her throat. What had she expected? That the impossible would happen and Ilios would declare his love for her? She was twenty-seven, not seventeen, and surely what had happened to her young sister had shown her the damage that could be done when a woman was foolish enough to believe that her love for a man had the power to change him, somehow conjure from him a reciprocal love for her.

Ilios did not love her. He had made that plain in the way that he had recoiled from her, rejecting her with that look of furious disbelief that had told her more clearly than any words that he not only didn't love her, but he actively wished she was not there.

CHAPTER FIFTEEN

LIZZIE suppressed a small guilty yawn, afraid she might actually fall asleep in her dinner if she wasn't careful.

She was regretting now having agreed that it was a good idea, at the reception a week before, when Ariadne Constantin had suggested that the four or them go for dinner together, to a new restaurant that had recently opened to rave reviews. Especially in view of the distance that Ilios had deliberately created between them. He barely looked at her any more, never mind spoke to her or touched her. There had not been any further invitations to accompany him on site visits during the day, and nor was he discussing any aspect of his life or his plans with her any more. It was, Lizzie acknowledged bleakly, as though he hated her being there and bitterly resented the fact he had had to marry her—even though it had been his own decision.

The food, a Greek take on Australian-Eastern fusion cooking, was delicious, and the light sauces accompanying the fish and meat courses mouthwateringly tempting, but Lizzie had no appetite for them. She was far too unhappy. Was her constant tiredness perhaps a symptom of the misery she was feeling? Was that why she yearned to close her eyes and blot out reality?

Just remembering the curtness in his voice and the way he had turned away from her now was enough to close up her throat and sting the back of her eyes with the embarrassing threat of unwanted tears. Her reaction was surely more that of a hormonal teenager than an adult woman, and certainly not one she could ever remember having before. But then she had never loved Ilios before.

Lizzie watched enviously as Ariadne and her husband got up to dance on the restaurant's small dance floor. It must be heaven to be held so close in the arms of the man you loved in a small and discreet public demonstration of the love between you. Her body trembled in response to the intensity of her emotions.

The Constantins were returning to the table. Stavros Constantin was ordering more wine. Lizzie shook her head when the waiter moved to fill her glass. She hadn't touched alcohol since the night she had drunk champagne and she and Ilios made love—had had sex, she corrected herself fiercely. That was all it had been—sex—lust—that was what she must remember. She certainly wasn't going to risk having a drink now. In her current emotionally vulnerable frame of mind there was no saying what she might attempt to do, or how much she might try to humiliate herself once they were alone together.

The other three drank their wine, then Ariadne got up, asking if, like her, Lizzie wanted to visit the ladies'.

Nodding her head, Lizzie got up too. Anything would be better than having to sit next to Ilios, knowing how eager he was to get rid of her.

Once in the cloakroom, Lizzie felt the tiredness that had threatened to overwhelm her earlier catch up with her again, causing her to smother yet another yawn. She apologised to Ariadne as she did so, hoping that the other woman wouldn't think her rude.

'Don't worry,' Ariadne responded. 'I understand. I was exactly the same when I was first pregnant with our son. I'd been expecting morning sickness, but instead what I got was sleeping sickness.'

Pregnant. The cloakroom spun dizzily round her and Lizzie had to cling to the basin.

Ariadne, obviously concerned, reached out to her.

'I'm all right,' Lizzie reassured her. 'It's just that I hadn't thought—'

She stopped abruptly, but Ariadne had obviously guessed the truth because she put her hand to her lips and then exclaimed, 'Oh! You didn't realise that you might be pregnant—and now I am the first to know and it should have been Ilios. Don't worry—I shan't say a word—not even to Stavros.' She gave Lizzie's arm a comforting little squeeze, and offered, 'If you would like, I could give you the name of my maternity doctor. He is very good.'

'That's kind of you, but...but I don't actually think that I *am* pregnant,' Lizzie fibbed. She was still in shock, battling to accept the reality of the situation, torn between tears of despair and joy. She longed with all her heart to believe that the man she loved would react to the news of the child they had created together with pride and love. But how could that happen when Ilios did not love her?

Pregnant. She was pregnant. It seemed so obvious now that she couldn't believe she had not realised for herself. What should she do? Ilios had a right to know, of course. What would he say? What would he do? He wanted sons. Would the knowledge that she was carrying his child soften his heart towards her or harden it? Lizzie wished she knew.

But if he rejected her and their child then at least his son or daughter would have a family who loved it in England.

A powerful surge of maternal need to protect her unborn child raced through her. Ilios might not want the child they had created together, but she would love it—doubly so, because she would love it for itself and because it came from Ilios.

Back at their table, she wanted to yawn again. On the other side of the table Ariadne smiled knowingly at her, telling her husband, 'Lizzie is tired. She isn't yet used to our habit of eating late, I expect. Ilios, you must take her home and look after her.'

Lizzie stiffened, horrified that despite her promise Ariadne might announce that she thought Lizzie was pregnant. But to her relief Ariadne announced that they too did not want a late night as her mother was babysitting.

They left the restaurant together, and said their good-byes in a flurry of hugs and kisses in the street next to their parked cars. Ariadne's warm hug for Lizzie was patently meaningful.

Leaning back against the comfortable support of the passenger seat of Ilios's car, whilst he drove them back to the apartment, Lizzie closed her eyes, her thoughts driven by panic and despair. She was pregnant. She was carrying Ilios's child. Despite the turmoil of her thoughts, somewhere deep inside Lizzie there was a small pool of calm and joy in the knowledge that she was carrying the most precious gift that life could give: the child of the man she loved.

CHAPTER SIXTEEN

LIZZIE gave Maria a wan smile as they stepped into the lift together. It was a week since she had realised that she was pregnant, and she still hadn't told Ilios. But then she hadn't really had much opportunity to do so, since he avoided her as much as he could. Lizzie wished that she was braver—that she had the courage to confront him, to tell him outright that he could treat her as he chose but his child had a right to his love. She had been out for a walk to try and clear her thoughts. Ilios was being so cold to her that she knew it was pointless her hoping that he would ever return her love.

The lift moved silently upwards. Lost in the despair of her own thoughts, Lizzie forgot to keep her back turned away from the glass wall and the yawning cavity below, the sight of which always made her feel nervous. She had suffered from a fear of heights for as long as she could remember, and the movement of the lift and its glass structure only made her feel worse.

A wave of dizziness engulfed her, making her lose her balance. The lift had stopped, but she felt too nauseous to move.

Maria took control, taking hold of her arm and supporting her as she guided her determinedly from the lift, across the hallway into the apartment. Lizzie felt too unwell to do anything but allow Maria to do so. A cold sweat had broken out on her forehead and her stomach was churning. When Maria released her to close the door, Lizzie slid to the floor in a dead faint.

When she came round Maria was kneeling on the floor beside her, her face flushed with excited delight as she a patted Lizzie's hand maternally and assured her, 'You do not worry. It is just the baby Ilios make with you makes you faint. He will be a big fine boy. Already he is causing his mama trouble. You stay there. I telephone Ilios and tell him to get doctor to come.'

'No!' Lizzie protested, horrified. 'No, Maria, please…' she begged her. This wasn't how she wanted Ilios to learn that he was to become a father. 'There's no need. I'm perfectly all right.' But it was no use. Maria already had the phone in her hand and was speaking at speed into it in Greek, gesturing as she did so.

Very carefully Lizzie got to her feet and made her way to the living room, where she sat down on one of the sofas. She still felt queasy, and slightly dizzy, but then she hadn't eaten any breakfast this morning. She'd planned to eat something whilst she was out, but she hadn't, and now she suspected the baby was making its displeasure known. A haunted smile touched her mouth as Lizzie remembered how firm she had been with Ruby about eating properly when she had been carrying the twins.

She could hear Ilios's voice in the hallway now, as he spoke in Greek to Maria. Her heart was jumping, her mouth dry. Matters had been taken out of her hands and there was no going back. Thanks to Maria, Ilios would now know that he was going to be a father. What would he say? What would he do?

The door opened and he came into the living room, striding towards her and then standing over her. He wasn't wearing a jacket, and his shirt emphasised the powerful width of his shoulders—shoulders that a woman could lean on, so long as that woman wasn't her.

'Maria says you fainted.'

Ilios's voice was harsh—with anger? Lizzie fought down the threatened return of her earlier nausea. Ginger biscuits—that was what she needed. They had worked for Ruby, she remembered.

'Is it true that there is to be a child?' Ilios demanded grimly.

Lizzie couldn't bring herself to speak. She could only nod her head, well able to imagine how unwelcome to him her confirmation would be.

Anger seized Ilios—a furious, savage, blinding rage that exploded inside him like a fireball, devouring reason, humanity and compassion. This was the very last thing he wanted—to be tied to anyone. And especially to this woman, who he had been fighting to keep out of his thoughts, his desires and his emotions, by anything, but most of all by a child. A living, breathing human life that would bind the three of them together with cords that no mere man had the power to break. Ilios wanted to bunch his fists and cry out to the gods his denial of this claim on him. He did not want it and never would.

'You did this deliberately—despite the fact that you knew I would not want it,' he accused Lizzie, conveniently forgetting that he himself had played the greater role in his child's conception. 'No doubt you were hoping to force me into accepting both you and your child—a child I expect you see as a meal ticket that will enable you to live in comfort for the rest of your life.'

Lizzie felt sick with grief and pain.

'No!' she told him. 'That is not what I thought.'

'No?' Ilios challenged her. 'Do you think I am such a fool that I can't see now what you *really* wanted when you claimed to desire me? What you really desired was what you are now carrying within you. My child—born into a legal marriage. A child that I cannot deny or refuse to accept. A child that will have a lifelong financial claim on me.'

'That's not true,' Lizzie denied frantically.

'You had it all planned, didn't you?' Ilios gave her a look of biting contempt. 'Well, I refute your claim and I refute your child. Both you and it are as nothing to me. Less than nothing.'

That was all Lizzie needed to hear. Ilios's cruel words had fallen on her like blows—blows she would not allow her child to bear.

She stood up, despite the fact that she felt so weak, and started to walk towards the door.

When she reached it she turned round and told Ilios proudly, 'Your child might be less than nothing to you, Ilios, but to me he or she is the most precious thing in my life. You're right. I *did* hope for lifelong security from you when I told you I desired you, even if at the time I didn't recognise it for what it was myself. But the lifelong security I wanted wasn't your money, it was your love—in exchange for my love for you. Now that you've made it plain that that can never be, I shall remove both my unwanted presence and your equally unwanted child from your life—permanently.'

'Good,' Ilios told her coldly. 'And the sooner the better.'

CHAPTER SEVENTEEN

ILIOS had gone out. Lizzie didn't know where. She wasn't going to cry. What would be the point? Instead she did everything that had to be done. She booked herself a seat on the first available flight, packed her trolley case. She wasn't going to take anything that had come to her via Ilios—except, of course, his child. But then he didn't want that child—had denied it, spoken callously and dismissively of it.

She was crying after all. Tears were flooding her eyes to run down her face before she could stop them. Carefully she wiped them away with a tissue.

She had done everything she needed to do, including calling herself a cab.

The intercom rang.

It was time for her to go.

She dropped the tissue beside the notepad next to the telephone, where she had written down her flight number, and headed for the door.

Would she have gone yet? Ilios hoped so, he told himself as he unlocked the door to his apartment and went inside.

But it wasn't pleasure or even relief that gripped him

and twisted his emotions with ruthless, painful intensity when he stood in the master bedroom. Only the lingering echo of Lizzie's scent remained to show that she had ever been there. On the bedside table on his side of the bed were her engagement and wedding rings. He picked them up. Lizzie had such slender fingers, elegant hands. The rings felt warm. Ilios curled his hand round them. Lizzie's warmth. An image slid into his head of Lizzie's hands holding their child, Lizzie's face looking down at it, her eyes warm with love.

Fresh anger filled him. Broodingly he pushed the rings into his pocket. What was the matter with him? He was behaving like…like a lovesick fool. He was the one who had wanted her to go. Who had forced her to go. Forced her to go even when he had seen how unwell she looked. What if she fainted again? What if she did? Why should he care?

Ilios walked into the dressing room and removed his jacket. A wisp of lace trapped in the closed doors of Lizzie's closet caught his eye. She'd obviously missed something when she'd packed. He pulled open the door, a fresh surge of anger burning through him when he saw all the clothes hanging there. The clothes he had bought her. What was she trying to prove? Did she really think he'd be impressed because she'd left them? Well, he wasn't. The truth was that he would far rather she had taken them with her. Why? Because he was afraid that they would remind him of her, and that he might start regretting what he had done?

Of course not. That was rubbish. Was it? Wasn't he already missing her? Hadn't he regretted his cruelty to her almost from the minute he had left the apartment?

Didn't the fact that he was here now, pacing the floor,

unable to work, unable to stop thinking about her, tell him anything about his own feelings? About her—Lizzie?

Lizzie.

Ilios sat down heavily in the chair next to the telephone, dropping his head into his hands in defeat.

Alone in the silent space which, despite all his attempts to stop it from being so, was filled with intangible memories of Lizzie's presence within it, Ilios glanced at the telephone. His body stiffened as he saw the piece of paper on which Lizzie had written her flight number and its time of departure. Another hour and she would be gone out of his life. There was a tissue beside the telephone marked with mascara—had she cried? Because of him? The sudden ring of the telephone filled him with a surge of fierce hope. Lizzie. It had to be.

He snatched up the receiver, his heart pounding as he demanded, 'Lizzie?' only to be flooded with disappointment when he realised that his caller was merely an acquaintance.

After he had got rid of him Ilios replaced the receiver and stood motionless, staring into space, whilst his heart thudded with sledgehammer blows that were pounding, beating into him the message, the knowledge that he had fought so hard to deny.

Pain wrenched through him, tearing at his heart, clawing at it, filling him with despair.

He loved Lizzie. He loved her and he had lost her.

Nothing was the same in his life because nothing could *be* the same. The anger he felt, the fury, the grim determination to destroy what had taken root in his heart, belonged not to a brave man but to a coward. It wasn't his love for Lizzie that was threatening his future, but his attempts to destroy it. As though light had replaced darkness Ilios could see now, when it was too late, how empty his life had been—and would be without her. In the short time they had been together she had changed him so completely, in so many different ways, that he felt he was still getting to know the person he now was—and he was in need of her support to help him do so. She had taught him so much, but there was still much he had to learn. How could he teach the sons who would follow him to be the men Ilios now knew he wanted them to be on his own? He couldn't. Those sons, just like him, needed Lizzie. They all needed her love.

When he thought of the sons he had planned to have, and the manner in which he had planned their conception, inside his head he saw them living in the shadows, deprived of the happiness they would have known had Lizzie been their mother. He wanted to stop time and turn it back, to that moment when he had still been holding her in his arms. He could have listened to what his own heart had been trying to tell him instead of resolutely denying it. Could have told her that he was nothing without her, and could have begged her to love him. Now it was too late.

Too late. Inside his head Ilios had an image of himself as a small child, standing on the quayside with Tino and his grandfather whilst he watched his mother and her new husband stepping onto his sailing boat. His mother had held out her arms to him, telling him to jump into them. He had desperately wanted to go to her, he remembered, but he had known that his grandfather disapproved of her remarrying.

'Mummy's boy, mummy's boy,' Tino had taunted him, and so he had hesitated, and then had had to watch his mother's smile disappear to be replaced by coldness as she turned away from him.

That had been the last time he had seen her. A month later she had drowned.

If he had jumped, if he had taken that risk, if he had trusted her love to keep him safe, how different would his life have been?

Too late.

Ilios reached for his mobile. For the man with courage there was no such thing as too late. There was merely further to travel to reach what he most wanted.

CHAPTER EIGHTEEN

HER flight had been called, but Lizzie had been attacked by a sudden surge of nausea that had forced her to make a dash for the ladies', where she now still was as she prayed for the threatening sickness to subside.

She hadn't texted her sisters yet. She was still trying to work out what to tell them. Another surge of nausea engulfed her.

Ilios was out of the helicopter as soon as it landed, ducking low to avoid the draught from its still-turning props as he ran across the tarmac and into the terminal building. He'd been lucky that the helicopter service he used had had a pilot on standby.

The gate for Lizzie's flight had closed, but Ilios wasn't going to let a little thing like that stop him. He'd hire a private jet and follow her all the way back to Manchester if he had to.

'Last call for Flight E20 for Manchester. Will passenger Elizabeth Wareham please report to Gate 10…'

Lizzie hadn't boarded? Ilios looked round the empty waiting area. Then where was she?

* * *

Lizzie grabbed her handbag and hurried out of the ladies'. Her sickness had finally subsided, but if she didn't hurry she was going to miss her flight.

They were calling her name again. Her old name, which she had realized with shock was still the name on her passport—the name to which she was now returning. It had only seemed a few yards when she had rushed down to the ladies', but now it seemed miles. There was the gate—and Ilios was standing beside it.

Lizzie came to an abrupt halt.

'I need to talk to you,' Ilios told her

'I'll miss my flight.'

Taking a deep breath, Ilios held out his hand to her.

'Please Lizzie.'

She wanted to refuse. She should refuse—for the sake of her baby if not for herself—but somehow she couldn't.

Ilios was taking advantage of her hesitation, telling the girl that she wouldn't be flying and assuring her that since she only had hand luggage there was no need for the flight to be delayed whilst her cases were unloaded.

'Let's go and sit down,' Ilios suggested. 'You shouldn't be standing so much, not when…'

He was expressing concern for them? For her and the baby?

That made her feel so shaky that she needed to sit down, Lizzie admitted, as she let him guide her to a chair and then sit down next to her.

'I was wrong to say what I did. Very wrong,' Ilios told her. 'I want you to stay. The fact that you are to have my child changes everything. Its place is here in Greece with me, and yours with it. You are both my responsibility. It is my duty to provide for you.' How stiff and cumbersome the words sounded, but he didn't know any other way to say what he wanted to say.

'Duty is no substitute for love, Ilios,' Lizzie told him. 'And I can't live in a marriage without love. Wanting something you can't have is corrosive. It embitters and destroys. Being trapped in a marriage that isn't wanted drives the one who doesn't love to crave their freedom, and from that contempt and hostility will grow. I don't want our child to grow up in that kind of environment, torn between two parents who are together only because of it. It is too much of a burden to place on a child. It's better that I leave.' She paused. 'Please don't make this harder for me than it already is. I'll tell him or her all about you—how special you are, how proud it can be to be your child and to have you as its father.'

She had to stop because of the emotion choking her throat. She wanted badly to touch him, to trace the shape of his face and give him her love—the love she knew he did not want.

'I'll tell it that you wanted us to be with you, and that it is my fault we aren't. And when I do I'll tell it too how much I love you, and how I couldn't bear to burden you with that love when I knew you didn't want it and hadn't asked for it. I can't promise, though, to tell it that its mother was foolish enough to mistake love for lust. I hope you will be happy, Ilios, and that life will send you someone you can truly love, because…'

'It already has—only I was too afraid to accept it, Lizzie.' He caught hold of her arm, his voice hoarse with desperation. 'I love you. Please give me a second chance. We belong together—you and me and our child.'

Lizzie shook her head. 'You're just saying that because of the baby. Because you think you have to. Because—'

Ilios stopped her. 'I'm saying it because it's the truth.'

One look at her face told him that no matter how hard he tried to convince her she was not going to believe him.

He took a deep breath.

'Lizzie, do you know why this—' he touched her still flat stomach '—happened?'

'Of course. It happened because I desired you.'

Ilios shook his head.

'No, it happened because I allowed it to happen— because secretly I wanted it to happen, even if I wouldn't let myself recognise that fact at the time. Something in me, something stronger and braver than I was, knew what I most needed.'

He was holding her hand in his own, making her feel safe and protected, making her wish…

'I admire you more than I believed it possible to admire anyone—man or woman. I respect you and I value you— as a person, not just as the woman I love. Before I knew I loved you I knew that I wanted you to be the mother of my sons. I knew that the night we made love. I knew it, and because I knew it I deliberately chose to ignore the fact that we weren't using any contraception. Even if I refused to recognise it at the time I know now that I wanted you to have my child, Lizzie. I wanted to tie you to me and I knew that you could not have a child and not love it. Please stay. Please stay and let me prove to you that I do love you. I need you, Lizzie. You've changed me, made me unrecognisable to myself, and I need you to help me understand the person I've become. I need you to show me how to be the man you want me to be. I grew up without learning what love is. I need your help so that I can understand it. You humble me, Lizzie—with everything that you are.'

Could she believe him? Dared she?

He was going to lose her. In his pocket he could feel her wedding ring, the diamond of her engagement ring. Impulsively he dropped down on one knee in front of Lizzie, and removed the rings from his pocket.

'Please wear these again for me, Lizzie—for me, and our child, and the other children I want us to have. Be my wife and my love. I need you, Lizzie. I love you.'

Lizzie reached out and touched the dark head, her love for him filling her.

'There's nothing I wouldn't give up to have your love, Lizzie, not even Villa Manos. You've taught me that love matters more than anything else.'

'You'd give up your inheritance? But it's a sacred trust.'

'I won't sacrifice my love or my children for bricks and mortar.'

Now she believed him. Now she knew that he loved her and the child they were to have.

'Oh, Ilios.'

She was in his arms, and he was kissing her with a fierce need that told her more than words just how he really felt about her.

'I couldn't have let you go,' he told her emotionally. 'My life is nothing without you to share it with me, Lizzie.'

'Nor mine without you,' Lizzie whispered back to him lovingly.

'Don't look at me like that,' Ilios begged her. 'Not until we get home and I can show you how very much I want you.'

'Home. What a lovely word that is,' Lizzie told him. '*You* are our home, Ilios—mine and our baby's. Nothing else and no one else matters.'

The look of devotion and love on his face was everything her loving heart had longed to see there—and more.

THE ITALIAN
DUKE'S VIRGIN MISTRESS

PENNY JORDAN

CHAPTER ONE

'ARE you Charlotte Wareham, the project manager from Kentham Brothers?'

Charlotte—Charley—Wareham looked up from her laptop, blinking in the strong Italian spring sunshine. She had only just returned from a snatched, very late lunch—a sandwich and a cup of delicious cappuccino in a local café. Her meeting with the two civic dignitaries responsible for the restoration project on a derelict public garden, to be completed for the five hundredth anniversary of the garden's creation, which she would be overseeing, had overrun badly.

The man now towering over her, whom she hadn't met before, and who seemed to have appeared out of nowhere, was plainly angry—very angry indeed—as he gestured towards the cheap faux stone urns and other replica samples she had shipped over for client inspection.

'And what, may I ask, are these vile abominations?' he demanded.

It wasn't his anger, though, that had a coil of

shocked disbelief tightening her whole body. Dimly she recognised that the sharp, swift pang of sensation possessing her was instinctive female recognition of a man so alpha that no woman could or would even want to deny him.

This was a man born to stand head and shoulders above his peers—a man born to produce strong sons in his own image—a man born to take the woman of his choice to his bed and to give her such pleasure there that she would be bound to him by the mere memory for the rest of her life.

She must have been sitting in the sun for too long, Charley decided shakily. Such thoughts were certainly not something she was normally prone to—quite the opposite.

She made a determined effort to pull herself together, putting her laptop down, rising from the faux stone bench on which she had been sitting, and standing up to confront her interrogator.

He was tall and dark and as filled with furious rage as a volcano about to erupt. He was also, as her senses had already recognised, extraordinarily good-looking. His olive-toned skin was drawn smoothly over the tautly masculine bone structure of his face, and he was tall, dark-haired, with the kind of arrogantly proud chiselled features that spoke of patrician forebears. His unexpectedly steely grey-eyed gaze swept over her with open contempt, his look like a sculptor's chisel, seeking the exact spot in a piece of marble where it was most vulnerable.

Charley tried to look away from him and found

instead that her gaze had somehow slipped to his mouth. Shocked by her own behaviour, she tried to drag her gaze away, but it refused to move. Prickles of warning quivered over her skin, but it was already too late. An unwanted jolt of awareness of him as a man had already struck through her like forked lightning coming out of a still, calm sky, and was all the more frightening for that unexpectedness. Her mouth had gone dry; a thousand tiny nerve-endings were pulsing beneath her skin. She could feel her lips softening and swelling as though in preparation for a lover's kiss, and he was looking at them now, his gaze narrowed and unreadable, but no doubt filled with arrogant disdain for her weakness. A man like this one would never look at her mouth the way she had looked at his. He would never be caught off guard by the sudden shock of knowing that his senses had torn free of his mind and were imagining what it would be like to feel her mouth against his.

Jerkily, her fingers trembling as she fought for self-control, Charley pulled down the sunglasses perched on top of her head to cover her eyes, in an attempt to conceal the effect he was having on her. But it was too late. He had seen it—and the contempt she could see hardening his expression told her what he thought of her reaction to him. Her face, her whole body was burning with a mixture of shocked disbelief and humiliation as she battled to rationalise and understand what had happened to her. She simply didn't *ever* react to men like that, and it shocked her that she had done so now—and to this man of all men. She had an unnerving need to touch her own lips, to see if they actually were as softly swollen as they felt.

What had happened must be some kind of reaction to all the pressure and stress she had been under, Charley tried to rationalise. Why else would she be reacting in this uncharacteristic and dangerous way? Her senses, though, refused to be controlled. The artist's eye within her recognised the raw male power of the body that was cloaked by his undoubtedly expensive charcoal-grey suit. Beneath his clothes he would have the kind of torso, and everything that went with it, that the medieval artists for which Florence was so justly famous had so loved to sculpt and paint.

Too late she recognised that he was still waiting for her to respond to his question. In a bid to regain the ground she felt she had lost, Charley lifted her small pointed chin and told him, 'I do work for Kentham Brothers, yes.' She paused, trying not to wince as she looked at the haphazard line of pots and statues, their shoddiness laid bare by the stranger's disdain, and then continued, 'And the "vile abominations", as you call them, are in fact very good value for money.'

The look of contempt that twisted his mouth into bitter cynicism—not just at the samples but also at her—confirmed everything Charley already knew about herself. The truth was that she was as lacking in true beauty, style and elegance, and every other female attribute there was that a man might admire as the samples were lacking in anything truly artistic. And it was that knowledge—the knowledge that she had been judged and found wanting by a man who was no doubt a true connoisseur of her sex—that prompted her to tell him defiantly, 'Not that it is really any of your business…' She paused deliberately before adding a questioning, 'Signor…?'

The dark eyebrows snapped towards the bridge of his arrogant, aquiline nose, the grey eyes turning molten platinum as he gave her an arrogantly lofty look and told her, 'It is not Signor anything, Ms Wareham. I am Raphael Della Striozzi—Duce di Raverno. Il Duce is the form of address most people of the town use to address me—as they have addressed my father and his father before him, going back for many centuries.'

Il Duce? He was a duke? Well, she wasn't going to let herself be impressed, Charley told herself, especially since he was obviously expecting her to be.

'Really?' Charley stuck her chin out determinedly— a habit she had developed as a child, to defend herself from parental criticism. 'Well, I should point out to you that this whole area is strictly off-limits to the general public, titled or untitled, for their own safety. There are notices in place. If you have issues with the restoration work which Kentham Brothers has been commissioned to do, I suggest that you take them up with the authorities,' she told him briskly.

Raphael stared at her in furious disbelief. She, this Englishwoman, was *daring* to attempt to deny him access to this garden?

'I am not the general public. It was a member of my family who originally bequeathed this garden to the town.'

'Yes, I know that,' Charley agreed. She had done her research on the garden very thoroughly when she had first been told about the contract. 'The garden was a gift to the townspeople from the wife of the first duke, in thanks to them for praying for the birth of a son after four daughters.'

Raphael's mouth hardened into a grim line, as he returned, 'Thank you, I am well aware of the history of my family.'

But it was only when he had looked into the matter more thoroughly that he had discovered the ornamentation this woman intended to replace with hideous examples of modern mass production had originally been created by some of the Renaissance's most gifted artists. Now abandoned, damaged and forgotten, the garden had been designed by a foremost landscaper of the day.

The realisation of how magnificent the garden must have been had stirred within him a sense of responsibility towards the current project. A responsibility he should have been aware of earlier, and which he now blamed himself for not shouldering before. The town might own the garden, but they carried the name of his family, and next year, when it was reopened to the public in celebration of its five hundredth year of existence, that connection was bound to be publicly referred to. Raphael took pride in the proper artistic maintenance of all the historic buildings and art treasures that had come down to him through his family, and the thought of the garden to which his family was connected being given a makeover more suited to an English suburban plot owned by people with dubious taste filled him with an anger that was currently directed towards Charlotte Wareham—with her make-up-less face, her sun-streaked mud-brown hair, and her obvious lack of interest or pride in her appearance. She was as ill equipped to match the fabled beauty of her renaissance peers as her revolting statues were of matching the magnificence of the originals that had once graced this garden.

He looked again at Charley, frowning as a second look forced him to revise his earlier assessment of her. Now he could see that her pink, lipstick-free mouth was soft, her lips full and well shaped, her nose and jaw delicately sculpted. He had initially thought her eyes, with their thick dark lashes, above cheekbones currently stained with angry colour, a light plain blue, but now, with her anger aroused, he could see they had become the extraordinarily brilliant blue-green of the Adriatic at its most turbulent.

It didn't matter what she looked like, Raphael told himself grimly.

Charley could feel her face starting to burn with memories of her parents warning her about thinking before she spoke or acted, and the unfeminine hastiness of her desire to answer back when challenged. She had believed that she had learned to control that aspect of her personality, but this man—this…this duke—had somehow or other managed to get under her skin and prove her wrong. Now she felt as though he had wrong-footed her, but she wasn't going to let him see that.

'Well, you may be the Duke of Raverno, but it says nothing in the paperwork I have seen about a duke having any involvement in this project. As I understand it, no matter what part your ancestors may have played in the garden in the past, it is the town that is now responsible for them and their restoration. You have no right to be here.'

She wasn't going to let him bully her, not for one minute—title or no title. She had had enough of that over these last few weeks, with her employer making her life such a misery that she longed to be able to hand in her notice. But she had to grin and bear it in the current financial climate. Her small household, which included her elder sister, her younger sister and her twin sons, desperately needed the money she earned— all the more so since her elder sister's interior design business was on the verge of collapse.

With so many people unemployed, she was lucky just to have a job—something her employer continually pointed out to her. She knew why he was doing that, of course. Times were hard; he wanted to cut back on his staff, and he had a daughter fresh out of university, working as an intern within the business, who'd thrown a complete hissy fit when she'd learned that Charley was going to be overseeing this new Italian contract.

If it hadn't been for the fact that she spoke Italian, and her boss's daughter did not, Charley knew she would already have lost her job. She would probably lose it anyway once this contract had been completed. So, she might have to let her employer treat her appallingly, because she desperately needed to keep her job, but she wasn't going to let this arrogant Italian do the same thing. Not when it was the town council she was answerable to and not him. And besides, challenging him made her feel much better about her unwanted awareness of him.

Raphael could feel the fury building up inside him—burning and boiling inside him like molten lava.

When the town council had announced that they planned to restore the dangerously dilapidated pleasure garden just outside the town walls, he had instituted a search of the ducal archives for copies of the original plans for the garden, initially simply out of curiosity, thinking they might assist with the renovation. However, when he had returned from Rome to discover that for financial reasons the town had decided to replace the statues and other features originally designed and created by some of Florence's greatest renaissance artists he had been appalled—and his temper had been left on edge by the council's assertion that the garden would either have to be restored within the small budget available or the site completely flattened, because in its present state it constituted a danger to the public. And now here was this Englishwoman, whose challenge to him was igniting his fury to near uncontrollable levels.

Raphael might not welcome what was planned for the restoration of the garden, but he welcomed even less the effect this young woman responsible for managing the restoration was having on him. Such was the intensity of his anger that it was fostering within him a desire to punish her for daring to provoke it in him. And that could not be allowed. Not now or ever.

Anger and cruelty were the twin demons that together created men whose savage legacy could never be forgotten or forgiven. And the propensity to exhibit them flowed as surely through his veins as it had done through the ancestors who had passed down that legacy to him—but with him that inheritance would end. He had vowed that as a thirteen-year-old, watching as his mother's coffin was placed in the family vault in Rome to join that of his father.

Raphael looked unseeingly towards the padlocked entrance to the gardens. He could feel the heavy, threatening shadow of those twin emotions at his back, following him, out of sight but always there, over his shoulder...

They ran through his family like a dark curse, waiting to escape. He had taught himself to imprison them with reason and ethical awareness, to deny them the arrogance and pride that were their life blood, but now, out of nowhere, simply by being here this Englishwoman had brought him to such a pitch of fierce passion, with her tawdry, ugly replicas, her lack of awareness of what the garden should be, that the key to freeing them was now in the lock without him even being aware of putting it there. Forcing back his urge to physically take hold of her and force her to study the original plans of the garden, to see the damage she would be doing to such a historical asset, was like trying to stem a river in full flood, straining every emotional and mental sinew he had.

The walls of his self-control had already been tested by his meeting with the town council as he had studied the plans they had so proudly showed him, while telling him what a bargain they had secured. And now here was this…this woman, so slender that he could have broken her with his bare hands, daring to deny him access to the garden his ancestor had originally created, expecting him to accept the shoddy, tawdry mockery of the artistic elegance and beauty that had once been.

'You have no right…' she had said. Well, he would *make* it his right—he would make the garden what it should be, and he would make her…

Make her what? A sacrifice to the darkness within his genes?

No! Never that. Nothing and no one would be allowed to threaten his control over that dark, dangerous capacity for savagely violent anger that ran through his veins and was patterned in his DNA.

He needed to speak to the local authorities and put before them the plan he was now formulating—for *him* to take control of the restoration project, so that it could be placed in more appropriate hands, and the sooner the better.

Unaware of what Raphael was thinking, Charley was both surprised and relieved when he started to stride away from her, moving to climb into a sleek, expensive-looking car parked several yards away, its bodywork the same steel-grey colour as his eyes.

CHAPTER TWO

CHARLEY looked worriedly at her watch. Where was the haulier the town officials had assured her would arrive to collect the supplier's samples? In another fifteen minutes the taxi booked to take her to the airport in Florence would be here, and Charley was far too conscientious to simply get into it without ensuring the samples were safely on their way back to the suppliers. She was beginning to wish now that she had spoken with the carriers herself, instead of accepting the city official's offer to do so for her.

Her earlier run-in with 'The Duke' had left her feeling far more unsettled and on edge than she wanted to admit. It had been a long couple of days, filled with meetings and site inspections, and the realisation of the enormity of the task of restoring the garden. Privately, it had saddened her to examine the overgrown, broken-down site and recognise how beautiful it must once have been, knowing that the budget they had been given could not possibly allow them to return it to anything like its former glory. And now, instead of being able to indulge in a few days of relaxing in Florence, soaking up everything it had to offer, she had to fly straight back to Manchester because there was no way her boss would allow her any time off. Not that she could have afforded to stay in Florence, even if he had been willing to let her take some leave. Every penny was precious in their small household, and Charley wasn't about to waste money on herself when they were struggling just to keep a roof over their heads.

A van came round the corner of the dusty road and pulled up virtually alongside her with a screech of tyres. The doors of the van were thrown open and two young men got out, one of them going to the rear of the vehicle to open the doors and the other heading for the samples.

This was the freight authority that had been organised? Charley watched anxiously, her anxiety turning to dismay when she saw the rough manner in which the young men were handling the samples.

But worse was to come. When they reached the open rear doors of the van, to Charley's disbelief they simply threw two of the samples into it, causing both of them to break.

'Stop it! Stop what you are doing,' Charley demanded in Italian, rushing to stand in front of the remaining samples.

'We have orders to remove this rubbish,' one of them told her, his manner polite, but quite obviously determined.

'Orders? Who from?'

'Il Duce,' he answered, edging past her to pick up another of the samples.

Il Duce! How dared he? Hard on the heels of her outraged anger came the knowledge that she must stop them—or face the wrath of both the supplier who had entrusted the samples to her and her employer.

'No. You can't do this. You must stop,' Charley protested frantically. There was close on a thousand pounds' worth of goods here, and the damage would be laid at her door. Out of the corner of her eye she saw a familiar grey car speed towards them, throwing up clouds of dust as its driver brought it to a halt on the roadside several yards away and then got out.

As soon as he was within earshot, Charley demanded, 'What's going on? Why are these men destroying the samples? The damage will have to be paid for, and—'

'They are acting on my orders, since I am now in charge of the restoration project, and it is my wish that they are disposed of.'

He was now in charge? It was *his* wish that they were disposed of? And would it also be his wish that she was disposed of—or rather that her services were dispensed with? Did she really need to ask herself that question?

Helplessly Charley watched as the final sample was loaded into the van.

'Where are they taking them? What you're doing is theft, you know.' She tried valiantly to protect the supplier's goods, but The Duke didn't deign to answer her, going to speak to the two young men instead. Charley looked at her watch again. She could do nothing about the samples now. But where was her taxi? If it didn't arrive soon not only would she be responsible for the loss of the samples, she would also miss her flight. She could just imagine how her boss was going to react. Only her fluency in Italian had prevented him from sacking her already, so that he could give his daughter her job.

She reached into her bag for her mobile. She would have to ring the council official who had organised the taxi for her.

The white van was speeding away, and The Duke had come back to her.

'There are matters we need to discuss,' he told her peremptorily.

'I'm waiting for a taxi to pick me up and take me to the airport.'

'The taxi has been cancelled.'

Cancelled? Charley was feeling sick with anxiety now, but she wasn't going to let it show—not to this man of all men.

'Follow me,' he commanded.

Follow him? Charley opened her mouth to object, and then closed it again as out of nowhere the knowledge came to her that this was a man who had the power to make a woman lose so much sense of herself that following him would be all she wanted to do. But not her, Charley assured herself—and yet wasn't that exactly what she was doing? Something about him compelled her to obey him, to follow him, as though…as though she was commanded by something outside her own rational control. Her whole body shuddered as immediately and physically as though he had actually touched her, and had found a reaction to that touch that she herself had not wanted to give. What was she *thinking*?

He was striding towards the car, leaving her with no option than to do as he had instructed her. He was opening the passenger door of the car for her.

He was taking her to the airport? And what had he meant when he had said that he was taking over the project?

She could all too easily picture him in Florence at the time of the Medicis, manipulating politics to suit his own purposes, with the aid of his sword if necessary, claiming whatever he wanted, be it wealth or a woman, and making it his possession. He had that air of darkness and danger about him. She shivered again, but this time not with angry resentment. This time the frisson of sensation that stroked her body was making her aware of him as a man, unnerving and alarming her.

He was not someone who would have any compassion for those weaker than him—especially if they were in his way, or if he had marked them out as his prey, Charley warned herself. Let him do his worst—think the worst of her. She didn't care. She had far more important things to worry about, like keeping her job and keeping her all-important salary flowing into the family bank account; like doing her bit and following the example of selfless sacrifice her elder sister Lizzie had set. Her sister always managed to make light of all that she had done for them, never revealing that she felt any hint of the shameful misery that Charley sometimes had to fight off because she had been forced to give up her private dreams of working in the world of fine art. Sometimes Charley admitted

she felt desperately constricted, her artistic nature
cruelly confined by the circumstances of her life.

Raphael slid into the driver's seat of the car, closing
the door and then starting the engine.

The town council had been only too delighted to
allow him to finance the restoration work on the
garden, and to hand the whole project over to him. Had
there been a trace of fear in their response to him as
well as delighted gratitude? They knew his family
history as well as he did himself. They knew that it
involved broken lives and bodies, and the inheritance
of blood that belonged to a name that still today caused
shudders amongst those who whispered it in secret
with fear and loathing. Beccelli! Who, knowing the
history of that name, would not shrink from it?

He could not do so, however, Raphael reminded
himself as he drove. He was forced every day of his
life to face what he was, what he carried within him
and its capacity for cruelty and evil. It was an inheritance that tortured and tormented those not strong
enough to carry it. Those who, like his mother, had
ended up taking their own life out of the despair that
knowing they carried such genes had brought. Raphael
stiffened against the unwanted emotional intrusion of
his own thoughts. He had decided a long time ago that
no one would ever be allowed to know how he felt
about his blood inheritance or the ghosts of his past.
Let others judge him as they wished; he would never
allow himself to be vulnerable enough to let them see
what he really felt. He would never seek their advice

or acknowledge their criticism. He had been left alone to carry the burden of what he was, his father having drowned in a sailing accident and his mother dead by her own hand—both of them gone within a year of one another just as he had entered his teens.

Until he had come of age trustees had managed the complex intricacies of his inheritance and its wealth. A succession of relatives—aunts, uncles, cousins— had made room for him under their roofs whilst he was growing up. After all, he was the head of the family whether they liked it or not. Its wealth and status, like its patronage, belonged to him alone.

In the way of such things, his great-aunt's death and the consequent gathering of the family had given his relatives an opportunity to bring up the subject of his marriage and the subsequent production of the next heir—a favourite subject for all Italian matriarchs with unmarried offspring.

It was no secret to Raphael that his father's cousin wanted him to marry her daughter, nor that the wife of his only male cousin, Carlo, often wondered if one day her husband or her son might stand in Raphael's shoes, should he not have a son.

Raphael, though, had no intention of enlightening either of them with regard to his plans. And they knew better than to press him too much.

The Beccelli family had been notorious for their cruelty and their temper. Raphael's own fear, however, lay not only with what he might have inherited himself but, even more importantly, with the genes that he would pass on, and those who might inherit them. In this modern world it might be possible to screen out those elements that combined to lead to a new life inheriting physical conditions that might damage it, but as yet there was no test that could pinpoint the inheritance of a mental and emotional mindset that would revel in cruelty, or protect a new life from the inner burden that came from knowing one's history.

They were travelling through the gathering darkness of the spring evening, and it was minutes before Charley caught a glimpse of a road sign that sent her heart thudding with renewed anxiety. She realised that they were going in the opposite direction from her expected destination.

This isn't the way to the airport,' she protested

'No.'

'Stop this car immediately. I want to get out.'

'Don't be ridiculous.'

'I am not being ridiculous. You have as good as kidnapped me, and my boss is expecting me to be back in England tomorrow.'

'Not any more,' Raphael informed her. 'When I spoke to him earlier he was most anxious that you should remain here—in fact he begged me to keep you and use you for whatever purpose I wished.'

Charley opened her mouth to object to the offensive connotations of his choice of words, and then closed it again when she saw the gleam in his eyes. He wanted to upset and humiliate her. Well, she wouldn't give him the satisfaction of letting him think that he had done so.

Instead she said firmly, 'You said that you have taken over the project?'

'Yes. I have decided to fund the restoration myself rather than allow my family's name to be connected with the kind of cheap, tawdry restoration you had in mind.'

'So you'll be cancelling our contract, then?'

'I would certainly like to do so,' Raphael agreed. 'But unfortunately it won't be possible for me to do that and find someone else to complete the work in time for next year's formal re-opening of the garden. However, I do have some concerns about your suitability to manage the project.'

She was going to be sacked.

'It seems to me that someone who gave up her Fine Arts degree halfway through to study accountancy instead is not the person to manage this project in the way I wish to have it managed.'

'My career choices have nothing to do with you,' Charley defended herself. She certainly wasn't going to tell him that after the deaths of their parents and the financial problems that had followed she had felt morally obliged to train for something that would enable her to earn enough to help her elder sister provide a home for them all.

'On the contrary, since I am now in effect employing you they have a very great deal to do with me. From now on you will work directly under my control and you will be answerable directly to me. Should I find that you are not able to satisfy me and meet the standards I set, then you will be dismissed. Your employer has already assured me that he has someone in mind to replace you, should that prove necessary.'

'His daughter,' Charley was unable to stop herself from saying furiously, 'who can't speak a word of Italian.'

Ignoring her outburst, Raphael continued, 'It is my intention that the garden will be restored as exactly as possible to its original design.'

Charley stared at him in the darkness of the car, the light from the moon revealing the harsh pride of his profile, etching it with silver instead of charcoal.

'But that will cost a fortune,' she protested, 'and that's just for starters. Finding craftsmen to undertake the work—'

'You can leave that to me. I have connections with a committee in Florence that is responsible for much of the work on its heritage buildings; it owes me favours.'

And she could just bet that calling in 'favours' was something he was very, very good at doing, Charley recognised.

'Your work begins tomorrow, when we will visit the site together. I have in my possession the original plans.'

'Tomorrow? But I was only supposed to be here for the day. I haven't got anywhere to stay, or…'

'That will not be a problem. You will stay at the *palazzo*, so that I can monitor your work and ensure that the garden is restored exactly as I wish. That is where we are going now—unless, of course, it is your wish that I ask your employer to send someone else to take over from you?'

Was that secretly what he was hoping? Well, he

was going to be disappointed, Charley decided proudly. She was as equally capable of managing a high-budget project as she was of managing a low-budget one, and in truth there was nothing she would have enjoyed more than seeing the garden come to life as it had once been, if only *he* was not involved. More important than any of that, though, was her need to keep on earning the money they all so desperately needed right now. She could not afford the luxury of pride, no matter how much it irked her.

The road began to climb up ahead of them, and on the hilltop, caught in the full beam of the rising moon, Charley could see the vast bulk of an imposing building dominating the landscape.

'That is the Palazzo Raverno up ahead,' Raphael informed her.

The façade of the building was illuminated by floodlights, and when they had finally came to a halt outside it Charley could see it was Baroque in style, with curved pediments and intricate mouldings displaying the deliberate interplay between curvaceous forms and straight lines that was so much a part of the Baroque style of architecture.

Despite her determination not to betray what she was feeling, when Raphael got out of the car and then came round to the passenger door to open it for her she was totally unable to stop herself from saying in disbelief, as she followed him up the marble steps, 'You live here? In this?'

Her awed gaze took in the magnificence of the building in front of her. It looked like something that should have belonged to the National Trust, or whatever the Italian equivalent of that organisation was.

'Since it is the main residence of the Duke of Raverno, and has been since it was first remodelled and designated as such in the seventeenth century, yes, I do live here—although sometimes I find it more convenient to stay in my apartments in Rome or Florence, depending on what business I am conducting.' He shrugged dismissively, making Charley even more aware of the vast gulf that lay between their ways of life.

'My nephews would envy you having somewhere so large to play in,' was all she could manage to say. 'They complain that there isn't enough room in the house we all share for them to play properly with their toys.'

'You *all* share? Does that mean that you live with your sister and her husband?'

Raphael didn't know why he was bothering to ask her such a question, nor why the thought that she might share her day-to-day life with a man, even if he was her own sister's husband, should fill him with such immediate and illogical hostility. What did it matter to him who she lived with?

'Ruby isn't married. The three of us—my eldest sister Lizzie, Ruby and I and the twins—all live together. It was Lizzie's idea. She wanted to keep the family together after our parents died, so she gave up her career in London to come back to Cheshire.'

'And what did you give up?'

The question had Charley looking at him in shock. She hadn't expected it, and had no defences against it.

'Nothing,' she lied, and quickly changed the subject

to ask uncertainly, 'Will your wife not mind you bringing me here into her home like this?'

'My wife?'

Raphael had been moving up the marble steps ahead of her, but now he stopped and turned to look at her.

'I do not have a wife,' he informed her, 'and nor do I ever intend to have one.'

Charley was too surprised to stop herself from saying, 'But you're a duke—you must want to have a son, an heir... I mean that's what being someone like a duke is all about, isn't it?'

Something—not merely anger, nor even pride, but something that went beyond both of those things and was darker and scarred with bitterness—was fleetingly visible in his expression before he controlled it. She had seen it, though, and it aroused Charley's curiosity, making her wonder what had been responsible for it.

'You think my whole purpose, the whole focus of my life, my very existence, is to ensure the continuation of my genes?' The grey eyes were burning as hot as molten mercury now. 'Well, I dare say there are plenty of others who share your view, but I certainly do not. I have no intention of marrying—ever—and even less of producing a son or any child, for that matter.'

Charley was too astonished to say anything. It seemed so out of character for the kind of man she had assumed he must be that he should not consider marriage and the production of an heir as the prime reason for his own being. That, surely, was how the aristocracy thought? It was the mindset that had made them what they were—the need, the determination to continue their male line in order to secure and continue their right to enjoy the status and the wealth that had been built up by previous generations. To hear one of their number state otherwise so unequivocally seemed so strange that it immediately made Charley wonder *why* Raphael felt the way he did. Not, of course, that she was ever likely to get the opportunity to ask him. That would require a degree of intimacy and trust between them that could never exist. He was obviously very angry with her—again—and as he took a step towards her Charley took one step back, forgetting that she was standing on a step and immediately losing her balance.

Raphael's reaction was swift, his hands gripping hold of her upper arms punishingly. Not to protect her from any hurt or harm, Charley recognised, but to protect himself from coming into unwanted contact with her. That knowledge burned her pride and her heart, reminding her of all those other times when men had dismissed her as being unworthy of their interest.

'You should take more care, Charlotte Wareham.'

'It's not Charlotte, it's Charley,' she corrected him, tilting her chin defiantly as she did so.

He was still holding her, and once again out of nowhere she was having to fight against the shock of suddenly experiencing an awareness of him that was totally alien to her nature. How could it have happened? she wondered dizzily. She just didn't feel like this ever—going hot and then cold, trembling with awareness, burning with the heat of sensation surging through her body as it reacted to his maleness.

She had taught herself years ago not to be interested in men, because she had always known that they were not interested in her.

She wasn't sure when she had first realised that in her parents' eyes she wasn't as pretty as either of her siblings. Once she had realised it, though, she had quickly learned to play up to the role of tomboy that they had given her, pretending not to mind when her mother bought pretty dresses for her sisters and jeans for her, pretending that being the family tomboy was what she actually wanted, telling herself that it would be silly for her to try to mimic her sisters when she was so much plainer than they were. It had been her father who had first started calling her 'Charley'—a name that suited a tomboy far better than Charlotte.

Over the years she had learned that the best way to protect herself from comments about her own lack of femininity and prettiness when compared with her sisters was to ensure that others believed she *wanted* to be what she was—that she wanted to be Charley and not Charlotte. But now, for some unknown reason, with Raphael's fingers curling into her flesh, his ice-cold grey gaze boring into her as though his scrutiny was penetrating her most private thoughts and fears, she felt a sharp stab of pain for what she was—and what she was not. If she had been either her elder sister Lizzie, with her elegance and her classically beautiful features, or her younger sister Ruby, with her mop of thick tousled curls and the piquant beauty of her face, he would not be looking at her as he was—as though he wanted to push her away from him and reject her.

Being so close to him was unnerving her—the sheer solid steel strength of his male body brutally hard against her own unprepared softness. Unwittingly her gaze absorbed the olive warmth of his throat above the collar of his shirt and then lifted upwards, sucked into a vortex of instinct beyond her control, blinding her senses to everything else as she fastened on the angle of his jaw, the pores in his skin, the shadow where a beard would grow if he wasn't clean-shaven. She wanted to lift her hand and touch him there on his face, to see if she could feel some slight roughness or if his skin was as smooth and polished as it looked. Her gaze lingered and darted across his face with lightning speed, swift as a child let loose in a sweet shop, eager to gather up forbidden pleasures as fast as it could.

How she longed to be set free to draw and paint this man's image on canvas, to capture the essence of his pride and arrogance so that all that he was, inside and out, was revealed, leaving him as vulnerable as neatly as he had just stripped her of her own defences. That mouth alone said so much about him. It was hard and cruel, the top lip sharply cut. In her mind's eye Charley was already visualising her own sketch of it, so engrossed in what was going on inside her head that when she looked at his bottom lip to assess its shape it was the artist within her that did that assessing, and not the woman. It was the woman, though, whose breath was dragged into her lungs and whose awareness was not of the lines and structure of flesh and muscle, but instead of the openly sensual curve and fullness of his lips. What must it be like to be kissed by a man with such a mouth? Would he kiss with the cruelty of that harshly cut top lip, demanding and taking his own pleasure? Or would he kiss with the sensual promise of that bottom lip, taking the woman he was kissing to a place where pleasure was a foregone conclusion and all she would need to measure it was the depth to which she allowed that pleasure to take her?

Charley's throat locked round the betraying sound of her awareness of him that rose in her throat, stifling and suppressing it. She pulled back stiffly within his hold, causing Raphael to immediately want to keep her where she was. Why? Because for a fraction of a second his body had reacted to her with physical desire? That meant nothing. It had been a momentary automatic reaction—that was all; nothing more. Raphael purposely kept his dealings with women confined to relationships in which both people understood certain rules about their intimacy being purely sexual and nothing more. He was committed to remaining single and child-free as a matter of duty and honour, and nothing was ever going to change that. Certainly not this woman.

And yet beneath his grip Raphael could feel the slenderness of her arm, and just registering that was enough to cause his thoughts to turn to how soft her skin would be, how pale and tender, with delicate blue veins running up from her wrist, the pulse of her blood quickening in them as he touched her. Her naked body would look as though it were carved from alabaster: milk-white and silkily warm to the touch.

Furious with himself for the direction his thoughts

had taken, Raphael pushed the tempting vision away, ignoring the eager hunger that was beginning to pulse through his body.

It was irrational and impossible that he should desire her. Even her name affronted his aesthetic senses and his love of beauty.

'Charley. That is a boy's name and you are a woman,' he pointed out to her, and then demanded, 'Why do you reject your womanhood?'

'I don't—I'm not,' Charley protested defensively. Why hadn't he let go of her? She knew that he wanted to do so. She could see it in his eyes, in the curl of his mouth, so cold and potentially cruel, and yet... A shudder of sensation she couldn't control swept through her as she looked at his mouth. What would it be like to be kissed by a man like him? To be held, and touched, caressed, wanted...?

A small sound locked her throat, her eyes darkening to such a dense blue-green that the colour reminded Raphael of the deep, clean, untouched waters in the small private bay below the villa he owned on the island of Sicily. The sudden swift hardening of his body before he had time to check its reaction to her caught him off guard, making him deride himself mentally for his reaction. He couldn't *possibly* desire her, he told himself grimly. It was unthinkable.

'No Italian woman would dress herself as you do, nor hold herself as you do, without any pride in her womanhood.'

He was being deliberately cruel to her, Charley decided. He must be able to see, after all, that she did not have the kind of womanhood it was possible to take pride in. She was plain and lanky, unfeminine and un-desirable—so much the complete opposite to the beauty her artistic senses admired and longed to create that it hurt her to know how far short she fell of her own standards. Secretly, growing up, she had believed that if she could not be beautiful then she could at least create beauty. But even that had been denied her. It was a sacrifice she had made willingly, for the sake of her sisters. They loved her as she was, and she loved them. That was what mattered—not this man.

And yet when he released her and was no longer touching her, when he looked at her as though he despised her, it *did* matter, Charley recognised miserably.

Following Raphael into the *palazzo*, Charley was conscious of how untidy and unattractive she must look, in cheap jeans that had never fitted properly, even when she had first bought them, and the bulky, out-of-shape navy jumper she had thought she might need if she had to visit the site, which she had worn over her tee shirt to allow her more packing space in her backpack. And her shoes were so worn that no amount of polishing could make them look anything other than shabby. But then she forgot her awful clothes as she took in the magnificence of the large entrance hall, with its frescoed wall panels and ceiling, the colours surely as rich and fresh today as they had been when they had first been painted, making her want to reach out and touch them, to feel that richness beneath her fingertips. The scenes were allegorical—relating, she guessed, to Roman mythology rather than

Christianity—and had obviously been painted by a master hand. Just looking at them was a feast for her senses, overwhelming them and bringing emotional tears to her eyes that she was quick to blink away, not wanting Raphael to see them. She tried to focus on something else, but even the marble staircase that rose up from the hallway was a work of art in its own right.

Raphael, who had been watching her, saw her eyes widen and change colour, her face lifting towards the frescoes with an awed joy that illuminated her features and revealed the true beauty of the delicate bone structure.

His heart slammed into his ribs with a force for which he was totally unprepared. The fresco was one of his personal favourites, and her silent but open homage to it echoed his own private feelings. But how could it be possible that this woman of all people, whose behaviour said that she had no awareness of or respect for artistic beauty, should look at the fresco and react to it with all that he felt for it himself? It shouldn't have been possible. It should not have happened. But it had, and he had witnessed it. Raphael watched her lift her hand as she took a step towards the nearest fresco, as though unable to stop herself, and then let it fall back. He hadn't expected it of her. She hadn't struck him as someone who was capable of feeling, never mind expressing such an emotion, and yet now he could feel her passion filling the distance between them. If he looked at her now he knew he would see her eyes had darkened to that stormy blue-green that had caught his attention earlier, and her lips would be pressed together—soft, sensual pillows of flesh, too full to form a flat line, tempting any man who looked at them to taste them…

Raphael cursed himself under his breath. He had been without a lover for too long. But he couldn't remember ever seeing anyone react quite so emotionally to the frescoes other than his mother, who had loved them and passed on that love to him. He could still remember how as a small child she had lifted him and held him so that he could see the frescos at close quarters, her voice filled with emotion as she talked to him about them. His life had been so happy then, so filled with love and security—before he had known about his dark inheritance.

So much beauty, Charley thought achingly. Her heart, indeed the very essence of her had gone hungry for such beauty for so long. In her imagination she tried to comprehend what it must have been like to be the pupil of such an artist, to have the privilege of watching him at work, knowing that one's own best efforts could never hope to match his smallest brush-strokes, feeding off the joy of witnessing such artistry. Only of course the great masters had never taken on female pupils—not even tomboy female pupils.

Once she had dreamed of working amongst great works of art in one of London's famous museums, as an art historian, but that dream had come to an end with her parents' death.

Dragging her gaze from the frescoes, she shook her head like someone coming out of a deep dream and said slowly to Raphael, 'Giovanni Battista Zelotti, the

most famous of all fresco painters of his era. He would
never tell anyone the recipe he used for his famous blue
paint, and the secret died with him.'

Raphael nodded his head. 'My ancestor commissioned him after he had seen the fresco he painted for
the Medicis in Florence.'

He looked at his watch, his movement catching
Charley's attention. His wrists were muscular, and the
dark hairs on his arm underlined his maleness, making
her stomach muscles tighten into a slow ache that per-
meated the whole of her lower body. What would it be
like to be touched, held by such a man? To know the
polished, controlled expertise of his stroke against her
skin…? And he would be an expert at knowing what
gave a woman the most pleasure… The slow ache
flared into something more intense, causing Charley
to catch her breath as she tried to hold her own against
her body's attack on her defences. It must be Italy that
was making her feel like this—Italy, and the knowledge that she was so close to the cities she had longed
to visit and their wonderful art treasures, not Raphael
himself. That could not be—must not be.

CHAPTER THREE

WARMTH, sunshine, a scent on the air coming in through the open balcony windows that was both un-familiar and enticing, and a large bed with the most wonderful sheets she had ever slept in. And despite everything she had slept, Charley admitted as she luxuriated guiltily in the delicious comfort of the bed and her surroundings, having been woken only minutes earlier by a discreet knock on her bedroom door, followed by the entrance of a smiling young maid with Charley's breakfast.

When Raphael's housekeeper had brought her up here last night she had felt slightly daunted, but to her relief Anna, as she had told Charley she must call her, had quickly put her at her ease, organising a light meal for her, and telling her that breakfast would be sent up to her room for her because 'Il Duce—' as she had referred to Raphael '—takes his breakfast very early when he is here, so that he can go out and speak to the men whilst they are working with the vines.'

Charley was, of course, relieved that she didn't have

to have breakfast with Raphael, and it wasn't because she was curious about him in any way at all that as she left the bed she was drawn to the balcony windows and the view of the vines she had already seen beyond the gardens that lay immediately below them. Slipping the band she used to tie her hair back off her face over her wrist, Charley padded barefoot to the balcony in her strappy sleep top with matching shorts—a Christmas present from the twins. The outfit was loose on her, due to the weight she had lost over these last anxious weeks.

It was wonderful to feel the warmth of the sun on her bare skin. Charley turned her face up towards it, and then tensed as she heard Raphael's voice and then saw him appear round the corner of the building, accompanied by another man with whom he was deep in conversation. Both men were dressed casually, in short-sleeved shirts and chinos, but it was to Raphael that her attention was drawn as the two men shook hands and the older man began to walk away, leaving Raphael standing alone. The blue linen of his shirt emphasised the tanned flesh of his bare forearms. A beam of sunlight touched the strong column of his throat. Charley had to curl her fingers in an attempt to quell the longing itching in them—not a desire to pick up a piece of charcoal and sketch his lean, erotically male lines, but instead a desire to touch him, to feel the warmth of the life force that lay beneath his flesh, to experience how it felt to be free to physically explore such a man.

Beneath the thin cotton jersey of her top her nipples

tightened, the small movement she made instinctively in rejection of her arousal dragging the fabric against their swollen sensitivity, conjuring up inside her head images of a male touch creating—indeed inciting—that sensitivity and then harvesting its sensuality, teasing her with skilled, tormenting caresses that played on her arousal, drawing it from her, making her want a closer intimacy. Behind her closed eyelids Charley could almost see the dark male hands tormenting her, making her yearn for their possession of her breasts. Instinctively she stepped forward—and then gasped, her eyes opening as she came up against the balcony railing.

Down below her Raphael looked up towards the balcony. It was too late for her to step back out of sight. He had seen her, and he would know that she had seen him. Suddenly conscious of how she must look, dressed in her sleepwear and with her hair all over the place, she plucked at the hairband on her wrist, her eyes widening in dismay as it slipped from her fingers and dropped through the railings, landing almost at Raphael's feet.

When he bent to pick it up Charley could see the fabric of his linen shirt stretch across his shoulders. It was such a male thing that—the breadth of a man's shoulders, the way his body tapered down in a muscular V-shape towards his hips, his chest hard and packed with muscles where her own was soft with the rounded shape of her breasts.

Raphael was straightening up, putting her hairband in his pocket, looking up at her, at her hair, her mouth, her breasts. Charley's toes curled into the mosaic-tiled floor of the balcony as she sucked in her stomach against the heat that flooded over her.

A mobile phone began to ring. Raphael's, she recognised as he removed it from his pocket and began to speak into it, turning his back to her and then beginning to walk away.

It was the warmth of the sun on her sunshine-starved body that had aroused her, not Raphael. He had just happened to be there at the same time—that was all, Charley insisted to herself as she stood under the shower, determinedly not thinking of anything other than the reason she was here in Italy.

Ten minutes later, having searched through her backpack three times, Charley dropped it onto the floor in defeat. How could she not have put in a couple of spare hairbands? She never wore her hair loose. *Never.* She preferred, *needed* to have it tied back and under control. She simply wasn't feminine enough to wear her hair loose in a mass of curls.

His call over, Raphael looked down at the hairband he had removed from his pocket, his body hardening as he studied it. Inside his head he could see Charlotte Wareham standing on the balcony, the bright morning sunshine turning the top and shorts she was wearing virtually transparent so that he could see quite plainly the flesh beneath them—her breasts round and full, shadowed by the dark aureole of flesh from which her nipples rose to push against the fabric covering them.

How different she had appeared then, without the concealment of the shapeless clothes she had been wearing the previous day. Raphael tried to dismiss the erotic image from inside his head, but instead his memory produced another picture, this time of Charlotte Wareham pressed against the balcony, her back arched, her eyes closed in a mixture of surrender and enticement, those long, long legs of hers parted, the sunlight revealing the neat covering of hair that protected her sex. How easy it would have been for a man to slide his hand up her thigh and beneath the cuff of her shorts, so that he could stroke that sensual softness and explore what it concealed. What she had been wearing—two small plain items of clothing, not suggestive at all, so one might think—had cloaked her body in such a way that their mere presence and proximity to her body had filled him with a fierce urgency to feast on all the delights her flesh had seemed to offer. He couldn't accuse her of being deliberately provocative, Raphael knew, and it brought a sharp edge to his irritation with himself to have to admit that against all the odds, and certainly against his normal code of behaviour, his mind had somehow developed a will of its own and had transformed clothes so ordinary into garments filled with sensual promise. Just remembering now the way in which the thin shoulder straps of her top had suggested they could be easily slid down her arms, to reveal the full promise of those dark hard nipples, filled him with angry rejection of his body's response to her. The soft, unstructured shape of the top itself, which had finished almost on her waist, revealing a glimmer of pale flesh, had urged him to lift it up and push it out of the way, so that he could see and touch the promised soft lushness of her body. And the shorts, baggy and loose-legged... A man could take his pleasure exploring whatever part of her he chose to reveal, knowing that he had the whole of her to access as and when and how he chose to do so.

Cursing himself silently again, Raphael commanded his self-control to dispel both his thoughts and the arousal they were creating. If he needed a woman then there were plenty available to him who would make more suitable bedmates than Charlotte Wareham.

Charley longed to fasten her hair and hold it gripped off her face as she stood in front of the desk behind which Raphael was seated. She had been summoned to his presence like a miscreant about to be punished—which, of course, as far as he was concerned was exactly what she was. She couldn't touch her hair, no matter how uncomfortable she felt with it tumbling down onto her shoulders, because if she did it might remind Raphael, and would certainly remind her, of the circumstances in which she had lost her hairband.

In an attempt to distract herself she studied her surroundings. The fact that the large room was on the ground floor of the *palazzo* indicated that its original purpose would have been for business to be conducted: orders given, favours sought and deals made—the administrative centre of the ducal estate.

The ceiling was decorated with painted lozenges depicting various hereditary arms and symbols. The polished wood of the library shelving which held huge leather-covered books, their gold lettering gleaming softly, added to the imposing air of the room. Traditionally it would no doubt have been here where those who administered the estate would come to present their accounts to the duke, to answer his questions and receive his praise—or his wrath.

Charley shivered. There was no doubt which of those things Raphael believed she deserved.

The heavy, ornately carved and inlaid desk, positioned to make the most of the light coming in through the narrow windows, was covered in papers.

Raphael looked briefly at Charley. She was wearing her hair down, and the sight of it, freshly washed, the delicately scented smell of it and of her reawakened the desire he had felt earlier. What was the matter with him? He was no mere hormone-driven boy, to be tempted and tormented by the thought of sliding his hands into those thick wild curls, of lacing his fingers through them as he covered her naked body with his own, arousing her as she had aroused him. Using the determination with which he had always so ruthlessly crushed any challenge or resistance to his self-control, Raphael closed down his unwanted thoughts as firmly as though he had trapped them behind an impregnable steel door. To allow himself to feel desire for Charlotte Wareham would be unacceptably inappropriate behaviour and, more than that, a weakness within himself that he was not prepared to tolerate. He had no idea why she should have such an effect on him. She was neither groomed nor elegant. She was not witty or sophisticated. In short, there was nothing about her that should have had any appeal for him.

All he could think was that somehow his body had been confused by the anger she aroused within him and was thus acting inappropriately. The reality was that Charlotte Wareham was proving to be a thorn in his side in more ways than one.

'I have copies here of the original plans for the garden. I want you to study them and see what is to be done within the garden.'

'Yes, Il Duce.' Charley responded through gritted teeth.

There was a small, dangerous silence, as though he knew how she had almost choked on delivering the title that in her own estimation reduced her to little more than a slave, forced to do his bidding, and how she had spoken the words with her angry contempt. She could see the thunder in the now dark grey eyes and she waited, knowing that she would be punished.

But when he spoke he shocked her by saying dismissively, 'You will address me as Raphael and not Il Duce.'

Use his name and not his title? Charley almost told him that she would do no such thing, but just in time realised how ridiculous such a piece of defiance would be.

'Now,' he continued, 'let me assure you that any attempt on your part to despoil the restoration of the garden with items of the sort I saw yesterday will result in your immediate dismissal. The garden will be restored to its full glory in every detail.'

Charley could almost feel the intensity of his commitment. If he could make that kind of commitment to a garden then how much more intense would be the commitment he made to the woman he loved?

Her body convulsed on a small betraying shiver. Once, a long, long time ago as a girl, before she had realised that tomboys were not the kind of girls the male sex wanted to protect, she had dreamed of growing up and being loved by a man whose love for her would be so strong that it would protect her always.

An aching sense of painful loss filled her. She would never know that kind of love—Raphael's kind of love.

Love? What on earth was going on? Love and this man had no place together in her thoughts. No place at all. She could not afford to be vulnerable. She was too vulnerable already.

A discreet but firm rap on the door broke across her thoughts and had Raphael turning towards it, commanding, 'Come.' It opened to admit his serious-looking male PA, Ciro, whom Charley had met earlier, when he had introduced himself to her and told her that Raphael was waiting to speak with her.

Ciro spoke quickly and quietly to Raphael, causing him to frown slightly and then tell her, 'I have to go and speak with the manager of the vineyard. I shall not be long. Ciro will arrange for Anna to have some coffee sent in for you whilst you wait for me to return.'

His words sounded polite enough, but Charley wasn't deceived. What they really were was an order to her that she was to remain here until his return— when no doubt she would be subjected to more contempt and more verbal castigation, she decided as

Raphael strode through the door his PA was holding open for him, leaving Ciro to follow him.

Thanking the maid for the coffee she had just brought, Charley picked up the cup the girl had filled for her, wrapping both her hands around it for comfort—like a child holding a comfort rag or toy, Charley thought, deriding herself for her own vulnerability.

As a child it had always seemed that she had been the one to get the blame for the accidentally naughty things the three of them had sometimes done—even when Lizzie had insisted that the fault was hers. There had been many times when she had gone to bed at night crying into her pillow in silent misery, feeling misunderstood, feeling she was less worthy of parental love than her two sisters. Now the way Raphael was treating her had evoked some of that long-ago misery and sense of injustice, adding to her existing despair.

She took a quick gulp of her coffee and then got up from her chair, putting the cup down as she was drawn to the sketches and plans laid out on Raphael's desk. Since they were of the pleasure garden, there was no reason why she should not look at them, she assured herself. She had, after all, seen the plans before, at home in England.

These, though, were not modern drawings, but sketches and watercolours of parts of the original garden, Charley quickly recognised, immediately becoming so absorbed in them that everything else was forgotten as she was mentally swept back to another century, enviously imagining what it must have been like to be involved in such a wonderful project. The plans and sketches alone were minor works of art in their own right, and Charley's fingertips trembled as she touched the papers on which those long-ago craftsmen had etched their sketches and detailed measurements of fountains, statues, colonnades and grottos.

A perspective overview showed the full layout of the garden. The formal sweep of a curved, colonnaded entrance opened in the centre, to draw the eye down a wide avenue planted with what looked like pleached limes. Either side of it the garden was intersected by narrower walkways, opening out into sheltered bowers decorated with seats and statuary, beyond which lay a stone fountain, in the middle of which was a huge piece of statuary. A paved terrace shaded by vines marked the boundary, where the land fell away with a view over an ornamental lake, complete with a grotto.

There were sketches for small, elegant pavilions, 'secret' water gardens designed to spring into life when the unsuspecting walked close to them. Charley ached with longing to have seen the garden following its completion. Raphael was right to say that trying to recreate such beauty using cheap manmade materials was an insult to the original artists.

She was so wrapped up in the world those long-ago craftsmen and artists had created that she didn't hear the soft click of the door opening, and was oblivious to Raphael's return and the fact that he was standing watching her as she stood looking down at the papers on his desk, her expression one of absorbed intensity.

Charley lifted her gaze from the desk, her eyes shadowed with all that she was feeling, lost in her own world—only to come abruptly out of that world when she saw Raphael.

How long had he been there? The way he was looking at her made her feel acutely vulnerable. She stepped back from the desk, so intent on escaping from his gaze that she forgot about the small table behind her on which the maid had placed the tray of coffee.

As she bumped into the table she dislodged the heavy thermos jug. Before she had time to react Raphael had reacted for her, reaching her side, pulling her away from the table just as hot coffee spouted from the jug and onto her jean-clad thigh.

She must have cried out, although she wasn't aware of having done so, because immediately Raphael looked down to where the hot liquid had soaked through her jeans, his sharp and almost accusatory, 'You have been burned,' causing Charley to shake her head.

'No. I'm all right,' she insisted.

Her face was burning with a mixture of emotions. Her leg was stinging painfully beneath the wet fabric of her jeans, but it was her own embarrassment at having been so clumsy rather than any pain that was making her feel so self-conscious. There was a small puddle of coffee on the snow-white starched linen tray cloth with its discreet monogram, and coffee on the floor as well, but thankfully it had missed the rug that covered part of the marble-tiled floor. Her parents would have shaken their heads if they had witnessed her mishap, pointing out to her that she was dreadfully clumsy. How she had longed to be deft and delicate in her movements, and not like the baby elephant her mother had always teasingly told her she was.

'It's my own fault,' she told Raphael. 'I shouldn't be so clumsy.'

Clumsy? Raphael frowned. She was tall, yes, but her hands and her feet were elegantly narrow, her body far too slender for her ever to be 'clumsy'. In fact if anything Raphael had noticed how controlled and economical her movements were, almost as though she was afraid to express herself.

'You'll want to get changed. I'll wait for you down here.'

'There's no need for me to change,' Charley told him. 'My jeans will dry.'

He was looking at her in a way that said very explicitly what he thought of a woman who cared so little for her appearance that she was content to continue wearing jeans that were stained with and smelled of coffee.

Gritting her teeth, Charley lowered her pride to admit, 'I haven't got anything to change into, since you insisted that I was to stay here instead of going home and then returning.'

Now that the immediate shock was receding Charley was beginning to realise that the scalding coffee had hurt her more than she had first thought. Her leg was throbbing and burning, the pain growing more intense with every passing second, but she was stubbornly determined not to let Raphael see that.

'Go up to your room,' Raphael commanded. 'I'll

speak to Anna about providing you with something to wear for now.'

It was easier to give in than to argue—especially with the pain growing more intense by the second, Charley admitted as she stood up. And then, to her shock, she felt her burned leg give way beneath her, causing her to stumble into Raphael's desk.

Raphael was on his feet immediately, opening a drawer in his desk, coming towards her as she clung to the edge of the desktop for support.

'No!' Charley protested, and protested a second time as she saw the scissors in his hand. But it was no use. He was cutting through the wet denim as ruthlessly as he would have cut down an enemy. The cool air on her burned flesh caused Charley to shudder. She felt slightly sick and light-headed when she looked at her leg and saw how the flesh had reddened and blistered.

Raphael's mouth tightened as he looked at the burned flesh. 'This needs proper medical treatment,' he announced grimly.

'No. I'm all right,' Charley insisted. 'I'll go upstairs and bathe it with some cool water.' She let go of the desk and took a couple of steps, the blood draining from her face as her body responded with a surge of pain.

Raphael had seen enough. Of all the stubborn, stupid women... Before Charley could stop him he was lifting her into his arms, his action forcing her to hold on to him tightly by putting her arms around his neck. He couldn't possibly be intending to carry her all the way to her room—but it seemed that he was, and

Charley could only guess at the power in the muscles cloaked by his fine linen shirt as he did so, as effortlessly as though she weighed little more than a child.

Once they were inside her room, Raphael placed her on the bed and then, after instructing her not to move, he left.

Strange how the pain had subsided whilst she was in Raphael's arms. But it had returned now, and if anything was even worse. It was ridiculous for her to feel as though she had been abandoned, and even more ridiculous—dangerously so—for her to wish that Raphael had stayed with her. Charley looked down at her lower body which, unlike her damaged leg, was still encased in her jeans. She wasn't helpless, she reminded herself. She sat up and started to ease her jeans off, wincing as the fabric brushed against her burned flesh.

'What the devil…? I told you not to move.'

Charley swung round. Raphael was coming towards her, carrying a first aid box.

'I've rung the doctor, and he should be here soon, but in the meantime the burn needs to be covered by a dressing.'

Raphael was kneeling on the floor next to her now bare legs, apparently oblivious to the fact that she had removed her jeans and was now only covered by the lacy briefs which had been Lizzie's Christmas present to her.

'There's really no need…' she began, but Raphael stopped her.

'On the contrary—there is every need,' he told her. She had removed her jeans, and now it wasn't just the slender length of her legs that was distracting him from his self-imposed task, Raphael acknowledged. He had seen women wearing far more provocative and revealing underwear than the lacy briefs that Charley was wearing, but right now the fact that he was acutely aware of what lay beneath the barrier concealing her body from him was having a very unwanted effect on him physically. Angry with himself for allowing his body to overcome his self-control, Raphael worked quickly to open the medical kit and remove the necessary dressing, keeping his gaze fixed firmly on the burned flesh of Charley's thigh, which had now begun to tremble slightly.

'The pain is getting worse?' he demanded.

Charley nodded her head. It was, after all, true that the pain was bad, but it was also true that it wasn't the pain that was causing her body to tremble. Nor was it the reason that the trembling increased when Raphael placed the dressing on her bare flesh. Her reaction to his touch horrified her. She was behaving like an adolescent with a crush.

'There—that should protect the burn until the doctor gets here to look at it properly.'

Charley nodded her head, managing a reluctant, 'Thank you.'

She felt shivery and sick, her nerves jangling—and not, she suspected, purely because of her burned thigh. This time it was a relief when Raphael left her.

CHAPTER FOUR

IT WAS another lovely sunny morning, her second here in Italy, in Raphael's *palazzo*, in what was in effect his bedroom, since he owned the *palazzo*. Goosebumps rose on her skin as though it had been touched, caressed. Helplessly Charley closed her eyes. It must be the painkillers the doctor had given her yesterday, after he had looked at her burn, re-dressed it and pronounced that she must spend the rest of the day in bed, not her wayward thoughts of Raphael.

She knew better this morning than to go and stand on the balcony in her sleepwear.

Instead of worrying about who owned the bed she slept in, what she should be doing was worrying about how she was going to manage without her jeans—the one and only garment she had with her to clothe the lower half of her body. She could hardly appear in public in the loose pyjama shorts she was currently wearing, although Raphael had said that he would speak to Anna on her behalf.

She owed Raphael a debt of gratitude for dealing

with the situation so properly and promptly. The doctor had told her that the burn could have turned very nasty indeed if it had been left unattended, as she would have chosen to do left to her own devices. Luckily it was not so severe that she would need skin grafts, but he had warned her that she might end up with an area of flesh that would forever be vulnerable to heat and sunlight.

Charley looked at her untouched breakfast tray. She was too on edge to eat. She pushed her hand into her hair to lift it off her face. She had lost a great deal since coming to Italy: her hairband, her jeans, her pride and even some of her self-respect. And hadn't she forgotten something? her conscience prodded. Charley defended her omission. Wasn't the list she had just given herself long enough? Did she really have to add to it that she was also in danger of losing the protection she had put in place around and within herself to stop her from feeling the pain of not being good enough, not being woman enough to merit male attention?

She looked round the room, desperate to find something she could focus on that would enable her to avoid dealing with what was happening to her. The room must have been remodelled at some stage, because its Baroque decor belonged to a later age than the *palazzo* itself. The softly painted grey-blue wooden panelling was decorated with gilded swags and cupids, and heraldic arms were carved into the imposing bedhead. Her bathroom contained a huge claw-footed bath, in addition to a more modern shower, and the room's walls were tiled in marble.

She heard someone knock on the bedroom door

and, assuming it was the maid coming to collect her untouched breakfast tray, went to open the door for her—only to discover that the person standing outside the door was not a maid, but Raphael. As he stepped into the room and closed the door behind him Charley saw that he was carrying a large, not very deep square box, stamped with an international delivery service's label, beneath his arm.

'Are you still in pain?' he asked. 'Dr Scarlarti has left with me some more medication if that is the case.'

Charley wasn't a fan of taking any kind of medication unless it was strictly necessary, so she shook her head, answering him truthfully, 'The skin is still slightly sore, but no more than that.'

The fact that he was in her room fully dressed, whilst she was wearing little more than a vest top and a pair of shorts not intended for public view, was making her feel far more uncomfortable than the burn on her leg. Raphael, on the other hand, looked perfectly at ease—but then Charley suspected he was far more used to being in a bedroom with a member of the opposite sex than she was. Just looking at him was enough to tell her that he was a sexually experienced man who must have shared his life and his bed with any number of willing women.

She gave an involuntary glance towards the bed, where Raphael had deposited the box he had been carrying, unable to stop her imagination from providing her with an image of him on a wide double bed, with the woman he had just pleasured lying in his arms. Her body had started to ache with heavy, sensual longing, and a pulse was beginning to beat low down in her body. A fierce stab of envy whipped through her. Somehow she managed to drag her gaze away from the bed, but looking at Raphael wasn't doing anything to banish either her inappropriate thoughts or the desire they were causing—far from it. How could she be experiencing something like this? It was humiliating—and dangerous.

It took Raphael's crisp, 'Why haven't you eaten your breakfast?' to bring her back to reality, turning her aching desire into prickly defensiveness.

'I wasn't hungry,' she told him.

'We've got a busy day ahead of us, and several acres of abandoned pleasure garden to walk through, provided your leg isn't causing you any pain, and that's something you won't be able to do on an empty stomach. I'll tell Anna to send up a fresh breakfast for you, and then you can meet me downstairs in say an hour's time.'

'I'll have to ask Anna if she can find me something to wear first,' she pointed out.

'That won't be necessary.'

'I can't go out like this,' Charley protested, and then wished she had not as her words caused him to give a probing, prolonged look at her legs. It made her quake inwardly in recognition of how much and how foolishly one part of her wondered what it would be like to have that probing look transformed to one of slow, sensual exploration, followed by the even more sensual stroke of his touch against her skin. Such dangerous, reckless thoughts were not to be encouraged.

'No,' he agreed, coming towards her, causing her to move back and then stop when she realised that she couldn't back up any further because the backs of her legs were already pressed against the bed.

When Raphael stood in front of her and leaned towards her Charley sank down onto the bed, her heart thudding with a mixture of expectation and apprehension, her gaze fixed on the second button of his shirt, not daring to move either up to the tanned bare flesh above it or down to the waistband of his jeans below it. He was reaching towards her—no, not towards her but past her, Charley recognised, dragging her gaze from his chest to his arm just in time to see him retrieving the package he had dropped on the bed earlier.

Mortified by her own misinterpretation of the situation, Charley scrambled to her feet.

'I took the precaution of ordering these for you,' Raphael was telling her impersonally, handing her the box. 'Hopefully they will fit.'

He was obviously waiting for her to open the parcel—so, turning her back to him as she placed the box back down on the bed, Charley proceeded to do so.

The first thing she noticed once she had removed the carrier's cardboard wrapping was that the elegant black box inside it was stamped in gold with the name of a world-renowned fashion designer. Her heart sank. How on earth was she going to pay for designer jeans?

Uncertainly she opened the box, her anxiety deepening when she realised that the tissue layers inside it didn't just contain a pair of jeans. There was also a tee shirt and what looked like a butter-soft, fashionably shaped tan leather jacket.

Dropping the lid back on the box, Charley turned to confront Raphael.

'I can't possibly wear these clothes,' she told him flatly. 'It's…it's kind of you to have thought of replacing my jeans, but these things…' She gestured helplessly towards the box, embarrassment burning her face. 'They're way outside my price range,' she was forced to tell him. 'I couldn't afford—'

'There is no question of you having to pay for them,' Raphael interrupted.

'What?' Charley was too overwrought to conceal her feelings. 'I can't let you buy clothes for me. It wouldn't be right.'

Raphael crossed his arms and gave her a haughty look of arrogant disdain.

'Where my affairs are concerned, I am the one who says what is and what is not right. I do not intend to waste time in resolving the issue of your tender pride whilst you wait for a member of my staff to source a pair of jeans for you. You will wear the clothes which I have provided. If wearing them is so offensive to you that you do not wish to keep them, when you return to England you may send them back to me—or give them to a charity.'

Charley tried to withstand the look he was giving her, but it was her gaze that fell away first, even though she managed to muster the determination to tell him, 'The jeans look smaller than my normal size. I don't think they will fit me.'

'On the contrary—they will be a perfect fit,' Raphael told her.

He was so arrogant, so sure of himself, so sure that he was right that Charley had what she knew was a childish urge to puncture that self-confidence.

'You can't possibly know that—even if you checked the size of my own jeans.' Designers were, after all, notorious for making their clothes smaller than those of less expensive manufacturers.

To her shock, instead of backing down Raphael gave her an even more haughty look and told her, 'I didn't need to check your jeans to assess what size you would need. I am a man, and despite the fact that you choose to inflict on your body clothes that smother it instead of enhancing it I am perfectly able to assess the shape and proportions of what lies beneath them.'

What was he saying? That he could see through her clothes to the body she had always been so anxious to protect from male appraisal and criticism? Flustered and defensive, Charley argued fiercely, 'That's not possible.'

Before she could stop him Raphael had taken hold of her—one hand holding her arm and preventing her escape, the other resting on her waist. Charley sucked in her breath. Why hadn't she thought to wear the towelling robe hanging up in her bathroom? Why hadn't she checked who was knocking on the door of her bedroom? Why had fate allowed her to be trapped in this untenable situation? Her heart was hammering into her ribs, tingles of awareness shooting to every part of her body from the pressure of Raphael's hand on her waist.

'From the span of my hand against the curve of your waist I can tell that your waist can't be much more than twenty-two inches,' he announced matter-of-factly.

A swift spasm of shocked recognition at his accuracy shook Charley's body—or was it the fact that Raphael's fingertip was moving in a straight line down over her still tensed stomach, causing rivulets of unwanted sensation to run from his touch with faster gathering force the lower his fingertip moved. Like lava from a long-suppressed volcano, they gathered speed and spread out, overwhelming the opposition of her tightened muscles and sending their message of aching arousal deep into her body. Surely it was only her own wanton imagination that was telling her that he had momentarily flattened the whole of his hand against her body, so that the heel of his palm momentarily pressed hard against the vulnerable flesh surmounting her sex? Shame, guilt and fear surged through her. How pitiful she was for actually thinking what she was thinking. She could understand why her body would be aroused by Raphael's touch, but how on earth could she imagine that he might want her?

Raphael was now drawing a line out to her hip bone and telling her coolly, 'Your hip measurement is approximately thirty-four inches.'

'Thirty-four and a half, actually.' Charley managed to find the courage to correct him.

'Which is still too narrow for your height.'

'Which you can also assess, no doubt?' Charley couldn't stop herself from snapping.

'Certainly,' Raphael agreed, releasing her arm to

step close to her and turn her round, holding her against his own body and directing her attention to the full-length mirror in front of her.

'I am six foot three, which means that you are around five foot nine—and you have long legs, in proportion to your height.' His hand brushed the top of her bare thigh, causing her to grit her teeth to control the shudder that gripped her.

Charley was beyond telling him that in fact she was five nine and a quarter. She was beyond doing anything other than staring with growing horror at the sharp peaking of her nipples beneath her thin top, the erotic contrast between their erect, eager stiffness and the swell and softness of her breasts filling her with humiliation.

'What I cannot understand,' Raphael continued as she battled to force herself to concentrate on what he was saying and not what his touch was doing to her, 'is why a woman—any woman—should want to conceal the beauty of the perfect form that nature has bestowed upon her with such ugly, concealing clothes.'

Distracted from her humiliation by the unexpectedness of his words, Charley struggled to assimilate them. Raphael was praising her body? Describing it as perfect? The body she had always felt so inferior? Her heart thudded against her ribs, making her dizzy with emotion. But wasn't it more likely that he had simply meant that the female form in general was beautiful and perfect, rather than meaning her body in particular?

Shakily, Charley tried to pull herself away from

him and turn round at the same time, but somehow all she managed to do was turn so that now she was face to face as well as body to body with Raphael, whilst his hands still held her hips. Automatically she looked up at him, her ability to breathe stifled by the way his probing gaze fastened on her mouth and stayed there. Immediately, as though commanded to do so, her lips parted, her breath coming quickly and urgently, lifting her chest in small unsteady movements. What would she do if he kissed her? She could feel his hands tightening against her body. What would it feel like to have them caressing her? Her whole body jolted as though it had received an electric shock so strong was its reaction to her own thoughts. She wanted to lean into him and offer herself to him. She wanted to curl her hand behind his head and bring his mouth down to her own. She wanted to feel his touch against her bare skin… She wanted…

Abruptly Raphael released her, and stepped back from her, leaving Charley to tell herself that she was glad that he had brought an end to her reckless and unwanted imaginings.

'Very well, then,' she told him, struggling for normality. 'I'll wear the jeans, but that's all. I don't need the jacket.'

Raphael had stepped into the shadow of the window and she couldn't see his expression properly.

'It is over two hundred years since the garden fell into disrepair,' he told her coolly. 'Many parts of it are thick with overgrown plants. You will need the jacket to protect you from thorns. Now, I shall expect you to be downstairs and ready to accompany me to the garden in one hour's time. Is that understood?'

Reluctantly Charley nodded her head.

As he walked down the corridor from Charlotte's bedroom there was only one image in Raphael's head, and one thought on his mind. The trouble was that the image and the thought were at war with one another. The image was that of Charlotte standing looking at him with defiant pride, her breasts rising and falling with the force of her emotions, her long legs going on for ever, making him ache to have them wrapped around his own body as the two of them lay together on the bed, her naked flesh warm and soft to his touch, her hands on his body, her mouth opening to his as he gave in to the aching need of his desire for her—a desire that in his imagination she shared and matched. He had never wanted a woman so much nor so illogically. Logically there was nothing about her that should have appealed to him—not physically, nor mentally, nor in any other way. His taste ran to soignée, elegant and mature women in their thirties, like him— women of the world, not fiercely passionate young women who dressed in ill-fitting clothes and upset and undermined a project of great personal importance to him. His mind told him that he should not want her, but his body told him equally powerfully that it did. In this instance, with something as important to him as the renovation of the garden at stake, it was what his mind was telling him that mattered, and it was on what his mind was telling him that he intended to focus.

* * *

Charley walked slowly over to the mirror and studied her reflection. Tentatively she touched her waist, and then, driven by an impulse she couldn't control, she pulled off her clothes. She couldn't remember the last time she had looked at her own naked body. How would she, when she normally avoided looking at it? It must be the sunlight that was giving her skin that soft glow, that sheen that said it wanted to be touched and admired. She lifted her own hand to her body, touching it as and where Raphael had done, trying to see it with his eyes, and then tensing. What was she doing? Wasn't the situation difficult enough for her already, without her adding even more potential discomfort to it?

She looked at the bedroom door, reminding herself that she didn't have much time to get downstairs if she was to keep to the schedule Raphael had given her.

Ten minutes later Charley looked down at the jeans she was wearing. They were a perfect fit—a far better fit and a far better cut than the ones she had been wearing, their slim shape emphasising the length of her legs and clinging to her hips.

She was also wearing the new tee shirt and the leather jacket, its fabric soft against her fingertips. When she'd looked at herself in the bedroom's full-length mirror she'd been caught off guard by the difference the new clothes made to her appearance. Even the hair clouding round her face looked different. Her reflection was more feminine somehow—but of course that was impossible. She was seeing what she wanted to see because of the way she felt about Raphael. Because, foolishly and dangerously, she wanted him.

Angry with herself, she used the dark brown ribbon that had been wrapped round the tissue-folded clothes to tie back her hair. She couldn't stay up here any longer. If she did Raphael might come and look for her—or was that what she secretly wanted? No! Grabbing her shoulder bag, she headed for the door.

Almost the second she stepped off the final marble stair and into the hallway the door to Raphael's office opened and he came out, acknowledging her presence with the briefest nod before heading for the open double doors through which the sunlight was streaming.

What had she been expecting? Charley asked herself as she lengthened her own stride to follow him. That he would make a comment about the way she looked? A flattering comment? She was far too sensible for that kind of silliness, and the slightly leaden feeling inside her chest cavity was not disappointment, but merely the effect of eating a cold croissant, Charley told herself firmly.

Raphael had already reached the Ferrari, and was holding open the passenger door for her, closing it firmly once she was in the passenger seat without having looked directly at her or even spoken to her.

She felt the car depress slightly as Raphael got in and started up the engine. The warmth of the sun had released the scent of the leather interior, along with a more subtle scent which her senses recognised as belonging to Raphael.

It didn't take them long to reach the outskirts of the town. The ruins of a medieval castle and its curtain wall, the ancient stone painted soft rose by the sun as they approached it across a flat agricultural plain filled with crops and livestock, were etched against the skyline. A single tower, ruined and roofless, pointed up towards the clouds.

'What happened to the castle?' Charley couldn't resist asking Raphael.

'It and the town were attacked and put under siege by a more powerful force than my ancestor had at his command. Fortunately he had friends who came to his aid and drove the attackers back, saving the town and the lives of my ancestors, but not the castle. It was as a result of that attack that the then duke decided to build a new home for himself, away from the town.'

Charley nodded her head as they drove into the town through an arched gateway in the medieval wall.

Ancient buildings leaned into one another as though for support on either side of the narrow cobbled street, and splashes of sunshine where it was intersected by another street turned the paving soft gold. High above their heads Charley could see lines of washing, and here and there a heavy wooden door was open to reveal a glimpse of a private courtyard basking in the sunlight.

She could smell fresh-baked bread, olive oil and herbs coming from the baskets of a group of elderly women dressed in black with faces seamed like walnuts, standing talking outside what was obviously a bakers, and then they were out of the narrow street and in the town square—the Piazza Grande.

In the centre of the square was an ornate fountain, and opposite the town hall there was what was obviously a market area, although there were no stalls on it today, so that she had a clear view of the pedestal topped by a life-size statue of an eagle.

'The eagle is part of our family emblem,' Raphael told her, following the direction of her glance. 'There is a legend that our land here in Tuscany was originally given to a Roman legionnaire who fought for Caesar and saved his life. This ancestor then adopted the Imperial Eagle from his legion's standard into his personal arms.'

Charley tried not to look as entranced as she felt. Imagine having that kind of lore as part of your personal family history. Had the mother Raphael had lost taken him on her lap and told him stories about his family's past? An ache of sadness filled her as she thought of her own childhood. It had been such a terrible time for them all when their parents had died— especially when they had learned that the lovely vicarage in which they had been brought up was heavily mortgaged, and that their parents had no savings nor any life insurance which might have eased their orphaned daughters' financial position.

The traffic had cleared and they were now travelling down another narrow street, and then through another archway in the town's wall. Charley gripped the sides of her seat as Raphael changed gear and the sports car surged forward.

The hard look he gave her derided her timidity as he told her, 'I don't know what kind of men you normally share a car with, but I can assure you that I am not the kind of driver who over-estimates his skill or takes foolish risks.'

'I'm not used to such a powerful car.' Or such a powerful man? Charley looked away from Raphael's face, only to realise that her gaze was slipping helplessly over the tanned flesh to his wrist as he manoeuvred the gear lever. Her foolish imagination was painting vivid images inside her head of Raphael's hand on her body. A surge of self-conscious heat burned through her. Why was he able to have such an effect on her? It had never happened before with any other man, and she didn't want it happening now. She could all too easily picture the mixture of arrogant disdain and mockery with which he would look at her if he knew what she was feeling. Her, a clumsy, unfeminine woman, untutored in the arts of feminine seduction, ill equipped to please a man of his undoubted experience? He would no doubt reject her desire for him with haughty contempt.

She had been so preoccupied with her own thoughts that it took her several seconds to realise that the car was slowing down and they had reached the entrance to the garden.

Charley looked at the dilapidated double colonnade that marked the entrance. Most of its columns were either missing or damaged, and over the top of it there was a tangle of overgrown wild vines on which the leaves were just beginning to open in the spring sunshine.

Silently Charley got out of the Ferrari when Raphael opened the door for her. Now, having seen the original drawings, she could well understand why

Raphael wanted to see the garden restored to its original glory.

'This way,' Raphael instructed, producing the key to unlock the bolts that secured the heavy wood doors.

CHAPTER FIVE

CHARLEY had seen the garden before, of course, but then Raphael hadn't been with her, she acknowledged nearly two hours later. She stood almost knee-deep in a tangle of undergrowth and weeds in the middle of what, according to the original plans, had once been a beautiful parterre garden, with neatly clipped borders and central features of cherubs playing musical instruments mounted on classically inspired plinths.

Standing here, in the middle of this ruined paradise, Charley was filled with sadness for the loss of so much beauty, and a yearning to do everything she could to restore it to what it should have been.

'There was a fountain here, according to the original designs, connected to the ornamental lake by a system of formal waterways and canals. If I remember correctly, your renovations called for the lake to be filled in.'

Raphael's comment brought her back to reality.

'It's filled with rubbish and leaking. It would cost nearly as much again as the town council had allowed for the entire renovation just to restore the lake and to put in the safeguards that modern laws demand,' she pointed out.

'It is my wish that everything will now be restored to match the original design—and that includes the lake.'

Raphael heard Charley sigh, and saw her look across the tangled mass of overgrowth and damaged masonry in the direction of the lake, now hidden from view.

'You do not agree with me, I take it?' Raphael demanded.

Charley turned towards him in astonishment.

'On the contrary—I can't think of anything that would be more rewarding than to see this place become once again what it was. It's a project anyone would give their eye teeth to be involved in…bringing to life something so wonderful.' Emotional tears momentarily blurred Charley's vision, as her feelings got the better of her. 'The people of the town are fortunate to have you to do something so generous, and I…I feel that I am fortunate too, to be a part of such a project,' she admitted.

Now it was Raphael's turn to look away from her. Her honesty surprised him. He hadn't been expecting it, and nor had he been expecting her open emotional reaction to the garden. Perhaps, after all, he did have the right person to manage the project—a person who had just shown him that she was capable of being touched to the deepest part of herself by what had once been and what was now lost. Such a person would give everything she had to give to a project that engaged her emotions. And to the man who engaged them as well?

Charlotte Wareham's sexual passions were hers to give to whomsoever she chose and no concern of his, Raphael reminded himself. It was as a project manager that he was interested in her, and not as a bedmate.

'If you're serious about the lake—' Charley began, breaking into the silence.

'I am.'

'My guess is that the restoration work will require the advice of proper experts who have experience in that kind of work. There is a team booked to come in and start clearing all the mess away, but I don't think they will be the right people to deal with the lake. It might be best to get in touch with... Well, in England I'd probably try English Heritage or the National Trust. Any organisation with artistic appreciation, that believes in the importance of preserving the heritage we've been left by artists of the past, couldn't help but want to be part of a project like this one. It would have been a dream come true for me when I was studying Fine Art.'

She was intelligent, and proactive, but above all her passion for the project was so strong that it shone from her eyes and could be heard in her voice. Why on earth would a woman who felt as she so obviously did give up her Fine Arts degree to study accountancy, and then take a job that involved her in projects calling for the appalling replicas he had seen her with? Raphael wondered, his probing mind curious against his better judgement. There was something here that didn't add up. His curiosity aroused, Raphael decided to put his suspicions to the test.

'Feeling as you so obviously do, it must have been

hard for you to give up your Fine Arts course?' he began, deliberately making his question sound casual.

Still wrapped in the emotions the garden had evoked, and in the understanding and harmony they had shared, Charley forgot to be on her guard, and responded without thinking.

'Yes, it was.'

She was shocked back to reality when Raphael asked, 'Then why did you?'

His question made her suddenly aware of the foolish relaxation of her guard, and she was doubly a fool for having let him see just how much the garden had affected her.

'You don't answer? Why not, I wonder? Is it perhaps because there is something you wish to hide? Perhaps it was not so much that you decided to change to another course, but that you were requested to do so by your tutors.'

Stung by Raphael's subtle allegation that she had had to drop her course because she had not been good enough, Charley told him fiercely, 'No. It was nothing like that.'

'Then what *was* it like? You are in effect now working under my command. I have a right to ask this question and to receive a truthful answer,' Raphael pressed.

Charley lifted her hands in a gesture of defeat.

'Very well then. If you must know, I applied for the course without telling my family what I was going to be studying. They thought… That is to say I really wanted to do an arts degree and study Fine Arts, but I knew my father would laugh at me, and say that I was far too much of a clumsy tomboy to be allowed anywhere near fine art. My sisters are both so pretty, and so feminine; I am the plain, awkward one of the family. I knew that for my own sake my father would try to persuade me to study something else—something more practical.'

Charley gave a small sigh, whilst Raphael digested her words in silence. He would certainly not have described Charley as either awkward or plain. It was true that hers was not the chocolate box variety of 'pretty', but in Raphael's estimation Charley possessed something far more potent. His body certainly thought so, from the way it responded to the delicate air of hidden sensuality she carried with her.

'But I was offered the course so they let me do it. I was less than a year into it when our parents were killed. Then we found out there was no money and that the house, our childhood home, was heavily mortgaged and would have to be sold. Lizzie, my elder sister, was working in London at the time for a top-notch interior designer, and then Ruby told us that she was pregnant. She was only seventeen. Lizzie and I both felt so guilty; she was practically still a baby herself. We had to do something. We couldn't just abandon Ruby and her babies as the babies' father had, so Lizzie moved back to Cheshire and set up her own small business, and...'

'And you decided to sacrifice your own plans in order to earn money to help support your family?'

'It wasn't a sacrifice,' Charley protested immediately. 'We wanted to stay together and support one another.'

'Maybe it wasn't a sacrifice then, but I think you feel that it is now,' Raphael corrected her. 'I think that now, here in Italy, you have become aware of all you have denied yourself.'

Charley couldn't look at him. Was it just her plans to take a Fine Arts degree and all that went with it to which he was referring? Or had he guessed about the other things she had denied herself—things like being free to be herself, and not the family tomboy, to explore and enjoy her sexuality as that self? She hoped not. That would be too humiliating for her to bear.

'Being in Italy has made me realise how much I would have enjoyed studying art,' she admitted in a stifled voice, unable to look at him as she did so. 'And of course the recession has changed things. Before it happened I told myself that if my job got too unbearable I could always leave and find another one, and that maybe one day I'd get the opportunity to study and travel, but now of course that's impossible. I do wish—' She stopped and shook her head. 'There's no point in talking about what one can't have, and I am very grateful to you for giving me the opportunity to work on something so very special.'

Inwardly Charley cursed herself. She had done it again—admitting that she was grateful to him, humbling and even humiliating herself, making herself far too vulnerable by her tacit admission that she so desperately wanted to be part of the renovation project. Maybe so, but at least she had been true to herself and to her own code, Charley comforted herself. She couldn't pretend that she had no wish to be involved in the project to renovate the garden when the exact opposite was the case.

Raphael turned away from Charley, not wanting her to see in his expression the feelings he didn't even want to acknowledge to himself. Her speech, her gratitude, the fact that her emotions about the garden were so in accord with his own, had rubbed against a vulnerable place within himself—a wound only half healed that he had believed until now was fully healed. Beneath the thin skin that covered that wound lay emotions and regrets so painful and dark that he could not bear to admit they were there. A whole adult lifetime dedicated to pretending that such a wound did not exist was now in danger of being ripped aside to reveal the truth. But that truth could not be acknowledged. He must adhere to the course he had set himself. He must not waver. Inwardly Raphael cursed Charley for the effect she was having on him, and damned himself for even thinking of weakening.

Raphael's silence made Charley feel anxious. Something had changed. She could almost feel the coldness now emanating from him, replacing what had previously been close to a shared openness about the importance of the garden. Now that was gone, and when Raphael swung back towards her, his expression shielded by the shadows, his voice was hard with warning as he told her, 'According to your project notes, you've allowed three months for clearing the site.'

Charley nodded her head.

'I want to see that work done in two months, not three.'

'That can't be done,' Charley protested. The intimacy they had shared earlier was over, she recognised, and Raphael was once again a man who was making it plain exactly how he felt about her and her ability to do the job he would no doubt have preferred to give to someone else.

'Anything can be done if one goes about it in the right way.' And that included finding a way to stop his senses from being so aware of her and his body from aching for her, Raphael reminded himself inwardly. 'As I have already told you,' he informed Charley, 'I expect my orders to be followed and carried out. There is no room on this project for a project manager who cannot achieve what needs to be achieved. If you feel you cannot do that…'

He was challenging her—setting her targets that could not be achieved because he wanted to get rid of her.

Well, she would show him.

'Very well,' she told him. 'But it will be expensive.' Now she was the one challenging him—to pay up or back down.

'Half as much again as you have already allowed for the cost of bringing in the extra manpower, but worth it for what it will save in time,' Raphael agreed with a dismissive shrug, before adding warningly, 'However, what is in question is not whether or not I am prepared to incur additional costs where I think it necessary but whether—or not—you are up to the task of managing this project.'

Charley had had enough. What had happened to their earlier harmony and the belief she had had then that he was prepared to give her a chance? They shared a recognition of just what the garden must once have been. Or had she just imagined it? Because she had wanted to connect emotionally with him? Charley's heart thudded into her ribs. That was nonsense. He meant nothing to her. It was the job that was important. Nothing else.

Was it? So why was she feeling so hurt and rejected, so sharply reminded of the way she had so often felt as a child, when her parents had compared her looks unfavourably to those of her sisters, making her aware that she was not good enough and that they wished that she was different—just as Raphael obviously didn't feel that she was good enough, and wished that the project was being managed by someone else.

It was such a blow after the intimacy and understanding she felt they had shared that Charley couldn't stop herself from bursting out, 'You want to get rid of me, don't you? You want me to fail. You want to bully me into saying I can't cope, just as my boss wants to bully me into handing in my resignation so that he can give my job to his daughter. Well, much as I'd love to oblige you both, and set myself free from the necessity of having to put up with you, I can't and I won't. I need this job, and I need it because, as I have already told you, without the money I earn from it my sisters and I could lose our home. Because of that I will manage this project successfully—no matter how hard you try to push me into leaving.'

Raphael turned away from her again. He was loath to admit it, but there was an element of truth in her accusation that he wanted to get rid of her. And not just because he doubted her ability to handle the project successfully. No, it was the effect she was having on him physically as a man that was the prime cause of his desire to get her out of his life. Raphael wasn't used to his body, his senses, challenging the rules he had made for the way he lived his life. The reality was that they had never done so before, and certainly not to the extent they were now—invading his thoughts and his judgement with their increasingly intense demands.

'There are other jobs,' he told Charley unsympathetically.

Charley looked at him in disbelief, and then shook her head.

'I don't know what world you live in,' she told him scornfully, 'but it isn't the real world. There's a recession on—but of course that won't affect people like you. Thousands of people are out of work, and thousands more—of which I am one—are living in fear of losing their job. If that wasn't the case do you think I would stay in this one?'

Now she had done it, Charley thought miserably, her anger giving way to anxiety as she recognised how outspoken she had been.

'I can manage this project successfully,' she told Raphael. 'And I *will* manage it successfully.'

The earlier harmony she had felt they shared had been nothing more than an illusion, Charley told herself bitterly—a trick and a trap into which she had fallen by allowing Raphael to get under her guard. Too late to regret now the information she had given him about herself; too late to tell herself that she should never have listened to her senses and her body instead of her head, when they had whispered excitedly to her of their reaction to Raphael. Her head knew perfectly well that there could be no intimacy—of any kind—between her and Raphael, no matter what her foolish senses might have wanted to believe. All she could do was make sure that she didn't make the same mistake again.

The garden covered several acres, and there were parts of it—like the part they were in now—that Charley hadn't seen on her earlier visit because access to them was so overgrown.

Striding ahead of her, Raphael had come to a halt outside the ruins of what had once been a pretty garden temple.

'Down here there is something I particularly want to discuss with you,' he told her, indicating a set of steps that led downwards to a heavy wooden door. 'But take care on the steps—they are damaged and slippery.'

Charley hesitated. She didn't like underground places—never had done since she had been accidentally locked in the vicarage's cellar as a child. But she knew she couldn't refuse without making a fool of herself and showing a vulnerability she did not want Raphael to see, so she followed Raphael down the stone steps, trying to control her reluctance and anxiety as he unlocked the door.

Just the sound of it creaking back on its hinges when Raphael pushed it open was enough to increase Charley's apprehension.

'Down here is the chamber containing the mechanism for the fountains. I've had someone looking at it, and it's still working, although the fountains and sprinklers themselves need repairing and restoring. Once they are in working order again they should prove a tremendous draw for visitors. One of the things I want to do—the only modernisation of the gardens I will permit—is the addition of lighting. The cabling for that will need to be put in at an early stage, and you will need to make arrangements for that.'

Charley nodded her head. He was quite right that specially designed lighting would enhance the garden.

'It is my intention that the money brought in via future visitors to the garden will go directly to the town, for the benefit of its people—especially the young people, to provide them with the opportunity to learn new skills. There is no industry here, no work for the young, and without them the town will eventually die.'

His altruistic plans surprised Charley. They seemed at odds with her own judgement of him—or was it just *her* he felt didn't deserve to earn a living?

Charley was just about to respond when she saw a small shadow flit past her out of the corner of her eye, followed by another.

'What…?' she began anxiously, but Raphael anticipated her.

'It is nothing to worry about,' he told her casually. 'It is only bats. They have made a home here. If you come down here and look closely you can see them hanging up in the roof. We've obviously disturbed them.'

Look closely? Charley shook her head, and then

whirled round as another bat flew past her, losing her balance on the crumbling stone as she did so.

Raphael must have moved quickly, because he had been several feet away from her when she had slipped and now he was holding her.

The bats were forgotten. All Charley could think about was her proximity to Raphael. Her heart was thudding into her ribs with a mixture of forbidden excitement and longing. She must not feel like this, she warned herself. She must not raise her head and look at him. She must not let her gaze rest yearningly on his mouth. She must not let her heart thud with anticipation and longing whilst she looked up into his eyes, her own eyes telling him what she most wanted.

She must not, but she was.

This was not what he should be doing, Raphael knew, but his hard grip on Charley's upper arms still softened into a hold that was more a caress, the pads of his fingertips smoothing the soft leather against her skin. He could see the pulse beating frantically in her throat, inciting him to capture it with his lips and then trace his way up to her mouth. He'd already lifted his hand, preparatory to cupping her face so that he could hold her still beneath his kiss. What harm would one kiss do? At least then he would know.

Know what? That he wanted her? He didn't need to kiss her to discover that.

Raphael was going to kiss her! Charley leaned helplessly towards him, and then stopped when he released her abruptly, almost thrusting her away from him.

'I thought you said that your leg was fine,' he said

angrily. 'If you are still having a problem with it you should have said so. The last thing I want is to have—'

'To carry me out of here?' Charley stopped him. She was shamefully close to tears, foolishly hurt by his anger and his lack of understanding. 'Well, you needn't worry. There's nothing wrong with my leg. The bats made me stumble, that's all.'

Carry her? The savage surge of physical reaction hardening his body at the thought of holding her in his arms increased Raphael's fury—not against Charley but against himself. He could feel it burning through him, beating at the defences of his self-control: anger against himself for not recognising that she might be in pain; anger against himself for wanting her; anger against the strictures placed upon him because of what and who he was, forbidding him from living as other men did. Anger, but not rage. Not that feeling he had sworn he would never allow to possess him ever again—that wall of savagery that had once risen up inside him, sweeping over him like a red mist, obliterating reason and humanity, possessing him with its violence, forcing him to accept the cursed reality of what he had inherited, the reality of what he was.

That feeling, experienced once and never forgotten by him, was his dark shadow—always with him, always reminding him, a warning of what might lie ahead of him in his future if it wasn't controlled. And who could say that it always would be? Who could say that it wouldn't grow and take over like some progressive disease? Like the form of madness that it was? So that he ended up not only risking passing on his own tainted inheritance to a future generation but also, in the grip of his own madness, destroying those he should most protect.

Images he had kept locked away burst past the doors he had closed against them. His mother's pretty sitting room, its air carrying her scent, the sunlight falling on the petit point that was her favourite hobby laid down on a small table, the chair on which she always sat whilst doing it beside the table.

Like a film inside his head Raphael could see himself reaching for that chair in a fit of anger—of madness—and then hurling it against the marble fireplace with such force that it had lain broken and splintered, its red silk seat covering resembling a pool of blood against the white marble.

No! The denial, silent and agonising, was wrung from deep inside of him, but Raphael knew that no amount of regret could take back what he had done in the savagery of his rage against his mother—the person who had loved him so very much and who had least deserved that rage. For the rest of his life he must be on his guard against that rage—against that madness ever possessing him again—and that meant controlling his emotions, not allowing himself to get close emotionally to anyone—for their own sake and protection.

CHAPTER SIX

IT WAS no use. She could mentally castigate herself as much as she liked for being too vulnerable to her emotions when she should have been listening to her head. Raphael was not someone she could afford to let her guard down around, Charley warned herself as she paused in front of the portraits of Raphael's parents—painted just after their marriage, so Anna had told her when she had asked about them.

She looked up at the portrait of Raphael's mother, dark-haired like her son, and dark-eyed like the husband whose portrait she was turning towards. What had struck Charley the first time she had seen the portraits was the shining happiness in Raphael's mother's eyes as she looked towards her husband, and the tenderness with which he looked back at her.

They had been very much in love, Anna had told her, the young Duchess having fallen in love with the twenty-two-year-old Duke at her own fourteenth birthday party, swearing that she would marry no one else. Witnessing now that look of shining love, and knowing of the grief that had driven her to take her own life after her husband's death, touched Charley's own emotions. Poor lady. And poor Raphael too? After all, he had lost his parents as she had lost hers, and at a much younger and more vulnerable age. She shrugged the thought away. She did not want to feel sorry for Raphael. She did not want to feel anything for him at all. Charley's heart started to beat unsteadily as she tried to deny what her body was telling her—that it was already too late for her to tell herself that.

She had spent the morning exchanging e-mails with the contractors who were to clear the site. It had taken some hard bargaining on her part to secure their agreement to do the extra work in the timescale Raphael had stipulated, and at a cost that was not excessive. She had also sourced three contenders for the lighting Raphael wanted installed, sending them copies of the original plans and asking for their suggestions for effective lighting and projected costs.

Raphael had sent for her, and no doubt he would want to know exactly how much progress she had made. Apprehensively and reluctantly, Charley knocked on the door to Raphael's office and then pushed it open.

'You wanted to see me?'

'Yes,' Raphael confirmed. 'I've been in touch with someone I know in Florence—a member of a committee responsible for the maintenance of some of the city's most historic buildings. He has supplied me with the contact details for both a landscape architect and the head of Florence's most prestigious academy for craftsmen. Men and women who study there learn the skills of traditional arts. My contact tells me that this is where we will find the very best sculptors to recreate the garden's ornaments. First, though, we shall need to convince Niccolo Volpari, who runs the school, that our project is worthy of his students.'

'That sounds excellent. If you give me his e-mail address I'll get in touch with him and arrange for him to come out and see the garden.'

Raphael shook his head.

'This is a very important and a very busy man. We will have to go to Florence to see him, not the other way around. The decision as to whether or not he will accept us onto his list of clients will be his and not ours,' he repeated. 'It is from the academy that the city of Florence finds sculptors and painters, gilders and carvers, stonemasons and master builders when any restoration work needs to be undertaken. It is Niccolo's teachers who will examine what is left of the garden's ornaments and then recommend the pupil who will replicate the damaged pieces.'

Raphael got up from behind his desk and walked towards the window. Charley watched him, her glance clinging to the broad span of his shoulders and the way his body tapered down to his hips. His shirt, which was no doubt handmade and expensive, somehow delineated the male shape of his body without in any way clinging to it as her avid gaze was doing. Why was it that Italian men, or at least this Italian man, seemed able to wear a pair of chinos in a way that focused female attention on the powerful muscles in his thighs?

The way his muscles moved when he moved filled her female mind with mental images of hard-muscled flesh, and the power it contained, its maleness emphasised by the dark silkiness of body hair.

Charley dragged her gaze away, panicking when it wanted to linger, as she heard Raphael speaking.

'Niccolo Volpari is insisting on seeing both of us. He is known for his eccentricity, apparently, where the projects he takes on are concerned, and I am told by those with whom he works that it would not do to refuse.'

And he had wanted to refuse, Raphael acknowledged—all the more so when he had discovered that members of a convention of Michelangelo admirers from all over the world were currently filling virtually every hotel bedroom in Florence.

'Unfortunately the only time he can see us is for dinner tomorrow evening, which means that we shall have to stay in Florence overnight—Italians do not eat until late in the evening.'

Unfortunately? Charley couldn't think of anything she'd rather do than have the chance to spend time in Florence. She might even be able to snatch enough time to visit its famous market and buy herself an inexpensive change of clothes to supplement the jeans and jacket Raphael had given her and her two tee shirts.

'We shall stay overnight in my Florence apartment.'

Now her excitement had become a complex mix of emotions, some of which were far too dangerous for her to want to question.

'We will leave first thing tomorrow morning. I warn you that my contact tells me that Niccolo Volpari does not suffer fools gladly, and he will have many questions he wants to ask, many tests the project will have to pass before he is satisfied and prepared to recommend that his artistes work on it. Their work is the best of the best, and he boasts that Michelangelo himself would not be able to tell the difference between his own *David* and a copy made by Volpari students. Now, what progress have you made with regard to the restoration of the lake?'

'I've been in touch with English Heritage and the National Trust, and they have given me the names of three Italian-based organisations that have the know-how to take on the project. I've e-mailed all three of them, but as yet I have not received a response. I've also informed the company clearing the site that you now want the work done in two months, and they have agreed to supply an extra team to ensure that that target is met. It will mean floodlighting the whole area, which will add to the cost, and paying overtime. I've got the figures here. I wanted to get your approval of them before I give them the go-ahead.'

Raphael reached the desk just as Charley was placing the papers on it. One of the papers slipped, and as she retrieved it somehow her knuckles inadvertently brushed against the soft fabric stretched against Raphael's thigh. The shock of sensation that burned through her was such that Charley immediately released the papers and withdrew her hand, not daring to look at Raphael, her whole body burning up with discomfort. Why on earth was she behaving like such a gauche fool? Her touch had been accidental, probably not even felt by Raphael, and yet here she was, behaving like a virgin who had found her hand resting unexpectedly on a full-on male erection, instead of an adult woman whose hand had merely brushed accidentally against a piece of fabric.

'I'm always so clumsy,' she heard herself saying apologetically. 'My parents were always telling me that.'

She started to bend down, to retrieve the piece of paper that was now on the floor, but Raphael stopped her, his voice harsh as he instructed, 'No, leave it. I'll look at it later. Right now I have some estate business to deal with, and some phone calls to make, and I am sure that you have work to do also.'

Hot-cheeked, Charley nodded her head and quickly made her escape from his office.

Raphael waited until Charley had gone before he bent down to retrieve the fallen piece of paper, his knuckles showing white through the tan on his skin as he did so. Had he allowed Charley to kneel down and retrieve the paper, as she had plainly intended to do, she would have seen quite plainly his arousal and known the cause of it. What manner of man was he that the mere accidental touch of a woman he desired was enough to breach the defences of his self-control?

Back in her room, Charley tried to concentrate on her work, knowing even as she did so that concentrating on anything other than the fool she had just made of herself was going to be impossible. Inside her head were images of Raphael: the way he stood, the way he moved, the way her imagination stripped the clothes from his body, the way her whole body had trembled when she had touched him. Charley gave a small groan of defeat. Thinking about work was impossible now that she had unleashed the dangerously sensual awareness of Raphael that was building inside her—wildly reckless and foolish thoughts of an intimacy between them that could never happen and that she should not even *want* to happen. But her body did want it to happen, and every day it wanted it to happen a little more. A little more? Didn't she mean an awful lot more? Charley questioned herself. She was like a girl in the grip of an impossible sexual crush on an idol, not a woman who ought to know better. Beneath her tee shirt her nipples peaked and ached on the surge of sexual longing that rushed through her.

Charley groaned again. She must not feel like this. She must not!

CHAPTER SEVEN

FLORENCE and Raphael! Florence with Raphael! Was she really sure that was a good idea? Charley asked herself. But then did she really have any choice? A shiver, half expectation, half dread, but wholly sensual, stroked taunting fingertips down her spine, immediately sending into disarray all the promises she had made herself the previous day about stopping herself from thinking about the effect he had on her sexually. Couldn't her body understand how humiliating it was for her to want a man who had made it plain how little time he had for her? Raphael did not want her in his life in any capacity at all, and he most certainly did not want her in his bed. Her breath caught on a savagely sweet ache of longing, which she had to fight to suppress. Why should Raphael want a woman like her—a woman devoid of beauty and female grace, a woman devoid of sexual expertise and sensual allure? He didn't, and he wouldn't, and if she had any self-respect she would find a way to stop herself from reacting to him in a way that could easily end up with her making a total fool of herself if she ever accidentally betrayed to Raphael himself what had happened to her.

What she should be doing was focusing on the job she had to do.

It wasn't even as though she could blame Raphael for the way she felt, or claim that he was the one who had deliberately made her feel the way she did. The truth was the opposite. Charley had grown up being honest with herself—especially when it came to her own shortcomings and failures. She couldn't blame Raphael for the fact that she was so acutely and intensely susceptible to him. The responsibility for that lay with her, and within her. But it wasn't too late for her to change things. She could draw a line under her vulnerability to him and set herself some new conditions and rules for the way she would permit herself to react to him. First and foremost amongst those rules would be at all times observing a proper professional attitude towards him, maintaining a proper professional distance between them. She could do it. She must do it, Charley told herself as she made her way downstairs. After all she had texted her sisters now, to tell them that she would be staying on in Italy to begin immediate work on the garden restoration, so it was too late to change her mind.

There was no sign of Raphael in the hallway, so whilst she waited for him Charley was free to study the frescoes in more detail, marvelling at the skill of the artist who had painted them. Every expression told its own story about the character who wore it, but it was the expressions on the faces of the three children grouped together that drew Charley. The tallest of them, a boy obviously meant to represent the young heir, had all of Raphael's arrogance and pride in his expression as he stood slightly in front of his mother and brother and sister, his clothes richer than theirs, his gaze fixed on the distant landscape, as though aware that one day those lands would belong to him. To his side, his sister, in her ermine-trimmed gown, was looking to her mother for approval as an envoy dressed in livery kneeled before her, offering her a roll of parchment on a shield—perhaps meant to signify a marriage agreement? Charley wondered. The youngest child, another boy, was seated on his mother's lap, reaching for the gold cross she was wearing. As a second son he might well have been destined for high office in the church, Charlotte recognised.

'The third Duchess with her children.'

The sound of Raphael's voice sent a frisson of forbidden pleasure curling down Charley's spine. Not trusting herself to turn round, she told him, 'The eldest son looks a little like you.'

'He was killed when the castle came under attack from enemy forces. He died defending his mother and his sister.'

Charley shivered. Raphael's words showed her that despite the air of arrogance and superiority the boy carried with him, underneath it he had still been vulnerable. Unlike Raphael, who she was sure would never be vulnerable to anything or anyone.

'You are ready to leave?'

Charley nodded her head, wondering as she followed him out to the waiting Ferrari what had caused the swift frowning look Raphael had given her.

It had rained in the night, and the morning sunshine was filling the air with the rich scent of damp earth and growing things—of life returning to the world after the darkness of winter.

At least now there was no need for her to feel deprived because her stay in Italy would be too brief for her to see all those things she longed to see, Charley told herself. There would be ample time for her to visit its cities and its art galleries, to breathe in its magic and fill her senses with its beauty.

The Ferrari made nothing of the kilometres, each signpost promising that they were getting closer to Florence.

'We shall go first to my apartment,' Raphael announced, 'since we shall be staying there.'

Charley's heart rolled over inside her chest. She didn't trust herself to say anything, but then what could she say? *I don't want to stay in your apartment because I want you and I'm afraid of betraying that to you?* Hardly.

The sound of Raphael's voice cut across her uncomfortable thoughts, giving her a welcome excuse not to dwell on them.

'This evening, as you know, we shall be dining with Niccolo Volpari, Antonio Riccardi, the landscape architect, and their wives.' Another frowningly assessing look, just like the one he had given her earlier when they had left the *palazzo,* raked her from head to toe, leaving her feeling vulnerable but reluctant to demand an explanation.

They had reached the outskirts of the city and were turning off the autostrada, heading for the River Arno.

'The Ponte Vecchio is to your left, beyond the Ponte alle Grazia,' Raphael informed her, as though guessing what was on her mind as they reached the river.

It made Charley feel dizzy to think of the history that lay before her, like a precious jewel waiting to be admired. Now Raphael was driving through a maze of narrow streets with names straight from history, bordered by buildings that had Charley silent with awe. In a small square she saw a sign for the Piazza della Signoria and the Uffizi, and her heart leapt with excitement. People, many of them tourists, Charley suspected, spilled from the pavements into the narrow streets. Car horns sounded, impatient Italian drivers gesturing from open windows, and a crocodile of uniformed schoolchildren caught her eye as the crowds and the traffic spilled out into another square dominated by an ancient church. To their left was the river, but Raphael turned right.

'This is the Via de' Tornabuoni,' he told Charley. 'At the next intersection you will see the Palazzo Strozzi, belonging to the family who once plotted against the Medicis and paid for their crime with banishment.'

The street was lined with imposing buildings, many of them housing designer shops, and the pavement was busy with elegantly clothed women who held themselves with that confidence that Charley thought uniquely continental. Charley was so busy watching one of them stepping out of a store that it took her by surprise when Raphael suddenly turned into a narrow opening between the buildings, guarded by a pair of heavily studded wooden doors. The doors opened automatically, allowing Raphael to drive in, then down a ramp into an underground car park.

'This building was rebuilt in the eighteenth century and originally came into the family via marriage,' he explained to Charley once they were out of the car and standing in a lift. 'It fell into disrepair after my parents' death. I had it restored, but decided to retain only two of its five floors and let out the others.'

The lift had stopped, allowing them to step out of it and into a magnificent eighteenth-century marble hallway, with curved niches containing polished marble busts, and a wrought-iron banister curling upwards with the marble staircase. But where Charley imagined gilt-framed traditional family portraits must have once hung on the staircase wall, the walls now had a distinctly modern air to them, with their dark grey paint and their white-framed black and white photographs of street scenes and buildings. The effect somehow suited the hallway. It certainly spoke of a man who had the confidence and the arrogance to follow his own artistic instincts rather than adopt those of someone else. She couldn't imagine herself having the confidence to impose such a modern style on a traditional building.

'I don't employ any staff here; I use a concierge service instead,' Raphael was informing her. 'I will show you to your room, so that you can leave your things there, and once you have done that I suggest you rejoin me in the living room, which is through that door to the left of us.'

She and Raphael were going to be alone in the apartment? Charley fought to remain composed as she followed Raphael towards the stairs, wide enough for them to climb side by side, thankfully with a good few inches between them.

The room Raphael showed her to was furnished in a French empire style and decorated in soft blue, grey and white. It had, as she discovered once Raphael had left her to 'make herself at home', a huge *en suite* bathroom, with an enormous claw-footed bath and several wall mirrors gilded with swags and cherubs. Charley could easily imagine someone like Napoleon's sister Pauline relaxing in the deep tub as she gloated over her brother's conquest of Italy. Despite its delicate colour scheme, somehow the rooms possessed an air of sensuality that reminded Charley of her own awkwardness. This was a bedroom for a woman confident in her sexuality—a purring, sensual seductress of a woman, who wore silks and satins and spent long, lazy summer afternoons lying in the arms of her lover.

Was this where Raphael brought his lovers? Sophisticated, knowing women who— Quickly Charley clamped down on thoughts she had no right to have, and which were an intrusion on Raphael's privacy that surely shamed her just as much as the betraying ache which had now started to pulse through her lower body. She must not let herself feel like this. She must not and she would not, Charley assured herself as she made her way back downstairs—just in time to see a small plump man stepping out of the lift to shake Raphael's hand.

'Charlotte, your timing is excellent,' Raphael told her. 'Come and meet my friend, Paulo Franchetti. It is Paulo who has acted as go-between for us with Niccolo Volpari.'

Impossible for her to pull away when Raphael reached out to take hold of her arm and draw her towards them.

'*Buongiorno*, Charlotte.' Paulo greeted her with a smile and a handshake.

Fifteen minutes later, after a brief discussion about the garden, Paulo left. Flicking back the cuff of his pale blue shirt, Raphael studied his watch and then told her, 'Soon we shall have some lunch, but first there is something else we have to do.'

Since he was already striding towards the main door to the hallway, plainly expecting her to follow him, there was nothing else Charley could do.

The moment he opened the door bright sunlight streamed in, making Charley blink.

'This way,' Raphael directed her, putting his hand beneath her elbow and taking the outside edge of the pavement. Somehow, almost miraculously, the crowd seemed to part to allow them through, and within a few short yards Raphael came to a halt in front of the plate glass windows of the store of an internationally famous Italian designer of women's clothes.

'You will need a working wardrobe commensurate with your position,' Raphael informed her. 'We may as well deal with that now, whilst we are here in Florence.'

Charley looked at him.

'I have plenty of clothes at home that my sisters can send out to me.'

Raphael raised one eyebrow in a way that made her face burn.

'Let me guess: these clothes that you have at home are dull, plain garments that are two sizes too big for you? *Si?* They will not be suitable for your new role. You will be dealing with artists and craftsmen who value beauty—Italian men,' he emphasised. 'It is vitally important, since you are representing me, that they respect you and recognise that you understand the importance of quality craftsmanship. To the master stonemason the correct drape of fabric against a woman's body is as important to his artistic eye as the correct choosing of a piece of stone, and that applies to all those with whom you will be dealing. In addition to that there will be many occasions on which I shall require you to accompany me to meetings and business dinners. Tonight, for instance, I do not want...'

'Me to show you up with my dull plain clothes?' Charley finished for him. 'Well, in that case I'm surprised you've brought *me* here instead of...of some elegant clotheshorse.'

'Why does the thought of wearing beautiful clothes fill you with such panic? Most women...'

'I am not most women, and it does not fill me with panic,' Charley denied. But of course he was right. She couldn't tell him, though, that she was afraid of beautiful clothes because she knew they would only underline how unworthy she was of wearing them.

'What I was actually going to say,' Raphael continued, 'was that most women would wish to be dressed
appropriately in the company of other women—particularly Italian women, who take a pride in their appearance. You will feel uncomfortable if you are not
comparably clothed.'

No, she wouldn't, Charley wanted to say, because
she knew how unsuited she was to the kind of Italian
elegance to which Raphael was referring.

'You have already agreed to work under my direction
and to abide by my conditions,' Raphael reminded her.

'As project manager, not in telling me what to wear,'
Charley retorted. 'Work clothes for me mean a sturdy
pair of boots and a properly fitting hard hat.' Was that
really pity she could see in Raphael's gaze?

'You shall have those, of course, but I hardly think that
even you would want to dress in such things for dinner.'

His words were a statement and not a question,
Charley recognised, and, much as she would have liked
to argue the point, Raphael was turning away from her,
nodding to the uniformed doorman to open the door
to the store, signalling that any attempt at rebellion on
her part simply would not be tolerated.

Now Raphael's hand under her elbow felt like a
form of imprisonment, but despite everything she
believed about herself, humiliatingly, Charley was
forced to admit that, when the sultry-looking sales assistant who had glided forward cast an assessing
glance over her, she was glad she was wearing good-
quality clothes—even though at the same time she felt
acutely conscious of how badly her looks and lack of

self-confidence at being in this most feminine of female places compared to that of the sales assistant. Not that the sales assistant spent much time in looking at her—she was far too busy looking at Raphael for that, Charley thought acidly. But then an older woman came forward, dismissing the other girl, smiling warmly but professionally at Raphael.

'My assistant is in need of a new wardrobe,' Raphael told the saleswoman. 'She will need everyday clothes, at least two business suits, and cocktail and evening dresses.'

No, Charley wanted to protest, not dresses. She never wore dresses. Her mother had always said that she was too much of a tomboy to wear them, and had laughed at her on the rare occasions when Charley had insisted that she wanted to be dressed like her sisters, telling her, 'Oh, poppet, you can't wear that.' Dresses— indeed all feminine clothes—were Charley's enemy. Just looking at them in shop windows brought her out in a cold sweat of remembered childhood humiliation.

The sales assistant's dark gaze, sent once in Charley's direction, didn't return to her as she nodded her head.

'Please come this way,' she invited them.

Within two minutes they were inside a private trying-on suite, complete with newspapers, magazines and a television, coffee having been ordered for them both.

Charley was then whisked into a luxuriously equipped large changing room, where she was measured by the saleswoman and then allowed to return to the main room of the suite, where Raphael was drinking his coffee whilst studying his BlackBerry.

Two young assistants were summoned and given a volley of instructions in Italian so rapid that Charley couldn't keep up with it, though she strained to catch the dreaded word 'dress' so that she could counteract it.

Swiftly, under the saleswoman's silent eagle-eyed inspection, the clothes rail which had been brought into the room was filled with clothes—beautiful, elegant clothes, in wonderful fabrics and sophisticated colours. Two trouser suits, both black; smartly tailored shorts in black, tan and white; tee shirts and knits; blouses… Charley's panic and dread were increasing with each new item added to the rail.

It was, of course, the evening dress that did it in the end: a swathe of cream silk satin, studded here and there with tiny crystals, the fabric so delicate that it fluttered sensually in the movement from the air-conditioning. Even without having seen it properly Charley knew instinctively that it was a gown designed for a woman who was confident of her own attractiveness—a woman who knew that when people looked at her the looks would be looks of admiration. She could just imagine the humiliation she would suffer if she allowed herself to be forced into such a dress; she would look idiotic, make a laughing stock of herself, the beauty and elegance of the dress simply underlining her own lack of them. The silk dress shimmered in front of her, warning her of the humiliation that was to come—inside her head she could hear her mother's voice, as she stood with Charley and her sisters in the

children's department of Manchester's poshest store—
Kendals on Deansgate—where she'd taken them to
buy Christmas party dresses. She had been seven,
Charley remembered.

She could see herself now, reaching out longingly
towards a deep sea-green shot taffeta dress with a black
velvet bodice and a wide sash, and then her mother had
exclaimed, 'Oh, no, Charley—you couldn't possibly
wear that.'

Just remembering the incident now, Charley could
feel the sting of humiliation burning up under her skin,
brought on by her mother's words and her own awareness of people turning to look at her, no doubt contrasting her with her pretty sisters.

Unable to stop herself, she stood up.

'I can't possibly wear any of these clothes,' she told
Raphael agitatedly, too wrought up to notice the
discreet manner in which the saleswoman had whisked
her assistants and then herself out of the room.

'Why not?' Raphael was in no mood for female
histrionics. He'd been awake in the early hours, questioning himself as to the wisdom of spending the night
alone in his apartment here in Florence with Charley,
and not very much liking the answers he had been
forced to come up with.

And now, when he had decided that he had no alternative other than to make the best of the situation
and see to it that she was properly prepared in every
way to do the job for which he had hired her, the last
thing he wanted was Charlotte behaving like a drama

queen over him providing her with the clothes she so obviously needed.

'*Why not*? Isn't it perfectly obvious?' Charlotte demanded bitterly. 'Just look at them, and then look at me. There's no way I'm going to try them on when I know I can't wear those kind of clothes. I'll look ridiculous and…make a fool of myself.'

Catching a note in her voice that was close to hysteria, Raphael put down the paper he had been reading and stood up, his irritation forgotten.

Charley was shaking, close to tears, and there was a look of deep self-loathing and misery in her eyes. The fact that her self-control was so obviously close to breaking was enough to arouse instincts within Raphael that he couldn't ignore or deny. How could he call himself a man and ignore her distress? His parents had brought him up to be chivalrous and protective of the female sex, and besides… But, dangerously, her distress was also awakening other instincts within him—the instincts of a man who desired a woman. Of the two of them, only he knew how close he was to taking her in his arms and holding her there—and only he must know, Raphael warned himself, because once he had taken her in his arms there would be no going back. His pulse and then his body quickened, confirming what he already knew.

'Why on earth should you think that?' he demanded, and the curtness his own conflicted feelings had injected into his voice increased Charley's misery.

There was a long pause whilst Charley looked away from him, and then, as though the words were being wrenched from her, she replied to him.

'Because I do—that's all.'

It was a child's reply, defiance—a defence against something too painful to reveal. Raphael knew that because he knew exactly how it felt not to be able to admit the true cause of an inner pain that had gone too deep for comfort.

Why had she said what she had? Why had she let him see her vulnerability? Why had she given him the weapon with which he could destroy her? It was too late now to ask herself those questions, Charley knew.

'I see.' Raphael paused. Charley trembled inwardly in the long pause whilst Raphael assessed the situation. What had he wanted most as a child, when confronted by his own pain and fear? Hadn't it been reassurance that there was in reality nothing to fear? A statement made confidently by 'a higher authority'? He had not received that reassurance because it had been impossible for his mother to deny the inheritance that was his, and even all her love had not been enough to protect him from that harsh reality. A woman's confidence in herself as a woman was everything. He had seen that in his mother, and somehow he wanted very much to restore it to Charley. But between that thought and acting upon it lay a no-man's land, and Raphael knew that he would be crossing a dangerous line within himself if he crossed that space.

He could stop. He could turn away from her. He could...

'Well, the choice is yours, but personally my judgement is that this dress would suit you very well indeed.

You have the figure for it, and you carry yourself well, with elegance—something that not all women do.'

Too late now. He had crossed it. And in doing so had set in motion the situation he had sworn to himself he would avoid.

Charley could only stare at Raphael, her lips parting and then closing again. Raphael had complimented her. Raphael had said she carried herself well—with elegance. Raphael believed she could wear the dress.

A feeling—dizzying, euphoric, boundless in all that it offered her—flooded through her like a dam breaking, washing clean everything that lay before it, carrying away in its flood the detritus of all that was rank, festering and poisoned, leaving her feeling so different, so lightened, that she looked down at herself in a bemused fashion, as though her body was unfamiliar to her and something she had to learn to know and understand. 'Elegance?' she repeated wonderingly.

Raphael nodded his head, and told her, 'Try on the clothes and see for yourself.'

There was no time for any further private conversation. The saleswoman had returned, accompanied by a girl carrying a fresh tray of coffee—a discreet excuse for having left them, to save *her* face, Charley recognised, as she allowed herself to be ushered back into the changing room.

Once there, Charley quickly discovered that there was far more to buying new clothes Italian-style than she had ever imagined. For a start, there was the make-up, applied deftly and determinedly by another impossibly pretty, slender girl dressed, as they all were, in black. Only when she was satisfied was Charley allowed to step into the first of the two black trouser suits and a cream silk shirt. All the time Charley was forbidden to look at her own reflection until everything was done. Was it for her benefit or Raphael's that her hair was brushed and tamed? Or was it more likely because of the size of the potential sale that she was getting all this attention? Charley couldn't help wondering, a little cynically. It didn't matter what the reason was in the long run because the result would be the same: she would look like a garish caricature; she already knew that.

Only when she was finally allowed to look in the mirror she didn't look like a caricature at all. Instead she looked... As she stared at her reflection, Charley blinked her mascaraed lashes uncertainly. Her lashes looked so long, and her eyes looked so...so big, their colour somehow deeper thanks to the subtle addition of expertly placed eyeshadow, she recognised distractedly. She was putting off the moment when she would have to look again at her whole reflection, just in case she had been wrong and the miracle that seemed to have taken place had been more of a mirage than a miracle.

Guardedly and carefully, fearfully almost, Charley let her focus move downwards, past her mouth with its soft sheen of warm pink lipstick, down to where the open neck of the silk shirt revealed the little hollow at the base of her neck in a way that made her want to touch the unfamiliar vulnerability it revealed. Still she was holding back from fully looking at herself. But the saleswoman was walking towards the door, and Charley knew that soon she would have to show herself to Raphael. She looked quickly into the mirror, holding her breath, and the air leaked from her lungs as she met the image looking back at her, and saw that the miracle had actually happened.

That *was* her—that immaculately groomed, slender-looking, feminine young woman with long legs and fragile wrist bones. What magic was this? How could a simple trouser suit bring about such a transformation? Or was she after all just imagining it? Seeing in herself what she so desperately wanted to see? Believing what Raphael had told her because she wanted to believe it? Torn between hope and doubt, Charley blinked away threatening tears. There was only one way to find out. It was said that the eyes could not lie— perhaps only when she stood in front of him would she really know what Raphael truly thought.

When she walked into the room he put down his paper and looked at her, but it was impossible for Charley to tell what he was thinking from his expression. Something—a small swell of chagrin and disappointment—formed inside her.

She turned on her heel—or rather on the heels she had been given to wear to try on the suit—totally unaware of the instinctive and wholly female affronted flounce in the movement of her body.

Raphael saw it, though.

'So are we agreed that I was right?' he said dryly.

Charley knew that he was, but she wasn't prepared to give in.

'My parents—' she began defensively, only to be stopped when Raphael spoke again.

'Whatever your parents or anyone else might have said, whatever they might have believed, ends now and is in the past. Only the weak blame their past for the faults they find in their present; the strong acknowledge the effects of their past and then move on from it. We are all free to choose whether we will be weak or strong.' His gaze challenged her to make her choice.

Charley took a deep breath. She felt dizzy again, light-headed, sort of untethered—as though something within her was floating free. As she struggled to understand what she was feeling she heard Raphael addressing the hovering saleswoman.

'We will take everything.'

'But I haven't tried everything on yet,' Charley tried to protest.

'There's no need. I am sure they will all fit perfectly—and besides, it's nearly two o'clock and as yet we haven't had any lunch.'

Charley could see that there was no point in trying to argue or protest.

By the time she had changed back into her own clothes everything was arranged. Her new things would be packed up and delivered to the apartment, and would be waiting for her when she returned there.

They had lunch in a small restaurant down an alleyway that opened out into a courtyard basking in sunshine, with tubs of spring flowers in bright bloom, but despite the relaxed ambience of the setting it wasn't a pleasant lunch. Raphael barely spoke to her, responding to her attempts to make conversation by asking him about the city with such terse replies that Charley lost her appetite, along with the desire to continue trying to converse with him. He was obviously bored with her company, and her heart turned over inside her chest and went leaden with pain when she saw him looking in the direction of a stunning redhead who was walking past their table. No doubt he was wishing that he was with the redhead instead of her, Charley guessed miserably.

She tried not to let her feelings show as he flicked back his cuff and glanced at his watch, as though impatient for their lunch to be over. She'd been a fool to hope as they left the shop that he might offer to show her something of the city.

It had been a mistake to bring Charlotte here to this small restaurant for lunch, Raphael recognised, irritated with himself for the way his desire for her was weakening him. The intimacy of the restaurant made him ache for the even greater intimacy of his bedroom, and Charlotte naked in his arms on the bed within it. There was no logical reason why she should have this effect on him. He had, after all, known and resisted far more openly sexual women. But the sunlight striking through the windows warmed the pale skin of her throat, making him want to touch it, to possess the tiny pulse he could see beating at its base, to possess *her*. This was madness. He couldn't allow himself to be controlled by his desire for her. It would be breaking all the rules he had made for himself.

'I have some meetings this afternoon.'

At last Raphael was speaking to her, even if his voice was abrupt and cold. Charley focused on him as he summoned the waiter and asked for the bill. Was it because of this morning and the clothes? Was he already regretting allowing her to work on the project? She made herself think about how she would feel if he were to change his mind. The surge of emotion within told her immediately. She wanted desperately to work on the garden project, she realised. She wanted to prove herself—wanted to be herself.

The same sense of shock and recognition she had felt staring at her new reflection in the mirror of the changing room hit her again now, bringing with it an awareness that deep down inside herself she had longed for the opportunity to overturn the conceptions about herself that imprisoned her; had secretly yearned not to be clumsy, awkward Charley, but someone else instead. Before she had told herself that that was impossible, that she was what she was. Now, though, she was suddenly able to see that Raphael had been right when he had said that what she had been was what others had forced on her. The prospect of shedding that persona and its restrictions might be uncomfortable and alarming, but it was also exciting, Charley recognised, and was filled with new possibilities, new goals, new ambitions—just as she had been filled with a sense of mingled anxiety and delight when she had come face to face with her new image in the mirror. She was filled with those same feelings at the knowledge of what she could be if only she had the courage to seize the opportunity life and Raphael had given her.

She had always longed to visit this part of Italy and now she was here; she had always ached and yearned for a job that would allow her to express herself artistically, and now she had one. She wanted desperately to learn more and grow as a person now she had that opportunity. Like tiny bolts of lightning her thoughts darted through her head, illuminating the darkest corners of her secret self. She could improve her Italian, explore the countryside, soak herself in Florence's artistic history, feel herself grow with the garden, do everything, *be* everything she had ever wanted to do and be. Except for wanting Raphael. That she could not and must not do. That was a closed door and must remain so. If with the birth of the new Charlotte that was happening within herself there was to come a desire to embrace her sexuality by taking a lover, then she must accept that that lover could not be Raphael.

The bill paid, Raphael told her, 'I suggest you spend the afternoon getting to know your way around the city, as that will be essential if you are to work efficiently. There will be occasions when you will have to come here alone—which reminds me that you will need a car.'

'Only something inexpensive...' Charley put in. She had cost him so much already, but she was determined that the work she would do for the garden would more than repay that expenditure.

'And small, please,' she added, remembering the narrowness of the streets.

A waiter was hovering, ready to pull out her chair for her, and Raphael stood up, signalling that it was time for them to leave.

As they walked out into the sunshine of the court-yard Charley warned herself that she would need to buy herself some decent sunglasses to replace the cheap pair she had brought from home. Raphael was already reaching for his—classically shaped, with a discreet Cartier logo—and their dark glass completely obscured his eyes. If he had already looked male and dangerous, the sunglasses brought a sharper raw edge to that look, making her heart turn over and her senses thrill with female sensual speculation and expectation. Coupled with a desire to make him equally aware of her it brought a new strand to everything else that she was dis-covering about herself. It was just as well, she decided, that Raphael quite plainly did not find her attractive—otherwise this new desire to explore and adventure could take her very quickly out of her depth, because if Raphael were to indicate that he wanted her, then…

Then what? Charley asked herself as they parted outside the restaurant and she turned to make her way to the square, following one of the many helpful signs. Then she would fling herself into a brief sexual affair with him with hedonistic abandon, relishing the oppor-tunity to give in to what she had already been feeling? Her heart thudded—not with apprehension and shock, but with excitement and anticipation.

Deep in her own thoughts, she didn't see the good-looking young man coming the other way until she had bumped into him. Flushed and guilty, she began to apologise, but instead of merely walking on the young man removed his sunglasses to smile at her, revealing white teeth. His voice was as liquid with warmth as the look in his eyes as he told her, simply and approvingly, *'Si bella, signorina,'* and then swept her with a look of meltingly delicious male approval before moving on.

He had been little more than a boy, really, probably still in his late teens, his early twenties at the most, with a mop of dark curls and that male lankiness that young men possessed, but his compliment had still boosted her confidence, Charley admitted as she continued to walk down the street.

Watching her from the pavement a few yards from the restaurant, Raphael frowned and then turned on his heel. What did it matter to *him* if other men found Charlotte Wareham attractive?

CHAPTER EIGHT

SHE had had a wonderful afternoon, Charley reflected as she sat in a small café, drinking her cappuccino. One glance at the queues of people waiting to visit some of Florence's most famous sites had told her that with only an afternoon at her disposal her time would be put to its best use if she simply wandered around and got a feel for the city—which was exactly what she had done. She had walked down from the Via de Tornabuoni to the River Arno, and then along its embankment until she reached the Ponte Vecchio, wandering by the long queues for the Uffizi to gaze in delight at everything in the Piazza della Signoria. Picking up a free map from a tourist office, she had strolled at her leisure, pausing frequently to admire her surroundings and to drink in the wonderful atmosphere of the city. Inside her head she had removed its modern-day crowds and re-peopled its streets with men and women of the Renaissance, imagining them going about their everyday business.

Now, though, it was nearly four o'clock, and she still had an hour to spare before she had to return to the apartment. A girl walking past, dark hair swinging on her shoulders like liquid silk, caught her attention. Italian women had such lovely hair... She reached up and touched her own. She'd tied it back again during the afternoon, but the new Charlotte who was emerging from the old Charley wasn't satisfied any longer with the plain practicality of simply pushing her hair out of the way. She wanted a hairstyle that matched her new self. She'd passed any number of hair salons on her stroll—but how to find the right one? She could see the store where Raphael had taken her down the street to her left. Determinedly, before her courage could desert her, Charley finished her cappuccino and, having paid for it, made her way towards it.

If the saleswoman who had served them earlier was surprised by her request she gave no sign of it, listening calmly instead, and immediately announcing that she knew the very place and that if Charley would kindly wait for a second she would telephone them herself, on Charley's behalf.

Which was how, nearly two hours later, Charley found herself stepping out of the salon with an elegant, sleek, not quite shoulder-length newly bobbed hairstyle, which she liked so much that she couldn't help sneaking glances at herself in shop windows, unable to resist moving her head just for the pleasure of feeling her hair swing so perfectly against her neck.

But she wasn't going to have much time in which to get changed for dinner. The new haircut had taken far longer than she had expected...

* * *

Raphael looked at his watch. Charlotte should have been back over an hour ago, and her failure to return— initially an irritation—had now grown into an anxiety that was manifesting itself within him as anger that he was fighting to control.

Anger. Just thinking about the dangers of allowing himself to feel such an emotion intensified what he was trying *not* to feel. Was this a manifestation of the madness that ran in his blood? A feeling of irritation that would ultimately grow into a monstrous, many-headed alien form within him that he could not control? That would make him lash out, at first verbally, then physically, hurting and then destroying those who aroused the rage that had taken possession of him? That rage had already possessed him once, and he had sworn that he would never allow it to do so again.

The buzz of the apartment's intercom, followed by the sound of Charley's voice, cut across his thoughts, replacing them with action as he moved quickly towards the door of his study-cum-office.

Standing on the step outside the imposing double doors in the still busy street, not hearing any response to her call, Charlotte was just about to try the intercom again when the door suddenly opened to reveal Raphael standing there.

'You were supposed to return here at five-thirty. It is now nearly seven o'clock.'

He was angry, Charley recognised. 'I know—I'm sorry,' she apologised. 'I got stuck in the hairdressers.

I didn't realise it would take so long, and I couldn't let you know as I don't have your mobile number.'

She'd been in a *hairdressers*? Raphael looked at the shining, elegant swing of her hair as she stepped out of the door's shadow, and was filled with an irrational surge of fresh anger as he recognised how much confidence and pleasure her new hairstyle was giving her, and that his concern for her wellbeing had been totally unnecessary.

'In future it would be as well if you remember that I don't pay you to visit hairdressers,' he told her harshly, adding, 'We have a vitally important business meeting in less than an hour's time, prior to which I had intended to run through a few things with you.'

Charley was completely mortified, all her pleasure in her new hairstyle lost, destroyed by the force of Raphael's anger.

'I'm sorry. I didn't think it would take so long. I wanted...' Her throat locked protectively around the words that would have humiliated her even more had she uttered them—told him that she had wanted him to look at her and admire her. Admire her or desire her? The confidence and happiness she had felt earlier had gone.

'I'll go and get changed,' she told Raphael in a flat voice that echoed what she was feeling.

Raphael watched her go, resisting the temptation to stop her and tell her—tell her what? That he wanted her? Wanted her when he knew that ultimately he might destroy her, and with her himself? The sooner everything was sorted out and he was able to leave her in charge of the garden project the better. He had work to do in Rome with regard to his business interests, which would keep him safely away from her for long enough for him to deal with his unwanted desire for her, Raphael assured himself.

In her bedroom, Charley undressed and then showered quickly, glad that the stylist had taken the time to show her how to dry and smooth her hair to keep it in polished perfection. She had taken the opportunity to ask the saleswoman at the designer store which of Charlotte's new outfits she would recommend for a smart business dinner engagement, and so, wrapped in a towel, she removed the clothes the saleswoman had suggested from the wardrobe in the dressing room off her bedroom and carried them carefully to place them on the bed.

The outfit was a slim-fitting sleeveless cream dress, over which went a soft, floating, seamed and tucked tunic top, with long sleeves that flared out at the wrist to almost cover her hands. The tunic reached almost to the hem of the dress, and the outfit was completed by a fine-knit silk jersey double-breasted cardigan jacket, cropped just above the waist.

A little dubiously Charlotte put each piece on, and then went and looked uncertainly in the mirror, exhaling a sigh of shaky delight when she saw that, far from looking as though she was dressed in an odd assortment of clothing, the finished effect was a breathtakingly delicate yet sophisticated blending of textures and fabrics.

Boosted by the new confidence, Charley slipped on the strappy wedge sandals that complemented the outfit, and picked up the pretty soft leather clutch bag that went with them. It was just about large enough to hold a notepad and pen, as well as her lipstick and comb. She headed for the door, stepping out onto the landing just as Raphael emerged from his own room.

Charley held her breath a little, wondering if he would make any comment about her appearance, and then told herself when he didn't that she wasn't really disappointed. He was wearing a light-coloured suit over a dark shirt—the effect, to her mind's eye, very Italian and very sexy.

As he waited for her at the top of the stairs he reached into his pocket and produced a small oblong package, which he handed to her, telling her, when she looked uncertainly at him, 'Scent. Later on you can choose your own, but for now this will have to do. No Italian woman considers herself properly dressed without her favourite perfume, and I'm aware that you don't wear any.'

Aware too, Raphael acknowledged inwardly, that the scent she always carried with her that was simply her own was becoming dangerously embedded in his senses. He had been glad of the shadows on the landing when she had come out of her room; he might have seen the clothes the saleswoman had chosen hanging on their rail, but the effect of the blending of different fabrics and textures of the outfit she was now wearing, and the way they both concealed and yet at the same time subtly hinted at the curves of her body, was one of sensual promise. And he would not be the only man to think that, Raphael knew. The feeling that speared through him was viciously sharp. *Jealousy?* He did not *want* other men to look at her with desire? He had no right to feel like that, Raphael told himself grimly.

Scent! She had not thought of buying any herself. Charley's fingers trembled as she removed the wrapping, just as they would have done if this had been a lover's gift—which of course it was not.

The liquid in the small glass bottle was the colour of warm amber. Very carefully Charley removed the top, breathed in the scent, and immediately fell in love. It transported her to summer gardens filled with fat, blooming heavy-petalled roses, their sweetness spiced with something alluringly exotic that made her think of Eastern harems and velvet nights.

She'd expected Raphael to choose her something modern and practical, but this surely was a scent designed for a woman who luxuriated in her sensuality—a scent she would wear in bed at night to clothe her naked body in temptation for her lover.

'If you don't like it—' Raphael began.

'I do,' Charley assured him, determinedly dabbing it on her throat and wrists in proof of her claim. 'It's heavenly—but there's no label on it.'

'It's from a *parfumier* who blends his own scents.' His manner was off-hand and dismissive, making Charley feel reluctant to pursue the subject, although she loved the scent so much she desperately wanted to know where it had come from. She already knew that when the bottle was empty she would want to replace it.

Charley had only just dabbed the scent on her wrists and throat, but already Raphael could smell its sensual mix of promise and passion and Charley herself. He had had to smell several different scents before he had found the one he had eventually chosen. Even though he had been aware of its sensuality, he hadn't, he admitted to himself now, been prepared for the effect it would have when mixed with the warmth of Charley's skin. His mother had always worn a rose-based scent, less sensual and more floral. He pushed away that memory. He didn't know why Charley's presence was making him think so often of his mother, and nor did he want to know.

CHAPTER NINE

IT MIGHT be over now, but Charley had had the most wonderful evening ever. The conversation had been every bit as intoxicating for her as the wine that had filled her glass. To be amongst people who were so knowledgeable about their craft, so filled with passion for all that it represented, and who treated her as their equal, had made her feel so complete and comfortable with herself that every minute of the evening had been a joy. The whole evening had been the most exhilarating and wonderful experience. Antonio and Niccolo were both in their early fifties, and their wives, Charley guessed, in their late forties, mothers of grown-up families. They had treated Charley with kindness, complimenting her on her appearance and asking her about her own family circumstances, issuing invitations for her to join their own family get-togethers whilst she was working in Italy, so that she would not feel alone. And Niccolo had assured Raphael that he was interested in the project, and would be willing to have his teachers and students involved in it. A coup in which Charley hoped she had played her part.

Now, though, they were back at the apartment, and Raphael hadn't said a word to her—his silence on the drive back a continuation of his behaviour towards her during the evening. Because he had been watching her? Assessing her? Testing her to see if she was up to the job of managing his project?

With her new-found confidence, instead of giving in to her anxiety she met it head-on.

'Something seems to be wrong. If it's because of the garden and my job, and you've changed your mind…'

She was not allowed to get any further. Raphael swung round and told her harshly, 'It isn't because of the garden, or your job. It's because of *this*.'

If he'd been fighting his desire for her only this evening he would have been able to control it. But he hadn't. He'd been fighting it for day after aching day, night after sleepless night, minute by minute, second by second, until the sheer weight of what he was trying to hold back was such that all it had taken was that one small extra burden of her question to tear down the walls he had built against her effect on him. In the few seconds of time it took him to reach for her a whole world of sensual images and longings flashed through him—an unstoppable avalanche of self-destruction he was powerless to stop.

Charley could hardly believe it. She was where she had so longed to be: in Raphael's arms, in his hold, his mouth hard on hers, her senses bursting into life. For a brief handful of seconds she was sharply aware of the soft darkness of the hallway, the smell of Raphael's cool cologne-scented skin contrasting with the heat they were generating, the rustle of their clothing, the soft sounds of pleasure she herself was making under Raphael's kiss and the sharp click of her heels touching the floor, because she'd raised herself up on tiptoe in order to get as close to him as she possibly could. And then she was aware of nothing other than the feel of Raphael's mouth on her own, the thrust of his tongue between her lips, and the surge of delight that invaded her body speared through her with a fierce urge to respond to him, to match him touch for touch and breath for breath.

This surely more than anything else was what she had been born for—what her senses had been designed for, what her inhibitions wanted to yield to. Curling her tongue against Raphael's in sensual pleasure, she pressed closer to him, feeling her breasts flatten against the hard muscular wall of his chest, knowing that her legs trembled as she leaned into him, knowing that inside herself she was softening and aching and wanting.

Her body's goal was Raphael's possession of it, and hedonistically, recklessly, perhaps even dangerously, she was welcoming every single sensation and thought that took her closer to that goal.

Lost in the heavy, pulsing need to give everything that she was, everything that she had, to the urgency driving through her, the sudden raw sound of Raphael's 'No!' as the harsh denial was ripped from his throat shocked her into frantic disbelief.

When Raphael released her and stepped back she swayed towards him, barely able to stand, her body shivering with rejection and the piercing, throbbing ache of denial, totally unable to comprehend why, having aroused her desire for him, he had now plunged her into such an aching agony.

'No? You can't say that. Not now—not after you've shown me that you want me and…and made me want you.'

She was so untutored in guile, so honest in what she thought and felt. Her words ripped into him, tearing apart the barrier he had tried to put between them.

'Want you?' Raphael laughed bitterly.

Until tonight, until he had seen her standing on the landing earlier, he had thought he had won, that he had subdued his desire for her—but all he had done was damp it down, and over the course of the evening, as he had watched her, it had leapt into fresh life like a wild fire, devouring everything that stood in its way.

'No, I do not want you,' he told her with brutal honesty. 'What I feel for you is no mere wanting. I wish to God that it were. I hunger for you. I ache for you and I crave you. But, since I have a rule of never mixing my business and my personal lives, those needs shall have to go unsatisfied. We will return to the *palazzo* in the morning, and then I shall leave for Rome.'

He was walking away from her, heading for the stairs. Charley licked her suddenly dry lips, and then, before she could change her mind, she ran after him, pushing past him on the stairs. She stood in front of him, spreading her arms so that he couldn't get past.

'Sometimes rules have to be broken,' she told him breathlessly. 'Sometimes things happen that we shouldn't try to control—things we are meant to experience, even if their pleasure is short lived.' She looked up at him. 'I want you to make love to me, Raphael. I want to know your hunger and your ache and your desire, because I feel them too.'

In the half-light of the hallway the shadows lent his face a haunted harshness, giving him the look of a man who belonged to another age, tormented and driven beyond his own limits.

'There can be no future for you with me,' he told her harshly.

'I am not asking you for a future.'

'Then what are you asking me for?'

'Tonight,' Charley told him softly. 'Tonight and nothing between us—nothing to stop us sharing the honesty of what we feel. When you said what you did earlier today, about my clothes and about my...my elegance, you started a process that has set me free to be myself. I want you to complete that process, Raphael.'

Charley could hear the increased pressure of his breathing even though he hadn't moved.

Holding his dark, unreadable gaze, she continued. 'I want you to take me and hold me. I want you to complete what you have begun, Raphael.'

His breathing had become a harsh sound of con-straint, his chest openly rising and falling with the pressure he was exerting over himself.

Charley let her own voice drop and soften to a husky, sensual whisper.

'I want us to break your rules, Raphael. I want us to have what we can have together tonight.' She took a step towards him and waited, her heart pounding.

Never in a thousand lifetimes had she imagined herself behaving like this with such sexual boldness, but now that she knew Raphael shared her desire she was prepared, whatever she had to risk, her whole body thrilling at the thought of what they could share.

When he reached out and circled her wrists with his hands, his fingers long and strong as steel when they snapped around her flesh, Charley's anticipation turned to dread. He was going to deny her—move her out of his way and step past her. His grip forced her arms down to her sides and held them pinioned there.

'One night?' he said softly. 'Do you really think that one night will be enough to sate the hunger you have aroused in me?' And then he was kissing her, fiercely and demandingly, and her own desire was leaping up inside her to meet the challenge of his.

CHAPTER TEN

THEY had reached the top of the stairs and they were
still kissing, but Charley had no awareness of them
having moved, no awareness of anything other than the
heat of Raphael's mouth on her own and the need
inside her that he was feeding.

Now, though, he had stopped kissing her. His hold
of her wrists was slackening, his thumbs finding the
excited race of her pulse and tormenting it with small
circling caresses.

'There can be no future in this,' he warned her, as
he had done before, emphasising the words as he
spoke them.

'I don't want a future,' Charley told him, and
believed it. 'I just want tonight and you.'

Raphael could feel the wild fire of unleashed
passion surging through his body. It was too much. He
couldn't deny her—or himself. The urge to hold her
body against his own, skin to skin, roared through him,
but somehow he held on to a final strand of self-
control—for her sake as much as his own.

'Very well, but there is one condition I must make—one assurance I shall need from you.'

Charley waited. What was he going to say? That she must not fall in love with him? She knew *that* without him needing to tell her.

Raphael expelled the air from his lungs and breathed in slowly.

'There must be no risk of there being any consequences to our actions in the form of a child.'

Why did his words strike against her heart like a sledgehammer blow? She certainly hadn't been thinking of conception or children when she had so boldly begged him to break his rule.

'Naturally I shall take precautions myself to ensure…'

'There's no need.' Charley stopped him. 'I'm on the pill.' It was the truth, even if the reason she was taking it was because the anxiety of the last year had meant that she needed to take it to correct her monthly cycle.

'Very well, but I must warn you that should you conceive the pregnancy will have to be terminated.'

Shock jolted through her, icy cold, in instinctive rejection of what he was demanding.

But it wasn't his child she wanted, she reminded herself, it was Raphael himself. And she did want him—desperately.

He should stop this right now, Raphael urged himself. It wasn't too late. He could turn away—refuse what she was offering him. *Refuse?* When his body ached like hell for her, and his senses were already anticipating every single pleasure they would give one another? He was beyond stopping himself, beyond listening to any inner warning voices, beyond even questioning just why this woman of all women should have the power to overturn all the boundaries he had set in place.

Charley moved uncertainly, a sharp point of light from the heavy chandelier that hung from the ceiling throwing the soft curves of her breasts into relief. Her nipples were pushing against the fabric of her clothes, tight and erect, their message of sexual arousal making Raphael's own flesh harden. He released Charley's wrist and lifted his hand to her body, rubbing the pad of his thumb against the cresting flesh, feeling his own body react to the visible shudder that gripped Charley as she moaned softly in response to his caress. It was too late to turn back—too late to do anything other than give in to the need driving through him.

'This way.'

Raphael was taking her to *his* bedroom. A new quiver of sensation ripped through Charley. Somehow the thought of Raphael making love to her in his bed rather than her own added an extra layer of sensuality and delight to what she was already feeling.

Elegant and smart, like photographs she had seen of seriously expensive boutique hotel bedrooms, Raphael's bedroom was decorated in shades of off-white, dark grey and aubergine, with heavy silk curtains striped in those colours to match the linens on the large double bed.

Not that Charley was in the right frame of mind to appreciate the decor, nor indeed had the time, for no sooner had Raphael switched on the low-level lighting, and she had stepped inside, than he closed the door and took her back in his arms.

The touch of his hand on her breast, expertly finding the hard rise of her nipple, made her shudder with fresh delight, but Charley's conscience was beginning to intrude on her pleasure. Reluctantly she broke the kiss to admit to him, 'There's something I ought to tell you.'

'What?'

'Well…' Charley wrinkled her nose. 'The truth is that I haven't had much previous experience. I don't want to disappoint you…'

She could see his chest rise and then fall again. Had she put him off?

'Much or any?' Raphael questioned her.

He was too astute. She had known that before.

'Any,' she admitted, before asking him, 'Does that change things and put you off?'

'Do you want it to?'

'No!' Charley told him vehemently.

'The pleasure we shall give each other and share will be unique to us, exclusive to us, as it is with any lovers. But, like any man, I dare say my ego will enjoy knowing that I cannot be compared to a previous lover and found wanting.'

Charley was so relieved that she burst out truthfully, 'I can't imagine any woman ever thinking that about you.'

Raphael exhaled slowly, recognising that deep down inside himself he had already suspected he would be her first lover. His heart slammed into the wall of his chest. He wanted to take hold of her right now, slide the clothes from her body and give in to his desire to take them both to a place where all that mattered was their shared need for one another.

The realisation rolled over him that he wanted her as he had never wanted any other woman—as he had never imagined wanting any woman—but all he said to her was, 'I shall do my best to be worthy of your faith in me.' He was unable to stop himself from adding under his breath, 'I just hope that my self-control is up to the challenge.'

His self-control? Charley trembled under the eager anticipatory tightening of her body. She felt, she thought dizzily, as though sensually, sexually, her desire for him had bloomed into a peak of lush, ripe readiness. Almost magically she was free of all restraints and inhibitions, just as though she had been reborn into the full flowering of her own sexuality. Because of Raphael. And not just because she wanted him, but because he had shown her that she could be free of the damaging beliefs of her past, that she could be whatever she chose to be.

Her body was singing with excitement and joy, aching deliciously and oh, so tormentingly with a thousand aches that instinctively she knew would meld into one piercingly intense surge of need beneath Raphael's touch.

She looked up at him and smiled.

'It isn't your self-control that I want,' she told him simply.

Raphael felt the breath shudder through his lungs, the savage thrust of his desire crashing through his barriers.

'You shouldn't say such things to me,' he warned her as he closed the distance between them.

'Why not?' Charley whispered the words against his lips. She was trembling so violently that she had to hold on to him for support.

'Because it's dangerous, because *you* are dangerous—dangerously enticing, dangerously sensual, dangerously tempting me to forget all the reasons why I should not be doing this,' Raphael whispered back.

His hands were moving over her, angling her within his hold so that he could shape and knead the soft fullness of her breast as he kissed her. Pleasure rushed through her—pleasure, excitement, and a need that had her finding his tongue with her own and caressing it, twining with it. Wild shudders of firework explosive delight showered her when Raphael stopped her, to turn her explorative caress into the shockingly deep thrust of his tongue within the softness of her mouth, his tongue and his hand against her breast working to a rhythmic beat that produced an aching echo of its urgency deep inside her. Helplessly Charley pressed closer to him, her hands moving feverishly over his chest and then his shoulders, frustrated by the barrier of his shirt.

As though he knew how she felt, he moved his lips to her ear, demanding, 'What is it you want?'

'I want to touch you, all of you, without your clothes,' Charley answered him immediately, her voice unsteady with the intensity of her longing.

'Then take them off for me.'

Undress him? A shock wave of raw need stormed through her, and then her fingers were tugging at his tie, trembling over his shirt buttons, only her longing to feel his bare skin against her own preventing her from being distracted by the way he was caressing her tight nipple whilst he held her shoulder with his free hand and slowly kissed his way along the side of her neck. At last she had his shirt unfastened, tugged out of the waistband of his suit trousers, and she was free to bury her face against the warm, muscular expanse of his chest with its soft covering of dark hair, breathing in the scent of him, pressing frantically hungry kisses on his bared skin, so completely lost in the pleasure of what she was at long last free to do that she was oblivious to the fact that Raphael had stopped kissing her and touching her, and was simply holding her whilst he struggled to control his breathing.

This was so much more than he had been prepared for—so much more than he had understood he could ever feel or want. Charley's open and uninhibited pleasure in what she was doing was undermining his self-control like the tide stealing away sand. Raphael cupped the sides of her head, arching his throat back in mute offering to the searing, scalding pleasure of her lips caressing his skin. An uncontrollable shudder of male pleasure seized him in its grip.

'Enough,' he told Charley rawly. 'Now it's my turn to undress you.'

Where she had been all fingers and thumbs, all out-of-control excitement and delight, Raphael was skilled. His touch was sure and knowing as he dealt with the layers of her clothes until she was standing in her underwear—the delicate silk and lace lingerie that had been delivered with her new clothes.

In one of the mirrors set on either side of the bed above the bedside tables Charley could see the pale shimmer of her almost naked body, glowing and pearlescent in the subdued lighting of the room, the slenderness and delicacy of her bone structure made more fragile by the solid muscularity of Raphael's torso beside it.

'We look so different,' she told him, her voice husky, softened by desire.

'But together we will make a perfect whole,' Raphael answered her.

As she watched their reflections she saw Raphael's hand lift to her breast, to push down the silk fabric and expose the dark flesh of her nipple, hard and tight with arousal. The sight of it, knowing what its arousal meant, sent an urgent frisson of longing down her spine. As though Raphael had felt it and knew its meaning, he traced a line of fiery erotic kisses along her shoulderblade, whilst his fingertips plucked and teased the eager longing of her nipple, causing starburst after starburst of pleasure to spread through her. But that pleasure was nothing compared to the dark agony of desire that flooded her when Raphael took her nipple into his mouth, tonguing it; stroking it; making her arch her body up to him in helpless supplication, whilst her veins ran with liquid heat and her whole body pulsed to the rhythm of her longing.

His mouth still on her breast, Raphael slid his hands

into the cut-away legs of her knickers, moulding and kneading the rounded cheeks of her bottom, making her press as close to him as she could as the ache between her legs intensified. She wanted him to touch her there. She wanted to press herself against him, to rub herself against him. She wanted— Charley gasped in shocked delight when Raphael lifted his head, his hand sliding between her legs, his fingers stroking the soft swell of flesh that covered her sex, pulling down the pretty confection of silk and lace so that in the mirror she could see the movement of his hand against her body, could see too that he was watching her just as she was watching him.

Slowly, so slowly that she had to hold her breath so as not to beg him to hurry, he parted the lips of her sex, causing a shudder of aroused delight to shake her body. Then she was arching with erotic shock when he stroked gently up and down the soft wet valley, and then pressed his fingers against the wellspring of her desire, rubbing it slowly, and then more swiftly, whilst she gasped and writhed and clung to him, her eyes wide with all that she was feeling. Her orgasm came so quickly and so intensely that it shook her from head to foot, and she needed the support of his arms to hold her as he kissed her and took the words of pleasure from her lips.

CHAPTER ELEVEN

STILL held in Raphael's arms, Charley could feel the hard, urgent pulse of his arousal against her as she relaxed into him, stirring a new surge of eager desire within her body that had her moving languorously against him; satisfied and yet at the same time aware of the capacity within her to be aroused to fresh need—aware too of a deep inner ache that had not been quenched.

What she had just experienced was the beginning, not the end, and the movement of her body against his was sending Raphael a deliberate message to that effect.

Even so he still hesitated, forcing down the impulse to carry her over to the bed and spread the softness of her body there beneath his own, so that he could enter her and lose himself in her in the way his flesh ached for him to do, but then Charley moved against him, pressing closer to him, snapping the tautly strung fragility of his self-control.

As though he had given his need words and spoken them to her, Charley whispered vehemently, 'Yes!' and within seconds he had removed the last of their clothes and they were on the bed, her body soft and eager beneath his hands.

This was wonderful, heaven, beyond anything she could ever have imagined. Raphael's skin felt like oiled silk beneath her explorative touch, his torso narrowing down to a flat belly, his body ridged with muscles beneath the warmth of his skin, and the reality of his erection a thousand times more breathtakingly erotic than any artistic phallic images she had ever seen. She reached out and stroked her fingertips along its length in wondering delight, gasping in sharp pleasure as her touch transferred the delicate stroke of Raphael's tongue-tip against her earlobe to the hard possession of his mouth against her nipple, his lips tugging on its pouting sensuality after its earlier pleasuring. Instinctively she closed her hand around him, her body shuddering as she felt the fierce pulse beating from his flesh into her own, and then arching on a spasm of sharp pleasure when his teeth grated delicately against the sensitive flesh of her nipple. Had she thought that she now knew desire? She had been wrong. What she had known had been merely the foothills of a far greater height.

Bending her head towards him, Charley whispered to Raphael.

'I was right. You are the most wonderful lover.'

'How can you know?' he mocked her softly, kissing the valley between her breasts and then making his way up towards her mouth.

'My body knows,' Charley answered him, 'and that is why it wants you so much.'

Ridiculous that a few words should have such an intense effect on him, Raphael knew. But they had. It was time. He couldn't wait any longer.

Cradling Charley against his side with one arm, he reached towards the drawer in the bedside table with the other.

Guessing what he was seeking, Charley placed her hand on his chest and shook her head, telling him fiercely, 'No. I want to feel you inside me—just you. Your flesh against mine as nature intended. Not—not a…a chemical barrier that isn't you… I'm on the pill so we're safe. I want to feel you inside me, Raphael,' Charley repeated determinedly. 'Just you—all of you…' She was kissing him in between her words: eager, passionate little kisses that, like her touch on his body, showed him how much she wanted him.

He should ignore her pleas. He should behave sensibly. He should ignore the way his body had reacted when she had said she wanted him inside her. He should…

'I want you so much,' Charley whispered.

It was too much, and too late to stop himself now, with the soft weight of her in his arms, her body lying eagerly open to his possession, her muscles closing tightly around him as he slowly thrust into her.

Charley shuddered and gasped, and then sighed with exalted pleasure, her hands gripping Raphael's shoulders as he moved slowly and carefully into her. Each sensation built on the pleasure of the one before it, as though she was climbing a set of steps. Her body protested, her muscles tightening to hold him where he was when Raphael pulled back a little, but his next thrust reassured her body that he wasn't leaving it, simply moving deeper and then deeper still, until she was moving with him, wrapping her legs around him, welcoming the increasing sensation of fullness and energy within her.

She was Eve and the apple—all the woman he could ever want, and impossible for him to resist. Her response to him was driving him both to want to conquer her and at the same time give all of himself over to her. His whole world had narrowed down to the bed and to her, one moment spread out beneath him, the next wrapped around him. The scent and sight of her, the sound of her pleasure, the feel of her skin under his hands, the hot, slick power of the way her body received and held him…

It was happening. It was coming. A flutter at first…but now the sensation gathered and gripped her. Charley sucked in a lungful of air and then tensed, her nails digging into the flesh of Raphael's shoulders as she looked up into his face.

His skin was sheened with sweat, the muscles in his arms corded and locked.

She held nothing back, Raphael recognised, concealed nothing. He could see the ecstasy in her expression as well as feel the surging rhythmic contractions of her orgasm. His own body trembled and then shook, his throat arching and his whole body pulled as taut as a bow in that final second before he joined her in his own release into pleasure.

CHAPTER TWELVE

CHARLEY looked up from the weekly progress chart she had been studying. It was three weeks now since Raphael had brought her back to the *palazzo* and left her there. She pushed back her chair from the pretty, delicately painted wood desk. She had been uncertain at first how Raphael would feel about the fact that Anna had given her as her office the pretty little sitting room which she had told her had last been used by Raphael's mother, but Anna had assured her that he wouldn't mind, that he had told her simply to make sure that Charley had somewhere to work.

Three weeks: twenty-one nights of unbearable aching longing, and twenty-one days of fighting to keep Raphael out of her thoughts.

She had had three wonderful days with him in Florence. Those she would never, ever forget. Three wonderful days and three even more wonderful nights: days during which Raphael had shown her his Florence, and nights when he had shown her the power of her own sexuality.

He might not have been a demonstrative lover in public, holding her hand and pulling her to him as she had seen one young man doing with his girl in the Boboli Gardens the afternoon Raphael had taken her there, but he had showed his desire for her in other more subtle ways—via a certain look, a certain touch—and there had definitely been no holding back from showing her his desire when they were on their own.

On their final morning before they had left the city she had been lying in his arms, after Raphael had made love to her. He had kissed her and smoothed the hair back off her face, telling her, 'You do understand, don't you, that what has happened here between us in Florence must belong only to Florence?'

Yes, she had understood—but that hadn't stopped her from asking him, almost begging him in desperation, even though she had already known what his answer would be, 'Will we come back?'

'No,' he had told her, with a finality that had cut into her like a knife slicing into her heart.

She had known, of course, that that would be his answer. He had told her from the start not to want anything more than they had had. Then she hadn't thought about the future—then she had been too driven by her desire for him to look deeper and see what was already growing beneath it. Then she hadn't realised that she had fallen in love with him. Not then, but she did now.

It wasn't Raphael's fault. It was her own. But knowing that didn't make her pain any easier to bear. She had tried to escape it by spending all her waking hours working. She was almost always the first at the garden in the morning and the last to leave at the end of the day, returning to the *palazzo* to write reports late into the evening, but not even that could keep Raphael out of her thoughts. He was there all the time, over-shadowing everything else, and Charley knew that he always would be.

The nights were worse than the days. She'd delay going to bed until the early hours, convinced that she would be so exhausted that she would sleep, and she did. But only for a while, waking up often to find her pillow wet with her tears, her body and her heart aching for Raphael.

Charley looked round the pretty, feminine salon. Whenever she imagined Raphael's mother here, perhaps sitting at the desk where Charley herself worked, writing her letters, another image would appear: Raphael himself as a young boy. Her heart turned over inside her chest, a yearning spreading through her. Now she could understand, as she had never understood before, the need of a woman to conceive the child of the man she loved. To have that child as a living, breathing memorial of what they had shared, to be loved and cherished as a precious gift.

But of course there could be no such gift for her. Her all too brief span of time in the paradise that being Raphael's lover had created for her was over. Raphael himself had closed the gates on their return.

Wearily Charley looked down at the desk. It was far too small really, for the amount of paperwork she had to deal with, but Anna had offered her this room so proudly that Charley hadn't had the heart to tell the housekeeper that she needed a working space that was more functional.

So far they were ahead of schedule with the work of clearing the garden in readiness for the actual renovation—although Charley suspected that sometimes the contractors would have preferred it if she didn't put in such long hours, assessing the progress of everything. But working herself hard was the only way she had of trying to stop the pain of loving Raphael.

In a few minutes she would go downstairs and drive out to the site, and then this evening she would update her schedules for the week and input them into her computer, ready to send to Raphael with her report as she had done for the previous three weeks. So far, though, Raphael had not e-mailed her back—not even to say that he had received her reports. Because he was afraid that if he contacted her she would plead with him as she had done in Florence? It was Charley's prayer that she would *never* humiliate herself and irritate Raphael by doing that.

There were moments when she longed for the comforting presence of her sisters, so that she could unburden herself to them and be comforted by them, but then there were other times when she simply couldn't bear the thought of disclosing her pain and the reasons for it to anyone, because it was so raw.

'All the statues have now been removed. Those that are only slightly damaged will be repaired in my workshops in Florence, whilst those that cannot will be measured and photographed so that exact copies can be made.'

Charley nodded her head as she listened to Niccolo giving her his progress report. It had been a long day, and now the warmth was dying out of the sun as it sank towards the horizon.

'You'll let me have a detailed report to pass on to Raphael?'

'Of course. No work will be done until he has sanctioned it. As you know, we've already photographed each piece of statuary, and the location where it was found.'

Charley nodded her head again. She too had taken photographs of everything, meticulously numbering them and pinpointing the sites on her own personal plan of the garden. She wasn't going to take any chances of being found wanting in her professional capacity, even if Raphael had found her not good enough to keep in his bed.

'We are doing very well. Raphael will have every reason to be extremely pleased with our progress,' Niccolo told her, as he left to return to Florence.

Half an hour later Charley too was ready to call it a day. The last rays of the setting sun were fading as she locked the heavy gates. It would be dark by the time she returned to the *palazzo*, where she would shower and eat and then start work on her evening's paperwork.

Since it was Friday, once she had updated everything she could e-mail it to Raphael—her treat of the week, her only precious contact with him. Just thinking about e-mailing him made her stomach muscles cramp with a mixture of pain and longing—and the desperate hope that he would e-mail her back.

How pathetic she was, Charley derided herself contemptuously. She looked towards the small Fiat Raphael had given her to drive, and then looked again in disbelief when she saw the sleek sports car parked next to it.

'Raphael...' Without thinking, desperate to get to him, she stepped into the road, oblivious to the car coming towards her until she heard the blare of its horn.

Raphael was out of the Ferrari in a flash, running faster than he had ever run in his life, grabbing hold of Charley and dragging her bodily out of the way as the car swerved to avoid her.

Charley felt the heat of its engine, the sting of the stones it threw up on her skin, and she heard the curses of the driver—but none of that mattered. All that mattered was that she was with Raphael. But he was shaking her, violently and almost painfully, over and over again, his face drained of colour, his hands hard on her arms as he demanded furiously, 'Why didn't you look before you crossed the road? Are you blind? What were you trying to do? Kill yourself?'

Charley had never seen him so angry. She could almost feel the heat and the power of his rage.

Shocked and frightened, more by her near-miss than by his anger, she trembled in his hold and begged him, 'Stop it.'

Immediately Raphael thrust her away from him, so hard that she staggered, and then leaned on the side of his car.

Reaction had begun to set in, reducing her to a shaking bundle of jelly-legged awareness of the danger she had been in.

'Get in,' Raphael ordered her, yanking open the door.

'I've got my own car,' Charley reminded him, but the last thing she felt like doing was driving.

'I'll arrange for that to be collected later.'

She was in the car, still feeling shaky and sick, wanting Raphael to hold her tenderly and comfortingly instead of being angry with her.

Raphael drove them back to the *palazzo* at speed, without speaking to her, and Charley was glad to be able to escape from him once they were inside, hurrying up to her room, wincing as she heard the furious slam of his office door on her way upstairs.

Ten minutes later, standing under the warm sting of the shower, Charley began to feel slightly better. Her shock had receded, leaving her to admit that she had been careless, and that she was lucky that Raphael had acted so speedily to save her from going under the wheels of the car. That was what loving the wrong man did for you. It made you so desperate to be with him that you forgot everything else. She had to find a way to stop herself from loving him. She must.

Wrapping a towel round her wet body, she headed for the bedroom—and then came to an abrupt halt when she saw Raphael standing there, waiting for her.

He was still angry. She could see that immediately.

'I'm sorry—' she began, but he stopped her.

'Sorry? Is that all you can say?' he demanded harshly. 'You damn nearly kill yourself and…' He was reaching for her again, but Charley stepped back from him.

'No!' she uttered, panicking, not trusting herself to

let him touch her, knowing that if he did she would end up begging him to stay with her.

Her denial was too much for Raphael. His heart was still thudding with the agony he had felt when he had thought the car would hit her. Everything he had told himself and taught himself was forgotten. He was a man denied what was rightfully his, the woman who was rightfully his—the woman fate had devised for him and bequeathed to him, the woman whose only previous 'no' to him had been a plea for him not to leave her.

Charley could almost feel Raphael's tension. It showed in his abrupt movements and in the dark grimness of his eyes, as though he was only just managing to hold back whatever it was that had turned them that colour. He looked...he looked like a man filled with suppressed anger, Charley recognised. And as he came towards her he was looking at her as though she was the source and the cause of that anger.

'What is it?' she asked apprehensively.

'What is it? It's *this*,' Raphael answered savagely, reaching for her, pulling her against his body and then bending his head to kiss her. Not as he had kissed her before, not as she had dreamed of him kissing her, but over and over again, as though he couldn't stop. Fierce, hard, demanding kisses, filled with a raw and angry pent-up passion that seared through her, igniting inside her an answering, equally primitive need.

Charley lost all sense of time as she clung to him, riding out the storm, letting him take what he wanted, glorying in the hard, imprisoning hold of his hands on her body that made her his willing captive. But at last she somehow managed to pull herself away from him to warn him, 'Anna will be bringing my supper.'

'Not now,' he told her, pulling her back towards him, his hand finding her bare thigh beneath her towel and caressing it, making her quiver with a thrill of yearning pleasure. 'I told Anna we are not to be disturbed. Your hunger for your supper will, I am afraid, have to go unsatisfied, because my hunger for you cannot bear any further delay.'

His hand had reached the top of her thigh; his voice was thick with emotion. Her heart was pounding with wild, out-of-control euphoria. He wanted her. Raphael wanted her.

Charlotte pressed herself closer to him in eager delight, another thrill running through her when he groaned and kissed her fiercely, the open agony of his longing matching everything that she herself felt.

Their mutual need was like a fireball, consuming them. Raphael was shedding his clothes as he caressed her with increasing urgency and intimacy. There was no time for the slow sensuality of leisurely love play, and no need either, Charley acknowledged. How could there be when she had spent the last three weeks aching for him? An ache that had become a tumultuous clamour of pulsing need, possessing the whole of her body even before she had seen how his hunger for her had brought Raphael to full and thick readiness. It was the sight of that readiness that sent her over the edge and into a place of wild, visceral need.

She could see the hot look of male urgency glittering in Raphael's eyes as he parted her naked thighs, the heat of his hand against her sex making her moan. The sound changed to a fevered gasp of almost too heightened pleasure when his fingers stroked the eager waiting length of her sex.

'I've lain awake night after night thinking of you like this—sweet and hot, wet and ready for me.'

Just the sound of his voice was enough to make her body convulse with longing.

There was no time for them to reach the bed—no thought in her head other than the need to have Raphael deep within her, filling her, completing her, driving her with each wonderfully powerful thrust of his body closer to the epicentre of the storm within her… Her legs wrapped around Raphael, her fingernails digging deep into his shoulders. His hands protected her back from the hardness of the bedroom door as they coupled wildly and fiercely. Charley could feel her body's possessive hunger for him as her muscles tightened around him, demanding that he take her deeper, harder, faster. Words formed by her aching need were gasped against his shoulder, his sweat-dampened throat. She could smell the aroused heat of his body, taste his need in the salty tang of his skin.

The end came quickly and almost violently, in a series of frantic mini-orgasms for Charley that built in intensity until Raphael tensed and made an agonised sound of release against her skin, his completion within her inciting a final orgasm that took her to new heights and held her there, whilst her body convulsed on wave after wave of pleasure.

Drained and trembling, Charley unwrapped her legs

from Raphael's body, too weak to stand unsupported on her own, simply leaning into him as he held her, their hearts pounding together in the aftermath of what they had shared.

They had eaten, showered, made love again—this time with Raphael slowly building her desire with sensuality and an awareness of her needs that had brought tears of emotion to her eyes.

'Stay with me,' Charley whispered as Raphael held her protectively in the curve of his body, and they both knew that it wasn't just for tonight that she wanted him to stay.

CHAPTER THIRTEEN

A SHADOW blotted out the morning sunlight warming her face, causing Charley to murmur a protest in her sleep. Just as she had done earlier, when he'd eased her out of his arms so that he could shower and dress, Raphael noted. The morning light fell harshly against the planes of his face, revealing a certain gauntness and weariness of spirit. He shouldn't have come here last night—shouldn't have left the safety of Rome even though it had become an imprisoning barren waste of aching. He had no right to take what he had given his vow to himself not to.

The temptation to simply walk away whilst Charlotte slept was almost overwhelming, but he made himself overcome it, leaning down to place his hand on her body—not on her bare rounded shoulder; he was far too raw to be able to trust himself to touch her skin to skin. Instead he placed his hand gently on the spot where her arm lay beneath the bedclothes.

Charley woke up immediately, her sleepy gaze

sharpening into focus, delight brimming in it as she sat up, exclaiming, 'Raphael!'

Everything about her demeanour spoke openly and joyously of her feelings. Raphael could see her love for him in the way she smiled at him, hear it in the upward lilt of her voice, feel it in the softly sensuous yearning movement of her body towards him.

He drew in a sharp breath and stepped back from the bed, turning away from her to look towards the window as he told her, 'I shall be returning to Rome in half an hour, but first I need to talk to you about last night.'

Charley felt the weight of his words as though they were the onset of an avalanche that was going to crush the life out of her. In the short space of time it took Raphael to say them, the happiness with which she had awoken had turned to fear.

'Last night?' she repeated.

Raphael nodded his head.

'Last night should never have happened. The blame for the fact that it did lies entirely with me. I should have had more self-control; I should not have come here and given in to my…need. It mustn't happen again. It will not happen again.'

Charley couldn't hide her distressed anguish.

'I don't understand,' she protested. 'You want me, and I want you.'

'Yes.'

Raphael's voice was terse. He wasn't looking at her, and Charley could see the way his jaw tensed.

'Then why can't we be together? I love you, Raphael.'

'Yes, I know, and that is part of the reason why it

must end. I cannot give you... There is no future for us. It is better, kinder, fairer to you, that we end things now.'

No future for them? Pain and anger filled Charley.

'Why is there no future for us? Because I'm not good enough for you, The Duke? Is that why you said what you did about me not conceiving your child? I'm not good enough to be the mother of a baby with your precious blue blood, is that it?'

She was working herself up into a fury because it was the only way she had of stopping herself from begging him to change his mind. She had to hold on to her anger because it was all she had to cling to.

'No. Never that.' Raphael swung round as he uttered the tormented denial, the sunlight revealing the new thinness of his face, his expression that of a man emotionally tortured beyond his own bearing.

'Tell me what it is, then,' Charley insisted. '*Tell* me.'

She could see his chest expanding as he took a deep, ragged breath.

'Very well, then. You saw for yourself how I reacted last night—how my anger overwhelmed me, how I took hold of you in anger and violence.'

'Because you were afraid that the car would hit me.'

'I wish I could believe it was only that that motivated me, but I cannot let myself accept that. Last night I broke every vow I have ever made to myself. It must never happen again. I am not saying that things must end between us because I do not want you to have my child, but because I will not put you in a position where I might hurt you. Just as I will not pass on to any child the poisoned inheritance that is in my own genes.'

Whilst Charley looked at him in shocked bewilderment, Raphael loosened the tension out of his shoulders with a tired movement.

'You will want to know what I mean?'

'Yes,' Charley agreed.

'It is a long story—as long as the history of my mother's family. She was descended from the bloodline of one of the most bloodthirsty of all the Beccelli family. During the fifteenth century his cruelty and sadism was such that it was expunged from all family documents. His greed knew no bounds. In order to empower himself he waged war on his neighbours, amongst them my mother's family, giving orders that the sons of the family should be killed along with their parents, whilst taking for himself their daughter to be married to one of his own sons—but not before he had raped her and impregnated her.'

Raphael heard Charley's indrawn gasp.

'His cruelty was unimaginable—the product of a twisted and sadistic mind. Finally he was brought to rough justice when he was murdered by his own sons, who then fell out amongst themselves, killing one another and leaving behind them the young raped bride who was carrying the child of her abuser. From that time down through my mother's family there have been those who have manifested sadism—men and women who have carried out acts of unspeakable cruelty. My mother's own great-grandfather was one of those people, as was a male cousin—who ended up being murdered in a brothel. There were other members of her family—less openly affected but possessed of terrible tempers, given to uncontrollable rages. Because of her dread of passing on the curse of that inheritance my mother had sworn never to marry or have a child, so that no future generations would be contaminated by her inheritance. But then she met my father. They were passionately in love with one another, and he persuaded her to marry him. She told me over and over again during my childhood how she had promised herself that she would not burden future generations with the burden she herself had had to carry, how madness brought on by guilt as well as sadism destroyed the lives of so many who shared her blood.'

Charley had to swallow hard before she could speak. Raphael's revelations had filled her with pity for him, and a fiercely protective love.

'But you are neither of those things,' was all she felt able to say. 'You are no sadist, Raphael, and you are not mad.'

'Not yet—although that is not to say that I will never be, nor that my child will not be.'

It took several seconds for the full horror of what he was saying to sink into Charley's mind.

'But you can't know that it will happen,' she managed.

'No. But, far more importantly I cannot know that it will not—and because of that I cannot take the risk, not for you and not for a child. Even if it is free of the taint of our shared blood, he or she in turn will have to carry the burden that will be born with them, and they will have to make the decision that I was not strong enough to make for them. It is my belief that in speaking to me as she did my mother was asking me to do what she had not been able to do.'

'But you are a duke, and without an heir...'

'I have an heir—the son of a cousin who is my closest male relative on my father's side, and so untainted.' Raphael dismissed Charley's statement. 'The reason I am telling you this is not because I want your pity but because I want you to understand why we cannot be together. Already you have witnessed my anger—how are we to know how that darkness within me might grow?'

'That was a completely natural reaction, and my fault.'

'No, last night is not the first time such a rage has possessed me. After my mother's death I went into her sitting room—the room she always loved best. I could almost see her sitting there in her favourite chair, but she wasn't there, and because of that I destroyed that chair by smashing it against the fireplace.'

'You were just a boy,' Charley protested. 'A boy who had lost both his parents and who was alone and frightened.'

Raphael turned to her, giving her a tormented look of mingled desire and denial.

'Do you not think I would like to tell myself that? That I would like to believe it? But I cannot. I must not. Because it may not be the truth, and because there is no way of knowing whether or not I possess my mother's family's curse.'

'I love you, Raphael, and I am willing to take the risk.'

'Maybe so, but I am not.'

'Because you don't love me?' Charley challenged

him. Surely if she could get him to say that he loved
her then she would be able to find a way to persuade
him to let her share his life?

'No, I don't love you.'

The pain that seized her was crucifying, unbearable.
Without knowing it she made a small sound, agonised
and heartrending. Raphael closed his eyes. He must not
weaken. It was for her sake that he was denying her—
for her future.

'Don't you think if I *did* love you that I would still
say there could be nothing between us? Don't you
think that if I loved you my concern would be for you,
for your ultimate happiness, your right to love a man
you will never need to fear—a man who can give you
the child or children that you will also love.' His voice
became harsher as he told her, 'I cannot and will not
imprison you in a relationship which ultimately you
will come to resent. I can't. I have told you that, and
if there were by some mischance to be a child...' He
paused and then told her heavily, 'It is my belief that
my mother took her own life after my father's death,
because she was afraid of being alone with the responsibility of what she might have passed on to me and
through me to generations as yet unborn.'

Charley's heart ached with compassion and love.

'I refuse to believe that you are affected by your
family's affliction, Raphael, and as for children—for
a woman who loves you, who truly loves you as I do,
you yourself would be enough,' she told him fiercely,
unable to keep her emotions out of her voice.

Now, at last, he turned fully to look at her. The

morning sunlight was cruel, revealing the toll his openness with her had taken on his haunted features.

'You cannot know that I will not be affected. Neither of us can. Do you think I want to see you recoil from me in horror and fear? To see the love shining in your eyes now turn to horror?'

Charley desperately wanted to go to him and hold him, almost as a mother might hold her child. He was the man she loved and he always would be. What he had revealed to her had only made her love him more, not less, just as it had made her want to share with him his exile from what other people took for granted.

'Raphael, please let me share this with you,' she begged him.

'No,' Raphael answered. 'To love someone and not yearn to create with them the miracle of a new life from that love is an act of denial beyond the limits of my own control. I may not have known that before, but I know it now. I learned that when I held you in my arms. I will not allow what I feel for you to chain you to me. Love—true, real love—has to be stronger than that. It must put what is right for the person loved above its own needs and desires.'

Raphael was saying that he loved her?

Joy lifted her heart—only for it to crash down again as she took in the full meaning of what Raphael had said.

'You cannot make that decision for me,' she told him. 'If you love me then—'

'Then nothing.' Raphael stopped her, his voice harsh. 'I cannot offer you my love and still think of myself as a man of honour. You must see that?'

'What I see,' Charley told him spiritedly, 'is that you are making us both suffer when we don't have to over an issue that may not even exist. I love you, Raphael. Of course I would love to have your child—but I will gladly and willingly sacrifice doing so to be with you and share your life.'

'I cannot allow you to do that.' His mouth twisted—the mouth she had kissed so passionately last night—and the lips that had touched her body so intimately, bringing her such pleasure, now held a cynical twist, causing her intense pain.

'Your own choice of words reveals the truth—you describe not having a child as a sacrifice,' Raphael told her. 'You cannot deny it. You used that description of your own volition.'

Charley could see that it was pointless for her to wish the word unsaid. She raged inwardly, blaming herself for her thoughtlessness, thinking how bitterly unfair it was that the whole of her future happiness should hang on one simple word.

'You may love me now, Charlotte,' Raphael told her, 'but there will come a time when the ache inside you for a child will be stronger than the ache inside you for me. I cannot let that happen. Not for my sake, but for yours. I am already guilty of allowing my own selfish need to overcome my principles, and in doing so I am hurting you. I shall not do so any more. When I return to Rome I will speak to my lawyer and to your employer, to arrange for someone else to take your place here, working on the project.'

Raphael ignored Charlotte's stifled protest.

'I shall, of course, compensate you financially…' he continued.

'Pay me off, you mean? Like a discarded toy you don't want any more? Is that how you always treat the women you sleep with, Raphael—by paying them off once you have had what you wanted from them?'

White-faced with grief, Charley flung the words at him, retreating to the top of the bed when he strode towards her, to grasp her shoulders and almost shake her.

'You will not say that,' he told her. 'You will not demean what we shared together and yourself by speaking in such a way. The money has nothing to do with our personal relationship. It is to compensate you because you will be losing your job.'

It was because his emotions were so raw that he was angry with her, Charley knew. The thought crossed her mind that if she increased that anger, if she really, really pushed him, then that emotion might spill over into a passion that would result in them making love, giving her a chance to prove to him that what they felt for one another was too strong to be ignored. Shame flooded through her. She must not taint what they had shared last night by attempting to manipulate him. She did not want her memories soured by her own shame.

Raphael released her, stepping back from her, removing the temptation to ignore her better self.

'It will take some time for everything to be sorted out—a couple of weeks at least, I imagine—and during that time it will be necessary for you to remain here at the *palazzo*.'

'And where will you be?' Charley had to ask him.

'I shall be in Rome. I cannot be here,' Raphael told her bleakly. 'Not now. It would be too much—for both of us. Do not look at me like that,' he warned her. 'I am doing this for your sake, and one day you will thank me for it.'

Charley shook her head, her vision of him blurred by the tears filling her eyes.

'No,' she told him brokenly. 'I will never do that, and I will never stop loving you.'

He was walking towards the door. She couldn't let him go.

'Raphael, please,' she begged him, running towards him, the sunlight splashing her naked body with golden light.

He had reached the door.

She put her hands on his arms and pleaded, 'We could be together. I understand now why the garden and its restoration is so important to you. It's because it is what you will give to posterity, isn't it? Instead of your children—your son. We could do it together, Raphael; together we could restore and create something of great beauty to give to your people.'

Charley felt the shudder that ripped through his body.

'Trust a woman to find some ridiculous and fictitious emotional fairytale and insist on substituting it for reason,' said Raphael, dismissing her statement, but he knew that she had touched a nerve. Her words were like the careful, gentle touch of an archaeologist, brushing away a protective covering to reveal something unbearably fragile beneath it. Only in his case what she had revealed was not some priceless piece of antiquity but instead his pitiful attempt to find a substitute in his life for all that he could not have—to find a purpose and a meaning that would compensate him for what he had to deny himself.

Charley's naked body was pressed close to his own, her face turned up to his, her gaze brimming with love and hope. All he had to do was open his arms to her and she would be his for ever. There would be no turning back. He would have her love to sustain him through the darkest of dark nights.

'A garden lives and breathes, Raphael, it gives love and joy to those who come into it. We could share that. It could be ours…'

The pain was almost too much for him. It reached out to every single part of him, along with the awareness of all that would be lost to him. He had to resist temptation. He had to endure the pain—for Charley. Desperately, Raphael formed a mental image of Charley—not as she was now, but as she would be holding her child in her arms, her whole body alight with the love she felt for it. Her child, but never, ever his.

'No!' he told her harshly, reaching for the door handle, forcing her to release him and step back from him.

It was over. There could be no going back.

CHAPTER FOURTEEN

SHE would be leaving Florence in ten days' time. Everything was arranged. She had her ticket; she would be picked up and driven to the airport—all she had to do was ensure that her paperwork was left in order and her appointments cancelled.

Charley started to pull open the drawer in the desk, to remove the desk diary she kept as an extra back-up reminder of the appointments stored electronically, determined to make sure that professionally nothing was overlooked. Her misery overflowed into irritation when the drawer wouldn't open properly. Kneeling down in front of the desk, she felt inside the drawer, quickly realising that the diary had become wedged against the underside of the desk. Picking up her ruler, she used it to try and prise the diary free, exhaling in impatient relief when she finally succeeded. The force of her probing, though, had sent the diary skidding right to the back of the drawer, with a definite thud of sound, obliging her to pull the drawer further out. Only when she did so, to her dismay, there was no sign of the diary and the back of the drawer itself was missing.

She had damaged Raphael's mother's desk. Horrified, Charley pulled the drawer out completely, and then frowned as she realised how much shorter it was than the full depth of the desk. Very carefully she slid her hand and her arm into the empty space where the drawer had been, feeling her way to the back of the space. It was more or less the same depth as the drawer, and indeed a good ten inches short of the depth of the desk. Curious now, Charley re-examined the space, pressing against the back wall and then exhaling in triumph when it suddenly gave way. It must be a hidden compartment, operated by a spring, and she must have inadvertently touched it when she had pushed her diary free. It was too deep for her to reach inside it, so she had to use her ruler again to edge out her diary and bring it within her reach. Only it wasn't just the diary she had edged out. There was something else as well: several thick sheets of expensive notepaper, poking out of an envelope that had obviously never been sealed.

Uncertainly Charley turned the envelope over, her heartbeat accelerating as she stared at what was written on it.

To my beloved son, Raphael…

Charley sank down onto the floor, still holding the envelope, her diary forgotten.

This was a letter to Raphael from his mother. It had to be. And she had no right to read it, but her hand was trembling so much that somehow the letter had begun to slip free of the envelope, the thick sheets sliding into her lap.

Putting down the envelope, Charley quickly picked the paper up.

Impossible now not to be aware of the elegant handwriting, of the date written at the top of the first sheet in dark ink.

The letter was nearly twenty years old, written quite obviously when Raphael had only been a boy. An aching longing filled her, a tender smile for the boy that Raphael must have been curving her mouth.

She looked down at the letter, the words written on it springing up as though demanding that she read them.

My dearest and dearly loved son—and you are that, Raphael, MY son, the son of my heart and my love. I am writing this letter to you in English because it is the language that my English governess taught me, as your father and I have taught it to you, so that we could all speak it together—our special 'secret' shared language. Your father is gone now, and my life without him is so empty. One day, when you yourself know true love, you will understand all that this means.

I write this letter now, knowing that it is what your father would want me to do. It is to be given to you when you come of age. We had planned to tell you together, and I fear I shall not have the strength to tell you on my own.

I beg you not to judge me too harshly, Raphael, for being too cowardly, too afraid of losing your love, to tell you the truth myself. The truth, though, must be told—for your own dear sake.

Now you are young, a boy still, but one day you will be a man, and when that time comes there are things that you will need to know.

She mustn't read any more, Charley told herself. She must fold up the letter and hand it to Anna to send on to Raphael. To continue to read something so obviously private was a gross invasion of the privacy of mother and son. And yet she was filled with a compulsion that she could not resist to read on.

Spreading out the heavy sheets of paper, Charley continued to read.

You know already of the terrible inheritance that has come down to me through my family. I have told you stories of lives ruined and destroyed, of the horror of the cruelty and madness that has surfaced in members of our blood, and part of the reason I have told you this is so that you will understand why your father and I chose to do what we have done.

You are my beloved son, Raphael, the greatest gift life has given me along with the love of your father. From the first moment of your conception, even before I held you in my arms for the first time, I loved you. You are my son, my child, even though the source that gave you life was not me.

I made a vow as a girl that I would not pass on to a child the burden that I had had to carry— the knowledge that whilst I had escaped the taint of our blood, my children, and their children after them might not do so. When your father and I married he knew of this vow I had made and he supported me in it. However, as the years went by I yearned increasingly to hold a child of our love in my arms. That need became a sickness in me for which I believed there could be no cure, until I learned that there was a doctor—not here in Italy but abroad—who had discovered a way to enable women who could not conceive natu- rally to have a child of their own. Initially your father was against such a thing, but he knew of my desperation, and so in the end he gave way, and we travelled abroad to see this doctor. He warned us that it would not be easy, nor the result guaranteed, but now I had hope—the hope of having a child from the love your father and I shared that would be free of my own blood.

So it was that your life began, with the gift of life from a childhood friend of mine of good family who had fallen on hard times. A woman with children of her own, who understood my need.

Those first early weeks when I knew that I carried you inside my body I hardly dared to believe that you actually were there. I was so afraid that I might lose you, but you yourself gave me strength, Raphael, because you were there, growing. You had not rejected me or spurned my body; instead you had made yourself part of me. I cannot tell you the joy I felt because you had accepted me as your mother, because you trusted me to protect you and provide for you. With every day that went by my strength grew because of your strength. I was so proud of you, so proud to be carrying you, your father's child, growing within me. Even before you were born I knew you and loved you.

To me you were mine every bit as much as you would have been had you been conceived from me. When after your birth you were placed in my arms I was joyful—not just because you were the image of your father, or even because I was holding you, but because I knew your life would be free of the shadows of my family past.

Over the years I have told you over and over again about that past, hoping that when the time came for me to tell you what I have written here you would understand and not turn away from me, or accuse me of deceit, no longer thinking of me as your mother. Even if you should do that, Raphael, you will always be my child, my so beloved son, who I carried with such joy and pride and who I have watched grow with equal joy and pride.

Charley lifted her head from the letter, biting her lip in an attempt to stem the tears spilling from her eyes. Every word she had written was filled with Raphael's mother's love for him, and reading the letter Charley had felt her emotion.

Why, though, had she hidden the letter away? There was no signature to it. Perhaps she had put it aside to be finished at a later date, but had not had the opportunity to do so?

How selfless a mother's love could be. Raphael's mother's desire to ensure that her son need not fear her past had come before her own obvious fear that the truth might come between them.

The truth!

Charley sat back on her heels. She was only just beginning to appreciate herself what the letter would mean—not only for Raphael himself, but also for them!

They could be together. Now there was nothing to keep them apart. Now they could love one another, without Raphael feeling that he was denying her anything.

She wanted to jump up and dance around the room. She was filled with energy and impatience. She would drive to Rome, take the letter herself to Raphael, so that she could be there when he read it. She knew that he would not reject his mother, that like her he would know how much and how selflessly she had loved him as her own child.

Her mind was racing ahead, making plans, but then abruptly a new thought struck her.

What if she was taking too much for granted? Raphael was a duke, the holder of an ancient title and estate, a member of a group of people who tended to marry within their own class in order to produce heirs.

Raphael might have seemed to care about her when he had believed that he must never have children, but what if his mother's revelations changed that? Just as he had put his concern for her future before his own feelings, wasn't it only right and fair that she should step back a bit now and allow him to come to her freely?

And if he didn't? If he should turn away from her? Charley shuddered under the misery of the pain that bit deeply into her. She had to do what was right—for Raphael.

An hour later she stood and watched as the courier drove away from the *palazzo,* taking with him the letter she had written to Raphael, enclosing his mother's letter to him, to be delivered by special delivery, no later than the morning.

She had been open and honest with him in her letter, admitting to reading what his mother had written, telling him how much she loved him and saying she hoped that now they could be together, but telling him as well that she would wait for him to make contact with her, and if he did not then she would leave for England, as arranged, and accept that their relationship was over.

She told herself she was worrying unnecessarily, because Raphael *did* love her. He had told her so himself. He had said, too, how much he wanted her as the mother of his children. It was foolish of her to have any doubts, but it was the right thing to do to wait for him to come to her to confirm his feelings for her.

By this time tomorrow he would be here, and she would be in his arms.

CHAPTER FIFTEEN

IT WAS over, Charley acknowledged bleakly, as the plane taking her home to Manchester began its descent through the grey clouds to the rain-soaked tarmac of the airport. Her throat felt raw from the tears she refused to allow herself to cry. Now, with them threatening again, she had to close her eyes tightly, no doubt making the man sitting next to her think she was a nervous passenger. Charley smiled wryly.

Right up until the last moment she had gone on hoping—right up until the car had arrived for her this morning and she had finally had to accept that Raphael did not want her.

It was ten days now since she had sent him the letters. At first with every new hour she had expected to see him arrive at the *palazzo*, to take her in his arms and tell her how much he loved her.

But when the hours and then the days began to pass, without him making any contact with her at all, her expectation had turned to despair. Unable to eat or sleep, she had watched hollow-eyed, night after night, unable to sleep, simply staring out through her bedroom window into the darkness, hoping against hope that he would appear.

His silence meant that her pride would not allow her to contact him again—not so much as an e-mail. What was the point when he had made it so very clear that he no longer wanted her?

Soon now she would be home. Home? There was no home for her now. It was hard for her to keep her misery at bay as the plane touched down. Her only true home, the only home she wanted, was within Raphael's heart, and there was no place there for her. She was an outcast, denied the only place she wanted to be, the only man she wanted to love.

The arrivals hall was busy with people pressing close to the barriers, eager to see the friends and family they were there to welcome. Charley barely spared them a glance. She hadn't warned her own family to expect her, clinging on right to the last second before her plane took off to the hope that by some miracle Raphael would not allow her to leave.

How foolish she had been—but at least she had her memories. She was past the waiting crowd now and in the arrivals hall proper, thronged with tired travellers intent on making their way to whatever transport they had arranged to get them from the airport to their homes. She would have to take a taxi—expensive, but fortunately the house she shared with her sisters in South Manchester wasn't very far from the airport.

She could hear the sound of movement behind

her—someone walking fast, someone reaching for her arm. No, not someone, she recognised weakly as she turned round. Not someone at all, but the only one.

'Raphael…' As she breathed his name Charley wondered if somehow he was merely a figment of her imagination, an image she had conjured up out of her own need—because how could he be here?

But he was, and he was pulling her into his arms and holding her there, his heart thumping heavily and fast against her.

'I can't believe you're here,' was all Charley could manage to say.

'Believe it,' Raphael responded. 'Believe it, and believe too that I will not leave your side until you have promised that you will never leave me again.'

'I thought it was what you wanted,' Charley tried to protest, but her heart wasn't in it—it was far too busy racing with joy and disbelief because Raphael was here, with her.

'You are what I want—all I want—all I will ever want. I can't go on without you. I thought I could, but I can't. Will you marry me, Charlotte Wareham? Will you come back to Italy with me and be my wife?'

He looked and sounded so humble, or at least as humble as it was possible for such a naturally proud man to be, that Charley suspected she would have forgiven him anything.

'There is nothing I want more than for us to be together, Raphael.'

'We will be married as soon as it can be arranged. I do not intend to risk losing you again.' He was holding her hand now, twining his fingers through her own, lacing the two of them together.

'I have been thinking about this matter of children,' he told her abruptly. He was looking at a point over her shoulder, and his jaw was tensing, Charley observed, as it did when he was trying to control his emotions.

'With modern-day medical science it is perfectly possible for us to have a child that will not carry my genes—a child, that will be born of you but will not carry my genes. A child that I will love as my own because it is part of you. That way I shall not be depriving you of motherhood. And, as for myself, if the day should come when it becomes evident that I have inherited my mother's family's curse then I shall end our marriage and give you your freedom.'

Charley stared at him in confused bewilderment, unable to say anything as the thoughts rushed around inside her head. Hadn't he read her letter?

'Did you get the letter I sent to you in Rome?' she asked him.

Immediately Raphael frowned.

'No. I left Rome three days after we parted. I could not work, I could not sleep—I could not do anything but think about you and all that I had lost. I own a small skiing chalet up in the mountains. I went there, intending to force myself to give up all thoughts of you, but instead I came to realise that I could not bear my life without you. I began to think that maybe you were right—that maybe my anger was not a sign of what I had inherited. I wanted to believe that more than you can know, because it was my way back to you. Then I told myself that we could still have a child—a child that would carry your genes only—and my hopes grew. All I wanted was to be with you, to talk with you and ask you to be my wife, but there was an accident on my way back to Rome.'

'An accident?' Anxiety sharpened Charley's voice. 'What happened? Are you all right?'

'It was my own fault. I was driving too fast, concentrating on being with you instead of on my driving. Luckily no damage was done other than to the Ferrari, but the hospital insisted on keeping me overnight in case I had concussion, even though I told them that it was vitally important that I be allowed to leave. Unfortunately I was too late. As I arrived at the airport your plane was taking off.'

'But you got here before me. How…?'

'I hired a private plane,' Raphael told her dismissively.

'Oh, Raphael.' Charley blinked back her tears. 'Are you sure about what you're saying? About us being together and everything?'

He didn't flinch.

'I mean every word I have said to you. I love you more than I ever thought it possible for me to love anyone. You are my life, my heartbeat, every breath in my body. You are everything to me, Charlotte, and without you I am nothing—there is nothing. Say you will marry me. Come home with me. Tell me that you love me.'

'I do love you, Raphael,' Charley confirmed, 'but there is something I have to tell you before we can talk about marriage—something important.'

She could see that he was concerned, even though he tried to conceal it from her.

'Very well, but we will discuss this oh, so important matter in the comfort of the plane and not here.'

That would mean going back to Italy with him, and if, once he knew the truth about his own birth, he should change his mind about wanting to marry her she would have to leave all over again. But how could she deny him what he was asking after what he had told her?

Unable to trust herself to speak, silently Charley nodded her head.

CHAPTER SIXTEEN

THE plane had taken off. They were alone in the comfort of its elegant interior, furnished more like a small sitting room than any kind of aircraft with which Charley was familiar.

The minute the steward had left them Raphael had taken her in his arms, kissing her so passionately and with such longing that Charley had been incapable of doing anything other than responding.

'I cannot wait for us to be alone,' Raphael told her. 'I cannot wait to make you properly mine again, to hold you in my arms and love you. We will spend tonight in Florence, at the apartment, and then tomorrow we will start to make the arrangements for our marriage.'

What if she simply didn't tell him? What if she begged him to stay with her until after they were married and he didn't see the letter until it was too late and he was committed to her? He had, after all, said that he loved her. Why should she risk losing him when she loved him so much?

Charley closed her eyes, willing away the temptation tormenting her.

'There is something you have to know…something you *must* know, just in case you should want to change your mind about marrying me.'

There—she had said it, and now Raphael was looking at her with that same haughty frown she remembered from the first time she had seen him.

'So what is this something—this secret from your past?'

'It isn't from my past, Raphael. It's from yours.'

Hardly daring to risk looking at him, in case she lost her courage, Charley plunged on.

'Whilst I was clearing my things from your mother's desk, by accident I found a concealed compartment. There was a letter in it. A letter your mother had written to you and for you. I shouldn't have read it, but I did… I sent it to you in Rome by special delivery. I hoped that when you'd read it you'd come to me, and when you didn't I assumed…that is to say…'

'A letter from my mother? How can that affect our plans to marry?'

Charley took a deep breath.

'Raphael, although you didn't know it when you made that suggestion, that selfless suggestion about us having a child, you were following in your own mother's footsteps. She loved you so much—so very, very much—her love for you shines out of her letter. Reading it made me cry. She carried you in her body, Raphael, she loved you as her child, but you were not her biological child. Like you, she did not want to take the risk of burdening a child with her own inheritance, and like you she made the decision to allow medical science to provide her with the means of giving birth to your father's child without that child having to carry her genes. The reason she told you so often about those genes was because she hoped that when you knew the truth you would understand that she had taken the steps she did take to protect you—because her love for you was such that she wanted you to be free of fear, for yourself and your descendants.'

Raphael's face was drained of colour and his mouth was set grimly. Charley's heart sank. Surely he was not going to reject his mother's love for him?

'And because of this you have doubts about marrying me?'

Charley was astounded.

'No, of course not. There is nothing I want more than to marry you. It is for *your* sake that I wanted you to know. Don't you see, Raphael? Your mother's letter changes everything. Now you are free to marry and have children, to have an heir, you can marry anyone you wish—someone far more suitable to be the mother of your son than I am.'

'More suitable? How could that be possible? There is no one more suitable to bear my children than you. How could there be when it is you that I love?'

'Oh, Raphael.'

She was in his arms, holding him as tightly as he was holding her, kissing him as passionately and hungrily as he was kissing her.

'You are my life,' he told her fiercely. 'My love and my life.'

They kissed again, sweetly and tenderly this time, their kiss a shared vow, a shared commitment to their love and their future together.

'When the garden is finished, could we name it for your mother, do you think?' Charley asked Raphael as he released her.

She could see the sheen of emotion in his eyes when he looked down at her.

'Yes,' he told her. 'We will name it for her in remembrance of the gift of love she gave to me when she gave me life.'

'How long do you think it will be before we are in Florence?' Charley whispered against his lips as she kissed him again.

'Far too long for the way I feel at the moment,' Raphael answered. 'Far far too long.'

Only it wasn't, and by the time the sun was setting they were standing together in the privacy of the bedroom where Raphael had first made love to her. The scent that was the only covering Charley was wearing filled the evening air.

'This was what I wanted when you gave it to me,' Charley told Raphael. 'I wanted to lie in your arms wearing only the scent and your touch.'

A delicate quiver of erotic pleasure ran through her when Raphael gathered her naked body against his own, and her love for him filled her when he told her huskily, 'I love you more than I can find the words to say. You have made me complete and brought light to the darkest places of my life. Now that you are mine I shall never let you go.'

'And I shall never want you to,' Charley promised him.

MARRIAGE: TO
CLAIM HIS TWINS

PENNY JORDAN

PROLOGUE

ALEXANDER KONSTANTINAKOS, powerful, formidable, billionaire head of an internationally renowned container shipping line originally founded by his late grandfather, stood in the middle of the elegantly luxurious drawing room of his home on the Greek Ionian island of Theopolis, his gaze riveted on the faces of the twin boys in the photograph he was holding.

Two black-haired, olive-skinned and dark-eyed identical faces looked back at him, their mother kneeling down beside them. The three of them were shabbily dressed in cheap-looking clothes.

Tall, dark-haired, with the features of two thousand years of alpha-male warriors and victors sculpted into the bones of his handsome face the same way that their determination was sculpted into his psyche, he stood in the now silent room, the accusation his sister had just made was still echoing through his head.

'They have to be your sons,' she had accused Nikos, their younger brother. 'They have our family features stamped on them, and you were at university in Manchester.'

Alexander—Sander to his family—didn't need to keep gazing at the photograph Elena had taken with her mobile phone on her way through Manchester Airport after visiting her husband's family to confirm her state-ment, or to memorise the boys' faces. They were already carved into his memory for all time.

'I don't know anything about them,' his younger brother Nikos denied, breaking the silence. 'They aren't mine, Sander, I promise you. Please believe me.'

'Of course they're yours,' Elena corrected their younger brother. 'Just look at those faces. Nikos is lying, Sander. Those children are of our blood.'

Sander looked at his younger sister and brother, on the verge of quarrelling just as they had always done as children. There were only two years between them, but he had been born five years before Elena and seven before Nikos, and after their grandfather's death as the only adult family member left in their lives he had natu-rally taken on the responsibility of acting as a father figure to them. That had often meant arbitrating between them when they argued.

This time, though, it wasn't arbitration that was called for.

Sander looked at the photograph again and then an-nounced curtly, 'Of our blood, but not of Nikos's making. Nikos is speaking the truth. The children are not his.'

Elena stared at him.

'How can you know that?'

Sander turned towards the windows and looked beyond them to where the horizon met the deep blue of the Aegean Sea. Outwardly he might appear calm, but inside his chest his heart was thudding with fury. Inside his head images were forming, memories he had thought well buried surfacing.

'I know it because they are mine,' he answered his sister, watching as her eyes widened with the shock of his disclosure.

She wasn't the only one who was shocked, Sander acknowledged. He had been shocked himself when he had looked at her phone and immediately recognised the young woman kneeling beside the two young boys who so undeniably bore the stamp of their fathering—*his* fathering. Oddly, she looked if anything younger now than she had the night he had met her in a Manchester club favoured by young footballers, and thus the haunt of the girls who chased after them. He had been taken there by a business acquaintance, who had left him to his own devices having picked up a girl himself, urging Sander to do the same.

Sander's mouth hardened. He had buried the memory of that night as deeply as he could. A one-night stand with an alcohol-fuelled girl dressed in overly tight and incredibly revealing clothes, wearing too much make-up, who had made such a deliberate play for him. At one point she had actually caught hold of his hand, as though about to drag him to bed with her. It wasn't something any real man with any pride or self-respect could ever be proud of—not even when there were the kind of extenuating circumstances there had been that night. She had been one of a clutch of such girls, openly seeking the favours of the well-paid young footballers who favoured the place. Greedy, amoral young women, whose one desire was to find themselves a rich lover or better still a rich husband. The club, he had been told, was well known for attracting such young women.

He had had sex with her out of anger and resentment—against her for pushing him, and against his grandfather for trying to control his life. He'd been refusing to allow him a greater say in the running of the business which, in his stubborn determination not to move with the times, he had been slowly destroying. And against his parents—his father for dying, even though that had been over a decade ago, leaving him without his support, and his mother, who had married his father out of duty whilst continuing to love another man. All those things, all that anger had welled up inside him, and the result was now here in front of him.

His sons.

His.

A feeling like nothing he had ever experienced before seized hold of him. A feeling that, until it had struck him, he would have flatly denied he would ever experience. He was a modern man—a man of logic, not emotion, and certainly not the kind of emotion he was feeling right now. Gut wrenching, instinctive, tearing at him—an emotion born of a cultural inheritance that said that a man's children, especially his sons, belonged under his roof.

Those boys were his. Their place was here with him, not in England. Here they could learn what it meant to be his sons, a Konstantinakos of Theopolis, could grow into their heritage. He could father them and guide them as his sense of responsibility demanded that he should. How much damage had they already suffered through the woman who had borne them?

He had given them life without knowing it, but now that he did know he would stop at nothing to bring them home to Theopolis, where they belonged.

CHAPTER ONE

CURSING as she heard the doorbell ring, Ruby remained where she was, on her hands and knees, hoping that whoever it was would give up and go away, leaving her in peace to get on with her cleaning. However, the bell rang again, this time almost imperiously. Someone was pressing hard on the bell.

Cursing again under her breath, Ruby backed out of the downstairs cloakroom, feeling hot and sticky, and not in any mood to have her busy blitz on cleaning whilst her twin sons were at school interrupted. She got to her feet, pushing her soft blonde curls off her face as she did so, before marching towards the front door of the house she shared with two older sisters and her own twin sons. She yanked it open.

'Look, I'm—' Her sentence went unfinished, her voice suspended by shock as she stared at the man standing on the doorstep.

Shock, disbelief, fear, anger, panic, and a sharp spear of something else that she didn't recognise exploded inside her like a fireball, with such powerful intensity that her body was drained of so much energy that she was left feeling shaky and weak, trembling inwardly beneath the onslaught of emotions.

Of course he *would* be dressed immaculately, in a dark business suit worn over a crisp blue shirt, whilst she was wearing her old jeans and a baggy tee shirt. Not that it really mattered how she looked. After all, she had no reason to want to impress him—had she? And she certainly had no reason to want him to think of her as a desirable woman, groomed and dressed for his approval. She had to clench her stomach muscles against the shudder of revulsion that threatened to betray her. The face that had haunted her dreams and then her nightmares hadn't changed—or aged. If anything he looked even more devastatingly handsome and virile than she had remembered, the dark gold gaze that had mesmerised her so effectively every bit as compelling now as it had been then. Or was it because she was a woman now and not the girl she had been that she was so immediately and shockingly aware of what a very sexual man he was? Ruby didn't know, and she didn't *want* to know.

The disbelief that had frozen her into silence had turned like snow in the sun to a dangerous slush of fear and horror inside her head—and her heart? *No!* Whatever effect he had once had on her heart, Sander Konstantinakos had no power to touch it now.

But still the small betraying word, 'You,' slid from the fullness of the naturally warm-coloured lips that had caused her parents to name her Ruby, causing a look of mixed contempt and arrogance to flash from the intense gold of Sander's eyes. Eyes the colour of the king of the jungle—as befitted a man who was in effect the ruler of the Mediterranean island that was his home.

Instinctively Ruby started to close the door on him, wanting to shut out not just Sander himself but everything he represented, but he was too quick for her, taking hold of the door and forcing it open so that he could step into the hall—and then close the door behind him, enclosing them both in the small domestic space, with its smell of cleaning fluid. Strong as it was, it still wasn't strong enough to protect her from the scent of *him*. A rash of prickly sensation raised the hairs at the back of her neck and then ran down her spine. This was ridiculous. Sander meant nothing to her now, just as she had meant nothing to him that night... But she mustn't think about that. She must concentrate instead on what she was now, not what she had been then, and she must remember the promise she had made to the twins when they had been born—she would put the past behind her.

What she had never expected was that that past would seek her out, and now it had...

'What are you doing here?' she demanded, determined to wrest control of the situation from Sander. 'What do you want?'

His mouth might be aesthetically perfect, with that well-cut top lip balancing the promise of sensuality with his fuller bottom lip, but there was nothing sensual about the tight-lipped look he was giving her, and his words were as sharply cold as the air outside the Manchester hotel in which he had abandoned her that winter morning.

'I think you know the answer to that,' he said, his English as fluent and as accentless as she remembered. 'What I want, what I have come for and what I mean to have, are my sons.'

'*Your* sons?' Fiercely proud of her twin sons, and equally fiercely maternally protective of them, there was nothing he could have said which would have been more guaranteed to arouse Ruby's anger than his verbal claim on them. Angry colour burned in the smooth perfection of Ruby's normally calm face, and her blue-green eyes were fiery with the fierce passion of her emotions.

It was over six years since this man had taken her, used her and then abandoned her as casually as though she was a…a nothing. A cheap, impulsively bought garment which in the light of day he had discarded for its cheapness. Oh, yes, she knew that she had only herself to blame for what had happened to her that fatal night. *She* had been the one to flirt with him, even if that flirtation had been alcohol-induced, and no matter how she tried to excuse her behaviour it still shamed her. But not its result—not her beautiful, adorable, much loved sons. They could never shame her, and from the moment they had been born she had been determined to be a mother of whom they could be proud—a mother with whom they could feel secure, and a mother who, no matter how much she regretted the manner in which they had been conceived, would not for one minute even want to go back in time and avoid their conception. Her sons were her life. *Her* sons.

'My sons—' she began, only to be interrupted.

'*My* sons, you mean—since in my country it is the father who has the right to claim his children, not the mother.'

'My sons were not fathered by you,' Ruby continued firmly and of course untruthfully.

'Liar,' Sander countered, reaching inside his jacket to produce a photograph which he held up in front of her.

The blood left Ruby's face. The photograph had been taken at Manchester Airport, when they had all gone to see her middle sister off on her recent flight to Italy, and the resemblance of the twins to the man who had fathered them was cruelly and undeniably revealed. The two boys were cast perfectly in their father's image, right down to the unintentionally arrogant masculine air they could adopt at times, as though deep down somewhere in their genes there was an awareness of the man who had fathered them.

Watching the colour come and go in Ruby's face, Sander allowed himself to give her a triumphant look. Of *course* the boys were his. He had known it the first second he had looked at the image on his sister's mobile phone. Their mirror image resemblance to him had sent a jolt of emotion through him unlike anything he had previously experienced.

It hadn't taken the private agency he had contacted very long to trace Ruby—although Sander had frowned over comments in the report he had received from them that implied that Ruby was a devoted mother who dedicated herself to raising her sons and was unlikely to give them up willingly. But Sander had decided that Ruby's very devotion to his sons might be the best tool he could use to ensure that she gave them up to him.

'My sons' place is with me, on the island that is their home and which ultimately will be their inheritance. Under our laws they belong to me.'

'Belong? They are children, not possessions, and no court in this country would let you take them from me.'

She was beginning to panic, but she was determined not to let him see it.

'You think not? You are living in a house that belongs to your sister, on which she has a mortgage she can no longer afford to repay, you have no money of your own, no job. No training—nothing! I, on the other hand, can provide my sons with everything that you cannot—a home, a good education, a future.'

Although she was shaken by the knowledge of how thoroughly he had done his homework, had had her investigated, Ruby was still determined to hold her ground and not allow him to overwhelm her.

'Maybe so. But can you provide them with love and the knowledge that they are truly loved and wanted? Of course you can't—because you don't love them. How can you? You don't know them.'

There—let him answer *that*! But even as she made her defiant stand Ruby's heart was warning her that Sander had raised an issue that she could not ignore and would ultimately have to face. Honesty compelled her to admit it.

'I do know that one day they will want to know who fathered them and what their family history is,' she said.

It was hard for her to make that admission—just as it had been hard for her to answer the questions the boys had already asked, saying that they did have a daddy but he lived in a different country. Those words had reminded her of what she was denying her sons because of the circumstances in which she had conceived them. One day, though, their questions would be those of teenagers, not little boys, and far more searching, far more knowing.

Ruby looked away from Sander, instinctively wanting to hide her inner fears from him. The problem of telling the boys how she had come to have them lay across her heart and her conscience in an ever present heavy weight. At the moment they simply accepted that, like many of the other children they were at school with, they did not have a daddy living with them. But one day they would start to ask more questions, and she had hoped desperately that she would not have to tell them the truth until they were old enough to accept it without judging her. Now Sander had stirred up all the anxieties she had tried to put to one side. More than anything else she wanted to be a good mother, to give her boys the gift of a secure childhood filled with love; she wanted them to grow up knowing they were loved, confident and happy, without the burden of having to worry about adult relationships. For that reason she was determined never, ever to begin a relationship with anyone. A changing parade of 'uncles' and 'stepfathers' wasn't what she wanted for her boys.

But now Sander, with his demands and his questions, was forcing her to think about the future and her sons' reactions to the reality of their conception. The fact that they did not have a father who loved them.

Anger and panic swirled through her.

'Why are you doing this?' she demanded. 'The boys mean nothing to you. They are five years old, and you didn't even know that they existed until now.'

'That is true. But as for them meaning nothing to me—you are wrong. They are of my blood, and that alone means that I have a responsibility to ensure that they are brought up within their family.'

He wasn't going to tell her about that atavistic surge of emotion and connection he had felt the minute he had seen the twins' photograph. Sander still didn't really understand it himself. He only knew that it had brought him here, and that it would keep him here until she handed over to him his sons.

'It can't have been easy for you financially, bringing them up.'

Sander was offering her sympathy? Ruby was immediately suspicious. She longed to tell him that what *hadn't* been easy for her was discovering at seventeen that she was pregnant by a man who had slept with her and then left her, but somehow she managed to resist doing so.

Sander gestured round the hall.

'Even if your sister is able to keep up the mortgage payments on this house, have you thought about what would happen if either of your sisters wanted to marry and move out? At the moment you are financially dependent on their goodwill. As a caring mother, naturally you will want your sons to have the best possible education and a comfortable life. I can provide them with both, and provide you with the money to live your own life. It can't be much fun for you, tied to two small children all the time.'

She had been right to be suspicious, Ruby recognised, as the full meaning of Sander's offer hit her. Did he really expect her to *sell* her sons to him? Didn't he realise how obscene his offer was? Or did he simply not care?

His determination made her cautious in her response, her instincts warning her to be careful about any innocent admission she might make as to the financial hardship they were all currently going through, in case Sander tried to use that information against her at a later date. So, instead of reacting with the anger she felt, she said instead, 'The twins are only five. Now that they're at school I'm planning to continue my education. As for me having fun—the boys provide me with all the fun I want or need.'

'You'll forgive me if I say that I find that hard to believe, given the circumstances under which we met,' was Sander's smooth and cruel response.

'That was six years ago, and in circumstances that—' Ruby broke off. Why should she explain herself to him? The people closest to her—her sisters—knew and understood what had driven her to the reckless behaviour that had resulted in the twins' conception, and their love and support for her had never wavered. She owed Sander nothing after all—much less the revelation of her teenage vulnerabilities. 'That was then,' she corrected herself, adding firmly, 'This is now.'

The knowing look Sander was giving her made Ruby want to protest—*You're wrong. I'm not what you think. That wasn't the real me that night.* But common sense and pride made her hold back the words.

'I'm prepared to be very generous to you financially in return for you handing the twins over to me,' Sander continued. 'Very generous indeed. You're still young.'

In fact he had been surprised to discover that the night they had met she had been only seventeen. Dressed and made-up as she had been, he had assumed that she was much older. Sander frowned. He hadn't enjoyed the sharp spike of distaste he had experienced against himself at knowing he had taken such a young girl to bed. Had he known her age he would have… What? Given her a stern talking to and sent her home in a cab? Had he been in control of himself that night he would not have gone to bed with her at all, no matter what her age, but the unpalatable truth was that he had *not* been in control of himself. He had been in the grip of anger and a sense of frustration he had never experienced either before or since that night—a firestorm of savage, bitter emotion that had driven him into behaviour that, if he was honest, still irked his pride and sense of self. Other men might exhibit such behaviour, but he had always thought of himself as above that kind of thing. He had been wrong, and now the evidence of that behaviour was confronting him in the shape of the sons he had fathered. Sander believed he had a duty to ensure that they did not suffer because of that behaviour. That was what had brought him here.

And there was no way he was going to leave until he had got what he had come for.

And just that?

Ruby shook her head.

'Buy my children, you mean?'

Sander could hear the hostility in Ruby's voice as well as see it in her eyes.

'Because that *is* what you're talking about,' Ruby accused him, adding fiercely, 'And if I'd had any thought of allowing you into their lives, what you've just said would make me change my mind. There's nothing you could offer me that would make me want to risk my sons' emotional future by allowing *you* to have any kind of contact with them.'

Her words were having more of an effect on him than Sander liked to admit. A man of pride and power, used to commanding not just the obedience but also the respect and the admiration of others, he was stung by Ruby's criticism of him. He wasn't used to being refused anything by anyone—much less by a woman he remembered as an over-made-up and under-dressed little tart who had come on to him openly and obviously. Not that there was anything of that girl about her now, dressed in faded jeans and a loose top, her face free of make-up and her hair left to curl naturally of its own accord. The girl he remembered had smelled of cheap scent; the woman in front of him smelled of cleaning product. He would have to change his approach if he was to overcome her objections, Sander recognised.

Quickly changing tack, he challenged her. 'Nothing

I could offer *you*, maybe, but what about what I can offer my sons? You speak of their emotions. Have you thought, I wonder, how they are going to feel when they grow up to realise what you have denied them in refusing to let them know their father?'

'That's not fair,' Ruby objected angrily, knowing that Sander had found her most vulnerable spot where the twins were concerned.

'What is not fair, surely, is you denying my sons the opportunity to know their father and the culture that is their birthright?'

'As your bastards?' The horrible word tasted bitter, but it had to be said. 'Forced to stand in second place to your legitimate children, and no doubt be resented by your wife?'

'I have no other children, nor any wife.'

Why was her heart hammering so heavily, thudding into her chest wall? It didn't matter to her whether or not Sander was married, did it?

'I warn you now, Ruby, that I intend to have my sons with me. Whatever it takes to achieve that and by whatever means.'

Ruby's mouth went dry. Stories she had read about children being kidnapped by a parent and stolen away out of the country flooded into her mind. Sander was a very rich and a very powerful man. She had discovered that in the early days after she had met him, when she had stupidly imagined that he would come back to her and had avidly read everything she could about him, wanting to learn everything she could—until the reality of the situation had forced her to accept that the fantasy she had created of Sander marrying her and looking after her was just that: a fantasy created by her need to find someone to replace the parents she had lost and keep her safe.

It was true that Sander could give the boys far more than she could materially, and the unwelcome thought slid into her mind that there could come a day when, as Sander had cruelly predicted, the twins might actually resent her and blame her for preventing them from benefitting from their father's wealth and, more importantly, from knowing him. Boys needed a strong male figure in their lives they could relate to. Everyone knew that. Secretly she had been worrying about the lack of any male influence in their lives. But if at times she had been tempted to pray for a solution to that problem she had certainly not envisaged that solution coming in the form of the boys' natural father. A kindly, grandfather-type figure for them was as much as she had hoped for, because after their birth she had decided that she would never take the risk of getting involved with a man who might turn out to be only a temporary presence in her sons' lives. She would rather remain celibate than risk that.

The truth, in her opinion, was that children thrived best with two parents in a stable relationship—a mother and a father, both committed to their wellbeing.

A mother and a father. More than most, she knew the damage that could be done when that stability wasn't there.

A sense of standing on the edge of a precipice filled

her—an awareness that the decision she made now would affect her sons for the rest of their lives. Shakily she admitted to herself that she wished her sisters were there to help her, but they weren't. They had their own lives, and ultimately the boys were *her* responsibility, their happiness resting in *her* hands. Sander was determined to have them. He had said so. He was a wealthy, powerful and charismatic man who would have no difficulty whatsoever in persuading others that the boys should be with him. But she was their mother. She couldn't let him take them from her—for their sakes even more than her own. Sander didn't love them; he merely wanted them. She doubted he was capable of understanding what love was. Yes, he would provide well for them materially, but children needed far more than that, and her sons needed *her*. She had raised them from birth; they needed her even more than she needed them.

If she couldn't stop Sander from claiming his sons, then she owed it to them to make sure that she remained with them. Sander wouldn't want that, of course. He despised and disliked her.

Her heart started to thud uncomfortably heavily and far too fast as it fought against the solution proposed by her brain, but now that the thought was there it couldn't be ignored. Sander had said there was nothing he would not do to have his sons living with him. Well, maybe she should put his claim to the test, because she knew that there was no sacrifice she herself would not make for their sakes—no sacrifice at all. The challenge she intended to put to him was a huge risk for her to take, but for the boys' sake she was prepared to take it. It was, after all, a challenge she was bound to win—because Sander would never accept the terms with which she was about to confront him. She was sure of that. She let out her pent up breath.

'You say the boys' place is with you?'

'It is.'

'They are five years old and I am their mother.' Ruby took a deep breath, hoping that her voice wouldn't shake with the nervousness she was fighting to suppress and thus betray her. 'If you really care about their wellbeing as much as you claim then you must know that they are too young to be separated from me.'

She had a point, Sander was forced to admit, even though he didn't like doing so.

'You need to be very sure about why you want the twins, Sander.' Ruby pressed home her point. 'And that your desire to have them isn't merely a rich man's whim. Because the only way I will allow them to be with you is if I am there with them—as their mother and your wife.'

CHAPTER TWO

THERE—she had said it. Thrown down the gauntlet, so to speak, and given him her challenge.

In the silence that followed Ruby could literally hear her own heart beating as she held her breath, waiting for Sander to refuse her demand—because she knew that he *would* refuse it, and having refused it he must surely be forced to step back and accept that the boys' place was with her.

Trying not to give in to the shakiness invading her body, Ruby could hardly believe that she had actually had the courage to say what she had. She could tell from Sander's expression that her demand had shocked him, although he was quick to mask his reaction.

Marriage, Sander thought quickly, mentally assessing his options. He wanted his sons. There was no doubt in his mind about that, nor any doubt that they were his. Marriage to their mother would give him certain rights over them, but it would also give Ruby certain rights over his wealth. That, of course, was exactly what she wanted. Marriage to him followed by an equally speedy

divorce and a very generous financial divorce settle-
ment. He could read her mind so easily. Even so, she
had caught him off-guard—although he told himself
cynically that he should perhaps have been prepared for
her demand. He was, after all, a very wealthy man.

'I applaud your sharp-witted business acumen,' he
told Ruby drily, in a neutral voice that gave away nothing of the fury he was really feeling. 'You rejected my
initial offer of a generous payment under the guise of
being a devoted mother, when in reality you were
already planning to play for higher stakes.'

'That's not true,' Ruby denied hotly, astonished by
his interpretation of her demand. 'Your money means
nothing to me, Sander—nothing at all,' she told him
truthfully, adding for good measure, 'And neither do
you. For me, the fact that you choose to think of my
offer in terms of money simply underlines all the reasons why I am not prepared to allow my sons anywhere
near you unless I am there.'

'That is how *you* feel, but what about how *they* might
feel?' Sander pressed her. 'A good mother would never
behave so selfishly. She would put her children's interests first.'

How speedily Sander had turned the tables on her,
Ruby recognised. What had begun as a challenge to
him she had been confident would make him back down
had now turned into a double-edged sword which right
now he was wielding very skilfully against her, cutting
what she had thought was secure ground away from
under her feet.

'They need their mother—' she started.

'They are *my* sons,' Sander interrupted her angrily. 'And I mean to have them. If I have to marry you to facilitate that, then so be it. But make no mistake, Ruby. I intend to have my sons.'

His response stunned her. She had been expecting him to refuse, to back down, to go away and leave them alone—anything rather than marry her. Sander had called her bluff and left her defenceless.

Now Ruby could see a reality she hadn't seen before. Sander really did want the boys and he meant to have them. He was rich and powerful, well able to provide materially for his sons. What chance would she have of keeping them if he pursued her through the courts? At best all she could hope for was shared custody, with the boys passed to and fro between them, torn between two homes, and that was the last thing she wanted for them. *Why* had Sander had to discover that he had fathered them? Hadn't life been cruel enough to her as it was?

Marriage to him, which she had not in any kind of way wanted, had now devastatingly turned into the protection she was forced to recognise she might need if she was to continue to have the permanent place in her sons' lives that she had previously taken for granted.

Marriage to Sander wouldn't just provide her sons with a father, she recognised now through growing panic, it would also protect her rights as a mother. As long as they were married the twins would have both parents there for them.

Both parents. Ruby swallowed painfully. Wasn't it

true that she had spent many sleepless nights worrying
about the future and the effect not having a father figure
might have on her sons?

A father figure, but not their real father. She had
never imagined them having Sander in their lives—not
after those first agonising weeks of being forced to
accept that she meant nothing to him.

She wasn't going to give up, though. She would fight
with every bit of her strength for her sons.

Holding her head up she told him fiercely, 'Very
well, then. The choice is yours, Sander. If you genuinely
want the boys because they are your sons, and because
you want to get to know them and be part of their lives,
then you will accept that separating them from me will
inflict huge emotional damage on them. You will understand, as I do, no matter how much that understanding
galls you, that children need the security of having two
parents they know are there for them—will always be
there for them. You will be prepared to make the same
sacrifice that I am prepared to make to provide them
with the security that comes from having two parents
committed to them and to each other through marriage.'

'Sacrifice?' Sander demanded. 'I am a billionaire. I
don't think there are many women who would consider
marriage to me a *sacrifice*.'

Did he really believe that? If so, it just showed how
right she was to want to ensure that her sons grew up
knowing there were far more important things in life
than money.

'You are very cynical,' she told him. 'There are any

number of women who would be appalled by what you have just said—women who put love before money, women like me who put their children first, women who would run from a man like you. I don't want your money, and I am quite willing to sign a document saying so.'

'Oh, you will be doing that. Make no mistake about it,' Sander assured her ruthlessly. Did she really expect him to fall for her lies and her faked lack of interest in his money? 'There is no way I will abandon my sons to the care of a mother who could very soon be without a roof over her head—a mother who would have to rely on charity in order to feed and clothe them—a mother who dressed like a tart and offered herself to a man she didn't know.'

Ruby flinched as though he had physically hit her, but she still managed to ask quickly, 'Were *you* any better? Or does the fact that you are a man and I'm a woman somehow mean that my behaviour was worse than yours? I was a seventeen-year-old-girl; you were an adult male.'

A seventeen-year-old girl. Angered by the reminder, Sander reacted against it. 'You certainly weren't dressed like a schoolgirl—or an innocent. And you were the one who propositioned me, not the other way round.'

And now he was going to be forced to marry her. Sander didn't want to marry anyone—much less a woman like her.

What he had seen in his parents' marriage, the bitterness and resentment between them, had made him vow never to marry himself. That vow had been the cause of acrimony and dissent between him and his grandfather, a despot who believed he had the right to barter his own flesh and blood in marriage as though they were just another part of his fleet of tankers.

Refusing Ruby's proposal would give her an advantage. She could and would undoubtedly attempt to use his refusal against him were there to be a court case between them over the twins. But her obstinacy and her attempt to get the better of him had hardened Sander's determination to claim his sons—even if it now meant using underhand methods to do so. Once they were on his island, its laws would ensure that he, as their father, had the right to keep them.

The familiar sound of a car drawing up outside and doors opening had Ruby ignoring Sander to hurry to the door. She suddenly realised what time it was, and that the twins were being dropped off by the neighbour with whom she shared school run duties. Opening the door, she hurried down the drive to thank her neighbour and help the twins out of the car, gathering up school bags and lunchboxes as she did, clucking over the fact that neither boy had fastened his coat despite the fact that it was still only March and cold.

Identical in every way, except for the tiny mole behind Freddie's right ear, the boys stood and stared at the expensive car parked on the drive, and then looked at Ruby.

'Whose car is that?' Freddie asked, round-eyed.

Ruby couldn't answer him. Why hadn't she realised the time and got rid of Sander before the twins came

home from school? Now they were bound to ask questions—questions she wasn't going to be able to answer
honestly—and she hated the thought of lying to them.

Freddie was still waiting for her to answer. Forcing
a reassuring smile, she told him, 'It's just…someone's.
Come on, let's get inside before the two of you catch
cold with your coats unfastened like that.'

'I'm hungry. Can we have toast with peanut butter?'
Harry asked her hopefully.

Peanut butter was his current favourite.

'We'll see,' was Ruby's answer as she pushed then
gently into the hall in front of her. 'Upstairs now, boys,'
she told them both, trying to remain as calm as she
could even as they stood and stared in silence at Sander,
who now seemed to be taking up a good deal of space
in the hallway.

He was tall, well over six foot, and in other circumstances it would have made her smile to see the way
Harry tipped his head right back to look up at him.
Freddie, though, suddenly very much the man of the
family as the elder of the two. He moved closer to her,
as if instinctively seeking to protect her, and some silent
communication between the two of them caused his
twin to fall back to her other side to do the same.

Unwanted emotional tears stung Ruby's eyes. Her
darling boys. They didn't deserve any of this, and it was
her fault that things were as they were. Before she could
stop herself she dropped down on one knee, putting an
arm around each twin, holding them to her. Freddie was
the more sensitive of the two, although he tried to conceal

it, and he turned into her immediately, burying his face in her neck and holding her tightly, whilst Harry looked briefly towards Sander—wanting to go to him? Ruby wondered wretchedly—before copying his brother.

Sander couldn't move. The second he had seen the two boys he had known that there was nothing he would not do for them—including tearing out his own heart and offering it to them on a plate. The sheer force of his love for them was like a tidal wave, a tsunami that swept everything else aside. They were his—of his family, of his blood, of his body. They were his. And yet, watching them, he recognised immediately how they felt about their mother. He had seen the protective stance they had taken up and his heart filled with pride to see that instinctive maleness in them.

An old memory stirred within him: strong sunlight striking down on his bare head, the raised angry voices of his parents above him. He too had turned to his mother, as his sons had turned to theirs, but there had been no loving maternal arms to hold him. Instead his mother had spun round, heading for her car, slamming the door after she'd climbed into it, leaving him behind, tyres spinning on the gravel, sending up a shower of small stones. He had turned then to his father, but he too had turned away from him and walked back to the house. His parents had been too caught up in their own lives and their resentment of one another to have time for him.

Sander looked down at his sons—and at their mother.

They were all their sons had. He thought again of his own parents, and realised on another surge of emotion that there was nothing he would not do to give his sons what he had never had.

'Marriage it is, then. But I warn you now it will be a marriage that will last for life. That is the measure of my commitment to them,' he told her, looking at the boys.

If she hadn't been holding the twins Ruby thought she might well have fallen down in shock—shock and dismay. She searched Sander's face for some sign that he didn't really mean what he was saying, but all she could see was a quiet, implacable determination.

The twins were turning in her arms to look at Sander again. Any moment now they would start asking questions.

'Upstairs, you two,' she repeated, taking off their navy duffel coats. 'Change out of your uniforms and then wash your hands.'

They made a dash past Sander, deliberately ignoring him, before climbing the stairs together—a pair of sturdy, healthy male children, with lean little-boy bodies and their father's features beneath identical mops of dark curls.

'There will be two conditions,' Sander continued coldly. 'The first is that you will sign a prenuptial agreement. Our marriage will be for the benefit of our sons, not the benefit of your bank account.'

Appalled and hurt by this fresh evidence of how little he thought of her, Ruby swallowed her pride—she was doing this for her boys, after all—and demanded through gritted teeth, 'And the second condition?'

'Your confirmation and proof that you are taking the birth control pill. I've seen the evidence of how little care you have for such matters. I have no wish for another child to be conceived as carelessly as the twins were.'

Now Ruby was too outraged to conceal her feelings.

'There is no question of that happening. The last thing I want is to have to share your bed again.'

She dared to claim *that*, after the way she had already behaved?

Her outburst lashed Sander's pride into a savage need to punish her.

'But you *will* share it, and you will beg me to satisfy that hunger in you I have already witnessed. Your desire for sexual satisfaction has been honed in the arms of far too many men for you to be able to control it now.'

'No! That's not true.'

Ruby could feel her face burning. She didn't need reminding about the wanton way in which she had not only given herself to him but actively encouraged him to take her. Her memories of that night were burned into her conscience for ever. Not one of her senses would ever forget the role they had played in her self-humiliation—the way her voice had sobbed and risen on an increasing note of aching longing that had resulted in a cry of abandoned pleasure that still echoed in her ears, the greedy need of her hands to touch and know his body, the hunger of her lips to caress his flesh and taste his kisses, the increased arousal the scent of his skin had brought her. Each and all of them had added to a wild torrent of sexual longing that had taken her to the edge of her universe and then beyond it, to a place of such spectacular loss of self that she never wanted to go there again.

Shaking herself free of the memories threatening to deluge her, Ruby returned staunchly, 'That was different…a mistake.' Her hands curled into her palms in bitter self-defence as she saw the cynical look he was giving her. 'And it's one that I never want to repeat. There's no way I'd ever want to share your bed again.'

Her denial unleashed Sander's anger. She was lying, he was sure of it, and he would prove it to her. He wasn't a vain man, but he knew that women found him attractive, and Ruby had certainly done everything she could that night to make it plain to him that she wanted him. Normally he would never have even considered bedding her—he liked to do his own hunting—but her persistence had been like a piece of grit in his shoe, wearing down his resistance and helping to fuel the anger already burning inside him. *That* was why he had lost control. Because of his grandfather. Not because of Ruby herself, or because the aroused little cries she had made against his skin had proved so irresistible that he had lost sight of everything but his need to possess her. He could still remember the way she had cried out when he had finally thrust into her, as though what she was experiencing was completely new to her. She had clung to him, sobbing her pleasure into his skin as she trembled and shuddered against him.

Why was he thinking of that now?

The savagery of his fury, inflamed by both her demand for marriage and her denial of his accusation, deafened him to the note of raw pain in her voice. Before he could stop himself he had taken hold of her and was possessing her mouth in a kiss of scorching, pride-fuelled fury.

Too shocked to struggle against his possession, by the time she realised what was happening it was too late. Ruby's own anger surged in defiance, passionate enough to overwhelm her self-control and battle with the full heat of Sander's desire to punish her. Desire for him was the last thing she had expected to feel, but, shockingly, the hard possession of Sander's mouth on her own turned a key in a lock she had thought so damaged by what he had already made her endure that it could never be turned again. Turned it with frightening ease.

This shouldn't be happening. It could not be happening. But, shamefully, it was.

Her panic fought with the desire that burned through her and lost, overcome as swiftly as though molten lava was pouring through her, obliterating everything that stood in its path. Her lips parted beneath the driving pressure of Sander's probing tongue, an agonised whimper of longing drawn from her throat. She could feel the passion in Sander's kiss, and the hard arousal of his body, but instead of acting as a warning that knowledge only served to further enflame her own desire, quickening the pulse already beating within her own sex.

Somewhere within the torrent of anger motivating him Sander could hear an inner voice warning him that this was how it had been before—this same furious, aching, agonised need and arousal that was possessing him now. It should have been impossible for him to want her. It should always have been impossible. And yet, like some mythical, dark malformed creature, supposedly entombed and shut away for ever, his desire had found the superhuman strength to break the bonds imprisoning it. His tongue possessed the eager willingness of the softness of her mouth and his body was already hard, anticipating the corresponding willingness of the most intimate part of her if he didn't stop soon...

Ruby shuddered with mindless sensual delight as Sander's tongue began to thrust potently and rhythmically against her own. Beneath her clothes her nipples swelled and hardened, their ache spreading swiftly through her. Sander's hand cupped her breast, causing her to moan deep in her throat.

She was all female sensual heat, all eager willingness, her very responsiveness designed to trap, Sander recognised. If he didn't stop now he wouldn't be able to stop himself from taking her where they stood, from dragging the clothes from her body in his need to feel her bare skin against his touch, from sinking himself deep within her and feeling her body close round him, possessing him as he possessed her, both of them driven by the mindless, incessant ache that he was surely cursed to feel for her every time he touched her.

He found the buttons on her shirt, swiftly unfastening them. The feel of his hands on her body drew Ruby back into the past. Then he had undressed her expertly and swiftly, in between sensually erotic kisses that had melted away her ability to think or reason, leaving her aching for more, just as he was doing now. His left hand lifted her hair so that he could taste the warm sweetness of that place just where her neck joined her shoulder.

Ruby felt the warmth of his breath against her bare skin. Flames were erupting inside her—the eager flames of denied longing leaping upwards, consuming her resistance. Mindless shudders of hot pleasure rippled through her. Her shirt was open, her breasts exposed to Sander's gaze.

He shouldn't be doing this, Sander warned himself. He shouldn't be giving in to the demands of his pride. But that was *all* he was doing. The heat running through his veins was only caused by angry pride, nothing else.

Her breasts were as perfect as he remembered, the dark rose nipples flaring into deep aureoles that contrasted with the paleness of her skin. He watched as they lifted and fell with the increased speed of her breathing, lifting his hand to cup one, knowing already that it would fit his hand as perfectly as though it was made to be held by him. Beneath the stroke of his thumb-pad her nipple hardened. Sander closed his eyes, remembering how in that long-ago hotel bedroom it had seemed as though her nipple was pushing itself against his touch, demanding the caress of first his thumb and forefinger, then his lips and tongue. Her response had been wild and immediate, swelling and hardening his own body.

He didn't want her, not really, but his pride was now demanding her punishment, the destruction of her claim that she didn't want him.

Ruby could feel herself being dragged back to the past. A small cry of protest gave away her torment.

Abruptly Sander thrust her away from him, brought back to reality by the sound.

They stood watching one another, fighting to control the urgency of their breathing, the urgency of their need. Exposed, raw, and in Ruby's eyes ugly, it was almost a tangible force between them.

They both felt the strength of it and its danger. Ruby could see that knowledge in Sander's eyes, just as she knew he must see it reflected in her own.

The weight of her shame ached through her.

Ruby's face was drained of colour, her eyes huge with shock in her small face.

Sander was just as shocked by the intensity of the desire that had come out of nowhere to threaten his self-control—but he was better at hiding it than Ruby, and he was in no mood to find any pity for her. He was still battling with the unwanted knowledge of just how much he had wanted her.

'You will take the contraceptive pill,' he told her coldly. His heart started to pound heavily in recognition of what his words meant and invited, and the ache in his body surged against his self-control, but somehow he forced himself to ignore the demands of his own desire, to continue. 'I will not accept any consequences of you not doing so.'

Never had she felt so weak, Ruby thought shakily— and not just physically weak, but emotionally and mentally weak as well. In the space of a few short minutes the protective cover she had woven around herself had been ripped from her, exposing her to the full horror of a weakness she had thought controlled and contained. It should be impossible for her to want Sander, to be aroused by him. Should be.

Reaction to what had happened was setting in. She felt physically sick, dazed, unable to function properly, torn apart by the conflicting nature of her physical desire and her burning sense of shame and disbelief that she should feel that desire… Wild thoughts jostled through her head. Perhaps she should not merely ask her doctor for a prescription for the birth control pill but for an anti-Sander pill as well—something that would destroy her desire for him? She needed a pill for that? Surely the way he had spoken to her, the way he had treated her, should be enough to ensure that she loathed the thought of him touching her? Surely her pride and the humiliation he had heaped on her should be strong enough to protect her?

She couldn't marry him. Not now. Panic filled her.

'I've changed my mind,' she told him quickly. 'About…about us getting married.'

Sander frowned. His immediate response to her statement was a fierce surge of determination to prevent her from changing her mind. For the sake of his sons. Nothing else. And certainly not because of the ache that was still pounding through him.

'So the future of our sons is not as important to you as you claimed after all?' he challenged her.

She was trapped, Ruby acknowledged, trapped in a prison of her own making. All she could do was cling to the fragile hope that somehow she would find the strength to deny the desire he could arouse in her so easily.

'Of course it is,' she protested.

'Then we shall be married, and you will accept my terms and conditions.'

'And if I refuse?'

'Then I will move heaven and earth and the stars between them to take my sons from you.'

He meant what he was saying, Ruby could tell. She had no choice other than to bow her head in acceptance of his demands.

He had defeated her, Sander knew, but the taste of his triumph did not have the sweetness he had expected.

'The demands placed on me by my business mean that the sooner the arrangements are completed the better. I shall arrange for the necessary paperwork to be carried out with regard to the prenuptial agreement I shall require you to sign and for our marriage. You must—'

A sudden bang from upstairs, followed by a sharp cry of pain, had them both turning towards the stairs.

Anxious for the safety of her sons, Ruby rushed past Sander, hurrying up the stairs to the boys' room, unaware that Sander was right behind her as she pushed open the door to find Harry on the floor sobbing whilst Freddie stood clutching one of their toy cars.

'Freddie pushed me,' Harry told her.

'No, I didn't. He was trying to take my car.'

'Let me have a look,' Ruby instructed Harry, quickly checking to make sure that no real damage had been done before sitting back on her heels and turning to look at Freddie. But instead of coming to her for comfort Freddie was standing in front of Sander, who had obviously followed her into the room, looking up at him as though seeking his support, and Sander had his hand on Freddie's arm, as though protecting him.

The raw intensity of her emotions gripped her by the throat—grief for all that the twins had missed in not having a father, guilt because she was the cause of that, pain because she loved them so much but her love alone could not give them the tools they would need to grow into well balanced men, and fear for her own self-respect.

His hand resting protectively on the shoulder of his son, Sander looked grimly at Ruby. His sons needed him in their lives, and nothing—least of all a woman like Ruby—was going to prevent him from being there for them.

Oblivious to the atmosphere between the two grown-ups Freddie repeated, 'It's *my* car.'

'No, it's not. It's mine,' Harry argued.

Their argument pulled Ruby's attention back to them. They were devoted to one another, but every now and again they would argue like this over a toy, as though each of them was trying to seek authority over the other. It was a boy thing, other mothers had assured her, but Ruby hated to see them fall out.

'I've got a suggestion to make.' Sander's voice was calm, and yet authoritative in a way that immediately had both boys looking at him. 'If you both promise not to argue over this car again then I will buy you a new toy each, so you won't have to share.'

Ruby sucked in an outraged breath, her maternal instincts overwhelming the vulnerability she felt towards Sander as a woman. What he was doing was outright bribery. Since she didn't have the money to give the boys one each of things she had impressed on them the need to share and share alike, and now, with a handful of words, Sander had appealed to their natural acquisitive instincts with his offer.

She could see from the eager look in both pairs of dark gold eyes that her rules about sharing had been forgotten even before Harry challenged Sander excitedly, 'When…when can we have them?'

Harry was on his feet now, rushing over to join his twin and lean confidently against Sander's other leg whilst he looked up excitedly at him, his words tumbling over themselves as he told Sander, 'I want a car like the one outside…'

'So do I,' Freddie agreed, determined not to be outdone and to assert his elder brother status.

'I'm taking both of you and your mother to London.'

This was news to Ruby, but she wasn't given the chance to say anything because Sander was already continuing.

'There's a big toyshop there where we can look for your cars—but only if you promise me not to quarrel over your toys in future.'

Two dark heads nodded enthusiastically in assent, and two identical watermelon grins split her sons' faces as they gazed up worshipfully at Sander.

Ruby struggled to contain her feelings. Seeing her sons with Sander, watching the way they reacted to him, had brought home to her more effectively than a thousand arguments could ever have done just what they were missing without him—not financially, but emotionally.

Was it her imagination, or was she right in thinking that already they seemed to be standing taller, speaking more confidently, even displaying a body language they had automatically copied from their father? A small pang of sadness filled her. They weren't babies any longer, *her* babies, wholly dependent on her for everything; they were growing up, and their reaction to Sander proved what she had already known—they needed a male role model in their lives. Helplessly she submitted to the power of the wave of maternal love that surged through her, but her head lifted proudly as she returned Sander's silently challenging look.

Automatically Ruby reached out to stroke the tousled dark curls exactly at the moment that Sander did the same. Their hands touched. Immediately Ruby recoiled from the contact, unable to stop the swift rush of knowledge that slid into her head. Once Sander's hands had touched her far more intimately than they were doing now, taking her and possessing her with a potent mix of knowledge and male arousal, and something else which in her ignorance and innocence she had told herself was passionate desire for her and her alone, but which of course had been nothing of the sort.

That reality had left her emotions badly bruised. His was the only sexual male touch she had ever known. Memories she had thought sealed away for ever were trying to surface. Memories aroused by that kiss Sander had forced on her earlier. Ruby shuddered in mute loathing of her own weakness, but it was too late. The mental images her memories were painting would not be denied—images of Sander's hands on her body, the sound of his breathing against her ear and then later her skin. But, no, she must not think of those things. Instead she must be strong. She must resist and deny his ability to arouse her. She was not that young girl any more, she was a woman, a mother, and her sons' needs must come before her own.

CHAPTER THREE

RUBY'S head was pounding with a tension headache, and her stomach cramped—familiar reactions to stress, which she knew could well result in her ending up with something close to a full-scale migraine attack. But this wasn't the time for her to be ill, or indeed to show any weakness—even if she had hardly slept since and had woken this morning feeling nauseous.

The twins were dressed in the new jumpers and jeans her sisters had bought them for Christmas, and wearing the new trainers she had spent her preciously saved money on after she had seen the frowning look Sander had given their old ones when he had called to discuss everything—'everything' being all the arrangements he had made, not just for their stay in London but for their marriage as well, before the four of them would leave for the island that would be their home. They were too excited to sit down, insisting instead on standing in front of the window so that they could see Sander arrive to pick them all up for their visit to London.

Would she have made a different decision if her

sisters had been at home? Ruby didn't see how she could have done. They had been wonderful to her, insisting that they would support her financially so that she could stay at home with the boys, but Ruby had become increasingly aware not just of the financial pressure they were under, but also the fact that one day surely her sisters would fall in love. When they did she didn't want to feel she and the twins were standing in their way because they felt duty-bound to go on supporting them.

No, she had made the right decision. For the twins, who were both wildly excited about the coming trip to London and who had happily accepted her careful announcement to them that she was going to marry Sander, and for her sisters, who had given her and the twins so much love and support.

The twins had reacted to the news that she and Sander were going to be married with excitement and delight, and Freddie had informed her hopefully, 'Luke Simpson has a daddy. He takes him to watch football, and to McDonalds, and he bought him a new bicycle.'

The reality was that everything seemed to be working in Sander's favour. She couldn't even use the excuse of saying that she couldn't take the boys out of school to refuse to go to London, since they were now on holiday for Easter.

When they went back to school it would be to the small English speaking school on the island where, Sander had informed her, those islanders who wished their children to grow up speaking English could send them.

The conversation she and Sander had had about the

twins' future had been more of a question and answer session, with her asking the questions and Sander supplying the answers. All she knew about their future life was that Sander preferred to live and work on the island his family had ruled for several centuries, although the container shipping business he had built up into a world-wide concern also had offices and staff at all the world's major commercial ports, including Felixstowe in England. Sander had also told her that his second in command was his younger brother, who had trained in IT and was based in Athens.

When it came to the boys' future education, Sander had told her that he was completely against them going to boarding school—much to her own relief. He had said that when the time came they would spend term time in England as a family, returning to the island when the boys were out of school.

In addition to the younger brother, Sander had informed her, he also had a sister—the same sister Ruby had learned had taken the photograph of the twins that had alerted Sander to their existence. Like his brother, she too lived in Athens with her husband.

'So it will just be the two of us and the boys, then?' she had pressed warily.

'That is the norm, isn't it?' he had countered. 'The nuclear family, comprising a father, a mother and their children.'

Stupidly, perhaps, she hadn't thought as far as how they would live, but the way her thoughts had recoiled from the reality of their new life together had shown her how apprehensive she was. Because she feared him, or because she feared wanting him? Her face burned even now, remembering her inability to answer that inner question.

It had been far easier to deal with the practicalities of what lay ahead rather than allow herself to be overwhelmed by the complex emotional issues it raised.

Now, waiting for Sander to collect them, with letters for her sisters explaining what she was doing and why written and waiting for them on their return to the UK—the situation wasn't something she felt she wanted to discuss with them over the phone—Ruby could feel the pain in her temple increasing, whilst her stomach churned with anxiety. Everything would have been so very different if only she hadn't give in to that shameful physical desire Sander had somehow managed to arouse in her. In her handbag were the birth control pills Sander had demanded that she take. She had been tempted to defy him, to insist that she could rely on her own willpower to ensure that there was no further sexual intimacy between them. But she was still horrified by the memory of what had happened between them in her hallway, still struggling to take in the fact that it had happened. The speed of it, the intensity of it, had been like a fire erupting out of nowhere to blaze so fiercely that it was beyond control. It had left her feeling vulnerable and unable to trust herself.

There must not be another child, Sander had told her. And wasn't the truth that she herself did not *want* to create another new life with a man who had no respect for her, no feelings of kindness towards her, and certainly no love for her? Love? Hadn't she grown out of the dangerous self-deceit of dressing up naked lust in the fantasy illusion of 'love'? Clothing it in the kind of foolish dreams that belonged to naive adolescents? Before Sander had kissed her she would have sworn and believed that there was nothing he could do to her, no intimacy he could enforce on her, that would arouse her own desire. But the searing heat of the kiss he had subjected her to had burned away her defences.

She hated having to admit to herself that she couldn't rely on her own pride and self-control, but the only thing she could cling to was the knowledge that Sander had been as close to losing *his* control as she had been of losing hers. Of all the cruel tricks that nature could play on two human beings, surely that must be the worst? To create within them a desire for one another that could burn away every shred of protection, leaving them exposed to a need that neither of them wanted. If she could have ripped her own desire out of her body she would have done. It was an alien, unwanted presence, an enemy within her that she must find a way to destroy.

'He's here!'

Freddie's excited announcement cut through her introspection. Both boys were racing to the door and pulling it open, jumping up and down with eager delight when the car door opened and Sander stepped out.

He might be dressed casually, in a black polo shirt, beige chinos and a dark tan leather jacket, but Sander still had that unmistakable air about him that said he was a man other men looked up to and women wanted to be close to, Ruby was forced to admit unwillingly. It wasn't just that he was good-looking—many men were that. No, Sander had something else—something that was a mixture of an aura of power blended with raw male sexuality. She had sensed it as a naive teenager and been drawn to him because of it, and even now, when she was old enough and wise enough to know better, she still felt the pull of his sexual magnetism, its threat to suck her into treacherous waters.

A shiver that was almost a mocking caress stroked over her, making her hug her arms around her body to conceal the sudden unwanted peaking of her nipples. Not because of Sander, she assured herself. No, it was the cold from the open door that was causing her body's sensitive reactions.

Sander's brooding gaze swept over Ruby and rested momentarily on her breasts. Like a leashed cougar, the desire inside him surged against its restraint, leaping and clawing against its imprisonment, the force of its power straining the muscles he had locked against it.

These last couple of weeks he had spent more hours than he wanted to count wrestling with the ache for her that burned in his groin—possessed by it, driven by it, and half maddened by it in equal parts.

No woman had ever been allowed to control him through his desire for her, and for the space of a handful of seconds he was torn—tempted to listen to the inner voice that was warning him to walk away from her, from the desire that had erupted out of nowhere when he had kissed her. A desire like that couldn't be controlled, it could only be appeased. Like some ancient mythical god it demanded sacrifice and self-immolation on its altar.

And then he saw the twins running towards him, and any thought of protecting himself vanished, overwhelmed by the surge of love that flooded him. He hunkered down and held out his arms to them.

Watching the small scene, Ruby felt her throat threaten to close up on a huge lump of emotion. A father with his sons, holding them, protecting them, loving them. There was nothing she would not risk to give her sons that, she acknowledged fiercely.

Holding his sons, Sander knew that there was nothing more important to him than they were—no matter how much he mistrusted their mother.

'Mummy says that we can call you Daddy if we want to.'

That was Freddie, Sander recognised. He had always thought of himself as someone who could control and conceal his emotions, but right now they were definitely threatening to overwhelm him.

'And do you want to?' he asked them, his hold tightening.

'Luke at school has a daddy. He bought him a new bicycle.'

He was being tested, Sander recognised, unable to stop himself from looking towards Ruby.

'Apparently Luke's father also takes him to football

matches and to McDonalds.' She managed to answer Sander's unspoken question.

Sander looked at the twins.

'The bicycles are a maybe—once we've found bikes that are the right size for you—and the football is a definite yes. As for McDonalds—well, I think we should leave it to your mother to decide about that.'

Ruby was torn between relief and resentment. Anyone would think he'd been dealing with the twins from birth. He couldn't have given them a better answer if she had scripted it herself.

'Are you ready?' Sander asked Ruby, in the cold, distant voice he always used when he spoke to her.

Ruby looked down at the jeans and loose-fitting sweater she was wearing, the jeans tucked into the boots her sister had given her for Christmas. No doubt Sander was more used to the company of stunning-looking women dressed in designer clothes and jewels—women who had probably spent hours primping and preening themselves to impress him. A small forlorn ache came from nowhere to pierce her heart. Pretty clothes, never mind designer clothes, were a luxury she simply couldn't afford, and they would have been impractical for her life even if she could.

'Yes, we're ready. Boys, go and get your duffel coats,' she instructed, turning back into the hall to get the case she had packed, and almost being knocked over by the twins as they rushed by.

It was Sander's fingers closing round her arm that saved her from stumbling, but the shock of the physical contact with him froze her into immobility, making her feel far more in danger of losing her balance than the twins' dash past her had done.

Her arm felt thin and frail, in direct contrast to the sturdiness of the twins' limbs, he thought. And her face was pinched, as though she didn't always get enough to eat. A question hovered inside his head...an awareness of deprivation that he pushed away from himself.

Although he was standing behind her she could still smell the scent of his cologne, and feel the warmth coming off his body. Inside her head an image formed of the way he had kissed her such a short time ago. Panic and fear clawed at her stomach, adding to her existing tension. She saw Sander's gaze drop to her mouth and her whole body began to tremble.

It would be so easy to give in to the desire clawing at him—so easy to take her as quickly and wantonly as the way she was offering herself to him. His body wanted that. It wanted the heat of her eager muscles wrapped greedily round it, riding his deepening thrusts. It wanted the swift, savage release her body promised.

It might, but did he really want the kind of cheap, tawdry thrill a woman like her peddled—had been peddling the night they had met?

Ruby's small anguished moan as she pulled free of him brought him back to reality.

'Is this your only case?' he demanded, looking away from her to the shabby case on the hall floor.

Ruby nodded her head, and Sander's mouth twisted with contempt. Of course she would want to underline her poverty to him. Marriage to him was her access to a brand new bank account, filled with money. No doubt she was already planning her first spending spree. He remembered how much delight his mother had always taken in spending his father's money, buying herself couture clothes and expensive jewellery. As a child he'd thought her so beautiful, too dazzled by her glamorous exterior to recognise the corruption that it concealed.

Sander was tempted to ignore the hint Ruby was plainly intending to give him and let her travel to the island with the single shabby case, but that would mean punishing his sons as well as her, he suspected—and besides, he had no wish to make his marriage the subject of speculation and gossip, which it would be if Ruby didn't have a wardrobe commensurate with his own wealth and position.

'Our marriage will take place this Friday,' he told her. 'On Saturday we fly to the island. You've done as I instructed with regard to the birth control pill, I trust?'

'Yes,' Ruby confirmed.

'Can you prove it?'

Ruby was outraged that he should doubt her, but scorched pride had her fumbling angrily with the clasp of her handbag, both her hands shaking with the force of her emotions as she delved into her bag and produced the foil-backed pack of pills, quite plainly showing the empty spaces from the pills she had already taken.

If she had hoped to shame Sander into an apology she soon recognised that one would not be forthcoming. A curt nod of his head was the only response he seemed willing to give her before he continued cynically,

'And, having fulfilled your obligation, you now expect me to fulfil what you no doubt consider to be mine, I expect? To furnish you with the wherewithal to replace your single suitcase with a full set of new ones and clothes with which to fill them.'

The open cynicism in his voice burned Ruby's already scorched pride like salt poured into an open wound. 'Your only obligation to me is to be a good father to the twins.'

'No,' he corrected her coldly, 'that is my obligation to them.' He didn't like her response. It wasn't the one he had expected. It didn't match the profile he had mentally drawn up for her. Somehow she had managed to stray from the script he had written. The one in which she revealed herself to be an unworthy mother, leaving him holding the high ground and the moral right to continue to despise her. 'There is no need to be self-sacrificing.' Her resistance to the role he had cast for her made him feel all the more determined to prove himself right. 'As my wife, naturally you must present an appropriate appearance—although I must caution you against buying clothes of the type you were wearing the night you propositioned me. It is the role of my wife you will be playing in future. Not the role of a whore.'

Ruby had no words to refute his contemptuous insult, but she wasn't going to accept his charity. 'We already have plenty of clothes. We don't need any more,' she insisted vehemently.

She was daring to try to reject what he knew to be the truth about her. She must be taught a lesson that would ensure that she did not do so again. She *would* wear clothes bought with his money, so that they would both know just what she was. He might be forced to marry her in order to be able to lay legal claim to his sons, but he wasn't going to let her forget that she belonged to that group of women all too willing to sell their bodies to any man rich enough to provide them with the lifestyle of designer clothes and easy money they craved.

'Plenty of clothes?' he taunted her. 'In one case? When there are three of you? My sons and my wife will be dressed in a manner appropriate to their station in life, and not—'

'Not what?' Ruby challenged him.

'Do you *really* need me to answer that question?' was his silkily derisory response.

The shabby case was in the boot of a very expensive and luxurious-looking car, the twins were safely strapped into their seats, her decision had already been made— and yet now that it came to it Ruby wavered on the front doorstep, looking back into the house.

'Where's your coat?'

Sander's question distracted her.

'I don't need one,' she fibbed. The truth was that she didn't have a proper winter coat, but she wasn't going to tell Sander that—not after what he'd already said. He was waiting, holding the car door open for her. Shivering in the easterly March wind, Ruby locked the front door. Her head pounding painfully, she got into the car. Its interior smelled of expensive leather, very different from the smell inside the taxi that had transported them back to Sander's hotel that fateful night...

Her mouth went dry.

The twins were both engrossed in the TVs installed in the back of the front seats. Sander was concentrating on his driving. Now wasn't the time to think about that night, she told herself. But it was too late. The memories were already storming her defences and flooding over them.

Her parents' death in an accident had been a terrible shock, followed by her sister's decision to sell their family home. Ruby hadn't realised then that their parents had died heavily in debt. Her oldest sister had tried to protect her by not telling her, and so she had assumed that her decision to sell the house was motivated by the decision to set up her own interior design business in Cheshire. Angry with her sister, she had deliberately chosen to befriend a girl new to the area, knowing that her sister disapproved of the freedom Tracy's parents allowed her, and of Tracy herself. Although she was only eighteen months older than Ruby, Tracy had been far more worldly, dressing in tight-fitting clothes in the latest and skimpiest fashions, her hair dyed blonde and her face heavily made-up.

Secretly, although she hadn't been prepared to admit it—especially not to her older sister—Ruby had been shocked by some of the disclosures Tracy had made about the things she had done. Tracy's goal in life was to get a footballer boyfriend. She had heard that young footballers in Manchester patronised a certain club in the city, and had asked Ruby to go there with her.

Alarmed by Tracy's disclosures, Ruby hadn't really wanted to go. But when she had tried to say so, telling Tracy that she doubted her sister would give her permission, Tracy had mocked her and accused her of being a baby who needed her sister's permission for everything she did. Of course Ruby had denied that she was any such thing, whereupon Tracy had challenged her to prove it by daring her to go with her.

She had been just seventeen, and a very naive seventeen at that, with her whole world turned upside down by events over which she'd had no control. But no matter how often both her sisters had reassured her since then that her rebellion had been completely natural, understandable, and that she was not to blame for what had happened, Ruby knew that deep down inside she would always feel guilty.

Before they'd left for Manchester Tracy had promised Ruby a 'makeover' and poured them both a glass of vodka and orange juice. It had gone straight to Ruby's head as she had never drunk alcohol. The drink had left her feeling so light-headed that she hadn't protested or objected when Tracy had insisted that Ruby change into one of her own short skirts and a tight-fitting top, before making up Ruby's face in a similar style to her own, with dark eyeliner, heavy thick mascara loaded on her eyelashes and lots of deep pink lipgloss.

The girl staring back at Ruby from the mirror, with her tousled hair and her pink pout had been so unrecognisable as herself that under the effect of the vodka and orange Ruby had only been able to stare at her reflection in dizzy astonishment.

She might only have been seventeen, but she had known even before she had watched Tracy sweet talking the bouncer into letting them into the club that neither her parents nor her sisters would have approved of her being there, but by then she had been too afraid of Tracy's mockery and contempt to tell her that she had changed her mind and wanted to go home.

She'd watched other girls going in—older girls than her, dressed up to the nines in tiny little tops and skirts that revealed dark sunbed tans—and she'd known instinctively and immediately that she would feel out of place.

Inside, the club had been hot and stuffy, packed with girls with the same goal in mind as Tracy.

Several young men had come up to them as they'd stood close to the bar. Tracy had refused Ruby's suggestion that they sit down at a tucked-away table with a derisory, 'Don't be daft—no one will see us if we do that.' But Tracy had shaken her head, ignoring the boys and telling Ruby, 'They're nothing. Just ordinary lads out on the pull.'

She'd bought them both drinks—cocktails which had seemed innocuous when Ruby sipped thirstily at hers, because of the heat in the club, but which had quickly made her feel even more dizzy and disorientated than the vodka and orange juice had done.

The club had been packed and noisy, and Ruby's head had begun to ache. She had felt alien and alone, with the alcohol heightening her emotions: bringing home to her the reality of her parents' death, bringing to a head all the despair and misery she had been feeling.

Tracy had started talking to a young man, deliberately excluding Ruby from their conversation and keeping her back to her.

Suddenly and achingly Ruby had longed for the security of the home life she had lost—of knowing that there was someone in her life to take care of her and protect her, someone who loved her, instead of getting cross with her like her elder sister did. And that had been when she had looked across the bar and seen Sander.

Something about him had set him apart from the other men in the bar. For a start he'd been far more smartly dressed, in a suit, with his dark hair groomed, and an air of command and power and certainty had emanated from him that Ruby's insecure senses immediately recognised and were drawn to... In her alcohol-induced state, Sander had looked like an island of security and safety in a sea of confusion and misery. She hadn't been able to take her eyes off him, and when he had looked back at her, her mouth had gone so dry with the anticipation of speaking to him that she had had to wet her lips with the tip of her tongue. The way that Sander's gaze had followed that movement, showing her that he was singling her out from all the other girls in the bar, had reinforced Ruby's cocktail-produced belief that there was a link between them—that he was drawing her to him, that they were meant to meet, and that somehow once she was close to him she would be safe, and he would save her from her own fears and protect her just as her parents had done.

She had no memory of actually going to him, only of reaching him, feeling like a swimmer who had crested turbulent waves to reach the security of a calm sea where she could float safely. When she had smiled up at Sander she had felt as though she already knew him. But of course she hadn't. She hadn't known anything, Ruby reflected bitterly now, as she dragged her thoughts away from the past and massaged her throbbing temple as Sander drove onto the motorway slip road and the car picked up speed.

CHAPTER FOUR

SANDER had booked them into the Carlton Towers Hotel, just off Sloane Street. They had an enormous suite of three bedrooms, each with its own bathroom, and a good-sized sitting room as well.

Ruby had felt dreadfully out of place as they'd walked through the downstairs lobby, compared with the elegantly groomed women surrounded by expensive-looking shopping bags who were having afternoon tea in the lounge. But she had soon forgotten them once they had been shown into their suite and she had realised that Sander would be staying in the suite with them.

Her heart was beating far too fast, her whole body suddenly charged and sensitised, so that she was far too aware of Sander. His presence in the room, even though there were several feet between them and he was fully dressed, somehow had the same effect on her body as though he was standing close to her and touching her. The sound of his voice made her think she could almost feel the warmth of his breath on her skin. Her body was starting to react even to her thoughts, tiny darts of sensation heightening her awareness of him.

He raised his hand, gesturing towards the bedrooms as he told her, 'I've asked for one of the rooms to be made up with twin beds for the boys.'

Inside her head she could feel that hand cupping her breast. Beneath her clothes her breasts swelled and ached whilst she tried desperately to stifle her body's arousal. Why was this happening to her? She'd lived happily without sex for nearly six years. Why was her body reacting like this now?

It was just reacting to memory, that was all. Her desire for Sander, like that memory, belonged to the past and had no place in the present. Ruby tried to convince herself, but she knew that it wasn't true. The fact that he could arouse her to intense desire for him was something she didn't want to think about. Her stomach was churning, adding to the feeling of nausea already being produced by her headache. She had actually been sick when they had stopped for a break at a motorway service station, and had had to purchase a travel pack of toothbrush and toothpaste to refresh her mouth. Now all she really wanted to do was lie down in a dark room, but of course that was impossible.

'You and I will occupy the other two rooms, of course,' Sander was saying. 'I expect that you will wish to have the room closest to the boys?'

'I could have shared a room with them,' was Ruby's response. Because sharing with the boys would surely prevent any more of those unwanted memories from surfacing? 'There was no need for you to book three rooms.'

'If I had only booked two the hotel would have assumed you would be sharing my bed, not sleeping with the twins,' was Sander's response.

Immediately another image flashed through her head: two naked bodies entwined on a large bed, the man's hands holding and caressing the woman, whilst her head was thrown back in wild ecstasy. Sander's hands and her head. Heat filled her body. Her own mental images were making her panic. What she was experiencing was probably caused by the same kind of thing that caused the victims of dreadful trauma to have flashbacks they couldn't control, she told herself. They meant nothing other than that Sander's unexpected and unwanted reappearance in her life was causing her to remember the event that had had such a dramatic effect on her life.

To her relief the twins, who had been inspecting the suite, came rushing into the sitting room. Harry ran over to her to inform her, 'Guess what? There's a TV in our bedroom, and—'

'A TV which will remain switched off whilst you are in bed,' Ruby told him firmly, relieved to be able to return to the familiar role of motherhood. 'You know the rules.' She was very strict about limiting the boys' television viewing, preferring them to make their own entertainment.

Sander's comment about the rooms had penetrated her mind and was still lodged there—a small, unnerving time bomb of a comment that was having an effect on her that was out of all proportion to its reality. The sound of Sander saying 'my bed' had made her heart jerk around inside her chest as though it was on a string—and why? She had no desire to share that bed with him; he meant nothing to her now. It was merely the result of only ever having had one sexual partner and being sexually inexperienced. It had left her reacting to a man saying the words 'my bed' as though she were a teenager, blushing at every mention of anything remotely connected to sex, Ruby derided herself.

'I thought we'd use the rest of the afternoon to get the boys kitted out with the clothes they'll need for the island. We can walk to Harrods from here, or get a cab if you wish.'

The last thing Ruby felt like doing was shopping, but she was determined not to show any weakness. Sander would only accuse of being a bad mother if she did.

Hopefully she might see a chemist, where she could get something for her headache. It had been so long since she had last had one of these debilitating attacks that she didn't have anything she could take for it. Determinedly trying to ignore her continuing feeling of nausea, she nodded her head, and then winced as the pain increased.

'The boys will need summer clothes,' Sander told her. 'Even in March the temperature on the island can be as high as twenty-two degrees centigrade, and it rises to well over thirty in the summer.'

Two hours later Ruby was battling between angry frustration at the way in which Sander had overruled all her attempts to minimise the amount of money he was spending by choosing the cheapest items she could find and a mother's natural pride in her sons, who had drawn smiles of approval from the assistants with their appearance in their new clothes: smart, boyish separates from the summer ranges that had just come in, and in which Ruby had to admit they looked adorable.

As a reward for their good behaviour Sander had insisted on taking them to the toy department, where he'd bought them both complicated-looking state-of-the-art boys' toys that had them both speechless with delight.

The whole time they had been shopping with the boys Ruby had been conscious of the admiring looks Sander had attracted from other women—women who no doubt would have been only too delighted to be marrying him in two days' time, Ruby acknowledged, and her heart gave a flurry of tense beats in response to her thoughts.

'I've got some business matters to attend to this evening,' Sander told her as they made a detour on the way back to the hotel to allow the boys to walk in Hyde Park—a suggestion from Sander which Ruby had welcomed, hoping that the fresh air would ease the pounding in her head.

After acknowledging Sander's comment Ruby focused on keeping an eye on the twins, who were walking ahead of them.

Sander continued. 'But first I've arranged for a jeweller to come to the hotel with a selection of wedding and engagement rings. I've also made an appointment for you tomorrow morning at the spa and hair salon in Harvey Nichols, and then afterwards a personal shopper will help you choose your own new wardrobe. I thought I'd take the boys to the Natural History Museum whilst you're doing that, to keep them occupied.'

Ruby stopped walking and turned to look at him, her eyes blazing with temper.

'I don't need a spa appointment, or a new hairstyle, or a new wardrobe, thank you very much. And I certainly don't want an engagement ring.'

She was lying, of course. Or did she think she could get more out of him by pretending she didn't want anything?

Oblivious to Sander's thoughts, Ruby continued, 'And if my present appearance isn't good enough for you, then too bad. Because it's good enough for me.'

Quickly hurrying after the twins, Ruby tried to ignore how unwell she was feeling. Even though she couldn't see him she knew that Sander had caught up with her and was standing behind her. Her body could feel him there, but stubbornly she refused to turn round.

'You have two choices,' Sander informed her coolly. 'Either you accept the arrangements I have made for you, or you will accept the clothes I shall instruct the store to select on your behalf. There is no option for you, as my wife, to dress as you are doing now. You are so eager to display your body to male eyes that you aren't even wearing a coat—all the better for them to assess what is on offer, no doubt.'

'That's a disgusting thing to say, and totally untrue. You must *know* the reason I'm not wearing a coat is—'

Abruptly Ruby stopped speaking realising that she had allowed her anger to betray her into making an admission she had no wish to make.

'Yes?' Sander probed.

'Is that I forgot to bring one with me,' Ruby told him lamely. The truth was that she had not been able to afford to buy herself one—not with the twins constantly outgrowing their clothes. But she wasn't going to expose herself to more humiliation by admitting that to Sander.

How could he be marrying a woman like this one? Sander wondered savagely. It would have suited his purposes far more if the report he had received from the agents he had hired to find Ruby had included something to suggest that she was a neglectful mother, thus giving him real grounds for legally removing them from their mother. The report, though, had done nothing of the sort—had actually dared to claim that Ruby was a good mother, the kind of mother whose absence from their lives would damage his sons. That was a risk he was not prepared to take.

Ignoring Ruby's defiant statement, Sander went on, 'The boys are approaching an age where they will be aware of appearance and other people's opinions. They are going to have to deal with settling into a different environment, and I'm sure that the last thing you want to do is make it harder for them. I have a duty to the Konstantinakos position as the ruling and thus most important family on the island. That duty involves a certain amount of entertaining. It will be expected that as my wife you take part in that. Additionally, my sister, her friends, and the wives of those of my executives who live in Athens are very fashion-conscious. They would be quick to sense that our marriage is not all it should be were you to make a point of dressing as you do now. And that could impact on our sons.'

Our sons. Ruby felt as though her heart had been squeezed by a giant hand. She was very tempted to resort to the immature tactic of pointing out that since he hadn't even been aware of the twins' existence until recently he was hardly in a position to take a stance on delivering advice to her on what might or might not affect them—but what was the point? He had won—again, she was forced to acknowledge. Because now she would be very conscious of the fact that she was being judged by her appearance, and that if she was found wanting it would reflect on the twins. Acceptance by their peers was very important to children. Ruby knew that even at the boys' young age children hated being 'different' or being embarrassed. For their sake she would have to accept Sander's charity, even though her pride hated the idea.

She hated feeling so helpless and dependent on others. She loved her sisters, and was infinitely grateful to them for all that they had done for her and the boys, but it was hard sometimes always having to depend on others, never being able to claim the pride and self-respect that came from being financially self-supporting. She had hoped that once the boys were properly settled at school she might be able to earn a degree that ultimately would allow her to find work, but now she was going to be even more dependent on the financial generosity of someone else than she was already. But it wasn't her pride that was important, Ruby reminded herself. It was her sons' emotional happiness. They hadn't asked to be born. And she hadn't asked for Sander's opinion on her appearance—or his money. She was twenty-three, and it was ridiculous of her to feel so helpless and humiliated that she was close to defeated tears.

To conceal her emotions she leaned down towards the boys, to warn them not to run too far ahead of them, watching as they nodded their heads.

It was when she straightened up that it happened. Perhaps she moved too quickly. Ruby didn't know, but one minute she was straightening up and the next she felt so dizzy from the pain in her head that she lost her balance. She would have fallen if Sander hadn't reacted so quickly, reaching out to grab hold of her so that she fell against his body rather than tumbling to the ground.

Immediately she was transported back to the past. The circumstances might be very different, but then too she had stumbled, and Sander had rescued her. Then, though, the cause of her fall had been the unfamiliar height of the borrowed shoes Tracy had insisted she should wear, and the effect of too many cocktails. The result was very much the same. Now, just as then, she could feel the steady thud of Sander's heart against her body, whilst her own raced and bounced, the frantic speed of its beat making her feel breathless and far too weak to try to struggle against the arms holding her. Then too his proximity had filled her senses with the scent of his skin, the alien maleness of hard muscle beneath warm flesh, the power of that maleness, both physically and emotionally, and most of all her own need to simply be held by him. Then she had been thrilled to be in his arms, but now… Panic curled through her. That was not how she was supposed to feel, and it certainly wasn't what she wanted to feel. Sander was her enemy—an enemy she was forced to share her sons with because he was their father, an enemy who had ripped from her the protection of her naivety with his cruel contempt for her.

Determinedly Ruby started to push herself free, but instead of releasing her Sander tightened his hold of her.

He'd seen that she was slender, Sander acknowledged, but it was only now that he was holding her and could actually feel the bones beneath her flesh that he was able to recognise how thin she was. She was shivering too, despite her claim not to need a coat. Once again he was reminded of the report he had commissioned on her. Was it possible that in order to ensure that her sons ate well and were not deprived of the nourishment they needed she herself had been going without? Sander had held his sons, and he knew just how solid and strong their bodies were. The amount of energy they possessed alone was testament to their good health. And it was *their* good health that mattered to him, not that of their mother, whose presence in his life as well as theirs was something he had told himself he would have to accept for their sakes.

Even so… He looked down into Ruby's face. Her

skin was paler than he remembered, but he had put that down to the fact that when he had first met her her face had been plastered in make-up, whilst now she wore none. Her cheekbones might be more pronounced, but her lips were still full and soft—the lips of sensual siren who knew just how to use her body to her own advantage. Sander had never been under any illusions as to why Ruby had approached him. He had heard her and her friend discussing the rich footballers they intended to target. Unable to find one, Ruby had obviously decided to target him instead.

Sander frowned, unwilling to contrast the frail vulnerability of the woman he was holding with the girl he remembered, and even more unwilling to allow himself to feel concern for her. Why should he care about her? He didn't. And yet as she struggled to pull free of him, her eyes huge in her fine boned face, a sudden gleam of March sunshine pierced the heavy grey of the late afternoon sky to reveal the perfection of her skin and stroke fingers of light through her blonde curls, Sander had sudden reluctance to let her go. In rejection of it he immediately released her.

It was the unexpected swiftness of her release after Sander's grip had seemed to be tightening on her that was causing her to feel so...confused, Ruby told herself, refusing to allow herself to use the betraying word *bereft*, which had tried to slip through her defences. Why should she feel bereft? She wanted to be free. Sander's hold had no appeal for her. She certainly hadn't spent the last six years longing to be back in his arms. Why should she, when her last memory of them had been the biting pressure of his fingers in her flesh as he thrust her away from him in a gesture of angry contempt?

It had started to rain, causing Ruby to shiver and call the boys to them. It was no good her longing for the security of home, she told herself as they headed back to the hotel in the taxi Sander had flagged down, with the twins squashed in between them so that she didn't have to come into contact with him. She must focus on the future and all that it would hold for her sons. Their happiness was far more important to her than her own, and it was obvious to her how easily they were adapting to Sander's presence in their lives. An acceptance oiled by the promise of expensive toys, Ruby thought bitterly, knowing that her sons were too young for her to be able to explain to them that a parent's love wasn't always best shown though gifts and treats, and knowing too that it would be part of her future role to ensure that they were not spoiled by their father's wealth or blinded to the reality of other people's lives and struggles.

Once they were back in their suite, in the privacy of her bathroom, Ruby tried to take two of the painkiller tablets she had bought from the chemist's she had gone into on the pretext of needing some toothpaste. But her stomach heaved at the mere thought of attempting to swallow them, nausea overwhelming her.

Still feeling sick, and weakened by her pounding headache, as soon as the twins had had something to eat she bathed them and put them to bed.

They had only been asleep a few minutes when the

jeweller Sander had summoned arrived, removing a roll of cloth from his briefcase, after Sander had introduced him to Ruby and they had all sat down.

Placing the roll on the class coffee table, he unfolded it—and Ruby had to suppress a gasp of shock when she saw the glitter of the rings inside it.

They were all beautiful, but something made Ruby recoil from them. It seemed somehow shabby and wrong to think of wearing something so precious. A ring should represent love and commitment that were equally precious and enduring instead of the hollow emptiness her marriage would be.

'You choose,' she told Sander emptily, not wanting to look at them.

Her lack of interest in the priceless gems glittering in front of her made Sander frown. His mother had loved jewellery. He could see her now, seated at her dressing table, dressed to go out for the evening, admiring the antique Cartier bangles glittering on her arms.

'Your birth paid for these,' she had told him. 'Your grandfather insisted that your father should only buy me one, so I had to remind him that I had given birth to his heir. Thank goodness you weren't a girl. Your grandfather is so mean that he would have seen to it that I got nothing if you had been. Remember when you are a man, Sander, that the more expensive the piece of jewellery you give a woman, the more willing she will be, and thus the more you can demand of her.' She had laughed then, pouting her glossy red lip-sticked lips at her own reflection and adding, 'I shouldn't really give away the secrets of my sex to you, should I?'

His beautiful, shallow, greedy mother—chosen as a bride for his father by his grandfather because of her aristocratic Greek ancestry, marrying his father because she hated her own family's poverty. When he had grown old enough to recognise the way in which his gentle academic father had been humiliated and treated with contempt by the father who had forced the marriage on him, and the wife who thought of him only as an open bank account, Sander had sworn he would never follow in his father's footsteps and allow the same thing to happen to him.

What was Ruby hoping for by pretending a lack of interest? Something more expensive? Angrily Sander looked at the rings, his hand hovering over the smallest solitaire he could see. His intention was to punish her by choosing it for her—until his attention was drawn to another ring close to it, its two perfect diamonds shimmering in the light.

Feeling too ill to care what kind of engagement ring she had, Ruby exhaled in relief when she saw Sander select one of the rings. All she wanted was for the whole distasteful charade to be over.

'We'll have this one,' Sander told the jeweller abruptly, his voice harsh with the irritation he felt against himself for his own sentimentality.

It was the jeweller who handed the ring to Ruby, not Sander. She took it unwillingly, sliding the cold metal onto her finger, her eyes widening and her heart turning over inside her chest as she looked at it properly for the first time. Two perfect diamonds nestled together on a slender band, slightly offset from one another and yet touching—twin diamonds for their twin sons. Her throat closed up, her gaze seeking Sander's despite her attempt to stop it doing so, her emotions clearly on display. But there was no answering warmth in Sander's eyes, only a cold hardness that froze her out.

'An excellent choice,' the jeweller was saying. 'Each stone weighs two carets, and they are a particularly good quality. And of course ethically mined, just as you requested,' he informed Sander.

His comment took Ruby by surprise. From what she knew of Sander she wouldn't have thought it would matter to him *how* the diamonds had been mined, but obviously it did. Meaning what? That she had misjudged him? Meaning nothing, Ruby told herself fiercely. She didn't want to revisit her opinion of Sander, never mind re-evaluate it. Why not? Because she was afraid that if she did so, if she allowed herself to see him in a different light, then she might become even more vulnerable to him than she already was? Emotionally vulnerable as well as sexually vulnerable? No, that must not happen.

Her panic increased her existing nausea, and it was a relief when the jeweller finally left. His departure was quickly followed by Sander's, to his business meeting.

Finally she could give in to her need to go and lie down—after she had checked on the twins, of course.

CHAPTER FIVE

'YOUR hair is lovely and thick, but since it is so curly I think it would look better if we put a few different lengths into it.' Those had been the words of the salon's senior stylist when he had first come over to examine Ruby's hair. She had simply nodded her head, not really caring how he cut her hair. She was still feeling unwell, her head still aching, and she knew from experience that these headaches could last for two and even three days once they took hold, before finally lifting.

Now, though, as the stylist stepped back from the mirror and asked, 'What do you think?' Ruby was forced to admit that she was almost lost for words over the difference his skill had made to her hair, transforming it from an untidy tumble of curls into a stunningly chic style that feathered against her face and swung softly onto her shoulders—the kind of style she had seen worn by several of the women taking tea at the hotel the previous afternoon, a deceptively simple style that breathed expense and elegance.

'I...I love it,' she admitted wanly.

'It's easy to maintain and will fall back into shape after you've washed it. You're lucky to have naturally blonde hair.'

Thanking him, Ruby allowed herself to be led away. At least she had managed to eat some dry toast this morning, and keep down a couple of the painkillers which had eased her head a little, thankfully.

Her next appointment was at the beauty spa, and when she caught other women giving her a second look as she made her way there she guessed that they must be querying the elegance of her new hairstyle set against the shabbiness of her clothes and her make-up-free face.

She hated admitting it, but it *was* true that first impressions counted, and that people—especially women—judged members of their own sex by their appearance. The last thing she wanted was for the twins to be embarrassed by a mother other women looked down on. Even young children were very perceptive and quick to notice such things.

The spa and beauty salon was ahead of her. Taking a deep breath, Ruby held her head high as she walked in.

Two hours later, when she walked out again with the personal shopper who had come to collect her and help her choose a new wardrobe, Ruby couldn't help giving quick, disbelieving glances into the mirrors she passed, still unable to totally believe that the young woman looking back at her really was her. Her nails were manicured and painted a fashionable dark shade, her eyebrows were trimmed, and her make-up was applied in such a subtle and delicate way that it barely looked as though she was wearing any at all. Yet at the same time her eyes looked larger and darker, her mouth fuller and softer, and her complexion so delicately perfect that Ruby couldn't take her eyes off the glowing face looking back at her. Although she would never admit it to Sander, her makeover had been fun once she had got over her initial discomfort at being fussed over and pampered. Now she felt like a young woman rather than an anxious mother.

'I understand you want clothes suitable for living on a Greek island, rather than merely holidaying there, and that your life there will include various social and business engagements?' Without waiting for Ruby's answer the personal shopper continued. 'Fortunately we have got some of our new season stock in as well as several designers' cruise collections, so I'm sure we shall be able to find everything you need. As for your wedding dress…'

Ruby's heart leapt inside her chest. Somehow she hadn't expected Sander to specify that she needed a wedding dress.

'It's just a very quiet registry office ceremony,' she told the personal shopper.

'But her wedding day and what she wore when she married the man she loves is still something that a woman always remembers,' the other woman insisted.

The personal shopper was only thinking of the store's profit, Ruby reminded herself. There was no real reason

for her to have such an emotional reaction to the words.
After all, she didn't love Sander and he certainly didn't
love her. What she wore was immaterial, since neither
of them was likely to want to look back in future years
to remember the day they married. Her thoughts had
produced a hard painful lump in her throat and an
unwanted ache inside her chest. Why? She was twenty-
three years old and the mother of five-year-old sons. She
had long ago abandoned any thoughts of romance and
love and all that went with those things, dismissing
them as the emotional equivalent of chocolate—sweet
on the tongue for a very short time, highly addictive and
dangerously habit-forming. Best avoided in favour of a
sensible and sustaining emotional diet. Like the love she
had for her sons and the bond she shared with her sisters.
Those were emotions and commitments that would last
for a lifetime, whilst from what she had seen and heard
romantic love was a delusion.

The twins were fascinated by the exhibits in the Natural
History Museum. They had happily held Sander's hand
and pressed gratifyingly close to him for protection, calling
him Daddy and showing every indication of being happy
to be with him, so why did he feel so aware of Ruby's
absence, somehow incomplete? It was for the boys' sake,
Sander assured himself, because he was concerned that
they might be missing their mother, nothing more.

Without quite knowing how it had happened, Ruby had
acquired a far more extensive and expensive wardrobe

than she had wanted. Every time she had protested or objected the personal shopper had overruled her—politely and pleasantly, but nonetheless determinedly—insisting that her instructions were that Ruby must have a complete wardrobe that would cover a wide variety of situations. And of course the clothes were sinfully gorgeous—beautifully cut trousers and shorts in cream linen, with a matching waistcoat lined in the same silk as the unstructured shirt that went with them, soft flowing silk dresses, silk and cotton tops, formal fitted cocktail dresses, along with more casual but still frighteningly expensive 'leisure and beach clothes', as the personal shopper had described them. There were also shoes for every occasion and each outfit, and underwear—scraps of silk and lace that Ruby had wanted to reject in favour of something far more sensible, but which somehow or other had been added to the growing rail of clothes described by the personal shopper as 'must-haves'.

Now all that was left was the wedding dress, and the personal shopper was producing with a flourish a cream dress with a matching jacket telling Ruby proudly, 'Vera Wang, from her new collection. Since the dress is short and beautifully tailored it is ideal for a registry office wedding, and of course you could wear it afterwards as a cocktail dress. It was actually ordered by another customer, but unfortunately when it came it was too small for her. I'm sure that it will fit you, and the way the fabric is pleated will suit your body shape.'

What she meant was that the waterfall of pleated

ruching that was a feature of the cream silk-satin dress would disguise how thin she was, Ruby suspected.

The dress was beautiful, elegant and feminine, and exactly the kind of dress that a woman would remember wearing on her wedding day—which was exactly why she didn't want to wear it. But the dresser was waiting expectantly.

It fitted her perfectly. Cut by a master hand, it shaped her body in a way that made her waist appear far narrower surely than it actually was, whilst somehow adding a feminine curvaceousness to her shape that made Ruby think she was looking at someone else in the mirror and not herself: the someone else she might have been if things had been different. If Sander had loved her?

Shakily Ruby shook her head and started to take the dress off, desperate to escape from the cruel reality of the image the mirror had thrown back at her. She could never be the woman she had seen in the mirror—a woman so loved by her man that she had the right to claim everything the dress offered her and promised him.

'No. I don't want it,' she told the bewildered-looking personal shopper. 'Please take it away. I'll wear something else.'

'But it was perfect on you…'

Still Ruby shook her head.

She was in the changing room getting dressed when the personal shopper reappeared, carrying a warm-looking, casually styled off-white parka.

'I nearly forgot,' she told Ruby, 'your husband-to-be said that you had left your coat at home by accident and

that you needed something warm to wear whilst you are
in London.'

Wordlessly Ruby took the parka from her. It was lined
with soft checked wool, and well-made as well as stylish.

'It's a new designer,' the shopper told her. 'And a line
that we're just trialling. She's Italian, trained by Prada.'

Ruby bent her head so that the personal shopper
wouldn't see the emotion sheening her eyes. Sander
might have protected her in public by pretending to
believe that she had forgotten her coat, but in private he
had humiliated her—because Ruby knew that he had
guessed that she didn't really possess a winter coat, and
that she had been shivering with cold yesterday when
they had walked in the park.

Walking back to the hotel wrapped in her new parka,
Ruby reflected miserably that beneath the new hairstyle
and the pretty make-up she was still exactly what she had
been beforehand—they couldn't change her, could not
take away the burden of the guilt she still carried because
of what she had once been. Expensive clothes were only
a pretence—just like her marriage to Sander would be.

For her. Yes, but not for the twins. They must never
know how she felt. The last thing she wanted was for
them to grow up feeling that she had sacrificed herself
for them. They must believe that she was happy.

She had intended to go straight to the suite, but the
assessing look a woman in the lobby gave her, before
smiling slightly to herself, as though she was satisfied
that Ruby couldn't compete with her, stung her pride

enough to have her changing her mind and heading for the lounge instead.

A well-trained waitress showed her to a small table right at the front of the lounge. Ruby would have preferred to have hidden herself away in a dark corner, her brief surge of defiance having retreated leaving her feeling self-conscious and very alone. She wasn't used to being on her own. Normally when she went out she had the twins with her, or one of her sisters.

When the waitress came to take her order Ruby asked for tea. She hadn't eaten anything all day but she wasn't hungry. She was too on edge for that.

The lounge was filling up. Several very smart-looking women were coming in, followed by a group of businessmen in suits, one of whom gave her such a deliberate look followed by a warm smile that Ruby felt her face beginning to burn.

She was just about to pour herself a cup of tea when she saw the twins hurrying towards her followed by Sander. His hair, like the twins', was damp, as though he had just stepped out of the shower. Her heart lurched into her ribs. Her hand had started to tremble so badly that she had to put down the teapot. The twins were clamouring to tell her about their day, but even though she tried desperately to focus on them her gaze remained riveted to Sander, who had now stopped walking and was looking at her.

It wasn't her changed appearance that had brought him to an abrupt halt, though.

In Sander's eyes the new hairstyle and pretty make-up were merely window-dressing that highlighted what he already knew and what had been confirmed to him when Ruby had opened the door of her home to him a few days earlier—namely that the delicacy of her features possessed a rare beauty.

No, what had caused him to stop dead almost in mid-stride was the sense of male pride the sight of the trio in front of him brought. His sons and their mother. Not just his sons, but the *three* of them. They went together, belonged together—belonged to him? Sander shook his head, trying to dispel his atavistic and unfamiliar reactions with regard to Ruby, both angered by them and wanting to reject them. They were so astonishingly the opposite of what he wanted to feel. What was happening to him?

Her transformation passed him by other than the fact that he noticed the way she was wearing her hair revealed the slender column of her throat and that her face had a bit more colour in it.

Ruby, already self-conscious about the changes to her appearance, held her breath, waiting for Sander to make some comment. After all the sight of her had brought him to a halt. But when he reached the table he simply frowned and demanded to know why she hadn't ordered something to eat.

'Because all I wanted was a cup of tea,' she answered him. Didn't he like her new haircut? Was that why he was looking so grim? Well, she certainly wasn't going to ask him if he approved of the change. She turned to the boys, asking them, 'Did you like the Natural History Museum?'

'Yes,' Harry confirmed. 'And then Daddy took us swimming.'

Swimming? Ruby directed a concerned look at Sander.

'There's a pool here in the hotel,' he explained. 'Since the boys will be living on an island, I wanted to make sure that they can swim.'

'Daddy bought us new swimming trunks,' Freddie told her.

'There should be two adults with them when they go in a pool,' Ruby couldn't stop herself from saying. 'A child can drown in seconds and—'

'There was a lifeguard on duty.' Sander stopped her. 'They're both naturals in the water, but that will be in their genes. My brother swam for Greece as a junior.'

'Mummy's hair is different,' Harry suddenly announced.

Self-consciousness crawled along her spine. Now surely Sander must say something about her transformation, give at least some hint of approval since he was the one who had orchestrated her makeover, but instead he merely stated almost indifferently, 'I hope you got everything you are going to need, as there won't be time for any more shopping. As I said, I've arranged for us to fly to the island the day after the marriage ceremony.'

Ruby nodded her head. It was silly of her to feel disappointed because Sander hadn't said anything about her new look. Silly or dangerous? His approval or lack of it shouldn't mean anything to her at all.

The boys would be hungry, and she was tired. She was their mother, though, and it was far more important that she focused on her maternal responsibilities rather than worrying about Sander's approval or lack of it.

'I'll take the boys up to the suite and organise a meal for them,' she told Sander.

'Good idea. I've got some ends to tie up with the Embassy,' he said brusquely, with a brief nod of his head.

'What about dinner?' Ruby's mouth had gone dry, and the silence that greeted her question made her feel she had committed as much of a *faux pas* as if she'd asked him to go to bed with her.

Feeling hot and angry with herself for inadvertently giving Sander the impression that she wanted to have dinner with him, she swallowed against the dry feeling in her mouth.

Why had Ruby's simple question brought back that atavistic feeling he had had earlier? Sander asked himself angrily. For a moment he let himself imagine the two of them having dinner together. The two of them? Surely he meant the four of them—for it was because of the twins and only because of them that he had decided to allow her back into his life. Sander knew better than to allow himself to be tricked by female emotions, be they maternal or sexual. As he had good cause to know, those emotions could be summoned out of nowhere and disappear back there just as quickly.

'I've already arranged to have dinner with an old friend,' he lied. 'I don't know what time I'll be back.'

An old friend, Sander had said. Did that mean he was having dinner with another woman? A lover, perhaps?

Ruby wondered later, after the boys had eaten their tea and she had forced herself to eat something with them. She knew so little about Sander's life and the people in it. A feeling of panic began to grow inside her.

'Mummy, come and look at our island,' Freddie was demanding, standing in front of a laptop that he was trying to open.

'No, Freddie, you mustn't touch that,' Ruby protested,

'It's all right, Mummy,' Harry assured her adopting a heartbreakingly familiar pose of male confidence. 'Daddy said that we could look.'

Freddie had got the laptop lid up—like all children, the twins were very at home with modern technology—and before Ruby could say anything the screen was filled with the image of an almost crescent shaped island, with what looked like a range of rugged mountains running the full length of its spine.

In the early days, after she had first met him, Ruby had tried to find out as much as she could about Sander, still refusing to believe then that all she had been to him was a one-night stand.

She had learned that the island, whose closest neighbour was Cyprus, had been invaded and conquered many times, and that in Sander's veins ran the ruling blood of conquering Moors from the time of the Crusades—even though now the island population considered itself to be Greek. She had also learned that Sander's family had ruled the island for many centuries, and that his grandfather, the current patriarch, had built up a shipping business in the wake of the Second World War which had brought new wealth and employment to the island. However, once she had been forced to recognise that she meant nothing to Sander she had stopped seeking out information about him.

'Bath time,' she told her sons firmly.

Their new clothes and her own had been delivered whilst they had been downstairs, along with some very smart new cases, and once the twins were in bed she intended to spend her evening packing in readiness for their flight to the island.

Only once the boys were bathed and in bed Ruby was drawn back to the computer, with its tantalising image of the island.

Almost without realising what she was doing she clicked on the small red dot that represented its capital. Several thumbnail images immediately appeared. Ruby clicked on the first of them to enlarge it, and revealed a dazzlingly white fortress, perched high on a cliff above an impossibly blue green sea, its Moorish-looking towers reaching up into a deep blue sky. Another thumbnail enlarged to show what she assumed was the front of the same building, looking more classically Greek in design and dominating a formal square. The royal blue of the traditionally dressed guards' jackets worn over brilliantly white skirts made a striking image.

The other images revealed a hauntingly beautiful landscape of sandy bays backed by cliffs, small fishing harbours, and white-capped mountains covered in wild flowers. These were contrasted by a modern cargo dock complex, and small towns of bright white buildings and dark shadowed alleyways. It was impossible not to be captivated by the images of the island, Ruby admitted, but at the same time viewing them had brought home to her how different and even alien the island was to everything she and the twins knew. Was she doing the right thing? She knew nothing of Sander's family, or his way of life, and once on the island she would be totally at his mercy. But if she hadn't agreed to go with them he would have tried to take the twins from her, she was sure. This way at least she would be with them.

A fierce tide of maternal love surged through her. The twins meant everything to her. Their emotional security both now and in the future was what would bring her happiness, and was far more important to her than anything else—especially the unwanted and humiliating desire that Sander was somehow able to arouse in her. Her mouth had gone dry again. At seventeen she might have been able to excuse herself for being vulnerable to Sander's sexual charisma, but she was not seventeen any more. Even if her single solitary memory of sexual passion was still limited to what she had experienced with Sander. He, of course, had no doubt shared his bed with an unending parade of women since he had ejected her so cruelly from both it and his life.

She looked at the computer, suddenly unable to resist the temptation to do a web search on Sander's name. It wasn't prying, not really. She had the boys to think of after all.

She wasn't sure what she had expected to find, but

her eyes widened over the discovery that Sander was now ruler of the island—a role that carried the title of King, although, according to the website, he had decided to dispense with its usage, preferring to adopt a more democratic approach to ruling the island than that exercised by his predecessors.

Apparently his parents had died when Sander was eighteen, in a flying accident. The plane they'd been in piloted by a cousin of Sander's mother. A shock as though she had inadvertently touched a live wire shot through her. They had both been orphaned at almost the same age. Like hers, Sander's parents had been killed in an accident. If she had known that when they had first met... What difference would it have made? None.

Sander was thirty-four, to her twenty-three; a man at the height of his powers. A small shiver raked her skin, like the sensual rasp of a lover's tongue against sensitised flesh. Inside her head an image immediately formed: Sander's dark tanned hand cupping her own naked breast, his tongue curling round her swollen nipple. The small shiver became a racking shudder. Quickly Ruby tried to banish the image, closing down the computer screen. She was feeling nauseous again. Shakily, she made her way to the bathroom.

CHAPTER SIX

'I NOW pronounce you man and wife.'

It was over, done. There was no going back. Ruby was shaking inwardly, but she refused to let Sander see how upset she was.

Upset? A small tremor made her body shudder inside the cream Vera Wang dress she had not wanted to wear but which the personal shopper had included amongst her purchases and which for some reason she had felt obliged to wear. It was, after all, her wedding day. A fresh tremor broke through her self-control. What was the matter with her? What had she expected? Hearts and flowers? A declaration of undying devotion? This was Sander she was marrying, Sander who had not looked at her once during the brief ceremony in the anonymous register office, who couldn't have made it plainer how little he wanted her as his wife. Well, no more than she wanted him as her husband.

Sander looked down at Ruby's left hand. The ring he had just slipped onto her marriage finger was slightly loose, despite the fact that it should have fitted. She was far too thin and seemed to be getting thinner. But why should her fragility concern him?

It didn't. Women were adept at creating fictional images in order to deceive others. To her sons Ruby was no doubt a much loved mother, a constant and secure presence in their lives. At their age that had been his own feeling about his mother. Bitterness curled through him, spreading its poisonous infection.

In the years since the deaths of his parents he had often wondered if his father had given in so readily to his mother's financial demands because secretly he had loved her, even though he'd known she'd only despised him, and she, knowing that, had used his love against him. It was a fate he had sworn would never be his own.

And yet here he was married, and to a woman he already knew he could not trust—a woman who had given herself to him with such sensuality and intimacy that even now after so many years he was unable to strip from his memory the images she had left upon it. He had been a fool to let her get close enough to him once to do that. He wasn't going to let it happen again.

Neither of them spoke in the taxi taking them back to the hotel. Ruby already knew Sander had some business matters to attend to, which thankfully meant that she would have some time to herself in which to come to terms with the commitment she had just made.

After Sander had escorted them to the suite and then left without a word to her, after kissing the boys, Ruby reminded herself that she had not only walked willingly into this marriage, she was the one who had first suggested it.

The boys were tired—worn out, Ruby suspected, by the excitement of being in London. A short sleep would do them all good, and might help to ease her cramped, nauseous stomach and aching head.

After removing her wedding dress and pulling on her old dressing gown, she put the twins to bed. Once she had assured herself that they were asleep she went into her own bathroom, fumbling in her handbag for some headache tablets and accidentally removing the strip of birth control pills instead. They reminded her that although Sander might have made her take them she must not let him make her want him. Her hands shook as she replaced them to remove the pack of painkillers. Just that simple action had started her head pounding again, but thankfully this time at least she wasn't sick.

She was so tired that after a bath to help her relax she could barely dry herself, never mind bother to put on a nightdress. Instead she simply crawled beneath the duvet on her bed, falling asleep almost immediately.

Ruby woke up reluctantly, dragged from her sleep by a sense of nagging urgency. It only took her a matter of seconds to realise what had caused it. The silence. She couldn't hear the twins. How long had she been asleep? Her heart jolted anxiously into her ribs when she looked at her watch and realised that it was over three hours since she had tucked the twins into their beds. Why were they so quiet?

Trembling with apprehension, she pushed back the bedclothes, grabbing the towel she had discarded earlier and wrapping it around herself as she ran barefoot from her own room to the twins'.

It was empty. Her heart lurched sickeningly, and then started to beat frantically fast with fear.

On shaking legs Ruby ran through the suite, opening doors, calling their names, even checking the security lock on the main door to the suite just in case they had somehow opened it. All the time the hideous reality of what might have happened was lying in wait for her inside her head.

In the dreadful silence of the suite—only a parent could know and understand how a silence that should have been filled with the sound of children's voices could feel—she sank down onto one of the sofas.

The reason the twins weren't here must be because Sander had taken them. There could be no other explanation. He must have come back whilst she was asleep and seized his opportunity. He hadn't wanted to marry her any more than she had wanted to marry him. What he had wanted was the twins. His sons. And now he had them.

Were they already on a plane to the island? *His* island, where he made the laws and where she would never be able to reach them. He had their passports after all. A legal necessity, he had said, and she had stupidly accepted that.

Shock, grief, fear and anger—she could feel them all, but over and above those feelings was concern for her sons and fury that Sander could have done something so potentially harmful to them.

She could hear a noise: the sound of the main door
to the suite opening, followed by the excited babble of
two familiar voices.

The twins!

She was on her feet, hardly daring to believe that she
wasn't simply imagining hearing them out of her own
need, and then they were there, in the room with her,
running towards her and telling her excitedly, 'Daddy
took us to a café for our tea, because you were asleep,'
bringing the smell of cold air in with them.

Dropping onto her knees, Ruby hugged them to her
not trusting herself to speak, holding the small wriggling
bodies tightly. They were her life, her heart, her everything. She could hardly bear to let them go.

Sander was standing watching her, making her acutely
conscious as she struggled to stand up that all that covered
her nudity was the towel she had wrapped round her.

Going back to her bedroom, she discarded the towel
and grabbed a clean pair of knickers before reaching for
her old and worn velour dressing gown. She was too
worked up and too anxious to get back to the twins as
quickly as she could to care what she looked like or what
Sander thought. The fact that he hadn't taken them as
she had initially feared paled into insignificance compared with her realisation that he could have done so.
Now that she had had a taste of what it felt like to think
she had lost them, she knew more than ever that there
was nothing she would not do or sacrifice to keep them
with her.

Her hands trembled violently as she tied the belt on

her dressing gown. From the sitting room she could hear the sound of cartoon voices from the television, and when she went back in the boys were sitting together, watching a children's TV programme, whilst Sander was seated at the small desk with his laptop open in front of him.

Neither of them had spoken, but the tension and hostility crackling in the air between them spoke a language they could both hear and understand.

Her headache might have gone, but it had been replaced with an equally sickening sense of guilt, Ruby acknowledged, when she sat down an hour later to read to the boys, now bathed and in bed. She watched them as they fell asleep after their bedtime story. Today something had happened that she had never experienced before. She had slept so deeply that she had not heard anything when Sander returned and took her sons. How could that be? How could she have been so careless of their safety?

She didn't want to leave them. She wanted to stay here all night with them.

The bedroom door opened. Immediately Ruby stiffened, whispering, 'What do you want?'

'I've come to say goodnight to my sons.'

'They're asleep.' She got up and walked to the door, intending to go through it and then close it, excluding him, but Sander was holding it and she was the one forced to leave and then watch as he went to kiss their sleeping faces.

Turning on her heel, Ruby headed for her own room. But before she stepped inside it her self-control broke and she whirled round, telling Sander, 'You had no right to take the boys out without asking me first.'

'They are my sons. I have every right. And as for telling you—'

Telling her, not asking her. Ruby noted his correction, consumed now by the kind of anger that followed the trauma of terrible shock and fear, which was a form of relief at discovering that the unthinkable hadn't happened after all.

'You were asleep.'

'You could have woken me. You *should* have woken me. It's my right as their mother to know where they are.'

'Your *right*? What about *their* rights? What about their right to have a mother who doesn't put her own needs first? I suppose a woman who goes out at night picking up men needs to sleep during the day. And knowing you as I do, I imagine that is what *you* do.'

Sickened by what he was implying, Ruby said fiercely, '*Knowing* me? You don't know me at all. And the unpleasant little scenario you have just outlined has never and would never take place. I have never so much as gone out at night and left the twins, never mind gone out picking up men. The reason I was asleep was because I haven't been feeling well—not that I expect you to believe me. You'd much rather make up something you can insult me with than listen to the truth.'

'I've had firsthand experience of the truth of what you are.'

Ruby's face burned. 'You're basing your judgement of me on one brief meeting, when I was—'

'Too drunk to know what you were doing?'

His cynical contempt was too much for Ruby's composure. For years she had tortured and tormented herself because of what she had done. She didn't need Sander weighing in to add to that self-punishment and pain. She shook her head in angry denial.

'Foolish and naive enough to want to create a fairy story out of something and someone belonging in reality to a horror story,' she said bitterly. Too carried away by the anger bursting past her self-control, she continued, 'You need not have wasted your contempt on me, because it can't possibly match the contempt I feel for myself, for deluding myself that you were someone special.'

Ruby felt sick and dizzy. Memories of what they had once shared were rushing in, roaring over her mental barriers and springing into vivid life inside her. She had been such a fool, so willing and eager to go to him, seeking in his arms the security and safety she had lost and thinking in her naivety that she would find them by binding herself to him in the most intimate way there was.

'So much drama,' Sander taunted her, 'and all of it so unnecessary, since I know it for the deceit that it is.'

'You are the one who is deceiving yourself by believing what you do,' Ruby threw at him emotionally.

'You dare to accuse *me* of self-deception?' Sander demanded, stepping towards her as he spoke, forcing her to step back into her bedroom. She backed up so quickly that she ended up standing on the trailing belt of her dressing gown. The soft, worn fabric gave way immediately, exposing the pale curve of her breast and the darker flesh of her nipple.

Sander saw what had happened before Ruby was aware of it herself, and his voice dropped to a cynical softness as he said, 'So that's what you want, is it? Same old Ruby. Well, why not? You certainly owe me something.'

Ruby's despairing, 'No!' was lost, crushed beneath the cruel strength of his mouth as it fastened on hers, and the sound of the door slamming as he pushed it closed was a death knell on her chances of escape.

Her robe quickly gave way to the swift expertise of Sander's determined hands, sliding from Ruby's body whilst he punished her with his kiss. In the mirror Sander could see the narrow curve of her naked back. Her skin, palely luminous, reminded him of the inside of the shells washed up on the beach below his home. Against his will old memories stirred, of how beneath his touch and against it she had trembled and then shuddered, calling out to him in open pleasure, so easily aroused by even the lightest caress. A wanton who had made no attempt to conceal the passion that drove her, or her own pleasure in his satisfaction of it, crying out to him to please her.

Sander drove his tongue between her lips as fiercely as he wanted to drive out her memory. The honeyed sensuality of her mouth closed round him, inviting his tongue-tip's exploration of its sweetest hidden places. The simple plain white knickers she was wearing jarred against the raw sexuality of his own arousal. He wanted her naked and eager, stripped of the lies and deceit with which she was so keen to veil her own reality. He would make her admit to what she was, show her that he knew the true naked reality of her. His hands gripped her and held her, moving down over her body to push aside her protective covering.

Her figure was as perfect as it was possible for a woman's figure to be—or it would be if she carried a few more pounds, Sander acknowledged. From her shoulders, her torso narrowed down into a handspan waist before curving out into feminine hips and the high, rounded cheeks of her bottom. Her legs were long and slender, designed to wrap erotically and greedily around the man she chose to give her the pleasure she craved. Her breasts were full and soft, and he could remember how sensitive her nipples had been, the suckle of his mouth against them making her cry out in ecstasy.

Why was he tormenting himself with mere memories when she was here and his for the taking, her body already shivering in his hold with anticipation of the pleasure to come?

She was naked and in Sander's power. She should fight him and reject him, Ruby knew. She wanted to, but her body wanted something else. Her body wanted Sander.

Like some dark power conjured up by a master sorcerer desire swept through her, overwhelming reason and pride, igniting a need so intense that she felt as though an alien force were possessing her, dictating actions and reactions it was impossible for her to control.

It was as though in Sander's arms she became a different person—a wildly passionate, elementally sensual woman of such intensity that everything she was crystallised in the act of being taken by him and taking him in turn.

It might be her wish to fight what possessed her, but it was also her destiny to submit to it as Sander's mouth moved from its fierce possession of hers to an equally erotic exploration of her throat, lingering on the pulse there that so recklessly gave away her arousal.

It was not enough to have her naked to his gaze and his touch. He needed to have the feel of her against his own skin. She was an ache, a need, a compulsion that wouldn't allow him to rest until he had conquered her and she had submitted to his mastery of her pleasure. He wanted, needed, to hear her cry out that desire to him before he could allow himself to submit to his own desire for her. He needed her to offer up her pleasure to him before he could lose himself within her and take his own.

He was caught in a trap as old as Eve herself—caught and held in the silken web of a desire only she had the power to spin. The savagery of his anger that this should be so was only matched by the savagery of his need for the explosion of fevered sensuality now possessing them both. It was a form of madness, a fever, a possession he couldn't escape.

Scooping her up in his arms, Sander carried Ruby to the bed, watching her watch him as he placed her on it and then wrenched off his own clothes, seeing the way her eyes betrayed her reaction to the sight of him, naked and ready for her.

Her eyes dark and wide with delight, Ruby reached

out to touch the formidable thickness of Sander's erection, marvelling at the texture of his flesh beneath her fingers. Engrossed and entranced, she stroked her fingertips over the length of him, easing back the hooded cover to reveal the sensitive flesh beneath it, not the woman she knew as herself any more, but instead a Ruby who was possessed by the powerful dark force of their shared desire—a Ruby whose breath quickened and whose belly tightened in pleasurable longing.

She looked up at Sander and saw in his eyes the same need she knew was in her own. She lifted her hand from his body, and as though it had been a signal to him he pushed her back on the bed, following her down, shaping and moulding her breasts with his hands, feeding her need for the erotic pleasure she knew he could give her with the heat of his lips and his tongue on her nipples, until she arched up against him, whimpering beneath the unbearable intensity of her own pleasure.

The feel of his hand cupping her sex wasn't just something she welcomed. It was something she needed.

Her body was wet and ready for him, just as it had been before. Just for a heartbeat the mistrust that was his mother's legacy to him surfaced past Sander's desire. There must not be another unwanted conception.

'The pill—' he began,

Ruby nodded her head.

A sheen of perspiration gleamed on his tanned flesh, and the scent of his arousal was heightening her own. It was frightening, this intensity of desire, this sharpening and focusing of her senses so that only Sander filled them. It had frightened her six years ago and it still frightened her now. The need he aroused within her demanded that she gave everything of herself over to him—all that she was, every last bit of her. The verbal demand he was making now was nothing compared with that.

'Yes. I'm taking it.'

'You swear?'

'I swear…'

Sander heard the unsteady note of need trembling in her voice. She was impatient for him, but no more than he was for her. He had fought to hold back the tide of longing for her from the minute he had seen her again. It had mocked his efforts to deny it, and now it was overwhelming him, the fire burning within him consuming him. Right now, in this heartbeat of time, nothing else mattered. He was in the grip of a force so powerful that he had to submit to it.

They moved together, without the need for words, movement matching movement, a duel of shared anger and longing. Her body welcomed his, holding it, sheathing it, moving with it and against it, demanding that he move faster and deeper, driving them both to that place from which they could soar to the heavens and then fall back to earth.

It was here now—that shuddering climax of sensation, gripping her, gripping Sander, causing the spurting spill of the seeds of new life within her. Only this time there would be no new life because she was on the pill.

They lay together in the darkness, their breathing unsteady and audible in the silence.

Now—now when it was over, and his flesh was washed with the cold reality of how quickly he had given in to his need for her—Sander was forced to accept the truth. He could not control the physical desire she aroused in him. It had overwhelmed him, and it would overwhelm him again. That knowledge was a bitter blow to his pride.

Without looking at her, he told her emotionlessly, 'From now on I am the only man you will have sex with. Is that understood? I will not have my wife shaming me by offering herself to other men. And to ensure that you don't I shall make it my business to see to it that your eager appetite for sexual pleasure is kept satisfied.'

Sander knew that his words were merely a mask for the reality that he could neither bear the thought of her with another man nor control his own desire for her, no matter how much he despised himself for his weakness.

Ruby could feel her face burning with humiliation. She wanted to tell him that she didn't understand what happened to her when she was in his arms. She wanted to tell him that other men did not have the same effect on her. She wanted to tell him that he was the only man she had ever had sex with. But she knew that he wouldn't listen.

Later, alone in his own room, Sander tried to explain to himself why the minute he touched Ruby he became filled with a compulsion to possess her. His desire for her was stronger than his resolve to resist it, and he couldn't. What she made him feel and want was unique to her, loath as he was to admit that.

CHAPTER SEVEN

GIVEN Sander's wealth, Ruby had half expected that they might fly first-class to the island—but what she had not expected was that they would be travelling in the unimagined luxury of a private jet, with them the only passengers on board. But that was exactly what had happened, and now, with the boys taken by the steward to sit with the captain for a few minutes, she and Sander were alone in the cabin, with its cream leather uphol-stery and off-white carpets.

'The money it must cost to own and run something like this would feed hundreds of poor families,' Ruby couldn't stop herself from saying.

Her comment, and the unspoken accusation it held, made Sander frown. He had never once heard his mother express concern for 'poor families', and the fact that Ruby had done so felt like a sharp paper cut on the tender skin of his judgement of her—something small and insignifi-cant in one sense, but in another something he could not ignore, no matter how much he might want to do so.

To his own disbelief he found himself defending his

position, telling her, 'I don't actually own it. I merely belong to a small consortium of businessmen who share and charter it when they need it. As for feeding the poor—on the island we operate a system which ensures that no one goes hungry and that every child has access to an education matched to their skills and abilities. We also have a free health service and a good pension system—the latter two schemes put in place by my father.'

Why on earth did he think he had to justify anything he did to *Ruby*?

It was dark when their flight finally put down on the island, the darkness obscuring their surroundings apart from what they could see in the blaze of the runway lights as they stepped down from the plane and into the warm velvet embrace of the Mediterranean evening. A soft breeze ruffled the boys' hair as they clung to Ruby's sides, suddenly uncertain and unsure of themselves. A golf cart type of vehicle was their transport for the short distance to the arrivals building, where Sander shook hands with the officials waiting to greet him before ushering them outside again to the limousine waiting for them. It was Sander who lifted the sleepy children into it, settling Harry on his lap and then putting his free arm around Freddie, whilst Ruby was left to sit on her own. Her arms felt empty without the twins, and she felt a maternal urge to reach for them, but she resisted it, not wanting to disturb them now that they were asleep.

The headache and subsequent nausea it had caused

her had thankfully not returned, although she still didn't feel one hundred percent.

The car moved swiftly down a straight smooth road before eventually turning off it onto a more winding road, on one side of which Ruby could see the sea glinting in the moonlight. On the other side of them was a steep wall of rock, which eventually gave way to an old fashioned fortress-like city wall, with a gateway in it through which they drove, past tall buildings and then along a narrow street which broadened out into the large formal square Ruby had seen on the internet.

'This is the main square of the city, with the Royal Palace up ahead of us,' Sander informed her.

'Is that where we'll be living?' Ruby asked apprehensively.

Sander shook his head.

'No. The palace is used only for formal occasions now, and as an administrative centre. After my grandfather died I had my own villa built just outside the city. I don't care for pomp and circumstance. My people's quality of life is what is important to me, just as it was to my father. I cannot expect to have their respect if I do not give them mine.'

Ruby looked away from him. His comments showed the kind of attitude she admired, but how could she allow herself to admire Sander? It was bad enough that he could arouse her physically without her being vulnerable to him emotionally as well.

'The city must be very old,' she said instead.

'Very,' Sander agreed.

As always when he returned to the island after an absence, he was torn in opposing directions. He loved the island and its people, but he also had the painful memories of his childhood here to contend with.

In an effort to banish them and concentrate on something else, he told Ruby, 'The Phoenicians and the Egyptians traded here, just as they did with our nearest neighbour Cyprus. Like Cyprus, we too have large deposits of copper here, and possession of the island was fought over fiercely during the Persian wars. In the end a marriage alliance between the opposing forces brought the fighting to an end. That has traditionally been the way in which territorial disputes have been settled here—' He broke off to look at her as he heard the small sound Ruby made.

Ruby shivered, unable to stop herself from saying, 'It must have been dreadful for the poor brides who were forced into marriage.'

'It is not the exclusive right of *your* sex to detest a forced marriage.'

Sander's voice was so harsh that the twins stirred against him in their sleep, focusing Ruby's attention on her sons, although she was still able to insist defensively, 'Historically a man has always had more rights within marriage than a woman.'

'The right to freedom of choice is enshrined in the human psyche of both sexes and should be respected above all other things,' Sander insisted.

Ruby looked at him in disbelief. 'How can you say that after the way you have forced me…?'

'You were the one who insisted on marriage.'

'Because I had no other choice.'

'There is always a choice.'

'Not for a mother. She will always put her children first.'

Her voice held a conviction that Sander told himself had to be false, and the cynical look he gave her said as much, causing Ruby's face to burn as she remembered how she had fallen asleep, leaving the twins unprotected.

Looking away from her, Sander thought angrily that Ruby might *think* she had deceived him by claiming her reason for insisting he married her was that she wanted to protect her sons, but he knew perfectly well that it was the fact that she believed marriage to him would give her a share in his wealth. That was what she really wanted to protect.

But she had signed a prenuptial agreement that barred her from making any claim on his money should they ever divorce, an inner voice defended her unexpectedly. She probably thought she could have the prenup set aside, Sander argued against it. Her children loved her, the inner voice pointed out. They would not exhibit the love and trust they did if she was a bad mother. He had loved *his* mother at their age, Sander pointed out. But he had hardly seen his mother or spent much time with her. She had been an exotic stranger, someone he had longed to see, and yet when he had seen her she had made him feel anxious to please her, and wary of her sudden petulant outbursts if he accidentally touched her expensive clothes. Anna, who was now in charge of the villa's household, had been more of a true mother—not just to him, but to all of them.

As Anna had been with them, Ruby was with the twins all the time. Logically he had to admit that it simply wasn't possible for anyone to carry out the pretence of being a caring parent twenty-four seven if it was just an act. A woman who loved both money and her children? Was that possible? It galled Sander that he should even be asking himself that question. What was the matter with him? He knew exactly what she was—why should he now be finding reasons to think better of her?

Sander looked away from Ruby and out into the darkness beyond the car window. The boys were soft warm weights against his body. His sons, and he loved them utterly and completely, no matter who or what their mother was. It was for their sakes that he wanted to find some good in her, for their sakes that his inner voice was trying to insist she was a good mother—for what caring father would *not* want that for his children, especially when that father knew what it was to have a mother who did not care.

Was it her imagination, or were the twins already turning more to Sander than they did to her? Miserably Ruby stared through the car window next to her. Whilst they had been talking they had left the city behind and were now travelling along another coastal road, with the sea to one side of them. But where previously there had been steep cliffs now the land rolled more gently away from the road.

It was far too late and far too selfish of her to wish that Sander had not come back into her life, Ruby admitted as the silence between them grew, filled by Sander's contempt for her and entrapping her in her own ever-present guilt. It was that guilt for having conceived the twins so carelessly and thoughtlessly that had in part brought her here, Ruby recognised. Guilt and her overwhelming desire to give her sons the same kind of happy, unshadowed, secure childhood in a family protected by two loving parents that she herself had enjoyed until her parents' death. But that security had been ripped from her. Her heart started to thud in a mixture of remembered pain and fierce hope that her sons would never experience what she had.

On his side of the luxurious leather upholstered car Sander stared out into the darkness—a darkness that for him was populated by the ghosts of his own past. In his grandfather's day the family had lived in the palace, unable to speak to either their parents or their grandfather unless those adults chose to seek them out. Yet despite maintaining his own distance from Sander and his siblings, their grandfather had somehow managed to know every detail of his grandchildren's lives, regularly sending for them so that he could list their flaws and faults and petty childhood crimes.

His sister and brother had been afraid of their grandfather, but Sander, the eldest child and ultimately the heir to his grandfather's shipping empire, had quickly learned that the best way to deal with his grandparent was to stand up to him. Sander's pride had been honed on the whetstone of his grandfather's mockery and baiting, as he'd constantly challenged Sander to prove himself to him whilst at the same time having no compunction about seeking to destroy his pride in himself to maintain his own superiority.

An English boarding school followed by university had given him a welcome respite from his grandfather's overbearing and bullying ways, but it had been after Sander had left university and started work in the family business that the real clashes between them had begun.

The continuation of the family and the business had been all that really mattered to his grandfather. His son and his grandchildren had been merely pawns to be used to further that cause. Sander had grown up hearing his grandfather discussing the various merits of young heiresses whom Sander might be wise to marry, but what he had learned from his mother, allied to his own naturally alpha personality and the time he had spent away from the island whilst he was at school and university, had made Sander determined not to allow his grandfather to bully him into marriage as he had done his father.

There had been many arguments between them on the subject, with his grandfather constantly trying to manipulate and bully Sander into meeting one or other of the young women he'd deemed suitable to be the mother of the next heir. In the end, infuriated and sickened by his grandfather's attempts at manipulation and coercion, Sander had announced to his grandfather that he was wasting his time as he never intended to marry, since he already had an heir in his brother.

His grandfather had then threatened to disinherit him, and Sander had challenged him to go ahead, telling him that he would find employment with one of their rivals. There the matter had rested for several weeks, giving Sander the impression that finally his grandfather had realised that he was not going to be controlled as his own parents had been controlled. But then, virtually on the eve of a long planned visit by Sander to the UK, to meet with some important clients in Manchester, he had discovered that his grandfather was planning to use his absence to advise the press of an impending engagement between Sander and the young widow of another ship-owner. Apart from anything else Sander knew that the young widow in question had a string of lovers and a serious drug habit, but neither of those potential draw-backs had been of any interest to his grandfather.

Of course Sander had confronted his grandfather, and both of them had been equally angry with the other. His grandfather had refused to back down, and Sander had warned him that if he went ahead with a public an-nouncement then he would refute that announcement equally publicly.

By the time he had reached Manchester Sander's anger hadn't cooled and his resolve to live his own life had actively hardened—to the extent that he had decided that on his return to Greece he was going to cut all ties with his grandfather and set up his own rival business from scratch.

And it had been in that frame of mind, filled with a dangerous mix of emotions, that he had met Ruby. He could see her now, eyeing him up from the other side of the crowded club, her blonde hair as carefully tousled as her lipglossed mouth had been deliberately pouted. The short skirt she'd worn had revealed slender legs, her tight top had been pulled in to display her tiny waist, and the soft rounded upper curves of her breasts had been openly on display. In short she had looked no different from the dozens of other eager, willing and easily available young women who came to the club specifically because it was known to be a haunt for louche young footballers and their entourages.

The only reason Sander had been in the club had been to meet a contact who knew people Sander thought might be prepared to give his proposed new venture some business. Whilst he was there Sander had received a phone call from a friend, urging him not to act against his own best interests. Immediately Sander had known that somehow his grandfather had got wind of what he was planning, and that someone had betrayed him. Fury—against his grandfather, against all those people in his life he had trusted but who had betrayed him—had overwhelmed him, exploding through his veins, pulsing against all constraints like the molten heat of a volcano building up inside him until it could not be contained any longer, the force of it erupting to spew its dangerous contents over everything in its path. And Ruby had been in the path of that fury, a readymade sacrifice to his anger, all too willing to allow him to use her for whatever purpose he chose.

All it had taken to bring her to his side had been one

cynical and deliberately lingering glance. She had leaned close to him in the crush of the club, her breath smelling of vodka and her skin of soap. He remembered how that realisation had momentarily checked him. The other girls around her had reeked of cheap scent. He had offered to buy her a drink and she had shaken her head, looking at him with such openly hungry eyes that her lack of self-respect had further inflamed his fury. He had questioned to himself why girls like her preferred to use their bodies to support themselves instead of their brains, giving themselves to men not directly for money but in the hope that they would end up as the girlfriend of a wealthy man.

Well, there had been no place in his life for a 'girlfriend', but right then there *had* been a rage, a tension inside him that he knew the use of her body in the most basic way there was would do much to alleviate. He had reached for his drink—not his first of the evening— finished it with one swallow, before turning to her and saying brusquely, 'Come on.'

A bump in the road woke the twins up, and Harry's 'Are we there yet?' dragged Sander's thoughts from the past to the present.

'Nearly,' he answered him. 'We're turning into the drive to the villa now.'

As he spoke the car swung off the road at such a sharp angle that Ruby slid along the leather seat, almost bumping her head on the side of the car. Unlike her, though, the twins were safe, protected by the arms Sander had tightened around them the minute the car had started to turn. Sander loved the twins, but he did not love her.

The pain that gripped her caught Ruby off guard. She wasn't jealous of her own sons, was she? Of course not. The last thing she wanted was Sander's arms around *her*, she told herself angrily as they drove through a pair of ornate wrought-iron gates and then down a long straight drive bordered with Cypress trees and illuminated by lights set into the ground.

At the end of the drive was a gravelled rectangle, and beyond that the villa itself, discreetly floodlit to reveal its elegant modern lines and proportions.

'Anna, who is in charge of the household, will have everything ready for you and the twins. She and Georgiou, her husband, who has driven us here, look after the villa and its gardens between them. They have their own private quarters over the garage block, which is separate from the villa itself,' Sander informed Ruby as the car crunched to a halt over the gravel.

Almost immediately the front door to the villa was opened to reveal a tall, well-built woman with dark hair streaked with grey and a serene expression.

It gave Ruby a fierce pang of emotion to see the way the twins automatically put their hands in Sander's and not her own as they walked with their father towards her. Her smile of welcome for Sander was one of love and delight, and Ruby watched in amazement as Sander returned her warm hug with obvious affection. Somehow it was not what she had expected. Anna—Ruby assumed the woman was Anna—was plainly far more to Sander than merely the person who was in charge of his household.

Now she was bending down to greet the boys, not overwhelming them by hugging them as she had Sander, Ruby noted approvingly, but instead waiting for them to go to her.

Sander gave them a little push and told them, 'This is Anna. She looked after me when I was a boy, and now she will look after you.'

Immediately Ruby's maternal hackles rose. Her sons did not need Anna or anyone else to look after them. They had her. She stepped forward herself, placing one hand on each of her son's shoulders, and then was completely disarmed when Anna smiled warmly and approvingly at her, as though welcoming what she had done rather than seeing it as either a challenge or a warning.

When Sander introduced her to Anna as his wife, it was obvious that Anna had been expecting them. What had Sander said to his family and those who knew him about the twins? How had he explained away the fact that he was suddenly producing them—and her? Ruby didn't know but she did know that Anna at least was delighted to welcome the twins as Sander's sons. It was plain she was ready to adore and spoil them, and was going to end up completely under their thumbs.

'Anna will show you round the villa and provide you and the boys with something to eat,' Sander informed Ruby.

He said something in Greek to Anna, who beamed at him and nodded her head vigorously, and then he was gone, striding across the white limestone floor of the entrance hall and disappearing through one of the dark wooden doors set into the white walls.

That feeling gripping her wasn't a sense of loss, was it? A feeling of being abandoned? A longing for Sander to return, because without him their small family was incomplete? Because without him *she* was incomplete?

As soon as the treacherous words whispered across her mind Ruby stiffened in denial of them. But they had left an echo that wasn't easily silenced, reminding her of all that she had suffered when she had first been foolish enough to think that he cared about her.

CHAPTER EIGHT

'I'LL show you your rooms first,' Anna told Ruby, 'and then perhaps you would like a cup of tea before you see the rest of the villa?'

There was something genuinely warm and kind and, well, *motherly* about Anna that had Ruby's initial wary hostility melting away as they walked together up the marble stairs, the twins in between them.

When they reached the top and saw the long wide landing stretching out ahead of them the twins looked at Ruby hopefully.

Shaking her head, she began, 'No—no running inside—' Only to have Anna smile broadly at her.

'This is their home now, they may run if you permit it,' she told her.

'Very well,' Ruby told them, relieved by Anna's understanding of the need of two young children to let off steam, and both women watched as the boys ran down the corridor.

'Looking at them is like looking at Sander when he

was a similar age, except that—' Anna stopped, her smile fading.

'Except that what?' Ruby asked her, sensitively defensive of any possible criticism being lodged against her precious sons.

As though she had guessed what Ruby was thinking, Anna patted Ruby on the arm.

'You are a good mother—anyone can see that. Your goodness and your love for them is reflected in your sons' smiles. Sander's mother was not like that. Her children were a duty she resented, and they all, especially Sander, learned young not to turn to their mother for love and comfort.'

Anna's quiet words formed an image inside Ruby's head she didn't want to see—an image of a young and vulnerable Sander, a child with sadness in his eyes, standing alone and hurt by his mother's lack of love for him.

The boys raced back to them, putting an end to any more confidences from Anna about Sander's childhood, and Ruby's sympathy for the child that Sander had been was swiftly pushed to one side when she discovered that the two of them were going to be sharing a bedroom and a bed.

Why did she feel so unnerved and apprehensive? Ruby asked herself later, after Anna had helped her put the twins to bed and she was in the kitchen, drinking the fresh cup of tea Anna had insisted on making for her. Sander had already made it plain that she must accept that their marriage would include sexual intimacy. They both already knew that she wanted him, and she had already suffered the humiliation *that* had brought her, so what was there left for her to fear?

There was emotional vulnerability, Ruby admitted. With her sexual vulnerability to Sander there was already a danger that she could become sexually dependent on him, and that was bad enough. If she also became emotionally vulnerable to him might she not then become emotionally dependent on him? Where had that thought come from? She was a million miles from feeling anything emotional for Sander, wasn't she?

Excusing herself to Anna, Ruby explained that she wanted to go up and check the twins were still sleeping as they had left them, not wanting them to wake alone in such new surroundings.

The twins' bedroom, like the one she was to share with Sander, looked out onto a courtyard and an infinity pool with the sea beyond it. But whilst Sander's bedroom had glass doors that opened out onto the patio area that surrounded the pool, the boys' room merely had a window—a safety feature for which she was extremely grateful. Glass bedroom doors, a swimming pool, and two adventurous five-year-olds were a mix that would arouse anxiety in any protective mother.

She needn't have worried about the twins. They were both sleeping soundly, their faces turned toward one another. Love for them filled her. But as she bent towards them to kiss them it wasn't their faces she could see but that of another young child, a child whose dark eyes, so like those of her sons, were shadowed with pain and angry pride. Sander's eyes. They still held that angry pride now, as an adult, when he looked at her. And the pain? Her question furrowed Ruby's brow. Emotional pain was not something she had previously equated with Sander. But the circumstances a child experienced growing up affected it all its life. She believed that wholeheartedly. If she hadn't done so then she would not feel as strongly as she did about Sander being a part of the twins' lives. So what had happened to Sander's pain? Was it buried somewhere deep inside him? A sad, sore place that could never heal? A wound that was the cruellest wound of all to a child—the lack of its mother's love?

Confused by her own thoughts, Ruby left her sleeping sons. She was tired and ready for bed herself. Her heart started beating unsteadily. Tired and ready for bed? Ready to share Sander's bed?

The villa was beautifully decorated. The guest suite Anna had shown Ruby, and in which she would have preferred to be sleeping, was elegantly modern, the clean lines of its furniture softened by gauzy drapes, the cool white and taupe of the colour scheme broken up with touches of Mediterranean blues and greens in the artwork adorning the walls.

From the twins' room Ruby made her way to the room she was sharing with Sander—not because she wanted to look again at the large bed and let her imagination taunt her with images of what they would share there, but because she needed to unpack, Ruby told herself firmly. Only when she opened the door to the bedroom the cases that had been there before had vanished, and from the *en suite* bathroom through the open door she could smell the sharp citrus scent of male soap and hear the sound of the shower.

Had Sander had her cases removed? Had he told Anna that he didn't want to share a room with her? Relief warred with a jolt of female protectiveness of her position as his wife. She liked Anna, but she didn't want the other woman to think that Sander was rejecting her. That would be humiliating. More humiliating than being forced in the silence of the night to cry out in longing to a husband who could arouse in her a hunger she could not control?

Ruby moved restlessly from one foot to the other, and then froze as the door to the *en suite* bathroom opened fully and Sander walked into the bedroom.

He had wrapped a towel round his hips. His body was still damp from his shower, and the white towel threw into relief the powerful tanned male V shape of his torso and the breadth of his shoulders, tapering down over strong muscles to his chest, to the hard flatness of his belly. The shadowing of dark hair slicked wetly against his skin emphasised a maleness that had Ruby trapped in its sensual spell. She wanted to look away from him. She wanted not to remember, not to feel, not to be so easily and completely overwhelmed by the need that just looking at him brought back to simmering heat. But she didn't have that kind of self-control. Instead of satiating her desire for him, what they had already shared seemed only to have increased her need for him.

Her own intense sensuality bewildered her. She had

lived for six years without ever once wanting to have sex, and yet now she only had to look at Sander to be consumed by this alien desire that seemed to have taken possession of her. Possession. Just thinking the word increased the heat licking at her body, tightening the pulse flickering eagerly deep inside her.

It was Ruby's fault that he wanted her, Sander told himself. It was she, with her soft mouth and her hungry gaze, with her eagerness, who was responsible for his own inability to control the savage surging of his need to possess her. It was because of her that he felt this ache, this driven, agonising urgency that unleashed within him something he barely recognised as part of himself.

Like a wild storm, a tornado threatening to suck them both up into its perilous grasp, Ruby could feel the pressure of their combined desire. Fear filled her. She didn't want this. It shamed and weakened her. Dragging her gaze from Sander's body, she started to run towards the door in blind panic. But Sander moved faster, reaching the door before her, and the impetus of her panic slammed her into his body, the impact shocking through her.

Tears of anger—against herself, against him, and against the aching desire flooding her—filled her eyes and she curled her hands into small fists and beat them impotently against his chest. Sander seized hold of her wrists.

'I don't want to feel like this,' she cried, agonized.

'But you do. You want this, and you want me,' he told her, before he took the denial from her lips with the ruthless pressure of his own.

Just the taste of her unleashed within him a hunger he couldn't control. The softness of her lips, the sound she made when he kissed her, the way her whole body shuddered against his with longing, drove him in what felt like a form of madness, a need, to a place where nothing else existed or mattered, where bringing her desire within the control of his ability to satisfy it felt as though it was what he had been born for.

Each sound she made, each shudder of pleasure her body gave, each urgent movement against his touch that begged silently for more became a goal he had to reach— a test of his maleness he had to master, so that he would always be the only man she desired, *his* pleasuring of her the only pleasure that could satisfy her. Something about the pale silkiness of her skin as he slid her clothes from it made him want to touch it over and over again. His hands already knew the shape and texture of her breasts, but that knowing only made him want to feel their soft weight even more. His lips and tongue and teeth might have aroused the swollen darkness of her nipples to previous pleasure, but now he wanted to recreate that pleasure. He wanted to slide his hand over the flatness of her belly and feel her suck it in as she fought to deny the effect of his touch and lost that fight. He wanted to part the slender thighs and feel them quiver, hear the small moan from between her lips, watch as she tried and failed to stop her thighs from opening eagerly to allow him the intimacy of her sex. He loved the way her soft, delicately shaped outer lips, so primly folded, opened to the slow stroke of his fingers, her wetness eagerly awaiting him.

A shocked cry of protest streaked with primitive longing burst from Ruby's throat as Sander gave in to the demand of his own arousal and moved down her body, to kiss the soft flesh on the inside of her thighs and then stroke the tip of his tongue the length of the female valley his skilled fingers had laid bare to his caress.

Waves of pleasure were racing through her, dragging her back to a level of sensuality where she was as out of her depth as a fledgling swimmer swept out by the tide into deep water. Each stroke of his tongue-tip against the most sensitive part of her took her deeper, until her own pleasure was swamping her, pulling her down into its embrace, until the rhythm it imposed on her was all that she knew, her response to it dictated and controlled by the lap of Sander's tongue as finally it overwhelmed her and she was drowning in it, giving herself over completely to it.

Later, filling her with his aching flesh, feeling her desire catch fire again as her body moved with his, inciting him towards his own destruction, Sander knew with razor-sharp clarity, in the seconds before he cried out in the exultation of release, that what he was doing might be trapping her in her desire for him but it was also feeding his need for her.

CHAPTER NINE

FROM the shade of the vine-covered pergola, Ruby watched the twins as they splashed in the swimming pool under Sander's watchful eye. It was just over six weeks now since they had arrived on the island, and the twins were loving their new life. They worshipped Sander. He was a good father, Ruby was forced to admit, giving them his time and attention, and most important of all his love. She glanced towards the house. Anna would be bringing their lunch out to them soon. A prickle of despair trickled down her spine as chilling as cold water.

This morning she was finally forcing herself to confront the possibility that she might be pregnant! The breakfasts she had been unable to eat in the morning, the tiredness that engulfed her every afternoon, the slight swelling of her breasts—all could have other explanations, but her missed period was now adding to the body of evidence.

Could she really be pregnant? Her heart jumped sickeningly inside her chest. There must be no more children, Sander had said. She must take the contraceptive pill. She had done, without missing a single one, but her symptoms were exactly the same as those she had experienced with the twins. Sander would be angry—furious, even—but what could he do? She was his wife, they were married, and she was having his child. A child she already knew he would not want.

Ruby could feel anxiety-induced nausea clogging her throat and causing perspiration to break out on her forehead. Was she right in thinking that Anna already suspected? Anna was an angel, wonderful with the children—almost a grandmother to them. After all, she had mothered Sander and his sister and brother. Somehow she seemed to know when Ruby was feeling tired and not very well, taking charge of the twins for her, giving her a kind pat when she fell back on the fiction that her lack of energy and nausea were the result of their move to a hot climate.

Sander was getting the twins out of the pool. Anna had arrived with their lunch. Determinedly, Ruby pushed her anxiety to one side.

Sander was used to working at home when he needed to, but since he had brought Ruby and his sons to the island he had discovered that he actually preferred to work at home. So that he could be with his sons, or so that he could be with Ruby? That was nonsense. A stupid question which he could not bring himself to answer.

Angrily he tried to concentrate on the screen in front of him. This afternoon he was finding it hard to concentrate on the e-mails he should be answering. Because he was thinking about Ruby? If he was then it was because of the conversation he had had with Anna earlier in the day, when she had commented on what a good mother Ruby was.

'A good mother and a good wife,' had been her exact words. 'You are a lucky man.'

Anna was a shrewd judge of character. She had never liked his mother, and she had protected them all from their grandfather's temper whenever she could. She had given him the only female love he had ever known. Homely, loyal Anna liked and approved of Ruby, a woman with more in common with his mother than she had with her.

Sander frowned. He might have seen the financially grasping side of Ruby that echoed the behaviour of his mother, but he had also seen her with the twins, and he was forced to admit that she *was* a loving and protective mother—a mother who gave her love willingly and generously to her sons…just as she gave herself willingly and generously to him…

Now what was he thinking? He was a fool if he started allowing himself to believe that. But did he want to believe it? No, Sander denied himself. Why should he want to believe that she gave him anything? Only a weak man or a fool allowed himself to think like that, and he was neither. But didn't the fact that he couldn't stop himself from wanting her reveal the worst kind of male weakness?

Wasn't the truth that even though he had tried to

deny it to himself he had not been able to forget her? From that first meeting the memory of her had lain in his mind like a thorn in his flesh, driven in too deeply to be easily removed, the pain activated whenever an unwary movement caused it to make its presence felt.

He had taken her and used her as a release for his pent-up fury after his argument with his grandfather, telling himself that his behaviour was justified because she herself had sought him out.

Inside his head Sander could hear his grandfather's raised voice, see the fist he had smashed down onto his desk in his rage that Sander should defy him.

Sander moved restlessly in his computer chair. It was too late now to regret allowing himself to recall that final argument with his grandfather and the events that had followed it. Far too late. Because the past was here with him, invading his present and filling it with unwanted memories, and he was back in that Manchester hotel room, watching Ruby sleep curled up against him.

His mobile had started to ring in the grey light of the dawn. She had protested in her sleep as he'd moved away from her but she hadn't woken up.

The call had been from Anna, her anxiety and shock reaching him across the miles as she told him that she had found his grandfather collapsed on the floor of his office and that he was on his way to hospital.

Sander had moved as quickly as he could, waking Ruby and telling her brusquely that he wanted her out of his bed, his room and the hotel, using her yet again as a means of expelling the mingled guilt and anger the phone call had brought him.

She had looked shocked and uncomprehending, he remembered, no doubt having hoped for rather more from him than a few brief hours in bed. Then tears had welled up in her eyes and she had tried to cling to him. Irritated that she wasn't playing by the rules, he had thrust her off, reaching into his jacket pocket for his wallet and removing several crisp fifty-pound notes from it. It had increased his irritation when she had started to play the drama queen, backing off from him, shaking her head, looking at him as though he had stamped on a kitten, not offered her a very generous payment for her services.

His terse, 'Get dressed—unless you want the hotel staff to evict you as you are,' had had the desired effect. But even so he had escorted her downstairs and out to the taxi rank outside the hotel himself, putting her into a cab and then watching to make sure that she had actually left before completing his arrangements to get home.

As it turned out his grandfather had died within minutes of reaching the hospital, from a second major heart attack.

In his office Sander had found the document his grandfather had obviously been working on before he collapsed, and had seen that it was a notice to the papers stating that Sander was on the point of announcing his engagement. His guilt had evaporated. His guilt but not his anger. And yet despite everything Sander had still mourned him. Evidence of the same weakness that was undermining him now with regard to Ruby. A leopard did not change its spots just because someone was foolish enough to want it to do so.

After his grandfather's death Sandra had renewed his vow to himself to remain single.

How fate must have been laughing at him then, knowing that the seeds of his own destiny had already been sown and had taken root.

He turned back to the computer, but it was no use. Once opened, the door to his memories of that fateful night with Ruby could not be closed.

The hotel bedroom, with its dark furniture, had been shadowed and silent, the heavy drapes deadening the sound of the traffic outside and yet somehow at the same time emphasising the unsteadiness of Ruby's breathing—small, shallow breaths that had lifted her breasts against her tight, low-cut top. The light from the standard lamp—switched on when the bed had been turned down for the night—had outlined the prominence of her nipples. When she had seen him looking at them she had lifted her hands towards her breasts, as though to protect them from his gaze. He could remember how that simple action had intensified his anger at her denial of everything she was about, infuriating him in the same way that his grandfather had. The raging argument he'd had with his grandfather earlier that day had still been fresh in his mind. The two angers had met and joined together, doubling the intensity of his fury, driving him with a ferocious and overpowering need to possess her.

He had gone to her and pulled down her hands. Her body had trembled slightly in his hold. Had he hesitated then, trying to check the raging torrent within him, or did he just want to think that he had? The image he was creating of himself was that of a man out of control, unable to halt the force of his own emotions. In another man it would have filled him with distaste. But Ruby, he remembered, had stepped closer to him, not away from him, and it had been then that he had removed her top, taking with it her bra, leaving her breasts exposed. His actions had been instinctive, born of rage rather than desire, but somehow the sight of her nakedness, her breasts so perfectly shaped, had transmuted that rage into an equally intense surge of need—to touch them and caress them, to possess the flaunting sensuality of their tip tilted temptation.

They had both drawn in a breath, as though sharing the same thoughts and the same desire, and the tension of that desire had stretched their self-control until the air around them had almost thrummed with the vibration of it. Then Ruby had made a small sound in the back of her throat, and as though it had been some kind of signal to his senses his self-control had snapped. He had reached for her, no words needed as he'd kissed her, feeling her tremble in his arms as he probed the softly closed line of her lips. She had deliberately kept them closed in order to torment him. But two could play that game, and so, instead of forcing them to give way, he had tormented them into doing so, with soft, deliberately brief kisses, until Ruby had reached for the back of his neck, her fingers curling into his hair, and whimpered with protesting need against his mouth.

Sander closed his eyes and opened them again as he recalled the surge of male triumph that had seized him then and the passion it had carried with it—a feeling he had never experienced either before Ruby or after her, surely originating from his anger against his grandfather and nothing else. Certainly not from some special effect that only Ruby could have on his senses. The very thought of that was enough to have him shifting angrily in his seat. No woman would *ever* be allowed to have that kind of power over him. Because he feared what might happen to him once he allowed himself to want a woman with that kind of intensity?

Better to return to his memories than to pursue *that* train of thought, Sander decided.

As they had kissed he had been able to feel Ruby's naked breasts pressed up against him. He had slipped his hands between their bodies, forcing her slightly away from him so that he could cup the soft weight of them. Just remembering that moment now was enough to bring back an unwanted echo of the sensation of his own desire, roaring through his body as an unstoppable force. It hadn't been enough to flick his tongue-tip against each hardened nipple and feel it quivering under its soft lash. Nothing had been enough until he had drawn the swollen flesh into his mouth, enticing its increased response with the delicate grate of his teeth.

He had heard Ruby cry out and felt her shudder. His hands had been swift to dispose of her skirt so that he could slide his hands into her unexpectedly respectable plain white knickers, to hold and knead the soft flesh of her buttocks. Swollen and stiff with the ferocity of his anger-induced arousal, he had lifted her onto the bed, plundering the softness of her plum painted mouth in between removing his own clothes, driven by the heat of his frustration against his grandfather, not caring about the girl whose body was underneath him, only knowing that within it he could find release.

Ruby had wrapped her arms round him whilst he had plundered her mouth, burying her face in his shoulder once he was naked, pretending to be too shy to look at him, never mind touch him. But he hadn't been interested in playing games. To him she had simply been a means to an end. And as for her touching him... Sander tensed his muscles against his remembered awareness of exactly what her intimate touch on him would have precipitated. His body had been in no mood to wait and in no condition to need stimulus or further arousal. That alone was something he would have claimed impossible prior to that night. No other situation had ever driven him to such a peak of erotic immediacy.

No other situation or no other woman? Grimly Sander tried to block the unwanted question. His subconscious had no business raising such an unnecessary suggestion. He didn't want to probe any further into the past. But even though he pulled the laptop back towards himself and opened his e-mails, he still couldn't concentrate on them. His mind was refusing to co-operate, returning instead to its memories. Against his will more old images Ruby began to surface, refusing to be ignored. He was back in that hotel bedroom in Manchester. Sander closed his eyes and gave in.

In the dim light Ruby's body had been alabaster-pale, her skin flawless and her body delicately female. The lamplight had thrown a shadow from the soft mound of flesh covered by her knickers, which he had swiftly removed. That, he remembered, had caused him to glance up at the tangled mass of hair surrounding her face, surprised to discover that the colour of her hair was natural. Somehow the fact that she was naturally blonde didn't go with the image she had created, with her thick make-up and tight, clinging clothes.

She had met his look and then looked away, the colour coming and going in her face as her glance rested on his body and then skittered away.

If her naturally blonde hair had been at odds with his assessment of her, then her breathy voice, unsteady and on the verge of awed apprehension, had been enough to fill him with contempt.

'You look very big,' she had delivered, within a heart-beat of her glance skittering away from his erection.

Had she really thought him both foolish and vain enough to be taken in by a ploy like that? If so he had made sure that she knew that he wasn't by taunting her deliberately, parting her legs with his hand.

'But not bigger than any of the others, I'm sure.'

She had said something—a few gasped words—but he hadn't been listening by then. He had been too busy exploring the wet eagerness of her sex, stroking his fingertip its length until he reached the hard pulse of her clitoris, and by that stage she had begun to move against his touch and moan softly at the same time, in a rising crescendo of excitement.

He had told himself that her supposed arousal was almost bound to be partly faked but unexpectedly his body had responded to it as though it was real. It had increased his own urgency, so that he had replaced his fingers with the deliberate thrust of his sex. She had tensed then, looking up at him with widened dark eyes that had filled with fake tears when he had thrust properly into her, urged by the wanton tightness of her muscles as they clung to him, as though wanting to hold and possess him. Their resistance had incited him to drive deeper and deeper into her, just for the pleasure of feeling their velvet clasp. He had come quickly and hotly, his lack of control catching him off-guard, her body tightening around him as he pulsed into her.

Sander wrenched his thoughts back to the present. What had happened with Ruby was not an interlude in his life or an aspect of himself that reflected well on him, he was forced to admit. In fact part of the reason he had chosen to lock these memories away in the first place had been because of his sense of angry distaste. Like something rotten, they carried with them the mental equivalent of a bad odour that couldn't be ignored or masked. If he judged Ruby harshly for her part in their encounter, then he judged himself even more harshly—especially now that he knew the consequences of those few out of control seconds of raw male sensuality.

It was because he didn't like the fact that his sons had been conceived in such a way that he was experiencing the regrets he was having now, Sander told himself. He owed them a better beginning to their life than that.

What was it that was gnawing at him now? Regret because his sons had been conceived so carelessly, so uncaringly, and in anger? Or something more than that? Regret that he hadn't taken more time to—? To what? To get to know the mother of his sons better or to think of the consequences of his actions? Because deep down inside he felt guilty about the way he had treated Ruby? She had only been seventeen after all.

He hadn't known that then, Sander defended himself. He had assumed she was much older. And if he had known…?

Sander stood up and paced the floor of his office, stopping abruptly as he relived how, virtually as soon as he had released her, Ruby had gone to the bathroom. He had turned on his side, ignoring her absence, even then aware of how far his behaviour had fallen short of his own normal high standards. But even though he had wanted to blot out the reality of the situation, and Ruby herself, he had still somehow been unable to stop listening to the sound of the shower running and then ceasing, had been aware against his will of her return to the bed, her skin cold and slightly damp as she pressed up against his back, shivering slightly. He had had no need for intimacy with her any more. She had served her purpose, and he preferred sleeping alone. And yet for some reason, despite all of that, he had turned over and taken her in his arms, feeling her body stiffen and then relax as he held her.

She had fallen asleep with her head on his chest, murmuring in protest in her sleep every time he tried to ease away from her, so that he had spent the night with her cuddled up against him. And wasn't it true that somehow she had done something to him during those night hours? Impressed herself against his body and his senses so that once in a while over the years that had followed he would wake up from a deep sleep, expecting to find her there lying against him and feeling as though a part of him was missing because she wasn't?

How long had he fought off that admission, denying its existence, pretending to himself that since he had returned to the island this time his sleep had never once been disturbed by that aching absence? He moved impatiently towards the window, opening it to breathe in fresh air in an attempt to clear his head.

What had brought all this on? Surely not a simple comment from Anna that she considered Ruby to be a good mother. A good mother *and* a good wife, he reminded himself.

His mobile had started to ring. He reached for it, frowning when he saw his sister's name flash up on the screen.

'Sander, we've been back from America nearly a week now. When are you going to bring Ruby to Athens so that I can meet her?'

Elena liked to talk, and it was several minutes before Sander could end the call, having agreed that, since he was due to pay one of his regular visits to the Athens office anyway, he would take Ruby with him so that she and Elena could meet.

CHAPTER TEN

SHE had better find out for sure that she was pregnant, and if so tell Sander. She couldn't put it off much longer, Ruby warned herself. She wasn't the only one to blame after all. It took two, and she *had* taken her birth control pills.

She had also been unwell, she reminded herself, and in the anxiety and despair of everything that had been happening in London she had forgotten that that could undermine the effectiveness of the pills. Surely Sander would be able to understand that? But what if he didn't? What if he accused her of deliberately flouting his wishes? But what possible reason could she logically have for doing that? He was a successful, intelligent businessman. He would be bound to recognise that there was no logical reason for her to deliberately allow herself to become pregnant. He might be a successful, intelligent businessman, but he had also been a child whose mother had betrayed him. Would *that* have any bearing on the fact that she was pregnant? On the face of it, no—but Ruby had an instinctive feeling that it might.

She would tell him tonight, Ruby promised herself, once the boys were in bed.

Her mind made up, Ruby was just starting to relax when Sander himself appeared, striding from the house onto the patio area, quite plainly in search of her. Her heart somersaulted with guilt. Had he somehow guessed? At least if he had then her pregnancy would be out in the open and they could discuss it rationally. It was only when he told her that his sister had been on the phone, and that they would be leaving for Athens in morning and staying there for the night, that Ruby realised, cravenly, that a part of her had actually hoped that he *had* guessed, and that she would be spared the responsibility of telling him that she had once again conceived.

Since he hadn't guessed, though, it was sensible, surely, to wait until they returned from Athens to tell him? That way they would have more time to discuss the issue properly. He would be angry, she knew that, but she was clinging to the knowledge that he loved the twins, and using that knowledge to reassure herself that, angry though he would no doubt be with her, he would love this new baby as well.

'I've got a small apartment in Athens that I use when I'm there on business. We'll stay there. The twins will be safe and well looked after here, with Anna.'

'Leave them behind?' Ruby checked. 'They haven't spent a single night without me since they were born.'

Her anxious declaration couldn't possibly be fake, Sander recognised. It had been too immediate and automatic for that. He tried to imagine his own mother refusing a trip to a cosmopolitan city filled with expensive designer shops to stay with her children, and acknowledged that it would never have happened. His mother had hated living on the island, had visited it as infrequently as she could, and he himself had been sent to boarding school in England as soon as he had reached his seventh birthday.

'Elena will want to spend time with you, and I have business matters to attend to. The boys will be far happier here on the island in Anna's care than they would be in a city like Athens.'

When Ruby bit her lip, her eyes still shadowed, he continued, 'I can assure you that you can trust Anna to look after them properly. If I did not believe that myself, there would be no question of us leaving them.'

Immediately Ruby's gaze cleared.

'Oh, I know I can trust your judgement when it comes to their welfare. I know how much you love them.'

Her immediate and open admission that she accepted not only his judgement for their sons but with it his right to make such a judgement was having the most extraordinary effect on him, Sander realised. Like bright sunlight piercing a hitherto dark and impenetrable black cloud. He was bemused and dazzled by the sudden surge of pleasure her words gave him—the feeling that they were united, and that she…that she *trusted* him, Sander recognised. Ruby trusted him to make the right decision for their sons. A surge of unfamiliar emotion swamped him, and he had an alien and overpowering urge to take her in his arms and hold her tight. He took a step towards her, and then stopped as his need to protect himself cut in.

Unaware of Sander's reaction to her statement, Ruby sighed. She was being silly, she knew. The twins *would* be perfectly safe with Anna. Was it really for their sakes she wanted them with her? Or was it because she felt their presence was a form of protection and was nervous at the thought of meeting Sander's sister? Had they had a normal marriage she would have been able to admit her apprehension to Sander—but then if they were in a normal marriage she would already have told him about the new baby, and that news would have been a matter of joy and happiness for both of them.

'You will like Elena—although, as I told her often when she was a little girl, she talks all the time and sometimes forgets to let others speak.' Anna shook her head as she relayed this information to Ruby. She was helping her to pack for the trip to Athens—her offer, Ruby suspected, more because she had sensed her trepidation and wanted to reassure her than because she really felt Ruby needed help.

'She is very proud of her brothers, especially Sander, and she will be glad that he has married you when she sees how much you love him.'

Ruby dropped the pair of shoes she had been holding, glad that the act of bending down to pick them up gave her an opportunity to hide her shock. How much she loved Sander? What on earth had made Anna think and say that? She didn't love him at all.

Did she?

Of course not. After all, he hadn't exactly given her any reason to love him, had he?

Since when had love needed a reason? What reason had she needed in that Manchester club, when she had looked across the bar and felt her heart leap inside her chest, as though he himself had tugged it and her towards him?

That had been the silly, naive reaction of a girl desperate to create a fairytale hero—a saviour to rescue her from her grief, Ruby told herself, beginning to panic.

Anna was mistaken. She had to be. But when she had recovered her composure enough to look at the other woman she saw from the warm compassion in her eyes that Anna herself certainly didn't think that she was wrong.

Was it possible? *Could* she have started to love Sander without realising it? Could the aching, overwhelming physical desire for him she could not subdue be caused by love and not merely physical need? He was, after all, the father of her children, and she couldn't deny that initially when she had realised that she was pregnant a part of her had believed she had conceived because of the intensity of her emotional response to him. Because she had been naive, and frightened and alone, she had wanted to believe that the twins had been created out of love.

And this new baby—didn't it too deserve to have its mother's body accept the seed that began its life with love?

'You will like Elena,' Anna repeated, 'and she will like you.'

* * *

Ruby was clinging to those words several hours later, after their plane had touched down in Athens and they were in the arrivals hall, as an extremely stylish dark-haired young woman came hurrying towards them, her eyes covered by a pair of designer sunglasses.

'Sander. I thought I was going to be late. The traffic is horrendous—and the smog! No wonder all our precious ancient buildings are in so much danger. Andreas said to tell you that he is pretty sure he has secured the Taiwan contract—oh, and I want you both to come to dinner tonight. Nothing too formal...'

'Elena, you are like a runaway train. Stop and let me introduce you to Ruby.' Sander's tone was firm but wry, causing his sister to laugh and then turn to Ruby, catching her off-guard when she immediately enveloped her in a warm hug.

'Anna has told me what a fortunate man Sander is to have married you. I can't wait to meet the twins. Wasn't I clever, spotting them at Manchester Airport? But for me you and Sander might never have made up your quarrel and been reconciled.'

They were out of the airport now, and Sander was saying, 'You'd better let me drive, Elena. I have some expensive memories of what happens when you drive and talk at the same time.'

'Oh, you.' Elena mock pouted as she handed over her car keys, and then told Ruby, 'It wasn't really my fault. The other driver should never have been parked where he was in the first place.'

Anna was right—she was going to like Elena, Ruby

acknowledged as her sister-in-law kept up a stream of inconsequential chatter and banter whilst Sander drove them through the heavy Athens traffic.

Elena had obviously questioned Sander about their relationship, and from what she had said Ruby suspected that he had made it seem as though the twins had been conceived during an established relationship between them rather than a one-night stand. That had been kind of him. Kind and thoughtful. Protecting the twins and protecting her. The warm glow she could feel inside herself couldn't possibly be happiness, could it?

The Athens night was warm, the soft air stroking Ruby's skin as she and Sander walked from the taxi that had just dropped them off to the entrance to the exclusive modern building that housed Sander's Athens apartment. They had spent the evening with Elena and Andreas at their house on the outskirts of the city, and tomorrow morning they would be returning to the island. Of course she was looking forward to seeing the twins, but... Was she simply deceiving herself, because it was what she wanted, or had there really been a softening in Sander's attitude towards her today? A kindness and a warmth that had made her feel as though she was poised on the brink of something special and wonderful?

Sander looked at Ruby. She was wearing a pale peach silk dress patterned with a design of pale grey fans. It had shoestring straps, a fitted bodice and a gently shaped slim skirt. Its gentle draping hinted at the feminine shape of her figure without revealing too much of it, and the strappy bodice revealed the tan her skin had acquired in the weeks she had spent on the island. Tonight, watching her over dinner as she had talked and smiled and laughed with his sister and her husband, he had felt pride in her as his wife, as well as desire for her as a man. Something—Sander wasn't prepared to give it a name—had begun to change. Somehow *he* had begun to change. Because Ruby was a good mother? Because she had trusted him about the twins' care? Because tonight she had shown an intelligence, a gentleness and a sense of humour that—a little to his own surprise— he had recognised were uniquely hers, setting her apart from his mother and every other woman he had known?

Sander wasn't ready to answer those questions, but he was ready and eager to make love to his wife.

To make love to her *as* his wife. A simple enough statement, but for Sander it resonated with admissions that he would have derided as impossible the day he had married her.

As they entered the apartment building Sander reached for Ruby's hand. Neither of them said anything, but Ruby's heart leapt and then thudded into the side of her chest. The hope she had been trying desperately not to let go to her head was now soaring like a helium balloon.

On the way up to the apartment in the lift she pleaded mentally, 'Please let everything be all right. Please let things work out for…for *all* of us.' And by all she included the new life she was carrying as well.

She *was* going to tell Sander, but today whilst she had had the chance she had slipped into a chemist's shop and bought a pregnancy testing kit—just to be doubly sure. She would wait until they were back on the island to use it, and then she *would* tell Sander. Then, but not now. Because she wanted tonight to be very special. Tonight she wanted for herself. Tonight she wanted to make love with Sander, knowing that she loved him.

In the small sitting room of the apartment, Sander removed the jacket of his linen suit, dropping it onto one of the chairs. The small action tightened the fabric of his shirt against the muscles of his back, and Ruby's gaze absorbed their movement, the now familiar ache of longing softening her belly and then spreading swiftly through her. Her sudden need to breathe more deeply, to take in oxygen, lifted her breasts against the lining of her dress, causing her already aroused and sensitive nipples to react even more to the unintentional drag of the fabric. When Sander straightened up and turned round he could see their swollen outline pressing eagerly against the barrier of her dress. His own body reacted to their provocation immediately, confirming the need for her he had already known he felt.

She couldn't stand here like this, Ruby warned herself. If she did Sander was bound to think she was doing so because she wanted him and was all too likely to say so. She didn't want that. She didn't want to be accused of being a woman who could not live without sexual satisfaction. What she wanted was to be told that he couldn't resist her, that he adored her and loved her.

Quickly Ruby turned towards the door, not wanting

Sander to see her expression, but to her astonishment before she could reach it he said quietly, 'You looked beautiful tonight in that dress.'

Sander was telling her she looked beautiful?

Ruby couldn't move. She couldn't do anything other than stare at him, torn between longing and disbelief.

Sander was coming towards her, standing in front of her, lifting his hands to slide the straps of her dress off her shoulders as he told her softly, 'But you will look even more beautiful without it.'

The words were nothing, and yet at the same time they were everything. Ruby trembled from head to foot, hardly daring to breathe as Sander unzipped her dress so that it could fall to the floor and then cupped the side of her face and kissed her.

She was in Sander's arms, and he was kissing her, and she was kissing him back. Kissing him back, holding him, feeling all her doubts and fears slipping away from her like sand sucked away by the sea as her love for him claimed her.

The sensation of Sander's hands on her body, shaping it and caressing it, carried her on a surging tide of her own desire, like a tribute offered to an all powerful conqueror. His lightest touch made her body shudder softly in swiftly building paroxysms of pleasure. She had hungered to have him desire her like this, without the harsh bitterness of his anger. In the deepest hidden places of her heart Ruby recognised that, even if she had hidden that need from herself. She had hungered, ached, and denied that aching—yearned for him and forbidden that yearning. But now, here tonight in his arms, the lies she had told to protect herself were melting away, burned away by the heat of his hands on her body, leaping from nerve-ending to nerve-ending. Beneath Sander's mouth Ruby moaned in heightened pleasure when his thumb-pad rubbed over her nipple, hot, sweet and aching need pulsing beneath his touch. Her body was clamouring for him to free it, to lay it bare to his eyes, his hands, his mouth, so that he could plunder its desire, feed it and feast on it, until she could endure the ache of her own need no longer and she clung to him whilst he took her to the heights and the final explosion that would give him all that she was and all that she had to give, make her helpless under the power of his possession and her own need for it, for him.

This was how it had been that first night in Manchester, with her senses overwhelmed by the intensity of what she was experiencing. So much so, in fact, that she had scarcely noticed the loss of her virginity. She'd been so desperate for his possession and for the pleasure it had brought her.

She was his, and Sander allowed himself to glory in that primeval knowledge. His body was on fire for her, aching beyond bearing with his need for her, but he wanted to draw out their pleasure—to savour it and store the unique bouquet of it in his memory for ever. He bent and picked her up, carrying her through into the bedroom, their gazes meeting and locking in the sensually charged warmth of the dimly lit room.

'I've never forgotten you—do you know that? I've

never been able to get your memory out of my head. The way you trembled against me when I touched you, the scent of your skin, the quick, unsteady way you breathed when I did this.'

Ruby fought to suppress her breathing now, as Sander caressed the side of her neck and then stroked his fingertips the length of her naked spine.

'Yes, just like that.'

Helplessly Ruby whimpered against the lash of her own pleasure, protesting that Sander was tormenting her and she couldn't bear any more, but Sander ignored her, tracing a line of kisses along her shoulderblade. When he had done that the first time she had arched her back in open delight, helpless against the onslaught of her own desire. Sander lifted her arm and began kissing the inside of her wrist and then the inside of her elbow. He had never known that it was possible for him to feel like this, Sander acknowledged. The sensual sweetness of Ruby's response to him was crashing through all the defences he had raised against the way she was making him feel.

He kissed her mouth, probing its soft, welcoming warmth with his tongue, whilst Ruby trembled against him, her naked body arching up to his, the feel of her skin through his clothes a torment he could hardly bear.

Ruby was lost beneath the hot, intimate possession of Sander's kiss—a kiss that was sending fiery darts of arousal and need rushing through her body to turn the existing dull ache low down within it into an open pulsing need. Her breasts yearned for his touch, her nipples throbbing and swollen like fruit so ripe their readiness could hardly be contained within their skin. She wanted to feel his hands on her body, stroking, caressing, satisfying her growing need. Wanted his lips kissing and sucking the ache from her breasts and transforming it to the liquid heat of pleasure. But instead he was pulling away from her, lifting his body from hers, abandoning her when she needed him so desperately. Frantically Ruby shook her head, her protest an inarticulate soft moan as she sat up in the bed.

As though he knew how she felt, and what she feared, Sander reached for her hand and carried it to his own body, laying it flat against the hard swell of his flesh under the fabric of his suit trousers, his gaze never leaving her face as it registered her passion stoked delight in his erection, and its sensual underlining of his own desire for her.

Very slowly her fingertips traced the length and thickness of his flesh, everything she was feeling visible to him in the soft parting of her mouth, the brief flick of her tongue-tip against her lips and the excitement darkening her absorbed gaze.

Impatiently Sander started to unfasten his shirt. Distracted by his movements, Ruby looked up at him and then moved closer, kneeling on the bed in front of him as she took over the task from him. She leaned forward to kiss the flesh each unfastened button exposed, and then gave in to the impulse driving her to know more than the warmth of his skin against her lips, stroking her tongue-tip along his breastbone, breathing in the pheromone-laden scent of his body as it shuddered beneath her caress. His chest was hard-muscled, his nipples flat and dark. Lost in the heady pleasure of being so close to him, Ruby reached out and touched the hard flesh with her fingertip, and then on an impulse that came out of nowhere she bent her head and kissed the same spot, exploring it with the tip of her tongue.

Reaction ricocheted through Sander, engulfing and consuming him. He'd been unfastening his trousers whilst Ruby explored him, and now he wrenched off what was left of his clothes before taking Ruby in his arms to kiss her with the full force of his building need.

The sensation of Sander's body against her, with no barriers between them, swept away what were left of Ruby's inhibitions. Wrapping her arms around Sander's neck, she clung to him, returning his kiss with equal passion, sighing her approval when his hands cupped her breasts.

This was what his heart had been yearning for, Sander admitted. This giving and receiving, this intimacy with no barriers, this woman above all women. Ruby was everything he wanted and more, Sander acknowledged, making his own slow voyage of rediscovery over Ruby's silk-soft body.

Sander prided himself on being a skilled lover, but he had never been in this position before. He had never felt like this before. He wasn't prepared for his own reaction to the way he felt. He wasn't prepared for the way it powered his own desire to a level he had never known before, threatening his self-control, creating within him a desire to possess and pleasure every part of her, to bring her to orgasm over and over again, until he possessed her pleasure and her with it. He wanted to imprint himself on her desire so that no other man could ever unlock its sweetness. He wanted *her*, Sander acknowledged, and he fed the fast-surging appetite of his own arousal on the sound of her unsteady breathing, interspersed with sobs of pleasure, as he sucked on the hard peaks of her nipples and kneaded the soft flesh of her breasts.

Ruby arched up towards him, her hands clasped on the back of his neck to hold him against her. She had thought that Sander had already taken her to the utmost peak of sensual pleasure, but she had been wrong. Now, with the barriers between them down, she knew that what had gone before had been a mere shadow of what she was feeling now. Lightning-fast bolts of almost unbearable erotic arousal sheeted through her body with every tug of Sander's mouth on her nipples, going to ground deep inside her, feeding the hot pulse already beating there, until merely arching up against him wasn't enough to appease the savage dragging need possessing her. Instead she had to open her legs and press herself against him, her breath catching on a grateful moan of relief when Sander responded to her need with the firm pressure of his hand over her sex.

Against his hand Sander could feel the heavy pulsing beat of Ruby's need. It drove the ache within his own flesh to a maddening desire to take her quickly and hotly, making him fight for the self-control that threatened to desert him when he parted the swollen outer lips of her sex to find the wetness within them.

It was almost more than Ruby could stand to have Sander touching her so intimately, and yet at the same time nowhere nearly intimately enough. His fingertip rimmed the opening to her sex. A fresh lightning bolt shot through her. She could feel her body opening to him in eagerness and hunger, heard a sound of agonised relief bubbling in her throat when Sander slid one and then two fingers slowly inside her.

He didn't need Ruby's fingers gripping his arm or her nails digging into his flesh to tell him what she was feeling. Sander could feel her need in his own flesh and hers as the movement of her body quickened and tightened. Even before she cried out to him he was aware of her release, and the quick, fierce pleasure of her orgasm filled his own body with fierce male satisfaction, swelling his sex to a hard urgency to play its part in more of that pleasure.

But not yet—not until he was sure that he had given her all the pleasure he could.

For Ruby, the sensation of Sander's lips caressing their way down her supine body was initially one of relaxed easy sweetness—a tender caress after the white-hot heat that had gone before it. She had no intimation, no warning of the fresh urgency to come, until Sander's lips drifted across her lower belly and the ache she had thought satisfied began to pulse and swell in a new surge of need that shocked her into an attempt to deny its existence.

But Sander wouldn't let her. Her protests were ignored, and the growing pleasure of her wanton flesh was cherished with hot swirls of desire painted on her inner thighs by the stroke of his tongue—a tongue that searched out her desire even more intimately, until its movement against the hard swollen pulse of her clitoris had her abandoning her self-control once more and offering herself up to him.

This time her orgasm was short and sharp, leaving her trembling on the edge of something more. Agonised by the ache of that need, Ruby reached out to touch Sander's body, but he stopped her, shaking his head as he told her thickly, 'No. Don't. Let me do this instead.'

She could feel the glide of his body against her own, his sex hard and slick, probing the eager moistness of hers, and her muscles quickened in eager longing, matching each slow, deliberate ever deeper thrust of his body within her own.

Aaahhh—how she remembered the first time he had shown her this pleasure and revealed its mystery. The way it had taken her beyond that small sharp pain which had caught at her breath and held her motionless beneath his thrust for a handful of seconds before her arousal had made its own demands on her, her muscles softening to enfold him, just as they were doing now, then firming to caress him, her body driven by its need to have him ever deeper within her.

This was what her body had yearned and hungered for—this completeness and wholeness, beyond any other, as she clung to Sander, taking him fully within her and holding him there, welcoming and matching the growing speed of his rhythm.

He was lost, Sander recognised. His self-control, his inner self stripped away, taking from him his power to do anything other than submit to his own need as it rolled over him and picked him up with its unstoppable force.

He heard himself cry out, a male sound of mingled agony and triumph, as Ruby's fresh orgasm took them both over the edge, his body flooding hers with his own release.

Her body still racked by small aftershocks of the seismic pleasure that had erupted inside her, Ruby lay silently against Sander's chest, heard their racing heart-beats gradually slowing.

Tonight they had shared something special, something precious, Ruby thought, and her heart over-flowed with love.

CHAPTER ELEVEN

THE twins' matter-of-fact response to their return to the island proved more than any amount of words how comfortable they had been in Anna's care during her absence, Ruby reflected ruefully in her bedroom, as she changed out of the clothes she had travelled home in. Sander had gone straight to his office to check his e-mails.

But getting changed wasn't all she needed to do.

Her handbag was on the bed. She opened it and removed the pregnancy testing kit she had bought in Athens. Her hands trembled slightly as she took it from its packaging, her eyes blurring with emotion as she read the instructions. Six years ago when she had done this she had been so afraid, sick with fear, dreading the result.

She was equally anxious now, but for very different reasons.

Things had changed since she had first realised that she might be pregnant again, she tried to reassure herself. When Anna had referred to her love for Sander, initially Ruby had wanted to deny it. But once that truth had been laid bare for her to see she hadn't been able to ignore it. Of *course* she loved Sander. The real shock was that she hadn't realised that for herself but had needed Anna to tell her. Now, just thinking about him filled her with aching longing and pain.

Maybe this baby would build the bridge between them, if she lowered her own pride and told him how she felt. She had begged him to give her the possession of his body—would it really be so very difficult to plead with him to accept her love? To plead with him that this child might be born into happiness and the love of both its parents? He loved the twins—surely he would love this child as well, even if he refused to accept her love for him? Telling herself that she must have faith that the love she had seen Sander give the twins would not be reserved for the twins alone, she walked towards the bathroom.

Ten minutes later Ruby was still standing in the bathroom, her gaze fixed on the telltale line. She had known, of course—impossible for her not to have done. But nothing was the same as visible confirmation. Against Sander's explicit wishes she had conceived his child. Ruby thought of the contraceptive pills she had taken so carefully and regularly every evening, in obedience to Sander's conditions for their marriage. Perhaps this baby, conceived against all the odds, was meant to be—a gift to them both that they could share together? She put her hand on her still flat body and took a deep breath. She would have to tell Sander now, and the sooner the better.

The sudden childish scream of anger she could hear from outside had her letting the test fall onto the marble surface surrounding the hand basin as she ran to the patio doors in the bedroom in automatic response to the outraged sound. Outside on the patio, as she had expected, she found the twins quarrelling over a toy. Freddie was attempting to drag it away from Harry, whilst Harry wailed in protest. Anna, alerted as Ruby had been by the noise, wasn't far behind her, and the two of them quickly defused the situation.

Once they had done so, Anna said matter-of-factly, 'You will have your hands full if it is twins again that you are carrying.'

Ruby shook her head. She wasn't really surprised that Anna had guessed. The homemade ginger biscuits that had discreetly begun to appear with her morning cup of weak tea had already hinted to her that Anna shared her own suspicions.

Sander pushed back his chair. They had only arrived at the villa an hour ago, and yet already he was conscious of an urge to seek out Ruby, and with it an awareness that he was actually missing her company—and not just in bed. Such feelings made him feel vulnerable, something that Sander instinctively resisted and resented, and yet at the same time he was opening his office door and striding down the corridor in the direction of their bedroom.

Ruby would be outside with the twins. As their father, he could legitimately get changed and go and join them. Doing so would not betray him. And if he was there as much so that he could be with Ruby as with his sons, then only he needed to know that. The conditioning of a lifetime of fearing emotional betrayal could not be overturned in the space of a few short weeks. Others close to him, like Anna and Elena, might admire Ruby and think her a good wife, but Sander told himself that he needed more proof that he could trust her.

He noted the presence of Ruby's open handbag on their bed as he made his way to the bathroom, but it was only after he had showered and changed that he noticed the discarded pregnancy test.

The first thing Ruby saw when she went back into the bedroom was Sander's suit jacket on the bed. Her heart started to hammer too heavily and far too fast, with a mixture of guilt and fear. She walked towards the bathroom, coming to an abrupt halt when she saw Sander standing beside the basin, holding the telltale test.

There was a blank look in his eyes, as though he couldn't quite believe what he was seeing. A blank look that was soon burned away by the anger she could see replacing it as he looked at her.

'You're pregnant.'

It was an accusation, not a question, and Ruby's heart sank.

'Yes,' she admitted. 'I thought I might be, but I wanted to be sure before I told you. I know what you said when we got married about me taking the pill because you didn't want another child—and I did take it,' she told him truthfully. When he didn't say anything, but simply continued to look at her she was panicked into pleading emotionally, 'Please don't look at me like that. You love the twins, and this baby, *your* baby, deserves to be loved as well.'

'*My* child? Since you have said yourself that you were on the pill, it cannot possibly be my child. We both know that. Do you really think me such a fool that I would let you pass off a brat conceived with one of the no doubt many men who happened to be enjoying your body before I found you? If so, then you are the one who is a fool. But you are not a fool, are you, Ruby? You are a venal, lying, amoral and greedy woman.'

The words exploded into the room like randomly discharged machine gun fire, meant to destroy everything it hit. Right now she might be too numb to feel anything, but Ruby knew that she had been mortally wounded.

'You obviously knew when you demanded that I marry you that you were carrying this child,' Sander accused her savagely.

He had claimed that he was not a fool, but the opposite was true. He had allowed her to tempt him out of the security of the emotional mindset he had grown up with and to believe that maybe—just maybe—he had been wrong about her. But of course he had not been. He deserved the punishment of what he was feeling now for dropping his guard, for deliberately ignoring all the safeguards he had put in place to protect himself. The bitter, angry thoughts raked Sander's pride with poison-dipped talons.

'I thought you had married me for the financial gain you believed you could get from our marriage, but I can see now that I didn't recognise the true depth of your greed and lack of morals.'

Ruby couldn't bear any more.

'I married you for the sake of our sons,' she told him fiercely. 'And this child I am carrying now is yours. Yes, I took the pill, but if you remember I wasn't well whilst we were in London. I believe that is how I came to conceive. In some circumstances a…a stomach upset and nausea can damage the pill's efficiency.'

'A very convenient excuse,' Sander sneered. 'Do you *really* expect me to believe it, knowing you as I do? You didn't marry me for the twins' sake, Ruby. You married me for my money.'

'That's not true,' Ruby denied. How could he think so badly of her? Anger joined her pain. Sander had called himself a fool, but *she* was the fool. For loving him, and for believing that she could reach out to him with that love.

'I know you,' he repeated, and hearing those words Ruby felt her self-control break.

'No, you don't know me, Sander. All you know is your own blind prejudice. When this baby is born I shall have its DNA tested, and I can promise you now that he or she will be proved to be your child and a true sibling to the twins. However, by then it will be too late for you to know it and love it as your son or daughter, Sander, because there is no way I intend to allow my children to grow up with a father who feels and speaks as you do. You love the twins, I can see that, but as they grow to be men your attitude to me, their mother, your suspicions of me, are bound to contaminate their attitude to my sex. I will *not* have my sons growing up like you—unable to recognise love, unable to value it, unable to even see it.

'Do you know what my worst sin has been? The thing I regret the most? It's loving *you*, Sander. Because in loving you, I am not being a good mother to my children. You've constantly thrown at me my behaviour the first time we met, accusing me of being some wanton who came on to you. The truth is that I was a seventeen-year-old virgin—oh, yes you may look at me like that but it's true—a naive and recklessly silly girl who, in the aftermath of losing her parents, ached so much for love to replace what she had lost that she convinced herself a man she saw across a crowded bar was her saviour, a hero, someone special who would lift her up out of the misery of her pain and loss and hold her safe in his arms. That was the true nature of my crime, Sander—idolising you and turning you into something you could never be.

'And as for all those other men you like to accuse me of being with—they never existed. Not a single one of them. Do you *really* think I would be stupid enough to trust another man after the way you treated me? Yes, I expect I deserved it for behaving so stupidly. You wanted to teach me a lesson, I expect. I'm only surprised, knowing you as I now do, that you seem unable to accept that your lesson was successful.

'There was only one reason I asked you for marriage, Sander—because I thought it would make you back off.

But then, when I realised you genuinely wanted the twins, it was as I told you at the time—because I believe very strongly that children thrive best emotionally within the security of a family unit that contains two parents who intend to stay together. I grew up in that kind of family unit, and naturally it was what I wanted for my sons.

'What you've just accused me of changes everything. I don't want you poisoning the boys' minds with your own horrible mindset. This baby *will* be their true sibling, but somehow I doubt that even DNA evidence will convince you of that. Quite simply it isn't what you want to believe. You want to believe the worst of me. Perhaps you even need to believe it. In which case I feel very sorry for you. My job as a mother is to protect all my children. The twins are two very intelligent boys. They will quickly see that you do not accept their sister or brother and they might even mimic your behaviour. I will not allow that to happen.'

Initially he had been resolutely determined to deny that there could be any truth in Ruby's angry outburst. But beneath the complex defence system his own hurt emotions had built up to protect him from the pain caused by his mother, tendrils of something 'other' had begun to unfurl. So small at first that he thought he could brush them away. But when he tried Sander discovered that they were rooted in a bedrock of inner need it stunned him to discover. When had this yearning to throw off the defensive chains that imprisoned him taken root? How could this part of him actually be willing to take Ruby's side against himself? Struggling against the opposing forces within himself, Sander fought desperately for a way forward.

This was so much worse than anything she had imagined might happen, Ruby acknowledged. She had feared that Sander would be angry, but it had never occurred to her that he would refuse to accept that the child she had conceived was his. She should hate him for that. She wished that she could. Hatred would be cleansing and almost satisfying.

She would have to leave the island, of course. But she wasn't going anywhere without the twins. They would miss Sander dreadfully, but she couldn't risk them starting to think and feel as he did. She couldn't let his bitterness infect them.

She turned to look through the still open patio doors, her vision blurred by the tears she was determined not to let him see.

'There's no point in us continuing this discussion,' she told him. 'Since it's obvious that you prefer to think the worst of me.'

Without waiting to see if he was going to make any response Ruby headed for the patio, anxious to put as much distance between them as she could before her emotions overwhelmed her and the tears burning the backs of her eyes fell.

From the bedroom Sander watched her, his thoughts still at war with themselves. Ruby had reached the top of the flight of marble steps that led down to the lower part of the garden.

Blinking fiercely to hold back her tears, Ruby stepped forward, somehow mistiming her step, so that the heel of her shoe caught on the top step, pitching her forward.

Sander saw her stumble and then fall, tumbling down the marble steps. He raced after her, taking the steps two at a time to reach her crumpled body where it lay still at the bottom of the first flight of steps.

She was conscious—just. And her two words to him as he kneeled over her were agonized. 'My baby…'

CHAPTER TWELVE

'SHE'S coming round now. Ruby, can you hear us?'

Her clouded vision slowly cleared and the vague outlines of white-clad figures formed into two nurses and a doctor, all three of them smiling reassuringly at her. Hospital. She was in hospital? Automatically she began to panic.

'It's all right, Ruby. You had a nasty fall, but you're all right now. We've had to keep you sedated for a few days, to give your body time to rest, and we've performed some tests, so you're bound to feel woozy and confused. Just relax.'

Relax! Ruby put her hand on top of the flat white sheet pulled tightly over her body. She was attached to some kind of drip, she realised.

'My baby?' she demanded anxiously.

The nurse closest to her looked at the doctor.

She'd lost her baby. Her fall—she remembered it now—had killed her baby. The pain was all-encompassing. She had let her baby down. She hadn't protected it properly, either from her fall or from its father's rejection. She felt too numb with grief to cry.

The nurse patted her hand. The doctor smiled at her.

'Your baby is fine, Ruby.'

She looked at them both in disbelief.

'You're just telling me that, aren't you? I've lost the baby really, haven't I?'

The doctor looked back at the nurse. 'I think we should let Ruby have a look for herself.' Turning to Ruby, he told her, 'The nurse will take you for a scan, Ruby, and then you will be able to see for yourself that your baby is perfectly well. Which is more than I will be able to say for you, if you continue to upset yourself.'

An hour later Ruby was back in her hospital room, still gazing in awed delight at the image she'd been given—an image which showed quite clearly that her baby was indeed safe.

'You and your baby have both been very lucky,' the nurse told her when she came in a few minutes later to check up on her. 'You sustained a nasty head injury, and when you were taken into hospital on Theopolis they feared that a blood clot had developed. It meant they would have to terminate your pregnancy. Your husband refused to give his consent. He arranged for you to be brought here to this hospital in Athens, and for a specialist to be brought from America to treat you. Your husband said that you would never forgive him and he would never forgive himself if your pregnancy had to be terminated.'

Sander had said that? Ruby didn't know what to think.

'I dare say he will be here soon,' the nurse continued. 'Initially he insisted on staying here in the hospital with you, but Professor Smythson told him to go home and get some rest once you were in the clear.'

As though on cue the door to her room opened and Sander was standing there. Discreetly the nurse whisked herself out of the room, leaving them alone together.

'The twins…' Ruby began anxiously.

'They know that you had a fall and that you had to come to hospital to be "mended". They're missing you, of course, but Anna is doing her best to keep them occupied.'

'The nurse was just telling me that it's thanks to you I still have my baby.'

'Our baby,' Sander corrected her quietly.

Ruby didn't know what to say—or think—so her emotions did both for her. Tears slid down her face.

'Ruby, don't,' Sander begged, leaving the foot of her bed, where he had been standing, to come and take hold of her hand, now disconnected from the drip she had been on as she no longer needed it. 'When I saw you falling down those steps I knew that no matter what I'd said, or what I thought I'd believed, the truth was that I loved you. I think I knew it that last night we spent in Athens, but I told myself that letting go of my doubts about you must be a slow and measured process. It took the realisation that I might have lost you to show me the truth. I deliberately blinded myself to what was real, just as you said. I wanted and needed to believe the very worst of you, and because of that—because of my fear of loving you and my pride in that fear—you and our child almost lost your lives.'

'My fall was an accident.'

'An accident that resulted from my blind refusal to accept what you were trying to tell me. Can you forgive me?'

'I love you, Sander. You know that. What I want now is for you to forgive yourself.' Ruby looked up at him. 'And not just forgive yourself about me.' Did she dare to say what she wanted to say? If she didn't seize this opportunity to do so she would regret it, Ruby warned herself, for Sander's sake more than for her own.

'I know your mother hurt you, Sander.'

'My mother never loved any of us. We were a duty she had to bear—literally as well as figuratively. My brother and sister and myself were the price she paid for my father's wealth, and for living the life she really wanted—a life of shallow, gaudy excess, lived in luxury at someone else's expense. The only time we saw her was when she wanted my father to give her more money. There was no room in her heart for us, no desire to make room there for us.'

Ruby's heart ached with compassion for him.

'It wasn't your fault that she rejected you, Sander. The flaw was within her, not you.'

His grip on her hand tightened convulsively.

'I guess I've always been distrustful of women— probably as a result of my relationship with my mother. When I saw you in that club I saw you in my mother's image. I didn't want to look beneath the surface. I believe now that a part of me did recognise how innocent and vulnerable you really were, but I was determined to reject it. I used you as a means of expressing my anger against my grandfather. My behaviour was unforgivable.'

'No.' Ruby shook her head. 'Under the circumstances it was predictable. Had I been the experienced party girl you thought, I suspect I would have known that something more than desire was driving you. We both made mistakes, Sander, but that doesn't mean we can't forgive ourselves and put them behind us. We were both defensive when we got married. You because of your mother, and me because I was ashamed of the way I'd behaved with you—giving away my virginity to a man who couldn't wait to throw me out of his bed and his life once he had had what he wanted.'

'Don't…' Sander groaned remorsefully. 'I'm sorry I said what I did about this new baby, Ruby. When you fell just before you lost consciousness you whispered to me—"my baby"—and I knew then that no matter what I had said, or thought I believed, the child inside you was mine, that it was impossible for it to have been fathered by anyone else. Can we start again? Can you still love me after the way I've behaved?'

In answer to his question Ruby lifted herself up off her pillows and kissed him gently, before telling him, 'It would be impossible for me not to love you, Sander.'

It was just over a month since Ruby, fully recovered from her fall, had returned to the island, and each day her happiness grew. Or so it seemed to her. Sander had already proved to her that he was a loving father to the twins, and now, in addition to proving to her that he intended to be an equally good father to the child she was carrying, he had also dedicated himself to proving to her that he was a wonderfully loving husband.

Lying next to him in their bed, Ruby felt her heart swell with joy and love. Smiling in the darkness, she turned toward Sander, pressing a loving kiss against his chin.

'You know what will happen if you keep on doing that,' he warned her mock-seriously.

Ruby laughed. 'I thought I was the one who was unable to resist you, not the other way round,' she teased as she nestled closer to him, the soft curves of her naked body a sweet, warm temptation against his own.

'Does it feel like I'm able to resist you?' Sander asked her.

His hands were already stroking her skin; his breath was warm against her lips. Eagerly Ruby moved closer to him. It was still the same—that heart-stopping feeling of anticipation and longing that filled her when she knew he was going to kiss her.

'I love you…'

The words were breathed against her ear and then repeated against her lips, before Sander finally slowly stroked his tongue-tip against them deliberately, until Ruby couldn't wait any longer and placed her hands either side of his head. Her lips parted, a little shudder of longing rippling through her.

The sound of the accelerated speed of their breathing mingled with the movement of flesh against fabric, soft whispering sounds of sensuality and expectant desire.

As always, the sweetness of Ruby's arousal increased Sander's own desire. She showed her love for him so naturally and openly, with her desire whispered in soft words of love and longing, and encouragement and promises filling the air, breathed against his skin in an erotic litany of emotion. He could now admit that part of him had responded to that in her from the very start, and had in turn loved her for it, even if he had barricaded that knowledge away from himself.

The shape of her body was changing now, and her pregnancy was a gentle swell that he caressed gently before he kissed her growing bump.

Looking down at his dark head, Ruby stroked the smooth flesh at the nape of his neck. She knew now how much both she and this new baby meant to him.

Lying down beside her, Sander cupped her breast, allowing his lips to tease her nipple provocatively, his fingertips drifting tormentingly across her lower belly in a caress he knew she loved. Ruby closed her eyes and clung to him, riding the wave of her own desire as it swelled and pulsed inside her, smiling at the now familiar torment of building pleasure, of raw, sensual need that Sander knew exactly how to stretch out until it became almost unbearable.

Sander knew that if he placed his hand over her mound now he would be able to feel the insistent pulse it covered—just as he knew that the unsteady increase in her breathing meant that the stroke of his fingers within her would bring her almost immediately to orgasm, and that after that orgasm he would re-ignite her desire so that he could satisfy them both with the thrust of his body within hers. He could feel his self-control starting to give way.

His hand moved further down her body. The soft, scented wetness of her sex and the way she offered it to him with such sensual generosity turned his heart over inside his chest. He looked up at her as he parted the folded outer lips. A shudder ripped through her eyes, dark and wild with need. His fingertips stroked slowly through her wetness and then back again, to rub against the source of her desire, hard and swollen beneath his touch, making his own body throb in increasingly insistent demand. His lips caressed her nipple more urgently, his gaze registering the flush staining her skin and the growing intensity of the small shudders gripping her body.

'San—der...'

It was the way she said his name that did it—a soft plea of longing plaited with a tormenting thread of enticement that smashed through what was left of his self-control.

Ruby shuddered wildly beneath the sensation of Sander's mouth on her skin—her breasts, her belly, her thighs, and then finally her sex, where his tongue-tip stroked and probed and possessed until the pleasure made her gasp and then cry out.

Sander couldn't wait any longer. As it was he had to fight against himself to draw out their shared pleasure instead of giving in to the demand of his own flesh and its need to lose itself within her, holding them both on the rack of their shared longing before finally thrusting slowly into her, letting the responsive muscles of her body take him and possess him until they were riding the pleasure together to the ecstasy of shared love and release.

'I love you.'

'I love you.'

'You are my life, my world, light in my darkness, my Ruby beyond price.'

Held safe in Sander's arms, Ruby closed her eyes, knowing that when she woke in the morning and for every morning, of their lives together, she would wake up held safe and loved.

EPILOGUE

'OH, RUBY, she's beautiful.'

Smiling proudly, Ruby looked on as her sisters admired their new niece, who was now just over one month old.

It had been a wonderful surprise when Sander had told her that he had arranged for her sisters and their husbands to visit the island, and Ruby thought it the best present he could have given her—barring, of course, his love and their new daughter.

'She's the image of Sander,' Lizzie announced, with an eldest sister authority that Ruby had no desire to refute.

After all, it was true that Hebe was the image of her father and her twin brothers, and, whilst Sander had said prior to her birth that if they had a girl he would like her to look like her mother, Ruby rather thought that he didn't mind one little bit that she was a dark-haired, dark-eyed daddy's girl.

'It looks as though she can wind Sander and the boys round her little finger already.' Charlotte joined the conversation, adding ruefully, 'I'm itching to cuddle her properly, but this one—' she patted the bulge of her seven-month pregnancy ruefully '—obviously doesn't want me to. He kicked so hard when I tried.'

'Ah, so it *is* a boy, then.'

Ruby and Lizzie pounced in unison, laughing when their middle sister tried to protest and then glanced toward her husband, Raphael. He was standing with Sander, and Lizzie's husband Ilios, who was holding their two-month-old son Perry with the deftness of experienced fatherhood. The three men laughed and talked together.

'Well, yes, I think so from what I saw at the last scan!' she admitted ruefully. 'Of course I could be wrong, and the truth is that Raphael doesn't mind whether we have a boy or a girl, although personally…' She gave a small sigh and then said softly, 'I know it's silly, but I can't stop myself from imagining a little boy with Raphael's features.'

'It isn't silly at all,' Ruby immediately defended her. 'It's only natural. I love the fact that the twins and Hebe look like Sander.'

'I feel the same way about Perry,' Lizzie agreed, adding, 'That's what love does for you.'

Automatically they all turned to watch their husbands. 'It's lovely that our three babies will be so close in age—especially as the twins have one another,' Ruby added.

'Sander is so proud of the boys, Ruby. And proud of you, for the way you brought them up alone.'

'I wasn't alone,' Ruby objected, pointing out emotionally, 'They and I had both of you to support us and love us. I could never have managed without you.'

'And we would never have wanted you to—would we, Charlotte?' Lizzie told her.

'Never,' Charlotte agreed, squeezing Ruby's hand.

For a moment it was just the three of them again, sisters bonded together by the tragedy they had shared, and by their love and loyalty for one another, but then Charlotte broke the silence, enclosing them all to say softly, 'I think we must have some very special guardian angels watching over us.'

Once again they looked toward their husbands, before turning back to one another.

'We've certainly been lucky to meet and fall in love with such very special men,' Ruby said.

'And all the more special because they think *they* are the lucky ones in having met us.' Lizzie shook her head and then said ruefully, 'None of us could have imagined how things were going to turn out when I was worrying so much about having to go out to Thessalonica.'

The look she gave Ilios as she spoke said very clearly to her sisters how much she loved her husband, causing both of them to turn and look at their own husbands with similar emotion.

'There is something other than how happy we are now that we do need to discuss,' she continued, explaining when Charlotte and Ruby looked at her, 'The house. Ilios insisted on clearing the mortgage for me, because at that stage I still thought that you would both need it, and I transferred it into your joint names. Since none of us need it now, what I'd like to suggest is that we donate it to charity. I've been making a few enquiries, and there is a Cheshire-based charity that provides help for single mothers. If we deed the house to the charity then they can either use it to provide accommodation or sell it and use the money in other ways. What do you think?'

'I think it's an excellent idea.'

'I agree.'

'So that's decided, then.'

'There might be one small problem,' Ruby warned. 'Since Ilios cleared the mortgage, I rather suspect that Sander and Raphael will want to match his donation.'

Once again all three of them looked towards their husbands, exchanging smiles when the men looked back.

Three such male and strong men—strong enough to admit that they had been conquered by love and to show openly just how much that love meant to them.

'We are so very lucky,' Ruby announced, knowing that she was speaking for her sisters as well as for herself.

Sander, who had detached himself from Ilios and Raphael and was on his way towards them, overheard her, and stopped to tell her firmly, 'No, it is we who are the lucky ones. Lucky and blessed by the gods and by fate to have won the love of three such true Graces.'

The World of Mills & Boon®

There's a Mills & Boon® series that's perfect for you. We publish ten series and, with new titles every month, you never have to wait long for your favourite to come along.

Blaze®

Scorching hot, sexy reads
4 new stories every month

By Request

Relive the romance with the best of the best
9 new stories every month

Cherish™

Romance to melt the heart every time
12 new stories every month

Desire™

Passionate and dramatic love stories
8 new stories every month